THE HATE OF LOVING YOU

MAYA HUGHES

1

BAY

The buses pulled up beside the beach front hotel Maddy and the band seemed to favor for their time in LA. My stomach knotted as the brakes of the bus squealed and the seal around the door hissed.

It had been twenty-five days since I left. Twenty-five days since I left him. Twenty-five days since my fear overwhelmed me and I ran. I ran so hard and fast, I've felt breathless since the day the wheels left the ground at the airport twenty minutes away. Twenty-five days since I made the biggest mistake of my life.

The guitar I'd thought I'd said goodbye to for once and for all in the trash can in front of my house in Greenwood sat beside me, wedged into the bench seat and bolted down table at the front of the tour bus.

My hand had shot over my mouth and my fingers had gone numb the second it arrived to me. Somehow he'd repaired it. The faint lines of the cracked wood were barely visible under the shiny heavy body of the guitar. It played differently, with a fuller, deeper sound. The piece I'd saved from the trash stayed tucked into the case that travelled with me everywhere.

My hands trembled and I stared out the windows toward campus. The glowing screen of my phone sat in my lap and I tried to come up with words, words that were different than the ones I'd written before I left. The words I'd typed out and deleted a hundred times, but was too scared to send.

Rain droplets dotted the tinted glass.

"Bay, here's your key." Maddy slid it across the tabletop. The laminated card stock folder sprung open. I had a collection now. A stack that I didn't quite know why I was keeping. Maybe as a keepsake. Maybe as a reminder that I'd done this. I'd gone on the road with one of the biggest bands in the world. I'd had my moment in the spotlight to look back on fondly when I was in the stands cheering him on.

But she didn't walk past me and move on to the rest of the guys.

"Holden, can you give these out for me?" She handed over the rubber banded bundle to Holden.

The bus cleared out and I stared at the keycard on the table like I'd forgotten what it was and how to use it.

"How are you feeling, Bay?"

My gaze snapped to hers and I shrugged, trying to pretend I wasn't coming apart at the seams. Trying to pretend I wasn't moments from breaking down just like I'd been over the past four weeks.

"I'm good. Just tired." The past month had been the most draining I'd ever experienced. Life on the road, I hadn't imagined it would be like this. The thrill of the show was an adrenaline boost straight to my heart, but everything else around it felt muted and drowned out. It felt like I was living someone else's life. Like a part of me had been stolen, no forfeited, and it dulled my senses and stole away the thing that lit my soul on fire. Dare and Keyton—one and the same, and no longer with me.

The monotony of the road was an oddity for sure. I'd puke before stepping on stage, Holden had started showing up with a trashcan after a near miss with his shoes. I'd get back on the tour bus after the shows and curl up in my bunk, unless we were stopping at a hotel for the night, and I wrote. I wrote so much my fingers ached from gripping the pen and strumming my guitar. I filled my notebooks like the grains on the hourglass were running out. And maybe they were.

"You seem more than tired." She sat beside me nudging me with her elbow.

"It's weird being back here so soon."

"It feels different even though it's been less than a month, doesn't it?"

I nodded, my throat tight. Keyton was out there in the city somewhere. I'd followed the games. I hadn't heard the announcers mention him in one yet, but I'd searched for him on the sidelines. The news Vince had been cut from the team made it to the regular news broadcasts after his drug-fueled bender and single car crash he'd walked away from. That was one less issue Keyton would have to deal with on the team, although maybe I was about to introduce another speed bump back into his life—me.

"Does this have anything to do with you maybe not wanting to get back on this bus tomorrow for the next leg of the tour?"

My head shot up. "What? No! I know this is an opportunity other people would kill for." Had I been that obvious? Had my doubts appeared in a bubble over my head I didn't know about.

"But you're not other people, Bay." Her gaze softened

and she folded her hands on the table top. "There's a laundry list of reasons to do what we do. The rewards are unimaginable and exhilarating, but if your heart's not in it —if your heart's somewhere else, then it'll never give you everything you need."

Inside my chest, the searing got worse, feeling like it would burn me up in a blink. I'd thought about him every night. Dreamed about him.

"What if my heart can't have what it wants? What if I've destroyed my chance to ever have it?"

Her lips parted and she held onto my hands. "Don't blame yourself for taking this chance, Bay. I know how hard it can be. I know what it can feel like to look into someone's eyes and feel like they can give you the world. But that's not always how it works. And if you keep waiting for someone to serve it up to you or be that for you, you're setting yourself up for disappointment.

"You're twenty-two. A lot can change in your life, but you need to be sure. You need to want this because it's not easy and it'll never be easy. But I'll support you no matter what you choose. The bus leaves at seven a.m. tomorrow. I hope you're on it, but understand if you're not." She slid out of the seat and walked down the aisle toward the front of the bus.

"Bay?"

I leaned out, looking down the aisle.

"If he's not there for you, you can always turn to the music. I've seen how you are when you create and it's a gift I don't want you to lock away." She disappeared down the stairs and I was left alone in the silence.

The scariness of what he saw when he looked at me was offset by the panic of not seeing him again. And Felicia sending my dad's guitar with a note that it was from Keyton had wrecked me. I trailed my fingers over the cracks and splinters lacquered and smoothed like I was looking at them through museum glass. Preserved to stay with me forever and that was how I'd felt when I held it with shaky hands trembling so hard, I'd put it away out of fear I'd drop it and break it.

One part of our past had been put back together and I'd broken us apart all over again.

Right after the show, I'd been locked away in my hotel room with ice cream and a hot water bottle on my lap, feeling like I was drowning in tears. They'd clogged my throat and burned my eyes. My skin was so hot, it felt like they'd evaporate off my cheeks, but they hadn't. But the rawness remained.

And now I was back. But what would I be returning to?

A lot could change in a month, just like all the complicated feelings I had for Keyton were deepened, expanded, filling all the spaces in my soul with a love I'd never experienced before, it also scared me more than I'd ever been scared before. Even scarier than him looming over me with the broken pieces of my dad's guitar in hand, even scarier than how much it hurt to walk away from him on the graduation field, and so much more scarier than opening myself up to him again.

But now I was back where I started and felt like an alien trying to learn how to communicate.

My phone still sat in my lap, the screen was now off and I looked down at my reflection. I didn't want to hurt him more than I already had.

I dragged myself out of the bus and grabbed my lone bag on the pavement beside it. The hotel door man held the door for me. Laughter and chatter from the hotel restaurant poured into the lobby. My ride up to my floor in the elevator was thankfully solo. The hotel halls were quiet. My door lock beeped and I was welcomed into yet another hotel room. The shine had worn off quickly after the first ten or twelve.

Not wanting to message him yet, I checked Knox's social media since Keyton didn't have any. There were pictures of him and Keyton moving into their new place and selfies with Knox's parents. They were from a few hours ago. The buildings in the background were on campus.

He was here. He was close.

I shot up off my bed and threw my shoes back on.

In the elevator, I tried to formulate a plan. Knox was updating regularly and posted a video of him standing on the beach with his parents smiling beside him. The beach I'd stared out at during my meeting with Maddy.

Anticipation hummed in my veins. They weren't far from here. In the lobby, I rushed toward the doors only to stumble back and jump behind a marble column.

Keyton walked in through the doors I'd come through less than an hour ago with Knox and Knox's parents.

My breath froze in my lungs like I'd been chucked onto an ice flow. Was this the universe telling me I hadn't ruined everything? Was this the universe forgiving my selfishness and cowardice?

He was in a white button-down shirt and black pants. He and Knox were dressed the same except for the colors of their shirts.

My heart ached and yearned for him. Sleeping alone in a bunk on a tour bus surrounded by strangers, I missed the strong comfort of his arms around me.

He laughed, and closed his umbrella. Knox's parents had

their own. He looked good. He was smiling. He didn't look tired or angry.

I wanted to run to him. I wanted to fling myself at him and tell him I was sorry. How sorry and wrong I'd been to leave the way I did.

Unable to stop myself, I took out my phone and tapped on his name. I'd stared at the empty text box for long hours backstage before a show, and longer hours on the tour bus, my body rocking to the roll of the road and my fingers unable to formulate a complete sentence to him.

But seeing him, I knew I couldn't stop myself. The unfairness of it all wasn't lost on me. I'd been the one to leave, but now I was coming back. Coming back for him.

With shaky fingers, I typed out the message.

Me: *I'm going to be in LA soon. I'd like to see you.*

His head dipped, the smile still there, and he kept up with the conversation. He pulled out his phone and stared at the screen. The smile dropped off his face and my stomach plummeted.

He stared at his phone for long soul-shredding moments.

So long I could feel the pulse of blood through my veins by how tightly I gripped my phone.

His fingers tightened around the edges.

Even from here, I could see the strain. I could feel the turmoil roiling inside him.

My vision blurred and a burning started at the back of my nose making my tears build in the corners of my eyes.

Knowing it was unfair. Knowing I didn't deserve it. Knowing this was a mistake I couldn't take back, but hoping with every cell in my body I could talk to him again, I sent another message.

Me: *Please.*

The dimmed screen lit up again in his grasp. Using his thumb, he turned it off and slipped the phone back into his pocket.

He rejoined his group and whispered to Knox. Knox's eyes widened and he looked back at Keyton.

"Mom and Dad, we have a change of plans for dinner. There's another great place we found around here during training camp, and think you'll love it."

His parents looked to him in surprise, but they slipped back into their easygoing banter and were back out the door.

It felt like someone had planted a boot in the center of my chest and wouldn't let up. Instead of going back to my room, I walked out following a minute or so behind.

They turned the corner when my feet hit the sidewalk. He never looked back and why should he?

I walked in the opposite direction toward the water.

Kicking my shoes off I let my feet sink into the damp sand and walked toward the water.

Not far from the lapping waves, I sat and brought my knees up and wrapped my arms around them. Wetness seeped into my jeans, inching its way around my hips, until the fabric was a sodden mess.

The wind breezed across the sand, sending shivers through my body. Waves crashed in the distance and I stared out at the darkness in front of me with only the moon and dots of lights floating on the horizon.

Hope that he'd answer my message died with every passing minute. Then everything around me was bathed in darkness.

The lights of the beachfront restaurant had been turned off right along with my hope.

Night stretched out in front of me with a sadness that

sunk bone deep. Wisps of color appeared in front of me, creating my silhouette in the sand. I unfolded myself, gasping at the pins and needles shooting through my body. The sun rose behind me, but it didn't bring the hopeful promise of a new day, only the emptiness that spread out in front of me, like my soul was becoming the shadow in the sand.

The battery icon on my phone turned an angry red. Percentage numbers ticked away down into the single digits. And no new notifications.

Numb, aching and relearning how to walk, I stumbled back into the hotel. Turning on the shower, I leaned into the burn and let it warm my skin, but it didn't reach inside. It couldn't warm me. Instead, I focused on what I had left.

The lyrics rolled through my head. Wrapped in a towel, I grabbed my notebook and let the words spill out of me. My tears mingled with the ink on the page.

I shoved my clothes back into my bag and headed downstairs walking to the loading bay where the bus was parked. The bottom compartment was opened, filled with bags and equipment.

Maddy walked down the stairs of the bus, her eyes wide. "You're here."

My shoulders shrunk and I stared at the concrete between us. "If that's okay with you."

She wrapped her arms around me, almost at eye level in her boots. "Of course it's okay. I was always happy to have you. I—" She let me go and took a step back. "I know this isn't the way you wanted this to go, but you're not alone. Remember the music and keep it close to you."

"I wrote some new songs." My voice broke on the last word.

His final gift to me. He'd unlocked the one thing that would take me away.

I'd console myself with the strings of my guitar, the melodies floating through my mind and the lyrics that reminded me of him.

If I couldn't have him in the flesh, at least I could in my dreams until I learned to let him go.

2

KEYTON

"I have enough money. I want to talk to Wisconsin." I doused my head in water and upped the speed on the treadmill for the last five minutes of my workout.

"Do you know how cold it is up there?" Ernie groused from the speaker of my phone.

My feet pounded on the treadmill in the second bedroom of my fifty-fifth-floor apartment with a view of the Philadelphia skyline. The TV flicked to the sports segment of the local news.

"I've dealt with cold before. You act like I haven't played in Wisconsin."

"Playing there and living there are two totally different things. Their salary cap isn't going to give us much wiggle room." Ernie's no-longer-a-pack-a-day, been-around-the-block voice rumbled.

"I don't care. If they'll play me, I want to see how the talks go." I notched the speed up another half step. After training camp, I'd pushed myself harder than ever, and I'd still been relegated to the bench. Second string after proving myself on the field, like an incredibly well paid mascot. It had its benefits, though, like starting a foundation reaching out to kids like me and setting them on a better path. Tonight, I had to take a couple who'd won an auction for my foundation to a Without Grey concert. Whenever I heard their music, I couldn't help but think of Bay.

It hadn't helped that their hits felt like they had been non-stop over the past few years, but their songs weren't the only reason I avoided the radio or kept my streaming channels to music from decades past.

Without Grey's music seemed to be inextricably enmeshed in my life, although I'd only met them a few times. But tonight, at their concert I'd be a good host to the auction winners. Their bid had been generous and would do all kinds of good.

Ernie's gruff voice broke through my trip down memory lane. "It's less money. Come on, Keyton, you're killing me here. I have three college educations to pay for."

"Your ten percent will more than cover it, and think about how many more endorsement deals we can get once I'm actually playing."

I'd thought there were no more second chances in football, but it turned out superstition had a way of making people rewrite all kinds of rules.

"Those deals I've negotiated are mighty nice already."

"Think about doubling it. So much more leverage, if I'm the one who makes the game winning catch or block."

"Or you break your leg again."

"That was three years ago." I jabbed the button, cranking up my speed trying to sweat out the frustration. Charlotte put me in during my first season after my trade to the Lions. I'd played in five games. We lost all five, but the clincher had been a brutal tackle that had left me with my leg in traction for two weeks before surgery and then months of rehab and physiotherapy. My trade to Miami the next season had been for almost nothing compared to most contracts, but I was fully healed and ready to play. They had other ideas on how to use me, and it wasn't on the field. But it added another ring to my shelf, and the good luck shine was back on me for the trade to Philly for my fifth season. The sixth started in less than a week.

"And the only season you don't have a championship ring for. No one wants to chance it. It's safer for you sitting pretty on the bench."

"I don't want to ride the bench anymore."

The wheels were turning on the other end of the line. "I still don't like it."

"You don't have to like it. I have to like it and I want to see what options I have."

Grumbles were all that came over the other end of the line. "Fine, but if they start screwing us around, we walk."

"We'll see what the offer is first and then decide if they're screwing us around or not."

Training camp was over. Another season was about to begin. Another year of wins. Another five months of being a useless waste of space.

Five championship rings sat in the safe in my closet. Five rings from three different teams. Speculation flew on whether I'd spend the next season in Philly or move on to greener, more lucrative pastures. The same thing had been repeating in my head since walking out onto the field amidst confetti, fireworks and a gleaming gold trophy lifted overhead.

Every year around this time, those memories resurfaced. The summer that changed my life. The summer I'd lost Bay and almost lost everything.

I jammed my finger into the cool down button and

slowed from my sprint to a jog and finally a walk.

Six years, two months, and three days.

The last time I'd seen her I'd told her I didn't want to go anywhere near that long without seeing her again, and my wish had been granted like one made on a monkey's paw.

She'd been in music videos, commercials, award shows, red carpets and charity events. I hadn't had to spend six years without seeing her. Instead, I got to see her what felt like daily, and it was worse—so much worse.

My phone lit up beside the water bottle slotted into the dashboard of the treadmill.

"Knox, what's up?"

"You're not going to give me the scoop?"

I laughed and jabbed the stop button. "A true reporter now, huh?" Grabbing my towel, I ran it over my neck and face.

"Only trying to prove my worth now that I'm off the field."

"Keep taking your shirt off and I'm sure the ratings boost from the ladies will secure your seat."

"The cookies have finally taken hold in the off-season." He sighed, but didn't sound the least bit remorseful. "The six-pack isn't what it once was."

Dumping my towel in the hamper, I kicked off my shoes and headed for the kitchen. The fridge was stocked with protein shakes and grilled chicken and vegetable dishes portioned out to my nutritionist's specifications.

"I can tell by your silence that you're staying in peak physical condition as always."

"Being prepared to head out on the field is half the battle." The other half was actually getting some playing time.

"You should be swimming in your money Scrooge

McDuck-style and shoving your face full of cake at every turn. How many guys make it to their sixth?"

"Probably a few kickers out there."

His laugh vibrated the phone in my hand.

I grabbed one of the green shakes and kicked the fridge door closed. "And how many guys have had less than a game of playing time in five seasons?"

"Are we having this conversation again? Take the money and run. Or don't. Other than that apartment Alice had you get you're probably still spending money like you were when you were on the practice squad."

The pristinely sophisticated apartment in the Four Seasons. Who even knew you could live in a hotel like this? I hadn't. The view was stunning. One Liberty Place gleamed right outside my window. The price tag for a year in this place had stung like a hive of bees finding out I was after their honey, but it had been a compromise. Alice hadn't wanted to move in here. She'd wanted a house. Somewhere with a yard. A place to start a family.

The apartment had been a compromise and the beginning of the end.

"Is there a conversation or just a lecture?"

"I'm worried about you, man."

"Don't be. I'm good. Never better. The foundation's going well. I have another purely ornamental position on another team poised to make it to the championship. I haven't had a fight in what? Four years." After over twenty years of friendship, he still worried about me like I was the kid hiding out in his basement in Greenwood. He didn't need to worry about me, but old patterns died hard—the same ones I'd worked on correcting. I couldn't blame him for having his own. At least his patterns didn't leave him with bruised knuckles and a busted lip.

"You know what I mean."

I knew.

A long deep exhale on the other end of the line. "Have you thought about getting in touch with her?"

"No." I had. So many times. So many nights I'd stared at the ceiling wanting to speak to her again. But there were too many reasons to let her live the life she was meant to live and never open myself up to the kind of pain that only came from nearly destroying yourself and someone else at the same time.

"Why not?"

"What good would it do?" All it would prove to me was how much things hadn't changed, and that was scarier than any door slamming in my face.

The doorbell rang.

I peered around out into the hallway. No one was allowed onto this floor without being on the list or living here, and my neighbors weren't exactly known for asking to borrow a cup of sugar. "I've got to go. Someone's at the door."

"Okay, see you next week. And think about it."

"I will."

I checked through the peephole and took a deep steady breath. Opening the door, I smiled at my visitor, who used to be much more than someone who'd ring the doorbell and wait for me to let them in.

Alice stood in the hallway. She wore the camel-colored coat I'd bought her last year, although the leaves had barely begun to turn. Her blonde, pin-straight hair was wrapped in a knot at the base of her neck.

The first time I'd seen her, I thought I was finally ready for something serious. She was beautiful, kind, and uncomplicated. After *that* summer, I'd exclusively dated women who could never be confused with Bay. I'd thought the drinks I'd had with Alice two years ago were progress in moving past all the crazy, complicated feelings surrounding Bay. They weren't.

"Can I come in?" She tugged on her earlobe, her earrings jingling.

I stepped back. "Of course."

Using the overpriced espresso machine, I made her a cappuccino the way she liked and set it down on the table, moving to the chair opposite her. The chair glided along the marble floor.

We hadn't spoken in months, even after the quiet way things ended between us. It had been nearly silent the night she left. No dramatic glass breaking, screaming, blood-thumping emotions. It had been over and we had both known it.

"How have you been?"

I took a swig of my green drink, needing to do something with my hands. We sat quietly at the table like two strangers left alone when their mutual friend left for the bathroom.

"Good. Great, actually." Her cup clinked against the saucer as she set it down. Awkwardness crawled the walls, trying to escape the discomfort of the room. Her smile was polite, sincere, but not the one she'd had for me when I'd told her about the place I'd found for us to live after the move. She still had her gloves and coat on, like she wanted to sprint from the room at a moment's notice.

Join the party.

Was it always this awkward with an ex? Not that it wouldn't have been a lot more awkward to be stuck in a room with Bay, but there had always been a familiarity with Bay, even when she was threatening to feed me my balls.

Alice and I been together for almost eighteen months. Now, three months after it had all fallen apart, it felt like we hadn't seen each other for years. Sitting across from her, it felt like we'd never been more than acquaintances.

"How have you been? I've heard more of the trade talks swirling around."

"I was on the phone with Ernie a little while ago. We're talking, but nothing definitive yet." The faucet dripped. Why had she shown up after months of nothing? My stomach knotted at the thought that she might want to get back together. We hadn't been right for each other. Nothing had shown me that more than her leaving having almost no impact on my life. She deserved better than someone who could watch her walk away and have it not slice them in half.

I grasped for something, anything to talk about. Like her new boyfriend, a wide receiver for New York. "Mac's in trade talks too, right?"

Her hands jerked and a few drops of her drink splashed to the chestnut table. "Sorry." She jumped up and grabbed a paper towel and sponge before returning to the table. Taking off her gloves, she ran the sponge over the spot and cleaned up behind it with the paper towel before depositing them both back in the kitchen. "He is. The deadline is in a few months, so they're trying to hammer it all out now."

Cleaning mode was her go-to when she was avoiding a topic. She'd always start with the fridge, my closet, then hers. You picked up on the little ticks after being with someone for a while.

"You can tell me, Alice."

She froze with her hand on the cabinet hiding the trash can. The door closed, whisper quiet. There were no banging doors here. Everything was muffled, muted, subdued, from the colors to the furnishings to the acoustics. It was all classic and timeless, and I was still afraid of spilling stuff on the couches.

Her back straightened and she turned around, walking toward me with glistening eyes. "I know it hasn't been long since we broke up. I didn't want you to find out from anyone else."

She released the hands she'd been clasping in front of her. A glinting diamond sat on her ring finger. It rivaled the size of the one I'd given her.

I took a moment. I didn't try to force myself to feel anything. I checked every emotion running through my head without trying to feel anything specific.

Standing, I lifted her hand and checked out the ring.

Her hand trembled and I covered it with mine. "I'm happy for you both."

She let out a watery laugh and wiped her eyes with the back of her free hand. "You are? I know it's too soon and I know it's crazy. I never—" Her eyes filled with absolute conviction. "I never went behind your back. I never even thought about anyone else when we were together."

"I know." Alice wouldn't do that. She was everything any guy could want in a girlfriend, or in a wife. Just not for me. Unfortunately, her heart had been totally in our relationship, and I'd thought mine had been too. It hadn't. "Don't worry about me. I'm happy for you. I've seen the pictures. You two look like the perfect fit."

"It's crazy how quickly it's all gone." She let out a wry chuckle, her eyes shining with disbelief and unadulterated joy. "One minute we were at the Headstrong Foundation gala and then we'd spent three weeks together non-stop. I moved in that month."

"Sometimes, when you know, you know." I tasted the

words on my tongue. There wasn't a hint of bitterness or the acrid bite of sadness and regret, only happiness that she'd found someone who could give her what she deserved.

That's when the sadness hit like a thud in the center of my chest, trying to crack through my sternum.

Alice slid her hand out of mine and wrapped her arms around me. "I hope you find her again."

"Who?" My muscles went rigid. I'd never spoken to her about Bay. I'd never spoken to anyone other than Knox about her. Not even to LJ, Berk, Reece and Nix. In all the digging tabloids had done over the years about her, other than a few fast trivia facts about the two of us attending the same high school and the coincidence of her first performance being at one of the many fights in my early career, there hadn't been any ties between us.

Alice dropped her arms and cupped my cheek. "The woman you were always wishing you were with when you were with me."

"I—"

There was no pain in her eyes. Sadness at the hint of what could've been, but not pain. "You don't have to say anything. I only want you to be happy. You tried so hard to give me all the things I wanted, but you need to make room for the things you want and deserve too."

My throat tightened, closing so speaking was impossible.

She stared at me with those clear blue eyes filled with caring and concern. Gently tilting my head, she pressed her lips against my cheek and hugged me. The wool of her coat scratched against my chin.

I wrapped my arms tightly around her back. I'd pinned so many hopes on our relationship, and now I'd seen how unfair it had been to her. She hadn't deserved to be my proving grounds for whether or not I was capable of change, but she hadn't come in here ready to punch me in the jaw, even after I'd called off our engagement. "Thank you, Alice."

"No, thank you. Without you, Mac and I wouldn't have met. I think that makes us even." There was a sheen in her eyes, but her smile was blinding.

I cleared my throat, truly happy for her. I'd had that feeling once—twice—but it hadn't been enough. I hoped it was for her. "When's the wedding?"

She shoved her gloves into her pocket. "At the end of the season."

"Do I get an invite?"

Her shoes scuffed on the floor. "If you want one, of course."

We said our goodbyes with another hug, and then I was back in my quiet apartment, all alone. For a long time the quiet had been a comfort, a refuge. It had meant the certainty that danger wasn't lurking around the corner, ready to breathe fire and leave me a charred mess.

I'd been that dragon for a while. When I'd sat in the empty training camp apartment that I'd trashed, with Bay's guitar gripped in my hand, I'd realized what I'd become. I'd realized it, but couldn't do anything to stop it. The spiral had continued for longer than it should have.

The looming Without Grey concert was dredging up all those old memories. My apartment didn't feel like a refuge —more like a hideout or a place where I'd been banished.

After living with the guys during college, with Knox after we went pro, and then moving in with Alice, an empty house no longer put me at ease. It was a reminder of everything I'd lost.

Now it felt hollow.

3

BAY

The lighting swept across the stage.

Without Grey launched into the second song before the end of their show.

Holden stepped in front of me, trying to hold my gaze through the sea of people on my team and rushing around backstage.

"Two songs tonight. The first will be Back Steps, the second will be selected from this list by a charity auction winner."

A hand reached down the back of my dress. Most people weren't used to hands being shoved into their clothes behind a dark stage, but after all this time, it barely registered on my odd radar. Hands were in my hair and someone touched up my makeup. I lifted a foot and straps were fastened around my ankles. I hated these shoes.

An in-ear monitor was put in place. I adjusted it, pressing it in further. The music from the instruments on stage flowed through the earpiece without any delay or crowd noise. I closed my eyes and took a breath. A calm flowed over me—until I was ripped out of it by a sharp stab in my side.

I sucked in a sharp breath, but contained my yelp.

"Sorry, one of your sequins came undone." Emily clenched two needles and thread in her hand.

I closed my eyes again, trying to center myself.

"Bay, can you open your eyes? I need you to look up, so I can finish your eyes."

I let out a sharp breath and did as I was told.

"Once the encore is finished, they're asking for pictures with the charity winner. You can say no, it's not part of the package, but I want to know what I should say if they ask." Holden stood beside me with the glow of the tablet lighting up his face.

"What's the charity?"

The final brush strokes, hair fluffs and dress fixes were finished and I wasn't being touched for the first time in what felt like hours. Being the center of attention wasn't always what it was cracked up to be.

He checked his tablet. "It's a charity focusing on children in domestic abuse situations. They donated over—"

"Of course. How much time will the schedule allow for tonight?"

"This is the last event for tonight, but we have the photoshoot at nine a.m. tomorrow, which means you need breakfast by five to get in your workout and then to hair and makeup."

"Can't we go for a just-rolled-out-of-bed look? That's in, right?" Having so many people around me felt claustrophobic, not to mention being sewn into clothes or pinched by giant metal clothes clips for the perfect fit. Sometimes I just wanted to wear sweat pants, finger comb my hair, and eat Cheetos for a whole damn week and not hear a word about it from anyone. The closest I got was the two days my period arrived and I felt like my internal organs were being ripped out, but on concert nights I had to chuck the hot water bottle by four p.m. and tough it out on stage.

"You're hilarious." His reply was deadpanned and flat.

I laughed. "The only thing making it tolerable is knowing you have to be up even earlier than me to get me there on time."

He grumbled under his breath.

I cupped my hand around my ear, nearly knocking tonight's makeup artist in the face. "Sorry, I didn't hear that."

He cleared his throat and leaned in closer. "I said you don't pay me enough."

"You weren't complaining when you were sipping that champagne someone sent to me last night."

"Keeping me tipsy is one way to keep me happy." He shrugged and scribbled across the tablet with his stylus.

My feet throbbed. My little toe screamed at me about the beautiful red-soled shoes covered in glittering crystals that made me at least six inches taller. Even I could admit that they looked stellar.

"Are you good today?" Holden eyed me. They all did.

"I'm fine. I feel good. It's not even my show. Two songs." I lifted one knee then the other, psyching myself up. They weren't here to see me. They were here to see Without Grey. Half an hour and I'd be back in the car, then back to my hotel where I could sleep.

On stage, the sweeps of the lights and strobes ended on the last note as all the guys jumped as one.

Camden took the water bottle and towel handed to him by a roadie who rushed out onto stage. He stuck the mic back into the mic stand and gulped down the water. He dragged the towel down his face and around the back of his neck.

During my shows, I literally had to stand in front of an industrial fan in the wings between song breaks. If I touched my face, I'd look like a demented clown from outer space.

"Testing. Can you hear everything okay?" A disembodied voice spoke through my ear piece.

My stomach did cartwheels into backflips. My fingers went numb. One of the roadies shoved a mic into my hand.

"Yes, I can hear everything."

"The levels are okay?" The tinny voice of the sound engineer pierced my ear.

"If you could bring down the treble a hair, it would be great."

"We have a very special treat for you Philly. We've known her for over a decade. She played guitar on Burnout way back on the Hometown Whispers album."

A murmur rippled through the crowd.

Maybe this time—nope. Holden was there with a trashcan.

Emily held back my hair.

I buried my head in the trashcan. What little food I'd wolfed down at dinner in the car ride over came right back up.

A towel was thrust in front of my face after the wrenching stopped. I dabbed at my mouth. Holden handed me a bottle of water with the lid already off. I gargled a little and spit it into the trashcan. He handed it off and everyone swooped back in front of me.

Emily held out a quick dissolve breath strip.

I slid it onto my tongue. The overpowering mint flavor was biting. "Sorry about that. I thought I was good tonight."

"It's okay. I made sure she only did the lip liner." She laughed.

Seemed everyone else had predicted this but me.

"So tonight, because you're the best damn audience in the world. We have—" Camden held out his arm toward my spot in the wings of the stage.

I plastered on my smile and stepped past my team of people, hustling forward to make my entrance. The hairs on the back of my neck stood up, not like they did before my shows, but like they did...

My gaze collided with his at the edge of the stage. He looked so different, but so much the same it was like a lance to my side. Six years. It had been six years since the night I'd told him I loved him again and left. Six years since the day my dad's guitar had ended up on my lap in the tour bus driving through Illinois on the way to O'Hare. The one Dare had taken from me. The one Keyton had returned. And six years since I'd sent him the text hoping to see him again and he'd shut me out.

Who was he now? Dare or Keyton? Or someone new all together?

"Bay!"

I faltered. My heel caught on one of the taped-down cables running across the stage.

His hands shot out, but I caught myself and turned it into a jog on stage, even as my toes screamed out their displeasure.

I lifted my arm high above my head and waved to the sea of people filling the stadium.

"Hello, Philly. You don't mind me crashing the party?" My stomach knotted and I glanced over my shoulder.

In the shadows at the side of the stage, he stood a head

above everyone else. His shoulders were even broader than before. A pro football career would do that to you.

Was his fiancée with him tonight? The pictures had been splashed all over the same sites as mine right after the Grammys. That had been a double-chocolate-chunk-brownie-ice-cream-sundae day. But he'd looked happy. They'd stared into each other's eyes and she'd showed off the blinding ring, resting her hand on his chest.

I'd gone out on stage during that first tour with Without Grey needing it to be worth what I'd lost, but the doubts I'd kept locked away in a safe I closed six years earlier pounded harder on the metal making it harder to hear my own thoughts.

Camden's voice broke me out of the memory maelstrom. "You plan on playing guitar tonight?" He turned and waved a roadie forward.

The stage vibrated under my feet from the cheers of the crowd.

My lips parted and I eyed the gorgeous Martin guitar slung over his shoulder and the one in the roadie's hands before glancing down at my hands. I shook my head and laughed. "Do these look like guitar-playing nails?"

Tomorrow I'd be shooting for a perfume campaign, and maintaining the nails was in the contract. It also meant I hadn't played for a few weeks. It felt like an eternity. I'd have to find out when the next break was. Maybe I could get them taken off, if I'd have more than a day or two to myself.

"They look more like super villain nails."

I shot him a fiercely playful look, rubbing them against my chin. "I have my moments. Now let's play something for your awesome fans who came out here tonight."

A few screams erupted from the crowd. "I love you, Bay." "I love your hair."

I waved again and threw in a hair flip for good measure. All the eyes on me made it hard to concentrate when I wasn't singing.

"Any requests?" Camden called out to the whole stadium with his arms out wide.

People yelled out every song on every album we'd released. And all the songs on the pre-approved list provided by Holden. I kept my gaze on the sea of people in front of me and the smile on my face.

But I felt his eyes on me, the ever-present heat of him peeling away layers of me I hadn't thought could be revealed, here in front of a crowd.

Without Grey came to a consensus, which just happened to be the already-designated song. Funny how that worked out. I got it. Even after only three albums, it was harder to remember the deeper cuts of specific albums if I hadn't sung them in a while.

The band celebrated the song choice, calling one of the loudest yellers from the crowd up onto the stage.

Chancing a glance, I peeked into the wings. He stood with the auction winners in a tailored suit. For someone of his build, buying something off the rack was impossible, unless he wanted to look like he was about to hulk out in it.

He hadn't changed much. He was older, more distinguished. High school tough and college brawn had turned into adult rugged. The clean-shaven look accentuated his jaw and the strong neck framed by a crisp navy collar.

Did he miss me?

An ache ricocheted through my chest. But he was engaged now, soon to be married. When was the wedding? Had it happened already? I'd promised myself I wouldn't look at another gossip site for the rest of my life after seeing the engagement news.

I turned back to the sea of shadowy people with their phone screens lit up like a field of lightning bugs. My stomach filled with the lightness and fluttering that hit me every time I stepped out onto stage, even well after the puking. This was the moment where I sang the songs which had been hummed throughout late nights in a studio or for hours on my tour bus. Having the words come alive was what made it all feel worth it.

But knowing those lightning bug phones out there had people attached to them brought the nervousness raging back. I gripped the mic tightly and closed my eyes, focusing on the lyrics, on the story that needed to be told even though I'd told it thousands of times already.

Austin counted off the beat with his drumsticks and we launched into the Sweetest Goodbye. It was a collaboration we'd done on my first album, which helped me climb the charts.

Every few bars, I couldn't help seeing if he was still there.

The auction winners danced and clapped, waving their arms overhead.

He stood beside them like a designated babysitter or bodyguard, not someone enjoying the show. Or maybe he had been, before I'd shown up.

Through the crowd's applause and cheering and the final drum beats, Lockwood ran over to get the song request from the auction winners, bringing them up to the front of the stage. I exchanged quick hugs with them as they vibrated with excitement, and glanced over at Keyton.

"We've got some great people here tonight, who gave a shit ton of money to the Headstrong Foundation. Give them another big Without Grey hell yes."

The sound blast from the crowd hit my stomach like

over-modulated bass. No one could ever say Without Grey fans weren't on board with charity.

Keyton stayed behind in the wings of the stage.

"We'd love to hear Craving Chaos." The twenty-something there with her parents shouted into the mic.

Camden turned to the rest of the band and me. "Do you think we can pull that off?"

I lifted my mic. "Hell yes."

Another roar from the stadium filled with twinkling lights from cell phones.

We dove straight in and I closed my eyes to beat back those nerves, although it was easier this time because he was here—not just in my head, but live and in the flesh.

I stepped to the front of the stage after the second song, swallowing against the lump wedged in my throat.

"How would you feel if I sang three tonight?"

The crowd screamed, rumbling the stage under my feet.

I could hear the voices of everyone trying to figure out what I was doing in my ear. Tugging out the monitor, I smiled wide and spun to Camden with a lip bite and a 'don't kill me.'

The hairs stood on the back of my neck. A throwback. Off my first album. Generally acoustic. His song.

Camden laughed and crossed the stage dipping his head, still so much taller than me in my heels.

I whispered in his ear. His eyes widened before he glanced over his shoulder at the wings and nodded, jogging to tell the rest of the guys. We'd played it a few times over the years. Easy key changes, a basic melody. It had been my first number one hit.

Closing my eyes, I wrapped both hands around the mic. The fabric of the mic sleeve matched my outfit. Holden had

had them made after the first five times the mic had flown out of my sweaty palms.

The guitar chord kicked off the song and I opened my eyes, staring out at the sea of people. After all this time, it was his eyes on me that got me through a show. No matter what happened, I knew that at least once there had been someone who'd watched me like there wasn't anyone else in the world.

I'd clung to that with deep breaths as I stood on stage after stage after the puking and strobing lights to kick off a show.

Tears clung to my eyelashes, but I blinked them back. This was why I didn't perform it live anymore. The overwhelming feeling of our past collided with my present, making it hard to breathe. But I needed him to hear it, needed him to know I still thought about him.

It was unfair and stupid just like I'd been all those years ago too afraid to be the center of his world. Too afraid to think too hard about what we could've been.

He was getting married. If I could just talk to him and tell him how happy I was that he'd found his calm sea that I'd never been able to be. Then I could close the door forever and know he'd found his happiness. Found his love.

"Thank you, Philly." I smiled and waved.

Turning toward the wings, his shoulder disappeared from behind the curtains and I found myself running toward the now empty, dark space.

His group walked away with a guy in a headset guiding them.

Music picked up again on stage.

"Da—Keyton!" My shout was drowned out by the kinetic drumming from Austin.

"Bay!" Holden rushed after me.

Going up on my toes in the heels like I had for the Chanel ad a few months ago, I sprinted after him. "Keyton!" His head tilted like he heard me, but he didn't stop or turn around.

Heads turned in my direction and I was lucky someone didn't tackle me to the ground for making so much noise.

Someone held back a black curtain for them.

My heart raced, pinging against my ribs. "Keyton!"

He stopped and turned. The people around him doing the same with questioning gazes.

I skidded to a stop in front of him, wobbling.

He made no move to stop me from face planting.

Staring at him, my mouth felt dried out like week-old contacts. It would've been good if I'd come up with something to say before right this second. *Shit.*

4

KEYTON

She stood in front of me, her chest heaving and her eyes a little frantic.

Up on stage, she had been mesmerizing, like always. In the dress, with the hair and makeup, the differences were stark. This polished and perfected version of Bay didn't hold a candle to the Goober-eating, hot-chocolate-making girl who'd stolen my heart with a single note.

"Hi."

The music drowned out most talking and noise backstage.

A squadron of people stood behind her with ear pieces and tablets. It was like Maddy had cloned herself and sent a whole team to take care of Bay.

A shrill voice burst through the three-second beat where we stared at each other. "I know I just saw you on stage, but I needed to tell you how big a fan I am. And I don't want to lose my chance this time." The twenty-two-year-old whose parents had bid on this auction prize gushed, grabbing onto Bay's hands and jerking her forward like she hadn't hugged her less than ten minutes ago.

I cringed at how much of an idiot I'd probably looked like. "Gary, Barbara and Bethany. This is Bay. But I'm sure you already knew that."

They had their phones out already taking pictures.

Bay's gaze turned to them and I could see the stage presence she'd perfected sliding into place. This was the face she wore for the hours while performing, standing on red carpets, and signing autographs. Her smile was genuine and pleasant, but still guarded.

I knew all about living a life where everyone wanted a piece of you.

After a round of pictures and autographs using markers that appeared in front of her from her people, her gaze kept darting to mine.

I waved over the production assistant who'd been guiding us. "Can you take them to the after party? I'll follow right behind."

My trio was guided toward the backstage party area, craning their necks to get another look.

The music on stage ended as Without Grey finished their second encore. Backstage became a flurry of activity with equipment being moved, cases popped open and instruments tucked away.

The blanket of noise around us felt close to silence without the stadium-filling music that had been cranked up only a few minutes ago.

A roadie walked by with two guitars held in each hand. They were electric acoustics, nothing like the one I'd pieced together in California.

My heart did a triple beat and I searched for words. "I got your note for the guitar." The last communication from her six years ago. The note I hadn't been able to respond to, just like the texts and her one final attempt at contacting me.

Sitting in the darkened apartment, trying to keep my life from falling apart, I'd stared at her guitar wishing it were broken again, wishing I hadn't hung so many hopes and dreams on what it would mean when it was finally finished.

"I—I can't tell you what it meant to get it back."

Instead of shoving those old feelings deep down, I let them wash over me. I didn't deny the pain that had once been so sharp, I'd checked over my body to make sure I hadn't been stabbed and not noticed. The rage and sadness threw me into a dark place if I denied it.

"I was happy to know it made it safely to you." With a nod, I turned.

Her hand shot out and grabbed onto my arm.

The pressure of her fingers on my arm, even through my shirt and blazer, sent blood screaming through my veins. Just those five points of contact felt like the first time I'd been touched in a long time. A long time since my heart raced without any physical exertion.

"Can we talk? Can we go somewhere and talk?"

Let me go, Bay. Just let me go. I stopped, but didn't face her. "I'm playing chaperone to the auction winners until midnight."

She stood in front of me blocking my path. "Do you want to have lunch? Tomorrow."

The guy with tousled hair and a blazer over his buttoned-down shirt stepped forward, clearing his throat. "You're booked from five a.m. to four p.m. tomorrow."

Her lips tightened before she bared her teeth in frustration. Looking to me, searching my face, pleading with her eyes. "Coffee then? Grab a sandwich or something?"

Denying her had never been my strong suit, but I needed to be strong now. "I don't think it would be a good idea." The work to get to where I was hadn't been easy.

There had been so much shit to wade through to be able to stand in front of her. But that only went so far. The season started in a couple days. Training camp was always a reminder of her that sent the memories ringing in my chest like a long-abandoned bell in a tower.

She grabbed onto my arm again, eyes begging. "Please. A cup of coffee. That's all I'm asking."

I released a deep breath, trying to keep myself level. Leaving should be easy. After our past, I shouldn't think twice, but things were never easy when it came to Bay.

"I can meet you for a coffee."

Her shoulders sagged and a smile burst free. "Really?"

"Sure, tell me when and where." I glanced over my shoulder to the escape route through the backstage walkway.

Her mouth opened before a frantic panicked look stole over her face. "Holden? Coffee tomorrow. Where can we do it?" She spoke to him, turning her body without taking her eyes off me like I'd take off sprinting out the door with the glowing exit sign over it.

She wasn't wrong.

It had crossed my mind. More than crossed my mind. It had flashed like a giant, blinking neon billboard: get the hell out of here.

Holden tapped out a few messages on his phone before showing it to her with his gaze laser-focused on me.

"Tomorrow at five at the Executive Lounge at our hotel, the Four Seasons on 19th Street. They have a full coffee bar and food menu."

There was an urgency in her voice. "Holden can—"

"I know where it is." It was my hotel. The one I'd lived in for the past year. My hotel where Bay was staying right now, only a few floors away. My heart rammed right into my ribs making it hard to pretend this didn't affect me.

"Oh, okay. Great." She seemed hesitant to let me go, watching me like she was studying my facial expressions to know if I'd show up or not.

"I've got to head back to my auction winners. Have a good night, Bay." Walking away with my heart in my throat, I steeled myself so I wouldn't look back.

Passing through the black curtain to the cordoned off area, I couldn't help myself. Barely looking past my shoulder, I stole a glance at her.

A squadron of people surrounded her, a lot like the first time I'd seen her backstage in a sea of suits. And just like before, she found me through their heads and our gazes collided.

A glimmer of a smile quirked the edges of her lips.

It was all I let myself have before disappearing behind the cloak of fabric headed to the after party.

Keeping the auction winners entertained helped occupy my mind, but my thoughts always came back to Bay, especially while they were off getting pictures taken with Without Grey.

A gentle hand landed on my shoulder. "Look at you, cleaning up way better than you have any right to."

I glanced down only a few inches for once, due to her five-inch heels, taking in the spitfire who'd made all Bay's dreams come true. And taken her away from me.

Those dueling emotions warred in my chest. "Hey, Maddy."

"Good to see you, Keyton." She raised up on her toes even when I stooped down to hug her. She kissed my cheek and leaned against the surprisingly sparsely populated backstage bar where I'd asked the bartender for a bottle and some glasses. "Did you see the show?" Her gaze flicked to the black curtained doorway.

"I saw her."

Some of the tension evaporated from her pose. "You did?"

"I did. We're having coffee tomorrow."

"That's great. Amazing." Her smile lit up neon-sign bright before dimming a hint. She stood straighter, smoothing her hands down a more relaxed look than she'd worn the last time I saw her. "I know things...I know things between you two were...unresolved."

"I think her letter came through loud and clear." Like a cannonball to the chest.

"She—" Maddy pinched her lips together. "Never mind." She exhaled on what sounded like a ghost of a laugh like some inside joke had been told that I wasn't privy to. "It's for you two to figure out. If there's one thing I've learned it's that no one can force two people to sort through their past before they're ready." A bartender set down the bottle of champagne in a bucket on the bar. My charges had returned from their photo op.

"Where are your seats?" Maddy carried the glasses back to the table and popped the cork on the champagne like she was popping a top on a soda.

"We were standing on the other side of the wings. I saw you talking on your phone and scribbling on your tablet the whole time."

"If I've seen one show, I've seen them all. After I make sure they're all stage and able to play, it's on to putting out the next fire."

Introducing herself, she filled the glasses, and I slid them across the table to my wards for the evening.

"I hope they're paying you well."

"They're paying me enough." The corner of her lips twitched. "And what about you, Mr. All-Star National Championship good luck charm? I feel like I should have the guys rub your head as we close out this tour and get started on the album."

"You're recording it here?" Passing interactions with Maddy were fine. She'd never done anything to me personally, other than make all Bay's dreams come true. Sometimes it was hard not to feel like she'd stolen her from me, which was a fucked up thing to think. But Maddy had a way of intertwining my life with Bay's. While she wasn't Bay's manager, she still seemed involved in Bay's life, which meant her being in the city more was a possibility.

Leaving was looking like a better idea every day. It wasn't running from my past if I flew, right?

"Yes. It's been a magical city for us all. After the nightmare of the last album, I'd have thought no one would want to be here, but it turned out the best for all of us, so here we are." Her wistful look transformed into one with a bit more needling behind it. "What are your plans? Moving onto greener pastures? Picking up another championship for the city?"

"You looking to sell me out to the paparazzi?" I gave her a playful nudge.

"Not unless you want me to." She winked. Her phone jumped on the table, screen flashing. She downed the rest of her drink. "Duty calls. Have a good one, Keyton." She pecked me on the cheek and rushed off toward the guys with headsets and clipboards headed her way.

After a few more minutes with my auction winners, my assistant, Gwen, showed up to coordinate all the parting gifts they'd won.

Just after midnight, like Cinderella leaving the ball, I put them into the black SUV headed back to their hotel.

"Headstrong Foundation needs you for two photoshoots for their annual donation campaign. I can squeeze both in after the first game of the season. Ernie sent me your itinerary for the meetings with Wisconsin, so those tickets are in your phone."

"Do I have anything tomorrow?"

"Not too much. Adidas wanted to schedule a call, so I had it on your calendar for four."

It would be the perfect excuse. Gwen could call and let Holden know that my call had run over and I couldn't make it. The perfect way to hide, unfortunately I wasn't doing that anymore.

"See if you can move it up to noon. I have a meeting at five."

Her gaze snapped back to her tablet. "What meeting? I don't have a meeting on here."

I laughed at the edge of panic creeping into her voice. "It's a personal meeting."

"Oh...oh!" Her eyes lit up. "Personal, like a date."

"Not a date."

My car pulled into the loading dock behind the stage where travel cases of equipment were being loaded into semi-trailers. I opened my door and she opened the front passenger side door and climbed in.

I leaned forward. "You know I feel like an asshole when you have me sit back here by myself."

"Keeping things professional, boss," she called out from the front.

"You just hate it when I'm staring at your tablet as you move everything around in my life like chess pieces."

"You're so nosy."

"It's my life." I peered between the front seats.

She held the tablet to her chest. "And you don't need to know about all the hiccups that arise along the way while I keep everything moving as it should."

Glancing over her shoulder, her eyes narrowed. "And I want to throw it out there—I look hideous in a floor length insulated jacket with fake fur lining around the hood. My lips are also prone to drying out and cracking when temperatures dip below -15 degrees."

"I see Ernie got to you, too." Sitting on the sidelines year after year had built up an insurmountable frustration from watching my team play and feeling responsible for what happened on the field, but not being able to do a damn thing to fix it. Most people would tell me to shut up and take the money, but I wanted—needed—to prove I had it in me to help my team with more than shouting encouragement from the bench.

"I'm only throwing it out there. In case you wanted to know."

We rode in silence the rest of the way to my apartment. Me alone with my thoughts, which returned to Bay. It had taken a few months for her texts to peter out once she left me in LA after the first one saying she might be coming back. They'd been dark months. And when she showed up at the loft Knox and I had been sharing in LA almost a year later, I'd sat with my back against the wall beside the front door gulping down a bottle of Jack with the buzzing of the intercom and her voice on the other end being drowned out by the clawing panic in my chest.

But tomorrow I'd see her again. I went in through the residents' entrance, not the hotel one where I might run into Bay.

In my apartment, I grabbed a bottle of water and stared

out at the glittering lights of the city. I'd had so many different views from wherever I happened to be. On the road, in my apartments, from the field in a stadium. My view now was different from LA. It was closer to Charlotte. There weren't massive sky scrapers for as far as the eye could see. The silver of Liberty One reflected my building back to me.

Being back in the city had been like returning to an old friend, and I didn't have many of those—just enough to count on one hand. Philly had been one of the first places I'd felt safe after leaving Greenwood. The first place I'd felt like I had a chance of escaping my past. It was fitting this was the place she'd reappear.

It was time to finally wade through the murky water of my past and find a salve for those old wounds I couldn't pretend were long-since healed.

5

BAY

The noise from the concert crowd leaving filled the sticky night air. A black SUV with tinted windows idled outside the artists' entrance to the arena. I climbed into the car and found my usual seat in the middle row behind the driver. It meant everyone else could talk around me about plans without me getting in the way.

We left for the hotel and I stared out the darkened windows. The anticipation of my coffee with Keyton tomorrow made it impossible to focus on whatever Holden was talking about. People walked in and out of bars, spilling onto the sidewalk, laughing and singing with friends. They smiled, ran around, joked like people in their mid-twenties should before all the true seriousness of life descended on them. Things like real relationships, kids, marriage.

Keyton was getting married. There hadn't been a ring on his finger. The wedding hadn't happened yet. Not that it mattered either way. But I still wanted to talk to him, and maybe finally give him answers he deserved.

The answers I owed him.

At the hotel, I was hustled through the parking garage entrance.

Holden swiped the key and pressed the PH button in the elevator. It shot up, popping my ears all the way.

The suite was a lot like every other one on the road, joining the blur of beds overflowing with pillows, room service meals and heavy security doors that always made me jump whenever they slammed shut.

"Night, Bay. Room service will be here at five, so don't stay up too late watching House Hunters because that's only"—he pushed back the sleeve to his blazer and glanced down at his watch—"six hours from now."

"Of course, I won't." I pressed against the door, slowly closing it with my cheek against the wood. "I'm going straight to bed."

He glared through the crack in the door. "You're a liar. I'll add an espresso to your breakfast order."

The silence of the room was deafening. All the chatter, pinging and vibrating phones disappeared, and I was left alone with the gentle hum of the heater. My legs nearly gave out and I sagged against the wall. I'd seen him. After all this time, I'd seen him in person.

Tomorrow we'd get to talk. Straightening, I walked deeper into the room.

Muted voices were a whisper through my door. They were silenced completely by the time I leaned against the high-backed chair in the living room area. My aching toes sunk into the plush carpet, freed for a short while from their sweaty prison.

Hobbling past the coffee table with vases of flowers and cards from fans and admirers, I grabbed the TV snacks from my stash and took the lukewarm fries from the room service tray with me. I changed while trying to come up with my big speech for tomorrow.

I ran through how it would go, like a dance routine the poor choreographers drilled into me.

I flopped on the bed, and the knot from my robe dug into my empty stomach.

Tearing into the bag of Cheetos, I spilled a few onto the white comforter. I brushed away the neon orange dust and sank deep into the extra-soft pillow-cloud mattress topper, surrounded by extra pillows like I'd built a fort. It was nothing like the beds Keyton and I had snuggled up in. The bed in my room back in Greenwood had been Ikea basic. The one in my apartment back in California had barely fit the two of us. Sometimes in these beds I felt like I could be lost forever and no one would find me.

I grabbed the remote and pulled my feet up, massaging them, and flicked through the VOD program Holden had set up in my room and the telltale musical intro. House Hunters.

With a jump shot from the bed, I sailed the finished Cheetos bag into the trash can in the corner. I'd gotten pretty good at bedroom basketball.

"Let me guess, you cultivate butterfly gardens and your husband studies unicorn science and your budget is $2.5 million dollars." The welcome distraction of formulaic TV helped soothe me after the high of performing and then being blindsided by Keyton.

The couple on TV rattled off some ridiculous careers, but their budget was only $1 million, so there was egg on my face.

This couple was settling down and buying a place. Putting down roots and starting a family. Sometimes they had families already. The past six years had gone by so quickly. Some days I was sure I'd wake up with a killer hang-over from the night I'd sung karaoke, and it would all have been a dream. Keyton would come to my door, and things would be different somehow.

But most mornings I woke up in a bed that wasn't mine, and someone had to write down the name of the city on a piece of tape at my feet on stage so I didn't say the wrong one.

Nowhere was my home.

Visiting my mom in her house in California was the closest I had to a home, but it wasn't the one we'd lived in with my dad, and it wasn't our place in Greenwood. I felt constantly off-kilter.

But tomorrow I'd get to see Keyton. I held onto that as I snuggled down deeper into my blanket fort. Five extra pillows and two comforters was always my special request. As diva demands went, it wasn't too extreme. I hadn't requested they repaint the room in every suite I stayed in like I'd heard some people did.

After enough episodes to know I'd hate myself in the morning, I turned off the lights and hugged a pillow to my chest, burying my face in it. Clean pressed linen. It wasn't the scent I missed the most. Not the scent he'd worn like it was sewn into his DNA. Not the scent I'd lost.

I'd cultivated the talent of sitting up straight while I napped, which meant I could do it while a team of people worked on my face to make me camera-ready. Sometimes I forgot what it was like to be out in public as me.

The makeup was gone now, rubbed off after the appear-ance and marketing photos for the upcoming tour. My face stung from the makeup remover and the extra scrubbing that had been required to get to the coffee meeting on time.

I'd been preoccupied all day.

But here I finally was, in the executive business lounge of the hotel. Not exactly the most warm and fuzzy place to meet. It was chilly, like overpowered business people with laptops whirring away would overheat the place—or maybe they didn't want anyone to stay for longer than it took to down the complimentary snack and coffee.

I squeezed my hands between my knees, rocking in my seat and trying not to look like I was ready to come out of my skin. In flats, black pants and a short-sleeved black sweater, I looked more like I was headed to an accounting interview than here to meet Keyton. There hadn't been any good wardrobe recommendations for 'first real meeting with the only guy you've ever loved who you walked out on before stumbling into stardom'.

Sitting at one of the eight two-seater tables in the lounge wasn't exactly incognito, but my options were limited. My nose still burned from the perfume shoot. Apparently dumping gallons of eye-stinging perfume all around the set increased the ambiance. One thing it definitely increased was my sneezing and watery eyes.

They'd be lucky if they got twenty good shots out of the four-hour shoot.

Every time the door to the business lounge opened, my heart raced. The executive lounge on the twentieth floor wasn't anything out of the ordinary, but it was quiet, with muted décor and gentle piano music. Quiet and sparsely populated.

Holden and Emily sat at a table on the other side of the room, close to the door, ready to intercept anyone who might have heard I was here and slipped past security. Their heads were together over their tablets, phones, leather folios, pens and markers, orchestrating my life.

The European leg of my tour started in a little over two months. I had an eight-week reprieve before the grind began again.

I held my mug with both hands. My leg bounced up and down, rattling ceramic containers of sugar cubes and sweetener packets.

There were a few businessmen sprinkled throughout the room, working on their computers and filling up on even more caffeine.

I'd ordered a hot chocolate. The last thing I needed was to be up even later tonight. It wasn't as good as mine, but I hadn't made my own in a long time. Had it been two years ago, when I'd been to my mom's house for Christmas before heading to Australia for a New Year's show?

In my head I repeated his name over and over. Keyton, not Dare. Keyton, not Dare. It was hard to separate the two in my head. I'd had so much history with Dare, and it hadn't been erased by a month with Keyton.

Knowing I'd be sitting across from Keyton for the first time in over six years had me keyed up more than the double shot of espresso I'd had at six a.m.

The door opened again, and I sat up straighter.

He was here in a navy blazer and jeans with a crisp white shirt. The boy I'd fallen for and the guy I'd loved back at UCLA had been replaced by a man.

"Sorry, I'm late." His lips curved, not into a full smile, but the way they did when I ran late to an interview or some other obligation that wasn't on the top of my list for the day.

I wasn't used to someone not being happy to see me.

It was a knock—not that I didn't deserve it. I'd been worried he wouldn't show up at all.

"D—Keyton." I shot up, rocking the table even more and sloshing some of my hot chocolate out of the mug. "You came."

"I said I would." He sat, unbuttoning the two buttons on his blazer and sliding into the seat, smooth as butter.

I sat back down and mopped up the splashes of hot chocolate from the table.

The server came over with a menu for him, but he waved it off. "I'll have a coffee, milk and sugar."

He folded his hands on the table top and leaned back. "Traffic was a bit of a mess getting here. Sorry for keeping you waiting."

"I haven't been here long." Only thirty minutes. It was my second hot chocolate. I would be peeing mini marshmallows later tonight.

"So..." He trailed off looking to me to start the conversation.

There were so many things I'd wanted to say to him since I left him in my dorm room. So many things I'd said in my texts and emails over that first year. Ones I couldn't even be sure he'd read—and wanted to say when I'd shown up in LA to try to see him again for the last time, racing back from Oslo during a gap in the tour. But I hadn't known if I'd ever get to say any of it to his face and what I'd needed to say to him then was different than what I needed to say now.

So I started with something safe. "Thank you again for the guitar. I can't tell you how much it meant to get it back."

"You never should've had to say goodbye to it." A sadness flickered in his gaze.

My chest tightened. It was hard to remember who had done what to whom at this point.

"I saw your play last season. Where you ran in a touchdown." The game had been on in the airport lounge. Had I been in Phoenix or Orlando?

"My one play." His laugh came out like a huff.

"If there could be only one, that was the one to have." I offered a weak smile and sipped from my mug, feeling like my heart was a sledgehammer trying to break my ribs. This wasn't how I'd expected the conversation to go. A night's rest hadn't helped put together the pieces of speeches I'd run through in my head before going to bed. There were things I wanted to say, and some of the words became a song in my chest, the low rumblings of a melody with the words just out of reach. Now we were talking about football.

His lips tightened, not with anger, but determination. Like he wasn't going to let me drag this out with more pleasantries. "You can say it all, Bay. We don't have to pretend we're just meeting up like old friends."

"Aren't we?" The first cracks were showing.

He tilted his head, staring straight into my eyes. His gaze was heated and full on, like high beams at midnight. "We were a lot of things, Bay, but I don't think friends was at the top of that list."

I set down my mug and picked at the napkin. Lyrics to a song began rolling through my head, about a life disappearing like a mirage right before your eyes when you finally have a chance to say the words you've been practicing for years, but nothing comes out.

"I've been in the same spot before, remember? All the speeches I'd had planned evaporated like that" —he snapped—"the second I stood face-to-face with you outside your apartment door."

"I sent you texts and emails—I even showed up at your apartment in LA."

He gazed into my eyes with an emotion that almost looked like pity. "I know."

That was a blow. I'd often gone back and forth on what was worse, knowing he'd seen my messages and ignored them or if he'd never seen them, but knowing he had was definitely worse. But I deserved it.

I stared down into my mug, swallowing past the tightness and gathered my courage to look back at him. "Any tips on how to get through this?"

His laugh was heartier this time. "No, all I know is it never goes to plan." His face gentled, softened, relaxed. It was open like he was trying to comfort someone he could tell was exceedingly embarrassed.

"I don't know how to function without a plan anymore."

"Neither do I. How about we start with something easy?"

I looked to him, trying to figure out what about this was meant to be easy. My stomach was chaos and my heart was a jackhammer. "How have you been?"

"Fine. How about you?"

"Keyton, be serious."

"You run into me backstage and are hit with all these regrets racing through your head, and you feel like you have to jump or you'll never get your chance to say the things you've been rehearsing. I'm letting you off the hook, Bay. I'm fine now. Football worked out—in a way." He shrugged.

"I haven't been in a fight in years. I see Knox often and have a few friends here. Sure, I went to a dark place after Felicia showed up with your letter or maybe I was always there but pretending I wasn't. It was bad for a long time. My life didn't dissolve and crumble when you left." A muscle in his jaw tightened and his faraway look knotted and twisted my stomach. Knowing I'd hurt him so deeply—someone I'd loved—someone I'd never stopped loving scared me.

My heart clenched, but I kept my gaze locked on his, not wanting to look away and hide my shame. I needed him to see that it was the hardest thing I'd ever done, walking out of that room and out of his life. And rushing back after a month to find him and knowing he didn't want to see me drove me straight into my work. I'd had to make it worth it. I'd had to try to make my work worth it when it felt like I'd lost a piece of my soul.

I'd picked up bits of news about him—not from searching or deep dives, but enough to keep some of my guilt from eating me alive. But I'd allowed myself one last trip after I'd found out where he was living. I'd stood on the LA street ringing the intercom until the sun set and my fingers ached. That was when I'd known I'd have to live with my choice, the one made out of self-preservation.

Every update I'd let myself peek at had been better than the last. Season after season had ended in a national championship. Trades with even bigger signing bonuses stacked up, and then finally there had been the news of his engagement. That had hit hard—so hard I'd staggered back, clutching at my chest when I'd read it. The phone slipped from my hand and I heard the screen crack, just like my heart.

I'd sworn off looking again after that. He'd found his happiness. They'd looked so happy together. I'd swallowed my regrets and held onto the fact that he'd found someone who could love him and who was good for him and was there for him, no matter how much it had torn me up.

"And now?"

The server came over with his coffee and creamer.

I slid the sugar toward him. There were no illusions about what this was for me.

He was soon to be married. Somehow I'd thought we'd

find our way back to each other in some way, but now it was finally time to have the conversation I hadn't been able to have back in my apartment and didn't even know if I'd have been strong enough to have when I came back.

"And now, things are still good."

Clasping my hands around my mug, I push the air from my lungs. "Your fiancée is beautiful. I saw a picture early last year."

He stopped drumming his fingers on the side of his mug and dropped his chin. "Is that why you invited me here? To find out about Alice?"

I jerked back. "What? No. I saw you and I wanted to talk to you. That's all. No expectations or obligations. I wanted to congratulate you to your face. It's been too long." I dropped my gaze to my cup before dragging it back to him. The crashing waves of sorrow and guilt I'd tried to pretend didn't touch me were still there. The lapping waves were getting stronger and soon I'd be waist deep with the undertow drawing me under. "And I know that's my fault."

"Alice and I broke up three months ago. She's getting married early next year."

A sound escaped my mouth that made more than a couple heads turn in our direction, including Holden and Emily.

Holden gripped the arms of his chair like he was ready to launch himself across the room.

A sharp shake of my head and he settled back into his seat.

Keyton glanced over his shoulder. "You brought back-up in case this went south?" He leaned all the way back in his seat with judgement written across all the fine ridges creasing his forehead.

I shot forward. "No, they're always there. Unless I'm at

my mom's or in my hotel room, one of them is always around. Comes with the territory." I shrugged. They were fixtures, and I'd forgotten what it was like to not have them there. They were a security blanket and buffer to the rest of the world. "It's not about you. It's about me."

He made a sound of 'good enough' before going back to his coffee. "How are you? Everywhere I look your face is on a billboard, commercial, bus shelter, perfume counter."

"Things are how they are. Living my dream, right?" My smile was brittle, so I took a sip of my hot chocolate.

"Looks like we both got exactly what we wanted?"

"Looks like it." I set down my mug and stashed my hands in my lap.

"And from your face I can tell you're loving every minute that this life has given you." Sarcasm clung to every word. "But you invited me, so I think it's time you tell me the whole story of the night you left me."

KEYTON

Bay's face flushed, but she didn't look away.

I stared into those brownie-batter brown eyes, wanting to peel back everything and show her the rawness I'd been working on healing for far too long. Sitting across from her, I wanted to hold her hand in mine, run my lips over hers. This was exactly why I'd avoided any contact over the past six years. But this was the chance I didn't ever think I'd get.

When I'd handed off the guitar to Felicia, I'd expected her to run back to me. I'd expected Bay to show up on my doorstep with the guitar in hand and tell me it had all been a mistake. One week had turned to two after Felicia let me know she'd sent it, and that's when things had gone from bad to worse. All those ugly words I'd known were true blared in my ears, and losing so much all at once—I'd only made it through to the other side by clinging to the cliff's edge with my fingertips.

And then she had come back, my muscles locked up and I couldn't make myself let her in.

Not after her first text in LA, which had been like a

pitcher of ice water over my head. There had been texts and emails that came after, but I couldn't make myself respond. Every time I felt like I'd be dragging her into the churning pit of my life and drowning her right alongside me. And after she showed up at my apartment in LA, I'd woken up covered in my own sick with Knox banging on the front door to our apartment where I'd passed out listening to the buzz from the intercom. He bruised his shoulder, busting the door down since I'd been passed out blocking his way inside.

She'd been gone by the time I staggered downstairs and looking at myself then still drunk, covered in puke and barely coherent, I knew she'd been right. I'd been too afraid of losing the sliver of a grip I'd had left.

For that year, outside of my time in the gym or on the practice field, I was a plane pointed straight down, engines full throttle, with the ground screaming toward me.

After hooking up with Monica, it had gotten easier to make it through. I wasn't on a roller coaster without my seatbelt buckled.

Bay drummed her fingers along the mug. "Maddy sent me a message when you were at the meeting with your coaches about the fight, and then later in the night—in the middle of the night, she sent another." Her gaze was trained on the slowly dissolving marshmallow foam in her hot chocolate. "It was an offer to perform with Without Grey in Seattle. And go on tour with them."

"That's a good start."

Sitting in front of her, I couldn't help but stare. I'd seen her so many times over the years. On TV, on magazine covers, billboards. Today was the first time I'd gotten to be this close to her for more than a few minutes in so long—too long.

"I couldn't turn down the opportunity."

"Do you remember what you put in your letter?" My throat tightened, clogged by the memories of sitting in my dark, destroyed dorm apartment, trying not to ruin what was left of my life. I set my elbow on the table and covered my mouth with my closed hand.

She ripped her gaze away from mine. "I might've blocked some of it out." Her bottom lip shook before she tucked it between her teeth.

Every word had been branded on my brain, etched and carved into the soft gray matter to the point that I was unable to forget them. Just like the ones she'd said to me standing on the sunny high school field in June ten years ago.

"Here are some of the highlights: By the time you're reading this, I'll be on a plane."

"There are so many things I've wished for since you've come back into my life. The number one is wishing it was the right time for us. But it isn't."

My stomach knotted and twisted like it had reading those words in my training camp apartment. How I'd repeated them in my head when it was in a trashcan or toilet or I finished off another bottle of alcohol.

"You are worthy of love and deserve someone who'll love you, but they can't be the one who fixes you. No one can fix us." I cleared my throat.

"I'm still working on figuring out who I am. I can't be the one to keep your head above water when I'm treading in my own ocean. I need to find my own path." How lost and scared she'd been had flayed me. It had ripped through so many wounds I'd thought I could ignore, until I couldn't.

"I wanted you to know without a doubt. I forgive you. But I can't be with you. I'm sorry." The rage and terrified feelings that had welled up for a long time after thinking about what she'd said weren't there anymore. Now I felt sadness that I'd backed her into that corner, that she'd felt responsible for me in a way she never should have. There was still anger and complicated feelings I'd probably never work through, but they didn't blind me, clouding my vision until I lashed out to escape feelings too sharp to handle.

She wiped at the corner of her eye and chewed her lips. "Going straight for the meat, huh? You'd be a great hard-hitting interviewer."

"Why not lay it all out there?" Yank on the release valve to quiet the buzzing in my ears. It was always better to get it out than to try to hold it in, try to stifle or smother the feelings.

Sniffling, she lifted her head. "I was scared." A long choppy breath escaped through her lips. She glanced around the room. "So scared."

The few men in suits and business casual gear sat at tables and desk cubicles, reading their papers, focused on their laptops, or eating their food. Some did all three at once, but they faded away when I was sitting at the table with her. The lump in my throat turned to an anvil. "Of me." How close I'd come to lashing out and hitting her in my blind fury kept me up at night for a long time after she left.

Her eyes shot to me and she shook her head. "Of our situation. Of how sure you were that being with me would solve all the problems you were trying to work through. The whole month, things seemed to be deteriorating for you, and I didn't know how to stop it except by leaving. When you first showed up you felt so different and the longer we were together, it felt like you were getting worse. Like I was making you worse."

She jabbed a finger at the center of her chest. Her throat muscles strained and she took a long sip of her drink.

"The fight...that was my powder keg." It should've been my wake up call, but it wasn't.

"You kept talking about how you didn't care about getting kicked off the team and you'd follow me around the country or wherever I needed to go, but I saw you play. I finally saw you play, and I saw how happy it made you. How you loved signing autographs and taking pictures with the fans. And I was afraid..."

"Of what would happen if it all ended for me. If I'd blow up and lose my shit—on you." Even thinking it soured my stomach. Bile churned and my mouth filled with pre-puke saliva. She'd worried I'd hurt her even more than I already had, and I hated that she'd probably been right.

Pain ripped across her face and her lips trembled, nostrils flaring. "Maybe a little bit. I'm sorry."

I ran my hand over the back of my neck, pressing down with my thumb to ease some of the pressure.

"It was smart, what you did." My jaw clenched and swiped my chin back and forth. The stories I'd told myself at the beginning of our summer had been a prime example of why I'd had no business trying to start anything with her.

"I get it." Staring into her eyes, I needed her to know how much I truly did. "I was way more broken than you had super glue for. Expecting what we had to fix any of the shit broken inside of me wasn't fair to me or you. There was only going to be so long you could've held me together before I lost it. Before I ripped straight through your life and mine and left you trying to put the fires out on the flaming pile I created in my wake.

"I don't blame you for running, Bay. I forgive you for

running. Because it was probably the only thing that could have kept me from becoming everything I'd ever hated."

A sound caught in her throat and she covered her mouth with both hands, tears overflowed and streamed down her cheeks. Her body lurched.

Behind me there was the twin sounds of chairs shooting back across the carpet and cracking into wood.

The old tingle crept up my spine, the one that made me want to face the incoming threat. Six years ago, I would have clenched my fists at my sides until blood pounded in my veins and the fog descended. Instead, I laid my hands flat on the table and kept alert, but not racing for the edge.

Bay glanced up with watery eyes and waved her hand, calling off her guard dogs. She grabbed a handful of napkins and rubbed them down her face, until red splotches covered her cheeks. Her shuddering breaths rattled the table.

"I was a codependent mess back then, shoving every feeling I had deep down until it was only a matter of time before it exploded and I repeated the same mistakes all over again." I'd been a fucked up kid playing pretend, almost flushing his future down the drain.

"I've been trying to convince myself for so long that I did the only thing I could have, but in my heart—in my heart I've never truly forgiven myself for what I did." She rested her hand, gripping the damp napkins on the table.

I ran my fingers over her knuckles, wanting to pick up her hand and press my lips against it. I wanted to make it all better. Her smooth tear-soaked skin was warm under my touch. Realizing what I was doing, I pulled back and dropped my hands into my lap.

A man stepped up to the side of the table. "Sorry to interrupt, but I wasn't sure if it was you until just now. My daughter is a huge fan. Could I have your autograph?" He shoved a pen and napkin in front of her.

Like he couldn't see we were having a conversation. Like she hadn't just been crying.

Bay's eyes widened, and she stared up at him like he'd asked for a kidney before slipping the mask back on. I could see the cracks. The red ringed eyes. The watery smile.

The way she switched told me this happened to her a lot. It pissed me off for her and hit a part of me that wanted to tell this guy to back off and leave her alone.

"Of course. Who should I make it out to?" She took the pen and paper from his hand.

He cleared his throat. "To Michael."

This asshole showed up while she was crying to get an autograph for himself. I unclenched my hands under the table and smoothed them down my legs, locking my gaze on to Bay. One signal and I'd get this guy out of here.

But she didn't signal. She pushed ahead with her lips molded into that plastic smile. Keeping her head down, she signed her name with a flourish and added in the personalization at the top.

"Could I get a picture too?"

She pushed her chair back. "Sure—"

"Sorry." Holden, the same guy from backstage at the concert, jumped in. He'd obviously known this had gone too far. He was the one to draw the line that Bay didn't seem able to draw for herself. "Bay's got to head off right now. But if you give me an address, we can send a VIP backstage tour swag pack to you--your daughter." He handed his card to the man, who kept looking over his shoulder as he walked away.

"Bay, we can move this to the suite, if that's okay with you." He tilted his head toward the windows facing the hallway. It swarmed with people. When I'd come down the hallway earlier, no one had been out in the vestibule area.

Now hotel security stood shoulder-to-shoulder, holding people back. The elevator doors opened and even more people poured out. Some came running down the hallways.

"Can we finish this in my suite? It's massive, not like a hotel room or anything. It'll just be quieter." She checked over her shoulder.

I wanted to shield her, to snap every phone pointed in her direction. Not because they were taking pictures, but because of her obvious discomfort. Couldn't they see she wasn't in the mood right now? She'd put on a brave face and tough it out, but her eyes were still puffy and red.

As bad of an idea as going to her suite was, I wanted her out of here.

Cell phones from all those inattentive businessmen came out. Whether they knew who she was or not, they knew something was going on, and we were the only two who didn't fit the profile of a normal visitor.

I wanted to get her out of here, to sweep her up and carry her away from all the eyes on her. That was precisely why this needed to be a one-time conversation to clear up old wounds. She didn't need me running in to save her from her own life.

"Sure."

Her shoulders relaxed and I was treated to a small smile that wasn't the least bit watery. "Great, and sorry about this. I know you probably get hounded too, though."

Flashes went off, and the security guards were quickly getting overwhelmed. Concern for her safety—not just now, but all the time—ratcheted up. Uneasiness coiled deep in my gut imagining her life like this all day, every day.

"Not like this." Sports fans were rabid, especially after

winning the championship last year. But none of the girls and women being held back now spared me a second glance.

Holden popped up behind Bay. "Follow me. We'll duck in through the kitchen into the staff elevator and get off on another floor, then double back to the penthouse elevator.

Bay looked to me and nodded.

"Let's go."

Holden took the lead with a member of the hotel staff and another two hotel security guards coming up behind me. Emily took the position behind Holden, and Bay and I walked side by side.

"Sorry about this." Bay leaned over and whispered once we were on the staff elevator. "It's an occupational hazard." The nervous smile did nothing to soothe my agitation over how quickly that clusterfuck had happened.

"This happens anytime you go out?"

"I don't go out much."

We walked through the deserted hotel floor to another bank of elevators. "I can see why."

Another set of elevator doors opened before our car arrived, and screams ripped through the enclosed space.

What felt like twenty people poured out, holding out posters, pictures, stuffed animals, and more for Bay to sign. For every few smiling and waving there were some who screamed her name like they didn't know how to form complete sentences, lunging toward her.

I looked between them and Bay's team to see how they were handling this. Bay's paper-thin smile was firmly in place and she flinched when someone tossed something to her. It landed at my feet. A plastic bobble head designed in her image.

My muscles tightened, and I braced myself.

Whenever I'd had run-ins with fans they generally had a lot to say. Especially if my luck hadn't worked that week in a game. Those days, it usually included the words "worthless," "sack," and "shit."

Behind the three hotel security guards and one other guy I hadn't noticed before, who kept catching Holden's eye, Bay signed autographs and scribbled her name down on whatever was thrust in front of her.

The elevator arrived and she made her apologies before being shuttled inside, leaving a couple of security guards behind.

A key swipe across the access pad in the elevator and we rose up to the top floor of the building.

"How'd they know what floor you were on?"

She chuckled. "The fans get crafty. Remember the ones in Rome, Holden?"

He rolled his eyes. "They snuck into the cleaning cart and surprised Bay in her bathroom after we made it off a ten-hour flight where she was fighting food poisoning the whole time."

Why was everyone acting like this wasn't a big deal?

Bay shook her head, throwing it back with her arms folded across her chest. "Let's just say, they got to see a whole new side to me. Those poor girls probably had their nose hairs singed off."

"And this happens regularly?" How the hell were they keeping her safe?

"That was a couple years ago. Since then, we've brought Eric on for full-time security coordination." Bay tapped his shoulder.

His cheek lifted in what I think was meant to be a smile.

We exited the elevator and walked into her suite. The suite was decorated in creams and whites, neutral tones.

Large windows like the ones in my apartment gave sweeping panoramic views of the city. There was a living room with low back chairs and a square coffee table in the center with a fresh flower arrangement.

It was quiet, and empty as far as I could tell.

Some of the tension left my body as we walked into the refuge after the chaos. It was like the music being cut in a stadium right before a field goal. Absolute silence after so much noise almost felt louder than the shouting.

Emily stepped in front of us. "What would you like to order? Anything?"

They both looked to me. "No, I'm good."

"I'm fine too."

Dropping her tablet to her side, she nodded. "Then we'll leave you to the living room. Holden and I will be in the office if you need anything, and Eric's outside."

Bay fidgeted with her hands. "Sorry again for what happened back there."

"It's not your fault."

"I mean, it kind of is." She tugged at her ponytail and eked out a huff of a laugh.

As much as she'd tried to play it off out there, she was nervous. Probably about more than just the fans, which seemed to be a normal part of her life. It was a reminder of so much of our history, how easy it still was for me to see her tells.

"I see you still do that when you're nervous."

She dropped her hand. "I guess I do. Although I usually have a gallon of hairspray and eight feet of extensions in my hair, so I don't get to do it too often."

"I thought suiting up before games was tricky."

"Platform heels, dresses I have to be sewn into. It gets pretty crazy sometimes. I'd thought the lounge would be safe, but someone always leaks things. I've learned that over the years." A cloud of sadness settled over her face.

It was a hard lesson no one should have to learn. I hated that she felt like she couldn't ever have any privacy or do things other people could, like have a cup of coffee with someone from their past.

"People sell you out often?"

The corners of her eyes crinkled. "More like almost always." She gestured toward the closed office doors Holden and Emily had disappeared behind. "Those are the only two people I've had around since the beginning. Not that some people haven't left for different gigs, but there have been a lot of people who want to make a quick buck by selling dirt. Not that there's much to tell."

"Why don't we sit and we can continue our talk?" I motioned to the four cream arm chairs around a frosted glass coffee table.

Bay nodded and took a seat.

I dropped into one across from her.

She nibbled her bottom lip. "Are you sure you don't want anything to eat or drink?"

"I'm good."

"Maybe for later?" A hopeful edge to her voice.

"I'm sure you're really busy, so I won't keep you, but there are some more things I wanted to say." Things I needed to say to stop being afraid to show her how screwed up I'd been. The fear of her finding out had made me panicky, on edge, and I needed to release all of that to move on. I needed to prove to myself that I could move on, even if every cell in my body screamed to touch her again.

Her palms pressed together and she wedged them between her thighs, scooting to the edge of her chair and nodding for me to go ahead. Her heels bounced up and down, but her gaze was locked onto mine.

My heart raced, but I held onto it and all the words I needed to say. I licked my lips. This was just as hard as those first words I'd needed to say to her back in California.

"Being open and vulnerable with you scared me, and I felt a lot of the same feelings I wasn't allowed to have growing up. They had been an invitation for abuse. They made it so easy for him to hurt me, so I covered them all over and tried to forget."

The bouncing of her knees stopped.

"But being around you and being with you—really being with you—brought back my feelings of losing control because I wasn't in control. I was in love. And you can't love someone when you're closed up and trying to hide. When you're putting on a brave face and only pretending you're giving them every inch of you and letting them into your heart."

"I—"

I cut her off, needing to tell her everything. "You couldn't be that person for me because I wasn't ready to be that person with you. So, no,"—I scrubbed my hands down my face—"as much as I wanted to hate you, as much as I wanted to smash that guitar all over again, as much as I wanted to run until I passed out in a gutter somewhere, I couldn't blame you. I can't blame you. I don't blame you. How could I expect you to love me when I hated myself?"

"What I wrote—"

"This isn't about what you said, Bay. This is about who I was and what I was dealing with. We were twenty-two, but we were kids and I was expecting you to fix me. That wasn't right. I was so afraid of failing, I was ready to throw it all away to follow you around and not let you out of my sight because I was afraid one day you'd look at me and realize how fucked up I was, because, guess what? I was still pretty fucked up."

I sucked in a lungful of air and released it. It felt like I'd said it all in one long breath, not wanting to chicken out and stop talking. I dragged my hands back and forth over my knees.

"I know that was a lot. And I feel you deserved to hear it."

Resting my hands on my legs, I let the tightness in my chest ease, replaced by a rightness of finally saying the words out loud. It was easy to confuse that rightness of saying what I needed to with a rightness at being here. I didn't belong here, I didn't belong with her. Old patterns were hard to break, especially ones you longed for, and I'd never longed for anyone as much as I had Bay. I felt it deep down in my bones, as though she'd been stitched into my DNA, even after all my talks with Monica and my engagement to Alice. But the whirlwind of her life brought things out in me that I couldn't go back to, which meant there was only one option. Leaving.

I stood from my seat. "Thank you for the invite for coffee."

She shot up. "Wait! You're leaving? That's it?" Her hands rose and fell at her sides.

"One soul-baring per day is my maximum."

"We can hang out. I'd love to hear what's going on in your life. Hell, we could watch Die Hard or something. I can get Holden to push the call we have later on." Her eager smile and hasty movements showed me how much she wanted me to stay.

"That's not a great idea."

The door to the office opened. "Don't mind me." Emily tiptoed from one door to the other.

"You've probably got a million things to do. The first game of the season's coming up on Sunday." Not that getting dressed and sitting for three hours took any energy at all, but I liked to be prepared.

An ache burned at the center of my chest to say yes. To sit and talk with her late into the night. To get to know each other all over again.

I walked past the living room furniture toward the door.

Bay's footsteps followed close behind.

Spending time with her was all I'd ever dreamed of for so many nights, but the ground I was standing on was still made of glass. Not the fragile splintering kind where the ledge was sharp and right at the edge of my toes. This was sturdy, but I could still see down to a place I didn't want to go again, and she was a one-woman sledgehammer.

"Maybe dinner?"

She had the life she deserved, and I wasn't going to be the guy to fuck any of it up for her. I wasn't sure I could be the guy she needed me to be when I couldn't even pull that off with Alice.

"I don't think it would be a good idea. Practices and games will be my life until January, maybe February if my magic touch holds."

The room quieted the same way a stadium of 40,000 people did when a player took a nasty hit.

She took a step back and dropped her head.

"You're right. Sorry for being so pushy." She slid back into the same smile I'd seen her use with the jerk guy downstairs in the lounge. "Thank you for agreeing to meet with me today. Thank you for your forgiveness." Her voice seemed to give out on that word. Her eyes glistened and the smile faltered. "And thank you for being so honest with me. I—I appreciate it." Jerking the door open, she stepped aside to let me go.

Her security guy stood from his chair beside the elevator.

I stepped in close and wrapped my arms around her. She smelled different. But the hint of raspberry was still there. Buried, but still there. I allowed myself a full three seconds before letting her go and stepping back. "Bye, Bay."

Through the rapidly closing door her words whispered through the air. "Bye, Keyton."

7

BAY

I stood with my back to the door.

He'd taken the first opening to leave and leapt at it. After what I'd done, I couldn't blame him. The first time we'd seen each other in California, I'd made it clear I had nothing to say to him.

And here I'd thought a few nice words and we could pick up right where we'd left off—where I'd left off. Where I'd left.

"Bay, sorry to interrupt, but the call we have—" Holden looked up from his tablet and dropped it to his side. "He's gone already?"

"Yeah, a lot to do to prep for the season." It sounded like someone else was saying the words—someone not trying to piece herself back together after the first real conversation she'd had in years. I ran my hands up and down my arms, trying to banish a chill in the perfectly temperature-controlled room.

Crossing the room, he set down the tablet that usually seemed permanently welded to his hand. "And you're not happy about that."

Was it written in Sharpie across my forehead?

I perched on the edge of the living room seats. "It felt so final. He'd never been so open about his feelings before. There wasn't anything cagey or guarded about him. He was an open book. It's what I'd always hoped he'd be, and here he was, and he pretty much sprinted from the room the second I mentioned having dinner or watching a movie."

"Maybe he needed to wake up early." Holden offered it up like I was sitting alone at a birthday party no one showed up to. "You can't say you've never had to cut a night short because of work the next day."

I brushed my fingers across my lips thinking about the last time mine had touched his while he slept. "He said 'bye, Bay' and it didn't hit me like 'we'll catch up later'. It sounded a lot like 'have a nice life'." My shoulders sagged and I slid off the arm of the chair into the seat like I'd been knocked down. I felt like I'd been sprinting the entire day and was finally collapsing.

"Do you want to start something with him?" He sat on the edge of the coffee table, eyes intent on mine. "I'm going to cancel the call."

The magnetic pull of Holden's tablet called to him, but he resisted and focused on me.

"No, I'm fine." I tried to straighten in the chair, but the heaviness in my chest didn't ease. How I felt inside must've been telegraphed on my face. Holden and I had a silent agreement that I'd do whatever it took to make my career a success.

"Pretty hard to have anything with someone who doesn't want anything to do with you." Dating hadn't been on my radar for a long time. Trying to date anyone in this business was a recipe for disaster. I'd seen it happen so many times, which was why the shock reverberated through me that I'd even want to try with Keyton. After everything that had happened between us, I'd be lying if I didn't say that a flare of hope was there when I found out he wasn't with Alice anymore.

Desperation called and they wanted their look back. I needed to suck it up and forget about it. We'd both gotten to say what we needed to say. This could be the end.

"But you'd like to, if he were up for it?"

"Why are you asking me these questions?" I snapped.

Holden sighed, shaking his head. "When was the last time you've been on a date, Bay?"

I flung my hand in his direction. "You'd know better than me."

He coughed into his hand and wiped the smile away. "July, a year ago."

"Ding ding ding. Get the man a prize." I injected a double dose of sarcasm into my voice. Let's focus on Holden and not me.

He leveled his gaze at me, quick and incisive. It was the kind of look that made me lock my muscles, so I didn't squirm. He wasn't falling for it.

"What's your point?"

He scooted to the edge of the table. "Maybe, just maybe, you're not ready for things to be over with him."

"Do you think I should get a burlap sack and kidnap him and force him to have dinner with me?" There were no options. Keyton didn't want options. There were some things all the fame and money in the world couldn't buy.

"All I'm saying is, you have people. Outrageously handsome, immaculately dressed, insanely charismatic, incredibly good-at-their-jobs people." He straightened his imaginary tie. "Your people can call his people and set something up."

"This isn't about photo ops or a red-carpet appearance." I looked over my shoulder at the door that had slammed closed behind him. "And I think I've lost my shot." My body sagged into the chair like a battery giving up its last 1%.

"It's been a long day. You're right about the call. Let's cancel. I'm going to bed."

"We fly to Atlanta tomorrow. We need to be at the airport at five. Three days there and then back here."

Another day, another airport. "Are we leaving my stuff here or do I need to pack up?" I dragged myself out of the chair like a slug on Ambien.

Holden's head tilted. "Go ahead and leave everything you won't need in Atlanta. I'll clear the extra days with the hotel. Get some rest. You look like you need it."

"Wow. Night, Holden."

Back in my room, I changed into my pajamas. What a mopey pain in the ass I was. This was the fucking dream. I got to share my music with the world. People not only knew my name, but screamed it, surrounding my SUV and losing their minds when they met me.

So why was the hour I'd spent with Keyton one of the first times in a long time I'd felt like I was experiencing something real?

～

The lights in the booth were dim, with only a low wattage bulb over my spot behind the mic. Cream soundproofing panels were attached to the wall, a lot classier than the gray egg-carton type in some studios.

This was a long way from the dank basement recording studio I'd worked at in college, and way more advanced than Freddie's place back in Greenwood.

I swayed, my head dipping, and stumbled back. Jerking forward, I grabbed onto the mic stand in front of me, nearly setting both it and me flying.

"Bay! Are you okay?" Holden's insistent, concerned voice boomed through the soundproofed booth intercom.

"I'm good!" I covered my mouth, yawning so wide my jaw ached.

"Let's call it."

"No, I can go one more time."

"You're good. It's the soundboard. Sorry you've been here so long. You should've told me you were tired."

All the eyes on the other side of the glass were focused on me.

"Nope." I stifled another yawn. "I'm totally fine."

He *hmm*ed before turning off the intercom.

I'd made the mistake of complaining that I was tired in my first touring year before my album came out. Double shows between opening for Without Grey and playing my own at smaller venues for thirty-seven days straight had culminated in a press tour and studio recording time. Naps were luxuries taken with a sweatshirt stuffed under my head on the floor, countertops, anywhere I could curl up and pass out for sometimes as little as twenty minutes.

Holden had wanted me to slow down, but we were both trying to prove ourselves. We'd pushed harder than ever before which had led me to the precipice of intense burnout right before the two months reserved for finishing my next album.

The stories that had floated around about my lack of professionalism and diva behavior had almost ruined all the goodwill Holden and I had worked on cultivating right before my album released. That was when I'd learned never to complain—at least not out loud. Always be ready to go for another take or another outfit change or another encore.

Somehow being at the center of attention in small settings like this was way worse than up on stage. On stage, the faces melded into one giant swaying organism that recited all my lyrics back to me. In here, I could see the dissection going on in everyone's head.

The manager, Holden, trying to decide how much harder to push me.

The assistant, Emily, trying to keep up with Holden.

The storied producer, Leon—we'd come down here to talk to him about my new album.

The label executive running numbers on how many units and streams I'd need in my last album on my current contract.

The studio producer who was just happy to be in the room. I'd felt the same when I'd worked in the studios. Sometimes things were a drag, but there were those magical unicorn moments where you felt like you were flying above the clouds watching a group of people breathe life into a unique creation.

My dad would've loved every minute of it. It still felt pinch-myself surreal that this was my life. All he'd wanted to do was get up on stage and play. Some nights he'd been able to do it before heading into the office the next day. He'd have been to every show, listened to every album on repeat. I knew he'd have been proud. This was a once-in-a-lifetime opportunity, and I continued to be determined not to squander it.

My suggestions and my thoughts for the album were shot down with a word from Leon, dismissed as trite and unoriginal. They had been running through my head for months, and the first time I'd spoken up, a man with more production Grammys than almost anyone alive had told me exactly how they were absolutely shit.

Instead of crawling under the console, I'd kept my head up, deferred to the master, and gone to my place in front of the mic.

This side of the glass was rough between working with new people, trying out new songs, seeing how well we all worked together. Part zoo exhibit, part child stuck in the corner, I waited for the intercom to click on from the other side.

Leon shot up from his seat. The veins on the side of his neck bulged. He flung his hands up and stormed out of the room.

His reputation wasn't overblown one bit. He might be a musical genius, but he was also a dick. But I'd work with him, if it got us the best new album for the fans.

My stomach churned, a cauldron of ill will at being subjected to his freak outs. It wouldn't be the first time I'd put up with someone like that to get the job done. It's what professionals did, right?

I slid my headphones off and looked to Holden.

The intercom clicked back on. Holden leaned over the console and looked straight at me, his lips pursed and jaw tight. "We're good for tonight."

Oh shit. The cauldron was overflowing with worry now.

I set the headphones on the mic stand hook. Rushing out into the hallway, I faced Holden. The studio door closing behind him.

"What happened? I said I could go for another, if we needed." I stared at the now-empty hallway behind him. "Is he that pissed?"

"Leon is Leon and you're tired." His jaw was still tight, but not angry.

"I'm not." Cupping both my hands over my mouth, I tried to swallow my yawn.

"You're one Red Bull short of a coma. Let's get you back to the hotel."

"Why'd he freak?"

"Don't worry about it."

Emily came out of the production side door with all our bags.

On the ride back to the hotel, the two of them tapped furiously on their phones and scribbled on their tablets. They were probably talking to each other.

A noise jingled through the interior of the black SUV. I stared out the window. When we'd gone inside, the sun had still been up. Now night life had taken over the city. Keyton would play tomorrow. I'd planned on checking the score before warning myself away from it.

I'd followed his career at the beginning. It had been a blow when I'd realized he'd been cut from the team and bumped down to the practice squad, an electric guitar swung straight at my chest. His career had been faltering while mine had been poised to take off. That had made it even harder to think about calling him up. What the hell was I supposed to say?

Now that he'd landed on his feet the question still reverberated in my head.

"Bay, it's your phone."

I jolted and looked down at my bag on my lap. Rummaging through it, I grabbed the glowing screen nestled between the notebooks tucked inside.

More at ease, I tapped the screen. "Hi, Mom."

"Hey, Superstar."

"Ugh, I hate it when you call me that."

"What else am I supposed to call you when I have to

call you on a different number every three months?"
There were barely more than three contacts in my phone.
My mom. Holden. And Emily. I almost never made calls.
None of the numbers were ever registered to me directly,
but six months had been the longest we'd gone without
the number leaking and the weird calls and texts flooding
in.

"Your daughter or Bay?"

"But you know both of those things. Sometimes you
need a reminder that you're my superstar."

I grinned. "Thanks, Mom. How are you doing?"

"Good. Enjoying my early retirement. Met a new guy."

A pang went straight to my chest. You could forget about
an old pain for a while, but something would hit it out of
nowhere and it came rolling in again. I missed my dad, and I
knew she did too, but she deserved to be happy. "Will I get
to meet him soon?"

"You will, if you're home for Thanksgiving."

I covered the end of the phone and whispered, "Thanksgiving?" to Holden.

He held up his hand, teetering it back and forth.
"Depends on whether we add extra shows or not. They've
sold out already and the arenas are looking to shift a few
things to squeeze more in. Tickets for most shows were gone
within two hours."

Arenas worth of people wanted to hear my songs. I
remembered how it had felt to wait with my laptop and a
phone, ready to click a button and snag a ticket for a musician I loved, and how much it had sucked when they'd sold
out. The tug-of-war to not let anyone down intensified.

"It's still up in the air. We leave for the European leg of
the tour at the end of October. We could fly you both out to
wherever I'll be."

"You don't even know?" She said it like I'd announced I'd forgotten my own name.

"I barely remember what day it is." I chuckled and tugged on the end of my ponytail. It was Sunday, right? No, Saturday.

"You tell Holden to stop running you so ragged." Her chiding Mom-tone wrapped around me like a weighted blanket.

I stifled another yawn. "He's not running me ragged. I'm totally fine."

"Says the young lady three minutes from passing out in the back of her SUV."

"How'd you know?"

"It's the only way you travel nowadays. Not that I can blame you. The Rio concert was kind of crazy."

A security miscommunication had led us down the wrong street and straight in the path of throngs of fans coming to the concert. Once they knew it was me inside, we'd almost been rocked off our wheels by people trying to get pictures and autographs.

"It was, but it was my own fault for trying to sign autographs in a crowd that big."

"I hope you're keeping safe."

I hated worrying her, but we'd been good about security. There hadn't been any weird letters or gifts sent in over a year. So far it was standard fan fanaticism and nothing bordering on dangerous. Even Eric had taken a more lax approach.

"Always."

"Well, my dates are open for Thanksgiving. But I'll have to check with Ray about his plans. He's got kids in the area, so I don't know if he'll want to travel around then. Will you be inviting anyone else to our dinner, no matter where we have it?" Her fishing expedition had the subtlety of a thirty-pound salmon to the face.

"No, Mom. No other guests."

"Why not? What about that Mark guy I see you in all the perfume counter ads with?"

I laughed. "Campaign photoshoots don't mean we're in a relationship." Plus, Mark's breath smelled like he'd eaten nothing but week-old tuna for the entire morning before we'd been plunked down in the middle of a desert set sharing a white chaise lounge. He might've looked pretty, but he wasn't a thrilling conversationalist, which was probably why I'd made it out of the shoot with my nose hairs intact.

"But you two looked so doe-eyed in those pics."

"It's called doing my job."

"What about the one from your music video? With the blonde hair?"

"He's an actor. Hired for the job." He'd been nice. No tuna breath there, but he'd also been engaged. His exceedingly nice girlfriend hadn't even glared at me once while we got into some totally above-board compromising situations.

"From the way you two were rolling around in the sheets, I thought maybe..."

I slapped my hand over my eyes, trying to hold back the cringe. "Stop watching my stuff."

"How can I not? It comes up on my YouTube recommended videos all the time."

"It's because you keep watching the videos."

"Well, how else am I supposed to see my daughter?" She laughed, but under the melodic sound there was a hint of truth.

There hadn't been any cookie-and-hot-chocolate mother-daughter mornings since I'd graduated. Over college breaks, we'd stayed up late or early depending on her shifts, watched movies, and eaten way too many cookies. The breakneck schedule I'd pushed myself on had left so much of my previous life in the rearview mirror. It was hard to stop a runaway train and nothing in my life felt like it was in my control anymore.

"I miss you too, Mom."

"It's my job as a mom to worry. First page of the manual they hand out at the hospital says 'get ready to worry more than you've ever worried in your entire life.'"

"Thanks for the parenting heads up."

"Are you doing okay?"

"I'm good. Tired, but good. Looking forward to a break after the tour is finished. Then we can do a girls' trip somewhere. Anywhere you want. Just the two of us for a few weeks." I didn't look up at Holden to see the bug-eyed panic scrawled all over his face.

"That sounds wonderful. I'm holding you to it."

"I know you will. I love you, Mom." The SUV pulled up to the front of the hotel.

"Love you, my superstar."

I ended the call and stuck the phone back into my bag.

Somewhere between being hustled out of the car and into the elevator, fatigue slammed into me like an overloaded amp. It barreled right into me, nearly knocking me off my feet.

Meetings on top of meetings. Fittings. Interviews. Hours in the studio. This wasn't the life I'd envisioned for myself. I'd thought I'd be performing in smoky bars, maybe get upgraded to a movie-theater-turned-concert-venue in towns all over the US, loading and unloading my own gear.

This was a life beyond my own imagination and I was living it every day. But I couldn't get rid of the gnawing feeling in my chest, the one that kept me up late at night, that I tried to fill with the home renovation chatter instead of falling asleep with my own thoughts.

That feeling screamed at me for being even the slightest bit ungrateful for everything I'd been given and all the people who counted on me. But at the end of the day, when I dragged myself into bed, it was the thing I'd always thought I'd have no trouble being—alone.

The loneliness was harder to push back. The quiet moments rang in my ears with the hollowness of the life created around me—the one where everyone knew my name, but no one knew me.

8

KEYTON

From the treadmill I stared out over the city soaking up the morning sun. Running wasn't an escape anymore—it was how every day started. It was a way to get some energy out, while I went through everything on the schedule that Gwen sent over.

Keep things calm, measured and uneventful. If I knew what I had coming up, I could disarm some of the old reflexes that came from not knowing what the hell was going on around me. I couldn't control it all, but I could make sure my reactions weren't coming from a place of being absolutely about to lose my shit. And it worked—most of the time.

But this morning I was restless. Bay's face when I'd left the other day had stuck with me on the elevator ride back to my apartment. The hotel had been swarming with fans. Security was higher than I'd ever seen it before.

Was she safe up there? Her floor had been quiet, but she had to leave at some point. Had she already gone?

I wanted to go back to her. Talk to her even longer. Take

her up on her dinner invitation. Taste the lips she'd been nibbling.

Jamming my finger into the stop button, I growled at myself. Stop it.

There was no point in going off on one of these tangents again. Bay had her life, the best life she could've ever dreamed of. So why was there a glimmer of sadness in her eyes?

Probably because she'd been sitting across from me, the guy from her past who'd always been nothing but trouble. But the replay of her face had stuck with me since I'd left her hotel room. I couldn't stop thinking about how good it had felt to run my fingers across her skin, even though it was only her knuckles.

More than a couple times in the past 36 hours, I'd walked to my apartment door before talking myself out of going back there.

After my shower, I pulled out the big guns. Inside my office, I pulled open the drawer in my desk and pulled out my supplies. Sunlight flooded in through the open curtains.

Flicking the lid on the wooden box, I searched for the right pencil.

With it clenched between my teeth, I flipped open the sketch pad.

Drawing helped. I didn't only draw Bay like I had in college. I drew things around me. Scenes that stuck in my head. Scenes from my past. Scenes from my present. The scrape of the pencil or charcoal against a pad of paper helped me process a lot of the shit flying ninety-miles-per-hour in my brain.

Today I drew her. I lost myself in the memories of seeing her up close for the first time in six years. Not when she'd been Bay ready to walk out on stage, but when she'd sat across from me with the hot-chocolate-stained lips.

The drawing took long enough that the side of my finger ached from gripping the pencil. By the time I set it down, the morning sun wasn't peeking out from above the horizon —it was searing in the sky.

I jerked forward in my seat to check the time. The stampeding heartbeat slowed. There were still three hours until I needed to be at the stadium.

Dragging my finger along the space where her hair cast a shadow over her forehead, I smudged the lines of her face and held up the paper.

She stared back at me. The glimmer hadn't been imagined. It had been there. And there was nothing I could do about it—nothing I should do about it.

We'd both made our choices. It was only fair we lived with them, no matter how much we hoped we could take it all back. There was no erasing the past.

After a shower, I made my breakfast and headed into work to sit on my ass and do nothing and hope whatever the hell had worked so far continued to work. Sometimes I felt paralyzed, like anything I changed in my game day routine might break the spell cast over my stadium presence. I'd given up on it because the rituals had gotten too obsessive. I couldn't control this. Everyone else thought I did, but it didn't mean I didn't want them to win. I just wished I could do something that actually mattered out there.

The first game of a brand-new season. Nervous energy led to seated leg bouncing, which led to pacing. All the calm from drawing had evaporated in a matter of hours. I left my apartment when the waiting became unbearable.

Inside the locker room, I suited up early.

Support and coaching staff strode through the room

with purpose. It was less of a room and more a hive. The physio rooms were off the main locker room, which weren't so much lockers as oversized cubbies. The conditioning and rehab rooms had all the latest recovery tech.

There were ice baths that felt like you were being stabbed all over your body with sub-zero icicles. Not that I'd needed them with my level of game play. I'd jumped into one once before a game in LA and ended up doing it before every game in order to not lose the mojo. When I'd moved on to Phoenix, I was sure to leave that out of my pre-game ritual.

Long gone were the days of needing to wash and take care of my own gear. It was all set out on the wide padded bench seat in front of the placard with my name.

Honeycombs of activity all connected together. Learning new stadiums, new coaching staff, and new teams every season or two always created a settling-in period, but this was my second season with Philly and the initial transition had been less scary than the others.

The locker room door opened, and the crew of guys who were the closest thing I had to family outside of Knox and his parents burst through the doorframe.

"Keyton," they shouted as one, like we hadn't seen each other a few days ago at the first pre-season game.

I ducked my head and braced myself for the dog pile.

They barreled into me, squeezing me and whooping about kicking some serious ass this season. Everyone had done the same thing during training camp and the pre-season games.

"You guys need to work on your hellos. No damaging the merchandise or maybe you won't get another ring." I shrugged them off with a laugh, smoothing down the hair they'd ruffled. Confidence always played a part in my role. If I swore it would happen, people around me fell in line.

Reece grinned, his green eyes twinkling with mischief. "Isn't that how we get that luck? Rubbing our fingers through your luscious locks?" He reached for my head again.

I slapped his hands away. "Not if you want to keep those hands for catching passes."

He grinned and untied his red-and-white Adidas before tucking them safely in his locker. The sneaker obsession hadn't died after college.

"Thanks for taking care of that number for me, man." Berk knocked into my shoulder with his fist.

Before I'd joined the team, it had been his number—a number that had meant a lot to him.

"You know I didn't ask them to make you give it up." He hadn't brought it up all last season, but I knew it had to have been hard for him.

He huffed and lifted his chin. "I know. But if it helps us win again this year, I'm good with it." A lopsided smile set my worries at ease.

"You'll get it back once I leave." My number stayed the same from team to team, no one wanting to upset the balance too hard in any one direction.

All three guys whipped back around from their various stages of stripping down or suiting up.

Berk stopped toeing off his beat-to-shit sneakers. "You're planning on leaving us already?"

"Four teams in six years. I've gotten used to it."

"But you got us to the championship last year." LJ stared at me with his eyes wide, like I'd be insane to leave. He was the only one who might have the slightest hint of understanding about what it was like to be on a team where you never got to play. Our old college coach had benched him for most of the last two seasons because of his best friend, the coach's daughter. They'd started out as just friends, but the turning point had probably come at some point around when I'd found him on his knees with her skirt bunched up around her hips 'checking for a bee sting'. They pretended to be just friends for a while longer before it all came out.

He'd been an absolute wreck that season when he could get barely a quarter of field time.

Try an average of less than a play most games.

"I know, it'll be good to get back on the field with you guys this season."

Reece tugged on his moisture-wicking shirt. "You looked great during training camp. I can't believe they don't have you starting."

I did. I was unproven. An unproven vet. "Such is the life of the human good luck charm." I got ready, putting on all my gear although I'd be lucky to set foot beyond the sidelines this game. 'Woe is me' felt wrong. So many guys would kill to be in my position. How many made it to their fifth season with only one injury?

Everyone stopped by the strength and conditioning coaches and physiotherapists. Reece had a clicky shoulder. Berk's hamstring was on the mend, and LJ's left knee had been giving him trouble. After my break in Charlotte there hadn't been anything serious, but I hadn't strained a muscle in three years.

When most guys were hitting the end of their pro run, I had fresh legs and arms—hell, my body was practically still covered in the plastic sheeting that was so satisfying to peel off the screen of a new phone.

Coach came in to give us a rousing speech about how this season would be our season again. I'd heard the speech many times before, and I didn't miss the gazes darting in my direction throughout it.

No shrinking back. No having guys doubt their chances out on the field. It was what I did. Even though I did fucking nothing. Inside, my heart raced like I was about to run out onto the field and snatch an interception from the air, but I kept the cool, confident exterior humming along.

"Suit up and let's show everyone what we're made of!"

His final shout of determination shot a spike of adrenaline through me, although I wouldn't be playing. The smells of pain reliever, leather, plastic pads, and determination hung in the air, and everyone was pumped.

A few minutes later, it was time to take our places in the lineup to head out to the sidelines. Guys bounced on the toes of their feet, sprung high into the air, or rocked back and forth, gazes fixed on the light at the end of the stadium-staff-lined tunnel.

Announcements echoed and reverberated down, bouncing off the painted cinderblock walls. I rested my bare fingertips against the wall, feeling the energy of the place. Everyone behind me did the same, and then the guys in front of me caught on and reached their hands out.

Every move I made before a game became a team ritual. Sometimes I was tempted to break out into the chicken dance.

LJ knocked into my shoulder. "You ready?"

A chuckle locked in my chest. "I'm always ready." To sit on the sidelines.

Guys up front took off toward the field and we followed along, fingers brushing against the wall, not losing contact until we raced out of the tunnel through the giant banner to kick off the season before finding our spots on the sidelines.

Around me, the stadium came alive like a writhing,

undulating beast. Fans were on their feet, screaming from the time they entered until they left. The city certainly had a way of welcoming its athletic heroes.

Goose bumps rose on my arms like cleats pressing into fresh sod.

I stared up at the stands and breathed in the sights and sounds. The whole place was coming alive.

The team huddled up, and I took my place amongst them. Slowly, a path parted through the huddle and I was nudged closer to the front. My helmet rocked and tapped as guys rubbed and patted it like I was a lucky charm. I'd learned after my first season to wear the helmet during the huddle or they'd rub a damn bald spot into my head.

Coach shoved his headset down around his neck and clapped his hands against his clipboard before addressing the team. "Let's get out there everyone and kick off this season the right way. Keyton's here with us once again, which means we're bringing home the ring in February. Do what needs to be done to get us all there and make this city proud!"

The team clustered even tighter before shouting 'we've come to win!' and breaking the huddle. Offensive and defensive lines broke apart, finding their coaches. The offense rushed out onto the field.

I pulled off my helmet and grabbed my seat on the edge of the bench.

Berk, Reece and LJ all had their time on the field.

But the win was tight. In the final seven seconds, a field goal sailed through the air of an almost-silent stadium, ready to snatch the game from the jaws of victory.

The wind gods were with us and it flew wide, glancing off the left upright.

Pacing on the sidelines turned to cheers. Towels were

whipped overhead and primal screams ripped through the stands. I'd hate to see what happened when we lost. It felt inevitable and like a ticking time bomb looming over my professional career.

I was debriefed, showered, changed and back out to my car before some of the fans had even left. We were all meeting up at Tavola for dinner after the game, which had become harder to get a table at than any five-star restaurant in the city. Good thing we knew the owner. Nix had left The Brothel before I moved in, but he helped keep up a steady supply of killer food for our house full of football players.

I'd settle into another season of reviewing tapes for games I wasn't in and reviewing opponents' tapes to study for games I wouldn't play in, but the thread of hope was there that I could make it onto the field this season. Not in the first city I'd ever considered home, but in Wisconsin.

Sitting in my car, I checked my messages. There was one from Gwen.

Gwen: Headstrong Foundation floored when they saw you in pics with Bay. Heads up, they're asking her to perform at the SeptemberWeen Carnival.

I stared at the screen, my heart hammering into over-drive. First, there were pictures of Bay and I floating around. They could only be from when we were having coffee. They had now been shared everywhere. Was the pain etched on her face as slicing as I'd remembered? As I'd drawn? How fucked was it that other people were trading in these pics like it was no big deal?

Second...

Me: Did she respond?

Gwen: They're still waiting to hear back from her people

I dropped my head back against the headrest.

She had to be inundated with requests like these. The

odds she'd remember my foundation were small. Her people would screen it out. Headstrong Foundation was a small, new organization. There were hundreds, if not thousands, doing the same thing and trying to make a difference, but she didn't have infinite time. It didn't mean she'd make room in her schedule for me.

It was dangerous hoping she would. When the door had closed behind me on Friday, I'd made peace with it being the last time I saw her. The protective streak and my old instincts had shown me that I still hadn't come as far as I'd thought.

But this was different. If she said yes, it might have nothing to do with me. Maybe it would be her charity check box for the year. Maybe she'd accept and walk away once she realized I was involved. Or maybe this was the universe giving us another chance. A second chance's second chance.

And maybe I would be ready this time.

9

BAY

The flight from Atlanta took off on time, even though there were delays on the main runways. The perks of flying private. Sometimes, though, I longed for a cramped middle seat, a hint of the normalcy I had once taken for granted.

Today's session with Leon had gone better than on Saturday and Sunday, but something felt off. I'd woken up in a cold sweat thinking about working with him for two months solid before launching into a new tour. He was one of the best. He'd come highly recommended. Every album he worked on went platinum. I'd be stupid to back out. I could suck it up and get the work done.

I trusted Holden with my career, and, at times, my life. I trusted him to guide me in the right direction, but it had been hard to settle into anything that felt like comfortable during those two sessions. But some things took longer to meld together than others. I'd work harder and do what I needed to fall in line. Leon didn't have a room full of Grammys because he didn't know what he was doing.

"Earth to Bay, will you be joining us this evening?"

Holden sat across from me at the four-seater table behind the long couch running along one side of the plane.

"Do you know the first time I got onto one of these, I thought I'd never be on one again?" The cream and gold interior screamed understated classic like the polo match in Pretty Woman. A fresh floral arrangement sat in a glass bowl on every table. Living in this bubble was weird.

"You definitely didn't act like it. You were a bit distract-ed." He set down his tablet and folded his hands on top of it. Over the years we'd both changed a lot. He'd gone from a fledgling manager under Maddy's wing to the solo wrangler of the Bay show. Maddy handled the big things, but Holden was my day-to-day number one. We felt like a team, both in way over our heads and keeping this ship plowing through the waves even though sometimes it felt like we had no idea where it might end up.

The watch he'd bought when we were in Paris peeked from beneath his crisp white cuff. Not a Rolex—that was far too common for Holden. It was a Patek Philippe. It cost more than a year of my college tuition, but it suited him.

He looked like he'd been born on a private jet. I didn't think I'd ever seen him in jeans before.

"I was distracted."

"A lot like you are now." He waved his hand in my direction.

"There's a lot on my mind." My reflection stared right back at me in the window.

"We have the second half of a three-continent, forty-eight-city tour to finish in two months, we need to finish up all the pre-work for the new album, decide on the promo tour and Maddy is going to want to talk to you about the contract negotiations for the new multi-album deal. There's not a lot of time for distractions."

"I know." Beyond my reflection, the dark sky was filled with clouds and stars seemed pinned to the horizon. There was always a lot to do. Half the time I didn't know what I'd be doing from day to day without Holden and Emily shepherding me from one location to the next. At each stop, I never knew the full extent of what was in store for me until I arrived. There wasn't enough time for that.

He let out a long, low breath, the kind that meant something big happened. I'd heard it right before he announced my album had gone to number one, but he also used it to tell me I'd gotten a threatening letter and Eric would need some backup to keep me safe for a few months a year ago. It was always a toss-up on what kind of news the breath brought.

"Lay it on me." I wiggled the fingers of both hands. "Stop holding back and freaking me out."

"We get a lot of requests for you to do benefits and charity work." He tapped his thumbnail against his lips.

That was his deep thought move. Not bad, not good. The benefits and charity requests were information I already knew. With my schedule like it was, we tried to fit in as many as we could. It wasn't always possible. But I couldn't relax yet.

He was never this cagey when it came to saying no, if we couldn't make it work. "A new batch arrived and I thought you should maybe make the decision this time around."

There was more to this. He didn't drop the serious face unless he was worried. The drone of the engines drowned out the clench in my heart.

Sliding the tablet across the table, he watched me.

What the hell could be on here that had him acting so weird? The names at the top were standard ones we'd worked with before, but his careful attention put me on edge.

I scanned down the list. The dates for many wouldn't work when lined up against my schedule. "Can we give them all a nice bundle of merchandise I can sign for their auctions or to giveaway? And maybe I could do a video call in or something."

"For all of them?" His pointed stare sent me back to the list.

Why didn't he just spit it out? I glared at him and looked back to the list, running through each one until the new name I'd missed before jumped out at me. Only it wasn't new. I'd heard it before.

My head shot up. "Is this his foundation? Keyton's?"

Holden nodded. "Yes."

"Did he ask for me?" Hope flared in my chest. "Did you do this? Did you contact them?"

He sighed shaking his head. "I didn't touch it after you said to leave it alone." His tone leeched disapproval.

"But I did make sure it was added to the list, just in case. Someone from their events department contacted Emily, possibly after the pictures of you two hit the web."

My hope plummeted just as quickly. He probably hadn't asked for me as a way to see me again. It had probably been his people.

The pictures of us were already swirling around online. His 'goodbye' felt final. I stared at the date. The end of next week. The rest of the schedule was laid out in black and white. Going would cause a bottleneck, which would mean mainlining Red Bull and coffee for a week, but I needed to do this. I needed to show him and myself that we'd made our amends and we could both move on. I didn't want either of us to have to carry this baggage around anymore.

"I want to do it."

"I figured." His head jerked in a sharp nod. "Already working on rearranging the schedule."

One week.

"There are a few press events they'll need you to do a week or so before."

"Whatever they need." I ran my fingers along the smooth edge of the table. "Do—do you know if he'll be there?" I was a stupid, hopeless idiot for doing this. For hoping to see him again and have an excuse to talk to him one more time. Maybe knowing it would be the last time would make it easier to watch him walk away from me.

Helping his foundation was the least I could do. No expectations. No strings attached.

"I don't know. I can confirm before we respond."

Shaking my head, I looked out the window. The weather didn't feel as bleak as it had before. "No, that's okay. I'll do it no matter what."

Even if he wasn't there. The least I could do was support a charity that meant a lot to him. My face and name could be used for something other than selling albums or magazine covers.

"And recording in Philly? How do you feel about that? At least for the partial tracks for the album."

"I thought you said we'd do it in Atlanta." We'd looked for rental houses so we wouldn't have to stay in a hotel the whole time. We'd talked about collaborations with local artists. This didn't make any sense.

Holden's head tilted and he leveled a long, assessing gaze at me. "I think Philly will be better for you. Plus, Without Grey recorded their last album there and they just went double platinum."

"What about all the things we signed off on in Atlanta?"

Panic gripped my chest. "Did Leon cancel the deal? Does he not want to work with me?"

We'd sat through two hours of meetings before signing a huge stack of papers at the end. I'd had to initial every page before handing it over to Holden.

"It wasn't his choice. It was mine. It's my job to take care of that stuff, isn't it? He had an oversized ego and a piss-poor attitude."

"But—" The argument died in my throat, totally wiped out by relief. Thinking of working with Leon so closely hadn't settled my nerves one bit. Recording in Philly meant being closer to Keyton. The jury was still out on whether that was a good thing or not.

"He wasn't going to help you get through the album any easier."

"He's one of the best in the business."

"So are you." He winked. "Plus, you'll be getting me a new watch for Christmas to make it up to me for sorting it all out."

"Don't you already have one?" I tapped my finger against the glass face of his watch.

He hissed and jerked his arm back, petting the brushed steel around the glass. "Don't ever touch a man's watch like that." Slipping a square cloth from his inside jacket pocket, he ran it over the face of his watch.

For a guy so into his clothes and watches, looking at him, I'd have thought he was an athlete for sure. A posh sort though. Maybe polo or crew. Something refined and too expensive for anyone without multiple zeroes in their bank account to even attempt.

"Where should I send the Christmas present? Are you going to visit your family?"

His wry chuckle was followed by an eyebrow jump. "Another fishing expedition?"

I rested my elbows on the table, leaning forward, happy to have the attention off me. "I could hire a detective, you know? Find out all your Holden Yates' mysteries."

"This threat again." He shook his head and barely contained his eye roll.

He'd perfected the manager, man-in-the-shadows mode.

"You know everything about me, and sometimes I feel like we've only just met from how little I know about you."

"You know tons. I'm an impeccable dresser." He tugged at the lapels of his blazer. "I can bench press two hundred pounds. I have outstanding taste in watches, wine and women."

"In that order."

His gaze narrowed. "One more word and I'll leave you on the tarmac. You'll have to find your own way back to the hotel."

I flipped open the notebook in front of me and scribbled down the words at the top of a new page. "Idle threats."

"No." He grabbed for the spiral bound paper. "Do not do it."

"'Glaring. Glowering. Growling.' The fans are going to eat this up." I played keep away with my notebook. "All about a gritty drifter crisscrossing the country, sorting through thrift stores for clothes and shoes."

He flopped back into his chair with his arms folded across his chest, his face a half step from a pout. "You wouldn't."

"Oh but I would, if you don't make like a piñata and start spilling some sweet secrets. One thing. I know you've got an older brother and a younger sister. Both parents are alive. At least they were two years ago. Outside of that, I feel like I know nothing about you."

"We spend eighteen hours a day together. You know all there is to know." He said it like we didn't all have a past. One that shaped and guided us no matter how much we pretended it didn't.

"I know you now. You know about all my baggage and secrets."

"Hard to miss them when you've literally written three albums spilling them for the entire world."

"Did you come straight from London to LA? Did you go to college in the UK?"

His head snapped up. "How did you know I lived in London?"

I rolled my eyes. "It's the only city where you disappear for hours on end when you're off the clock. Plus, I saw you from the balcony the last time we were there. You were saying goodbye to four or five people. I figured if you knew that many people there, you'd probably lived there."

"The one time you weren't watching House Hunters... I lived there. Went to boarding school from the time I was fourteen. It wasn't long enough to pick up the accent though."

"Instead you went with an 'old money from the Northeast' accent."

"I don't have an accent."

"Not so much an accent, but an air. Carefully crafted."

His huff of amusement turned into a smile. "Oh, how it has been. Now you have your one bit of information. I lived in London."

"What? No, I found that out on my own. I need something else. Come on, I'm starved for information."

"Fine, I hate pizza."

I gasped. "Get the hell out!" I pointed to the airtight plane door. "Who even are you?" Clutching my notebook to my chest, I shook my head and stared back at this alien imposter who'd been in my presence for the past six years.

"But you've eaten it in front of me."

"Do you know what happens when you turn down pizza for not liking it? Eight thousand questions. I've been known to choke it down or take a couple bites and throw it away when I have my opening."

"I feel like I don't even know who you are."

"My dirty secret is out."

"I'll never look at you the same again."

"You wanted me to come clean, and now I have. The page, please." He beckoned me to hand it over, waggling his fingers.

Ripping the page from the notebook, I grabbed my pen.

Holden ripped up the page and tucked the pieces in his pocket.

At the top of the next page, I scribbled down 'Pizza Hater' at the top.

"What are you doing?"

I held it close to my chest. "Nothing."

He shoved out of his seat and using two fingers, motioned between his eyes and me, signaling he was watching me.

Keeping my innocent look, I didn't look down until he disappeared into the bathroom.

He was the closest thing I had to a friend nowadays. Every so often Piper sent an email or a text, and we met up when I was in town, but she had a life and a family. It felt like whenever I showed up, the circus was in town. I didn't want to lose her. She was one of the few people who still treated me like me, like the old Bay from before my life became my life. Felicia was the same. The RA whose bed I used to sit on, trying not to tear my hair out over econ homework, always felt like someone I could turn to, although the texts had gotten less frequent.

Time zones and travel made it hard enough to maintain friendships.

Barging into her life whenever it was convenient for me made me feel like the worst friend in the world. 'Hey, I'm free. Drop everything and come hang out with me because I missed you.' It wasn't a good look.

Even my messages to Spencer were few and far between. He was busy with his own tour. He never asked for anything —no requests for tickets or connections. I'd gone through two phones since we'd last talked earlier this year. That he'd been so shocked when I sent him a message hurt a little. It was like he'd forgotten we'd once even known each other, let alone been friends.

Holden and Emily were with me day after day, part of the madness my life had become.

But weren't friends supposed to be people you didn't have to pay to stick around?

Tomorrow, we'd hear back from Headstrong Foundation.

I'd have to figure out how to get Keyton to spend a little more time with me, and how to let go of the only man I'd ever loved.

10

KEYTON

The season opener and another game. The board meetings for Headstrong Foundation. The meetings with my agent and coaches from Wisconsin. The last few days had been jam-packed, and the September-Ween Carnival was four days away.

Talks had progressed with Wisconsin. It wasn't a done deal by any stretch of the imagination, and there were only two months before the trade window closed and I'd lose yet another season. At every turn, people kept reminding me how monumentally stupid it was to leave the cushy niche I'd carved out for myself.

"You're insane, kid."

"Maybe, but it's what I want."

There was a lot of grumbling on the other end of the line.

"If they come in at my minimum number, just take it. Don't haggle. Don't check in with me. Just say yes. You're my agent and I'm directing you to do this as your client."

Even more grumbling with a few choice words added in. "You're the boss."

Hanging up, I stared out the windows at the slivers of sunlight breaching the horizon.

Every morning I woke up with the sun and got on the treadmill in my empty gym in my empty apartment. These days, I wasn't trying to wear myself out running until it felt like my legs would fail and my lungs would burst. That didn't make it any less essential. It wasn't like I was getting a workout on the field.

My sketch pad had been getting a workout. I'd even graduated to charcoals with some bigger paper. Canvases sat unwrapped beside my front door. These feelings were growing, and the need to make the scenes bigger grew every day.

Sitting on the wooden bench beside my free weights, I tapped on a name in my contacts and waited for it to connect.

"Hey, Keyton. It's been a while." Almost three months. Around the time Alice and I broke up.

"Hey, Monica. The season's starting. Things get busy."

"How's the running?"

"Just finished."

"Okay good, I hoped that was why you were panting and not some other reason..." Her voice trailed off.

"Come on, Monica."

"No, please, don't." Deadpanned and dry as a decade-old raisin.

I flung my towel into the hamper and laughed. "You have a dirty mind to rival most guys on the team."

"So I've been told. Is that why we're talking today?"

"No, it's about Bay."

"Ah, Bay. That's a name I haven't heard in a while."

I swear I heard her pen click. Notebook pages were probably being flipped open. "I saw her. A week ago."

"And you waited a whole week to call me? Impressive."

"Our first run-in was an accident, and we had coffee the next day. It was supposed to be a one-time thing, but...I keep feeling like there is more we should've said." Gwen hadn't let me know if Bay had accepted the invitation. Once she realized it was for my foundation, she'd probably have Holden light the invitation on fire after how I'd bolted from her hotel suite.

"Why not go find her and talk some more?"

"It's not that simple."

"It can be."

"Can you try not to sound like a wise old owl right now?"

"No." Glad she was willing to help me out. "Tell me why talking to her has you on edge."

"Backsliding. Freaking out again." Ruining both our lives. We'd both dodged a Dare-sized bullet six years ago in California.

"She's not Alice. I know you know that. But you're different, right? And she's different. Why not come at this like you're meeting a new person? Your pasts will always be there, but there's no sense in catastrophizing speaking with her when you don't even know who she is right now, and she doesn't know who you are. Maybe you'll both hate each other."

"I don't think that's possible."

"Anything is possible, even things going well. Every time you imagine the worst, imagine the opposite as an option as well."

In my mind, I tried to picture what could be and it scared me how much I wanted it.

"I'm jealous of this party you're throwing later this week. Did my invite get lost in the mail?"

"Fly up here and I've got a ticket waiting for you."

"Asshole, you know I don't fly."

"Maybe you should talk to someone about that fear of yours…"

"The highlight of my day. You giving me crap about being afraid of flying."

"It's your only flaw."

She snorted. "Always a charmer. If you need to talk more, you know I'm here. But don't let your fear of the possibilities kill what could be a new start for the two of you."

"It's one meeting. Maybe."

"Maybe not…"

"Bye, Monica."

"Bye, Keyton."

The next couple days were gone in a blink. Hours had been swallowed up by the Texas game, which we'd won, hanging out with the Fulton U guys, reviewing hours of tape for our upcoming games and practice sessions, and Headstrong Foundation work. Hours I'd tried to keep focused on what was ahead of me.

Hours I'd tried not to dream of Bay.

Tickets had sold well for SeptemberWeen. Who didn't love feeling good about donating to charity while also getting tanked? Today was the last push before we closed ticket sales on Friday morning.

Over the years, we'd kept the location of the event secret as a way of building buzz around it. Attendees were told to meet at one location and were then sent the address thirty minutes before the party began.

It got people excited to be in on a secret no one else knew about. Once news leaked that Bay had been invited to perform, the secret location became a security must. I hoped they weren't disappointed and would demand refunds, if she didn't accept. Of course she wouldn't accept. Not after the way I'd left her hotel suite.

The SeptemberWeen team had spent the last week scrambling for a new location just in case, which meant we had a few more tickets available. I hoped I hadn't botched the whole event and ruined everyone's hard work.

But today wasn't SeptemberWeen. It was a final push for SeptemberWeen and highlighting a lot of the good done by so many people who cared. Growing up, I couldn't have believed there were this many people out there who cared for kids who weren't theirs. Knox's parents felt like an anomaly, but there were more great people out there.

They needed all the support they could get to keep helping even more kids like me.

Sometimes I felt so far away from the kid I was in Greenwood, and other days I swore I'd crack my eyes and be back in my bedroom with the padlock on the door.

Right now, I didn't feel like that kid.

The Headstrong Foundation conference rooms on the two floors we occupied had been transformed into a TV and photo studio to film all the promotions. Walls were covered in fabric, everything outside the halo of lights overhead was black, extra electrical cables and cords were run in and taped down to the floor, and lights were everywhere.

The open door leading to the hallway was the only source of light other than the rigs flooding the space like spotlights.

My suit was tailor-made. Not just altered, but made from scratch to fit my exact measurements—but at this moment, I felt like someone had squeezed me into a women's size 2 dress from The Gap.

At least I wasn't wearing a tie. Not that it was doing me any favors.

Interviews didn't faze me anyone. At least I didn't think they did. But talking about the game and talking about myself were two different things. Monica and I had talked about it a lot, and it was finally time. I'd never be free of my past if I spent all my time trying to pretend it didn't happen.

One of the audio techs attached the mic to the lapel of my blazer.

Gwen hovered behind him. "You have the Sports Central interview now and then you're doing a promo that'll air tonight and we'll post online to let people know there are still VIP tickets left and to tell them Bay will be performing."

My head snapped up. "Bay?" She'd accepted.

After not hearing back from Gwen, I'd thought the goodbye in Bay's hotel suite would be the last time we saw each other. I'd prepared myself for it and made my peace with it. I'd been wrong.

"I know! It's insane. The foundation hired an event coordinator, Everest, who has some connection to her people and put in a Hail Mary invite. It took some back and forth with her people, but she said yes. Can you believe it? We should've charged more for the tickets." Gwen was buzzing with excitement. She'd been pissed she'd missed Bay back at the concert.

My brain shot into overdrive. I would be seeing her again. At least twice. My heart drummed in my chest. "Bay's coming today and she's performing at the SeptemberWeen Carnival."

Gwen checked her tablet. "Yes. She should be here any minute. Her manager, Holden, said they were running a few minutes late after she left the studio. We've confirmed with

Bay's team that we can offer another level of tickets for a meet and greet with her."

"Taking this on at the last minute is a big favor. Let's not overwhelm her with extra requests." The shock of Gwen's announcement hadn't worn off yet. My lips felt numb. I hadn't prepared myself. I hadn't had time to run through how this day would go when I saw Bay again.

"Holden is the one who suggested it to boost the revenue for the event. We can offer it as an add-on for anyone who's purchased tickets already."

Holden was offering her up for even more beyond what we'd asked for? How much was the guy pushing her?

Bay was going to be here. Bay was going to be at SeptemberWeen.

A guy with a headset stepped up before her. "Mr. Keyton, we're ready for you."

I sat in the chair under a silver-lined umbrella. The lights blinded me to much else in the darkened room, but I could feel all eyes on me. There were seven people in the room: the ones handling the cameras and audio, Gwen, the interviewer, and others for whatever task was needed for the event to run smoothly.

My neck heated under my collar and I flexed my hands on my legs.

More noise came from the hall and a herd of people popped into view, walking past the door before doubling back.

In the middle of all the people on phones and tablets was Bay, backlit, features obscured by the shadows. She was here.

Every time I saw her felt like the first time watching her on her back steps. It dragged me out of whatever I was going through and toward her. I just wanted to be near her.

Gwen rushed over and spoke with the new arrivals in hushed tones.

The interviewer with perfectly placed hair and a country club look sat across from me with notecards and stuck the earpiece in place. After introducing himself and walking me through the bullet points of the fluff piece, he sat in the chair opposite me.

"We're here tonight supporting a wonderful cause, and we have with us the belle of the proverbial football ball, Darren Keyton. Thank you for speaking with us. You've been called many things over your last five seasons. The Championship Curiosity, The Winning Wonder, and my personal favorite, The Football Four-Leaf Clover."

"I've heard those a few times in my career." At least he hadn't gone with glorified mascot or overrated ornament.

"While we could go on and on about your special brand of championship team magic, we're here to talk tonight about a charity you began shortly after your trade to Philadelphia a little over two years ago. Why is it that you've taken such an interest in youth outreach? And why in Philadelphia after playing for teams in LA, Miami and Charlotte?"

"I went to school here and have a good group of friends in the area, so this was a natural place to want to begin the work of Headstrong Foundation. There are a lot of worthy causes in the world and it's hard to choose only one. So I worked with a team—" My throat tightened. Past the lights and people standing in the room, I could feel Bay watching me.

The prepared interview answers I'd gone over with the Foundation's public relations team didn't feel right. Monica and I had gone over this. There was nothing for me to hide about this.

"There is a personal connection for me. When I was growing up, I dealt with a lot of abuse from my father." The lights felt like they were searing into my skin. Blistering hot under my collar. I rubbed my hands down my pant legs. "It was physical—and mental. And it took me a long time to come to terms with the impact it had on me as a person and as a man." I licked my lips.

Glancing up, I saw Bay stepping further into the room, out of the shadows. Her shocked expression was even deeper than everyone else's.

I smoothed my hands along my thighs, letting my fingers drag over the soft fabric, and took a deep breath when I wanted to switch to the heavy breaths like I was about to take on an opponent on the field. Drawing in another breath, I focused on the interviewer.

"It took a lot of time and a lot of mistakes over the years to come to terms with my childhood. I hurt a lot of people along the way as well, people who never deserved it and shouldn't have been saddled with my baggage. If it weren't for a few people in my life who have believed in me and helped me along the way, I wouldn't have made it to where I am today.

"I don't want any kid out there dealing with hardships to feel like they can't talk about it or that they shouldn't talk about it. And I want to do everything I can to help them get all the resources they need to have a healthy, happy life."

The room was pin-drop silent. A few people who worked in the organization even exchanged looks. I'd never been so open about what I'd gone through, but the final step to moving forward had to be sharing my story to ease some of those feelings that crept up in me. The release was there, a freedom in not having to cling so tightly to my past. It was a past I'd only shared with a few people, but one that might help some other kid out there, or convince someone with a fatter wallet than mine to give them what they needed.

"I need other people out there to know there's no shame in what they went through and they don't have to struggle through it alone."

Across from me, the interviewer recovered and snapped his jaw closed. "Thank you for sharing your story with us today."

"Thank you for bringing light to the work being done by everyone—not just me—at the Headstrong Foundation."

"Your work will change lives."

I nodded, hoping he was right. Maybe it would give someone out there hope that they could find a life beyond their current situation, one where they didn't have to carry the weight of so much fear, guilt and sadness with them all the time. I was still working on it myself. I cleared my throat, trying to punch through the tightness. "All we're doing is giving kids the support and help they need and the tools to get out of the situations they're stuck in." My throat felt like it was on the verge of crushing itself.

"Thank you very much and to all the viewers out there. I've been told there are still a limited number of seats available. But by the time this airs, I imagine it'll be even fewer once the announcement goes out that Bay will be performing."

I zoned out for the rest of the interview, while he gave out all the details of the event, and focused on the woman in the corner.

The one signing autographs for people flooding the hallways in all directions.

The one I'd be beside for a photoshoot in the next room.

The one who kept peeking over at me.

After shaking hands with the interviewer, I stood and let

them take off the mic equipment. The interview team left the room, but Bay was still inundated with more people than I'd seen in the two hours I'd been in the building.

Did she ever get more than a few minutes alone?

Gwen hovered outside of the light rig range. "We're shooting the online promos right now." She glanced to her side where Bay stood with her squad of people. "But we have a couple minutes. I'll clear the hallway." She extricated Bay from the crowd, shooing them all from the room before closing the door and taking off with Holden. Now Bay was inside on her own. And all the attention was focused on me.

The heat from the lights still set up at eye level for the seated interview didn't heat my body nearly as much as being alone in the room with her did.

Crossing the space between us, she ducked beneath the lights and reflectors set up for the perfect shot.

"That was brave." She stared at me with a hint of apprehension, like she wasn't quite sure how I'd feel after such a public declaration.

A little worried, but lighter than ever.

"It wasn't brave. It was the truth. I should never have been scared of the truth."

"It takes a lot to be that open with people."

"You get up on stage night after night, singing songs straight from your heart." Songs about me.

"Sure, but I can pretend they're from my imagination. Things the muse cooks up and leaves on my doorstep with a nice bow on top." She offered a small smile.

"I'm sure they've helped someone. Just like I hope what I said today will help another kid out there just like me."

"I'm sure it will. How could it not? You spoke from your heart. Gwen told me you just found out I'd be coming today. Sorry to spring—"

The door behind her swung open. I tensed, ready to block whoever barged in.

Gwen stood in the half open doorway. "We're ready for you two." She looked between us. "If you're ready..."

Bay turned fully facing her. "Yes, of course. Are you ready?" Her gaze swept to mine.

"Yeah, let's go." With the ghost of a touch at the small of her back, we walked to the next room for an indeterminate amount of time for a photoshoot—together.

K eyton's assistant lead us to the room for the photoshoot. His hand brushed against my back, lighting me up with an awareness and fluttery feelings, the kind I never got when working with another professional draped all over one another. But none of those other professionals had been him.

I needed to get myself together. No one had told me he'd be here today, not that I shouldn't have expected to run into him at some point when performing for a foundation he'd created.

Somehow, I'd thought I'd be more prepared. I'd been thrown into countless rooms with three minutes of preparation and had to fly by the seat of my pants. This wasn't any different. I'd keep repeating it in my head until the mantra took hold.

Not freaking likely.

His interview had caught me off guard. His honesty back at my hotel hadn't been a one-time thing. Talking so nakedly about what he'd gone through growing up—once again, my heart ached for the scared little boy who'd grown into an angry teenager and then into the guy I'd met in California. Now he'd become the man I kept peering over at.

His jaw wasn't clenched, and there were no stressed tendons in his neck.

He turned his head, eyes widening when he caught me staring at him. "Sorry for the short notice on this."

"I—It's okay. I told them I was up for whatever they needed."

Now his jaw tightened. "Is 'yes' the only answer you know?" There was an odd stiltedness to his question. Would he prefer I was a prima donna who needed all requests to be submitted in writing in triplicate a week in advance?

"No." My lips twitched.

He relaxed. "Thank you for being here today. It means a lot to me."

Breathlessness robbed the words from my throat, and I nodded.

Gwen stepped in front of us. "We'll get you two beside each other with a few props. Video first and then some photos. We'll need a few minutes to change the lighting. Quick, short lines and the photographer will try to have you both out of here as quickly as she can with minimal embarrassment." She handed us both a card and let out a slightly hysterical laugh before running away. It wasn't a fangirl starstruck laugh; I'd heard those a thousand times before. This was something else.

The room buzzed with activity the way every set did. There were so many people behind the camera. Hair, makeup, lighting, sound.

"She seems nice." I scanned the card with the lines printed in size 22 font. Memorizing them like I did my lyrics, I set them to a melody, so everyone wasn't hanging around waiting for me to say my lines correctly.

"Gwen is my right-hand woman. She's been working for me for three years." He searched over his shoulder for her.

Had that work relationship ever progressed beyond just work? People often made assumptions about me and Holden, who was off in the corner pretending he didn't have a watchful eye on everything going on in the room while also scrolling through his tablet.

"It's hard to find good people."

"She's been with me through three moves so far."

"And she doesn't mind following you all over the country?"

"Not with how much she gets paid. Those red-soled shoes don't come cheap."

The bright color peeped out from under every step. Nope, I wasn't jealous. He could sleep with whomever he wanted. So why did it feel like taking a mic stand to the chest?

"That's like Holden and his watches."

Keyton shot me a look.

Gwen returned. "We have these for you. They'll match, so we don't have to worry about any color clashes with your outfit." She hefted a furry costume unicorn head and handed it over to me.

Now the laughter made complete sense. Was this a weird embarrassment play? Make me uncomfortable and keep me looking like an absolute idiot?

The weight hit my hands and sent me pitching forward. Keyton and Gwen both lurched forward to steady me. "People wear this on their heads? It's so heavy."

Shifting it, I stood straight. They let go of me, Keyton's hands lingering longer than Gwen's.

She'd been carrying both heads like they were made of

paper mâché. Holden better watch out. She could probably challenge him in a bench press competition.

"And we've got this one for you, boss." She held out a furry alligator head with one freaking hand.

He took it from her like it was nothing.

Show-offs. I tried not to grumble.

"Are we hosting a furry convention or a costume party?" He examined the mossy green head.

"We're improvising with what we have on hand." She walked back to the table. "Or would you prefer the leather bondage gear option." The silver loops and rings from the outfit clinked against each other doing their best heavy metal wind chime impersonation. She grumbled under her breath. "This is what happens when you send a new intern out on a job without explicit instructions. So this is what we have..."

He stared at me wide-eyed.

"Furries." We said at the same time.

The embarrassment-soaked laughter broke some of the tension.

The director for our impromptu shoot came over and showed us our marks.

We recited the lines ten or twenty times before they got whatever footage they needed. After every one, Gwen pranced over and handed us a new prop. She took Keyton's coat and gave him a new one.

All their moves were choreographed without a word. He handed her his cufflinks and rolled the sleeves of his button-down shirt to the elbows.

The flare of jealousy was hard to explain. Hard to tamp down. Hard to ignore.

I had no claim to him. Not like he had to me, even all these years later. The indelible mark he'd left on me back in

Greenwood had been reinforced in LA. Whereas I'd been one of many, firmly in the rearview mirror of his life.

He'd been engaged. If that didn't spell moved on, I don't know what did. Hell, it screamed it through a megaphone into my ear.

Emily and Holden jumped in for touch ups here and there.

"Bay?" Keyton touched my shoulder.

I jerked, focusing on him again. Going through the motions had become second nature. I hadn't even noticed the lighting guys changing the lights and the video camera being stowed.

"Sorry, what did you say?"

"We can sit for a few minutes while they change the lights." He motioned to the two folding chairs beside the folding table with some of the props on them.

I sat and tucked my hands between my legs, trying not to let the awkwardness eat me alive.

"It's great you've got Gwen here to handle all your needs." My smile was tissue paper thin.

His head tilted. One eyebrow dropped a hint. "She's indispensable. I couldn't do half the things I do without her."

"Must be great to have someone like her you can rely on no matter what?" Why am I saying this? If he is with Gwen, why the hell do I want to know? It's none of my business. I have no claim to him.

He owes me nothing.

I'm here for his foundation and there's nothing more attached to it.

His eyes narrowed. "She's great at her job. Why do you keep asking me so many questions about Gwen? What about Holden? How long have you two been together?"

"He was there the night I left LA." A sinking feeling engulfed my stomach. It was part of our story. The ones I'd recited to reporters and interviewers and other managers who'd tried to swoop in as my star rose. The story of me and Holden being a team from the beginning. But I'd forgotten I wasn't talking to anyone. I was talking to him.

His bare forearms flexed. "You walked out of your apartment while I was sleeping and hopped right into an SUV with him?"

I stared down at my hands pinched between my thighs. This was what I got for opening that Pandora's Box. "No." I glanced up. "He was on the plane Maddy arranged to take me to Seattle."

"Wow, so a whole thirty-minute trip to the airport." His voice was a hair off a growl.

"Forty if you count the trip to Felicia's to drop off the letter." Pushing. Prodding. Poking. I couldn't help it. How long had this Gwen situation been a thing? Didn't he just have a fiancée?

His jaw clenched. "What's it been like having him by your side all these years taking care of you through your rise to stardom?"

Like he didn't have someone taking care of all his needs too. "He's been great to have around in all the stressful situations I've been thrown into over the years."

Keyton jerked back like I'd thrown a punch.

Oh shit. "I didn't mean—I wasn't—" And now I was the dick—again. Had I ever stopped being the dick? "That wasn't a comparison comment."

A muscle in the side of his jaw jumped. "Don't worry about it."

He felt so put together now. So in control and completely over what happened between us, like it hadn't irrevocably changed him down to the cellular level like it had me. It had leveled me. Throwing myself into work was the only thing propping me up.

The rough time he'd mentioned over coffee wasn't a flicker in his gaze, but now he was wound up, all tension and tightness.

Guilt crashed into me that I was searching for the cracks in this new version of him rather than being happy he'd found his way out of the haze that often overtook him.

And I was happy for him.

"I wasn't going in for a dig." I reached for him before pulling my hand back. We weren't that close anymore.

"Don't worry about it." He shot me a glance, like he couldn't look at me full on.

That he couldn't share an intimate moment with me stirred an irrational irritation. He could talk to me so openly and it didn't mean anything to him other than moving past what we'd had.

"We're ready for you both." Gwen stood in front of Keyton, holding out his coat.

He smiled at her and rolled his sleeves back down, taking the cufflinks she had in her outstretched palm. He fastened them, then took his jacket from her and slid it on.

We stood beside each other like wooden soldiers. And I hated it. As much as I'd promised myself it was only for the foundation, of course I was here because I wanted to see him again. Be near him again. Talk to him again.

"Why don't you just ask what you want to ask?" He wrapped his arm around my shoulder.

The strong warmth of his fingers around my shoulder sent smoky flares racing up and down my arm.

My shoulder pressed against his chest and I fought against the urge to lean into him like I had so many times before. I wanted to wrap my arms around his waist from the front and press my cheek against his chest, listening to his heartbeat pound against my ear.

The flash went off. We both smiled for the camera as an incendiary crackling rippled through the set.

I kicked my heel up and widened my smile until my cheeks hurt. "What do you think I want to ask?"

His arm snaked around my waist, pulling me tight against him.

The brush of his fingers barely missing the gap between my sweater and waistband as the fabric shifted, and I cursed the near miss, wanting to feel his touch against my bare skin.

Through barely parted lips, he leaned in. The heat of his breath skirting across my cheek. "You want to ask if Gwen and I are sleeping together."

"You can sleep with whoever you want to. I'm sure you do." I snapped back too quickly, like I'd had the comment locked and loaded. The grating anger warring with my frayed nerves from his closeness pissed me off even more.

The flashes continued to go off and we kept posing, following the photographer's direction without really hearing him. My body was on autopilot while my mind fixated on the man beside me. Every brush, every touch, every look made it harder to remember there were other people in the room—other people like Gwen.

Why was I making a big deal about this? He could screw half the Eastern Seaboard and it wasn't my business. So why did it feel like someone was trying to scoop out my heart with a rusty spoon?

Maybe because I'd thought I'd gotten over it. I thought I was totally okay with him being engaged and moving on. I'd talked myself into believing it. Then, when I'd found out he wasn't engaged, I'd thought I had a chance. It had been a stupid, hopeful flare from my boat of one out in the middle of the dark, inky night. I'd hoped that seeing him again had all been for a reason, a way for us to come back together, but maybe it just wasn't.

A bitter laugh brewed in my chest. Looks like the pop princess didn't get everything she wanted.

Turning, I faced him, unable to keep up this pretense and needing to know what I was getting myself into by performing at SeptemberWeen. I needed to rip that expectation band-aid off right now.

Dropping my voice even lower, I whispered the words I was afraid to have answered. "Are you and Gwen sleeping together?"

His eyes bored into mine. "Are you and Holden? Have you and Holden..."

I was tempted to say, 'I asked you first.' Looking into his eyes, I could see the burning need to know the answer as keenly as I did, and it brought with it another spark of stupid hope. "No. Never. He's my best friend at this point, but it's a line we've never thought about crossing."

He faced forward and put his arm around my shoulder again, leaning in close. This time his lips brushed the shell of my ear. "Same."

The relief was swift and complete. Like a coil I hadn't realized I'd been tightening since I first saw them together, it exploded in my chest, not with pain, but with an unbridled, uncontainable joy. "Okay."

"Okay." He parroted back.

I opened my mouth, the sounds dying there. What exactly was there to say? Maybe grab him and find a closet somewhere?

The photographer clicked one last, I'm sure stellar,

picture of me with a bad case of fish mouth. "Thank you both so much." She walked over and shook our hands. "It was amazing to meet you. I'm honored."

We both went into professional mode. Thanking him and everyone else in the room. Oh yes, there were other people in here. My darting glances toward D—Keyton were met with his own. Every time, someone drew my attention right as his gaze collided with mine. These were fleeting moments. Stolen seconds.

A crowd of people arrived to break things down and have us sign releases. Every so often, there would be a clearing in my people and he'd be there dealing with his own people.

Holden touched my elbow and lead me toward the door. "We've got to get back to the hotel. You've got to get to the studio tonight and we only have it reserved for four hours."

I put the brakes on, twisting to see Keyton, only to find him being led out of another door. Disappointment thudded in my stomach.

Timing, am I right? Sometimes it felt like we'd never get it right, like we'd never have more than a few minutes to actually talk to each other alone before we were interrupted or one of us was whisked off to somewhere else.

There was always SeptemberWeen. Maybe we could steal more than a few moments together. For what? I wasn't sure, but the hope that I'd soon find out burned brighter and deeper than it had in a long time.

12

BAY

Bent over the sink in my hotel suite bathroom I dragged the washcloth over my face. It wasn't one of theirs. I'd never subject the poor housekeeping staff to the gallons of bleach that would be needed to wash a pound of makeup out of the fabric.

The whole room was marble and chrome, with a walk-in shower and a soaking tub. I'd have taken a bath tonight, but I'd been worried I might fall asleep in there.

This week was SeptemberWeen. I'd see Keyton again. I hated that I didn't have any way to get in touch with him. The number I'd had for him back in LA had been changed long ago. I found that out the hard way when one of my last messages to him had gone to a new person with the number who'd told me to stop texting their grandfather.

Getting in contact with someone had never been an issue before. Holden would track down the number or it would be one of the four people I spoke to semi-regularly. But I didn't want Holden getting his number for me. I wanted to ask him for it. Or better yet, have him offer it to me.

I shook my head and set the black washcloth on the counter beside me, grabbing a face towel. No, that wasn't why I was doing his event.

Water dripped down my chin onto my t-shirt.

Movement behind me caught my eye in the mirror.

Holden stood in the doorway with his suit jacket off and his top button undone. He looked rumpled.

I turned, my stomach beginning the first turns of a knot. "What is it?"

He sighed. His lips pinching together. "I've been working on this for over a week now." He dropped to the edge of the tub big enough to hold three people.

"Tell me."

Staring up at me, worry and disappointment radiated in his eyes.

"You're scaring me." My muscles at the base of my jaw tightened. I gripped the edge of the counter. "Did something happen to my mom?"

He loosened his tie. "It's Piper's birthday."

I slumped against the sink.

"Way to scare the shit out of me." My laugh was muffled as I patted the hand towel across my face. "It's December 12th. Mark's got it all planned out." I looked at his reflection.

The muscle on the side of his jaw flexed. "And you won't be able to go."

Dropping the towel to the counter, I turned to Holden. "No. No. We talked about this. It's been on the schedule for months. Since I missed her last one. I promised Mark I'd be there." After missing Parker's third birthday when I'd been in town, her last birthday, and my birthday celebration that I'd invited her along to before bailing at the last minute, I wasn't going to miss this.

He shoved his hand into his hair and slipped the rest of

his tie knot off, letting it dangle around his neck. "I know. It's a date with a huge red block around it. But the shift in the schedule, all the rearranging—you have a contract obligation to be in Sydney to fulfill and the knock-on effect with the shifts we've made over the past week has pushed things." He shrugged, an ineffectual, floundering shrug of defeat. "The 12th is the only day we can do it before the end of the year."

"But...Australia's ahead of Seattle. We can hop on a flight and get there."

He shook his head.

"Don't shake your head. We have to try." A hint of desperation entered my voice, a cover for the frustration and sadness. I'd promised. My promises weren't worth much nowadays. Outside of work, it felt like they were broken more than they were kept.

"I have!" He shot up from his spot gripping the edge of the tub. "I have, Bay." His voice gentled.

"Maybe..." I licked my lips and grasped for something. Anything, but I barely knew where I would be beyond tomorrow, let alone how to rework the 5000 things it felt we did every day. Clasping my hands together, I knocked them against my forehead. *Think, Bay. Think.*

"Trust me. I've gone over this a hundred times. I've looked at the flight routes. Flying private doesn't help. We can't make it there and get you back to Vienna in time for the next show on the 13th."

I sagged against the sink. "But I promised Mark." The words sounded weak, just like all my promises before.

"I know. And I'm sorry I couldn't pull this off." A pained expression streaked across his face. "I know you've been trying to get there for the past two years."

"Three." I stared at the grey splintering pattern of the

white marble tiles. "It's been three years I'll have missed now." I tugged on the end of my ponytail. "Do you know where my phone is?" Glancing up, I almost winced at how sad he looked. Was it a reflection of my own face?

He nodded and walked out.

My feet brushed against the carpet on the way to the green high-backed chair in the seating area of my room.

Back in a flash, he held out my phone. "I can do it. I can call Mark."

"No, it needs to be me. She's my friend, remember?" An even worse one would send someone else to do her dirty work.

"Do you need anything?"

"A time-turner?"

He searched his pockets before showing me his empty hands.

We traded humorless laughs.

"No, I'm good. I'm going to sleep after this."

"Five a.m. the trainer will be here, and then we've got a full day."

"When don't we?"

He stopped, grabbing onto the doorframe looking like there was more he wanted to say.

"It's okay, Holden. I'll do it." My shoulders folded in and I gripped the phone tighter.

His head dropped and he left the room, not letting the door slam behind him. Instead, it latched quietly, leaving me alone with my phone.

I paced the floor, staring at my screen for so long it dimmed. Tapping in my passcode, I closed my eyes. She was my oldest friend. My best friend at one point. It was only a matter of time before I became that person she once knew.

Mark picked up on the first ring and called out to Piper.

In the background, kids laughed and yelled, adding to the general commotion of a happy, lively house. "Hey, sweetheart. I've got to take this. I'll be right back." A door closed. "Hey, Bay. What's up?"

I grabbed my ponytail and ran my hands over it. "Hey, Mark."

"You can't make it, can you?" Disappointment blanketed the sentence, smothering it.

He already knew. That was who I was now. The promise breaker. The one who could never be counted on to pull through. No wonder he'd wanted to make it a surprise. He did what any good husband would do. He protected his wife from letdowns and sadness.

I rushed into apology mode. It was all I had left. "We tried everything. Absolutely everything. I'm so sorry."

"I know. She knows you're busy. She'd have loved to see you, but she'll understand."

"Once I'm finished with this tour, I swear we'll finally get to see each other for more than a few minutes backstage. When do you guys leave for your next assignment?" Jumping in with those promises yet again.

"January."

The tour didn't end until July. Making promises I couldn't keep wouldn't make either of us feel any better right now. "We'll see what happens."

"Parker loved his train set. Thanks for that." His sweetness hurt my heart even more. After letting down his wife and mother of his kids here he was trying to make me feel better about dropping the ball once again.

"Of course." I fought against the crack trying to creep into my voice. "The birthday boy deserved an extra-special gift. I'll take care of the whole party."

"You don't have to do that. You know we don't invite you just to get you to pay for things."

"I know." The crack broke through. I muted the phone and cleared my throat, staring at the ceiling blinking back the tears.

"We'll miss you. Parker keeps asking when you'll be staying in your room again."

A watery laugh burst from my lips. "Parker has a thing for five a.m. wake-up calls. Not that I mind." Last year I'd stayed at their house for the weekend—just a quiet weekend at home with them. We'd grilled. The kids had run around on the slip-and-slide and we'd all hung out together being normal. With my regular schedule calling for five a.m. wake-up calls, Parker and I became dawn buddies, reading, making pancakes for everyone, and goofing off.

"I'm sorry, Mark." The tears burned in the corners of my eyes.

"I know, Bay." His voice brimmed with understanding, which only made it worse.

Ending the call, I collapsed into the chair and launched my phone across the room like it was the collection of glass and metal's fault. Bending at the waist, I wrapped my arms around myself and buried my face in my knees.

If I cried too loudly, Holden or Emily would hear and then they'd come bursting in trying to fix things. I couldn't fix this. I couldn't get to my best friend's birthday party. I couldn't even guarantee I'd see my mom for Thanksgiving.

Going back into the bathroom, I washed my face again, this time using the hotel washcloth. I stared at myself in the mirror.

I had all the fame in the world. All the money I could ever want. And I was all alone in my hotel room.

I sat on the end of my bed and rummaged through my bag until my fingers brushed against the tattered and worn notebook. Less than a few months old, it felt a lot like the ones that had taken me years to fill.

Pulling it out, I grabbed a pen and uncapped it with my teeth.

I scribbled down the title on top of the page. *"lost."*

After writing until my head throbbed, I retrieved my phone from the floor and curled up in bed.

Maybe it made me a narcissistic asshole, but I pulled up YouTube, typed in my name followed by 'covers'. It was a reminder to me of why I did this, why I loved making music. Why I couldn't stop.

The results popped up in the hundreds of thousands. Needing to hear someone else sing the words, I typed in a song that had been playing louder in my head recently. Dare.

I nearly dropped my phone when one of the top results popped up. Spencer from only a few nights ago at a show.

Scrambling up, I sat with my back against the headboard.

"I've got a song for you tonight that some of you might know." He had a fun and commanding stage presence. His guitar was slung across his shoulder. The venue looked standing room only. Even out of focus with a little shaky cam, his joy up on stage was magnetic. "It's an older one, a deep track off an album I've loved since the day it came out, and I wanted to play it for you tonight."

His was an acoustic version of the song, a lot like the one I'd sung in front of all of Greenwood High, but so much better, and nothing like the version recorded for the album.

In a few solid notes, his voice rumbled and rolled, sending goosebumps prickling my skin.

As people in the crowd realized what song it was a few whistled and others clapped.

He hit the high notes in his octave and his fingers flew across the strings of the guitar. He brought my song to life, making it his own. He added his own stamp, his own voice to the lyrics and story, making them all new.

By the time he'd sung the last note I'd forgotten it had ever been mine.

I went to my messages.

Me: Can I interest you in a pirate party?

I'd almost drifted off to sleep when the reply rolled in.

Spencer: Bay?

I forgot he probably didn't even have my new number.

Me: Yes! Unless you're regularly being invited to pirate parties nowadays.

Spencer: LOL! Not too often. How are you doing?

Me: Not too bad. Awesome cover of Dare! That was insane.

The crowd had eaten it up. The lyrics with his vocal tone gave the whole song a different vibe. More hopeful. Maybe that's why I'd liked it so much.

Spencer: Oh shit. How'd you know? Not that I'm trying to be shady or anything. Do I have a cease and desist coming my way?

That he felt even a hint of worry about it, further reinforced how terrible of a friend I'd been. He used to sing all the time in the studio, trying to get me to belt it out along with him.

Me: No! Of course not. I saw it on YouTube.

Spencer: You're cool with me singing it?

His hesitancy hurt.

I needed to be a better friend, anyway I could.

Me: Of course. It was phenomenal! I loved what you did with the chorus.

Spencer: I didn't want to be a blatant song thief.

Me: You're not. I loved it. You're still touring. Where are you now?

Spencer: Right now, sitting in the back of the van between a couple amps on the way to the motel. Just finished breaking down all the gear from my show.

Part of me wished I hadn't skipped over those moments, the messy, fueled-by-adrenaline late nights into early days. I'd been on tour buses from the beginning. And the stage had only gotten bigger, ready to zero in on any mistakes or missteps.

Me: Are you on the East Coast?

Spencer: Headed that way. Is that where you are?

Me: In Philly for a few more weeks off and on, then headed to Europe for the last leg of my tour

Spencer: Awesome, Bay! I'm in Philly soon, I think. After my shows in Richmond and DC. Schedules get crazy sometimes.

I'd have to ask Holden to check his schedule. Maybe if he was passing through we could meet up. Familiar faces were hard to come by.

Me: Tell me about it

Spencer: I'm sure yours involves a lot more than a broken-down van and selling merch after shows until 2am

Me: You know none of this would've been possible if you hadn't told Walter about Without Grey

Spencer: No, he was interested even before that. I just knew you wouldn't jump up on the console and shout about it like I would've. We're at the motel. I need to unload this stuff onto the trailer. It was nice hearing from you

Me: Sorry, I've been MIA

Spencer: I get it. You're busy. Don't worry about it

Me: Night

The nostalgia train had pulled into the station and it

wasn't leaving. I grabbed my notebook again and went back to those late nights in the cramped studio with almost no ventilation where we'd listened to squawking for hours upon hours.

I remembered the times he'd snuck in a whole tub of ice cream under his sweatshirt in the middle of May.

Those had been simpler times. Being an adult had turned out a lot different than I'd thought back when I dreaded being stuck in a cubicle working on spreadsheets for the rest of my life.

Now, this was all I knew. It was the only life I'd ever lived. What could I even do other than sing and perform? I certainly couldn't head back to the accounting firm to sweat it through profit and loss statements. Sitting around for the next fifty years doing nothing didn't hold any appeal, but neither did pulling a Mick Jagger and trying to keep up the same pace for the next five decades.

The complications had only grown since that fateful summer when my life had changed irrevocably. The biggest change was the man I'd be seeing in two days.

Knowing I'd be seeing Keyton again had kicked all those memories into high gear. So much of our time apart was still colored by our time together.

Now it wouldn't be a shock when I saw him next. I had a date and time. Anticipation crept under my skin and infiltrated my brain.

Taking the spin Spencer had put onto my words, I jotted down more lyrics. This time it wasn't for me up on the stage; it was in the same vein Spencer had sung in.

Maybe next time I saw him I'd give them to him. A gift for being my friend, even though I sucked at it. And hell, maybe the songs sucked too.

I went on the trip down memory lane, revisiting how

hard it was to look back and realize you could never know in that moment how precious any of it was, and how we were destined to repeat the same mistakes with our present.

13

KEYTON

The regular school buses idled in the meeting point parking lot. Quaint and kitschy was how everyone labeled them, they were also damn cheap, which meant more money toward the rest of SeptemberWeen and our initiatives.

As much good as tonight would do, it wasn't on the fore-front of my mind, which probably added another line to the "reasons I'm a terrible person" list. But tonight I'd get to see Bay. During the photoshoot, her anger had been unexpected. Even more unexpected was how I'd matched it so quickly and easily with a question I'd pretended hadn't been rolling around in my head.

How close was she with Holden? I hadn't expected her to feel the same way about Gwen. The air had been cleared, but as things always went with her, we hadn't had any time.

Once I'd gotten back to the room where Bay and I had taken the pictures, she'd already been spirited away.

She wasn't here yet, which meant I needed to play the gracious host. Greeting people and posing for pictures went with the territory. Gwen called my Men in Black costume a cop-out, but I hadn't had to find one or add another thing to her list.

She'd been working with the Events Committee alongside SWANK, the event planning company brought in to handle the logistics and scope of an event with over six hundred guests.

Knox rolled in, almost knocking me off my feet with a hug. His wig tickled my face and neck. "Hell of a party you've got going on." He surveyed the parking lot packed with cars.

"Glad you made it, man." I clapped him on the back.

"I missed it last year, I wasn't missing it this year." He grinned, whipping his arms out to the side.

"Who the hell are you?"

He looked down at himself and back up. "I'm the Goblin King."

"It looks like you've stuffed a goblin in those tights. How the hell did you even get them on?"

Adjusting the codpiece, he glared. British-aristocracy-meets-80s-glam-rocker squeezed into tights no football player should be squeezed into was a sight to behold. "It's an authentic part of the costume and it took an entire mini bottle of baby powder to squeeze into it, but it was worth it. Check this out." He pulled out a clear ball and rolled it over his palms. It was a palmed-sized version of a glass orb that would sit in the middle of a psychic's table.

"How long did it take you to practice that one?"

He dropped his shaking head. "Hours. But without practices and games, I'm scrambling not to go crazy." The ball—definitely not glass—dropped and bounced under a neighboring car.

People were dressed in costumes from unoriginal to

insanely intricate. Some ghosts were sprinkled in amongst alien invaders complete with body paint and prosthetics.

His mini-performance over, his face sobered. "I saw Bay was going to be performing."

I rocked back on my heels and smiled, and shook hands with some passing fans. "She is."

He leaned in closer. "How are you feeling about that?"

"Is that why you came down here? To check on me?" Once again Knox was looking out for me. The old me would have gotten defensive or angry about it. Having people around who worried about me wasn't anything I'd take for granted again. But I hated that he still felt like at any moment the new me might dissolve away, and there might have been a flash of annoyance.

"No, but I know how things went the last time you two were together." And he'd been there to help me keep the pieces together just enough to make it through the worst of it. He'd seen how bad it could've gone.

"We had coffee a little over a week ago and saw each other at the promo shoot for tonight. We're fine." Less fine, more walking a tightrope of what-the-hell-was-happening. In the lead-up to seeing her again, I'd tried to pretend it wasn't a big deal and I could handle it, but right now, I didn't feel like I knew with any certainty how tonight would go.

"Whatever you say, just know I'm here, if you need me."

"I know, man." I grabbed his hand and locked thumbs before pulling him in again for a hug. "You're my best friend, of course I know that."

"Just making sure." He eyed me.

Gwen, sporting a red wig and the perfect Miss Frizzle dress complete with a Magic School Bus purse for all her assistant needs, stalked over to me. "The first buses will leave in ten minutes. It's a thirty-minute ride. Do you want to be on the first bus or the last?"

"I'll take the last one." Bay was supposed to follow the last bus there. Her schedule had been tight leading up to this evening, and rather than chance them getting lost on the way out to the secluded location, we'd offered to guide them.

All I was doing was making sure she made it okay. I'd have done it for anyone helping make this the best charity party of the year.

"Everest from SWANK and Gale are handling everything at the farm, so I'll jump on one of the first few buses to see if there's anything else they need."

I leaned in closer. "You can have some fun tonight. Make sure you pencil that in." Tapping on her tablet, I didn't even try to hide my smile.

She cracked a smile—barely. "Don't worry, you're paying me double for the extra help."

"That'll make it even better when you grab a few drinks while still on the clock."

"I'll think about it." She walked off toward the lines forming outside of the three other buses loading people, some with costumes so big they had to use step ladders through the emergency exit doors at the back.

"Hey, Keyton." A familiar voice shouted across the packed parking lot, turning more than a few heads.

LJ and Marisa were dressed as matching zombies, complete with undead makeup, blood, and a bag of squishy brains. Berk and Jules were Captain America and Peggy Carter. They wove between the parked cars to get to me. "Guys, you remember Knox?" More waves and handshakes for my oldest friend and family, and my newest.

Berk hugged me, patting me on the back. "Where's the VIP bus?!"

"Your chariot awaits." I pointed to the yellow and black metal tubes idling half the parking lot away.

"Don't worry, Keyton. I've got a can opener to pry him out of those seats." Jules wrapped her arms around me before letting go. "You've outdone yourself this year. It must've been a lot easier planning all this from here instead of halfway across the country."

LJ and Marisa hugged me too. He stepped back and wrapped his arm around Marisa's shoulder. "I feel like it's getting bigger."

Marisa's whispered mumble to LJ wasn't as low as she thought, or maybe that was her point. "That's what she said."

I'd miss them. Whether it was Wisconsin or another team, playing together and being in the same city wasn't likely to be a long-term thing. It would suck leaving them behind again.

"Holy shit, it's the Goblin King." Jules's wide-eyed outburst sent more than a few heads turning. "Bravo. Complete commitment. Love the eyeliner."

Knox preened, his already massive chest puffing out even more. "Why thank you." He punctuated it with a flourish-filled bow.

Berk stared at the parking lot filled with people whose tickets were being checked as they were loaded into the buses. "No one will ever doubt you know how to throw a party."

"None of it's me. Headstrong Foundation does all the work. I just show up."

Berk patted my shoulder and squeezed. "All this self-deprecation is making my teeth hurt it's so sweet. Funding all that work means you get at least some of the praise. Deal with it."

"I could say that to you guys too. Thank you for the generous donations."

LJ landed a soft punch to my other shoulder. "Come on, you know we did it for the tax write-offs."

Marisa swatted LJ's arm. "Ignore him. We were happy to do whatever we can. There are even a couple kids I've gotten museum internships for next year. Everyone is excited to help."

"Nix has a few working in his restaurant and said it's working out great."

Getting emotional over people helping out was an occupational hazard of being a part of Headstrong Foundation, but seeing the guys here supporting it made the little kid I'd been feel a hell of a lot less alone.

The next batch of buses pulled away.

"You guys can hop on any of the buses. Knox, you too."

"I can hang out with you a while longer." Knox piped up. Probably waiting to do Bay recon.

I loved him, but I wasn't going to go full werewolf the second I saw her. This would be the third time we'd seen each other. I'd made it through each time without baying at the moon.

Marisa threaded her fingers through LJ's, resting on his shoulder and looked to me. "What about you?"

I rocked from foot to foot, watching the entrance to the parking area. "I'm taking the last bus, but you don't have to wait around for me."

Some partygoers approached and asked for pics. The three of us posed for a few pics and signed a couple autographs. I couldn't help but notice the way this was different than when Bay was rushed. We were part of a team. Sure, one of us might've had a great play—well not me, but one of the guys—but they wanted our signatures because we were on a team they loved. I was a bit more recognizable because of my 'good luck' status, but it was almost never the kind of visceral, spotlighted attention Bay got.

Berk wrapped his arm around Jules's waist. "We'll wait for you." He nuzzled the side of her face and I couldn't help but feel the flares of sadness and jealousy itching at my skin.

These guys had both found the women who they couldn't live without. They'd all fallen into a happy normalcy where they woke up next to a great person who'd be by their side no matter what.

A few more fans came up to us as we hung out in the parking lot. It felt a bit like a time warp. I'd gone back in time, leaning against cars in the Greenwood parking lot, talking and laughing with my teammates and friends, but without all the baggage I'd had back there. A different kind of life.

The last two buses idled, waiting for stragglers. There weren't any this year. Apparently, having a Grammy-winning juggernaut performing was a surefire way to get even the fashionably late to show up early.

"Should we go...?" Jules jerked her thumb toward the rubberized stairs leading to the padded bench seats.

Crunchy gravel ground under the tires of the slow-moving vehicle. A black SUV pulled into the parking lot.

The clenched tightness in my chest relaxed and redoubled.

My group all looked to me and I realized I'd gripped tight to the side mirror of the car I'd been leaning against. She was here.

The back passenger door popped open. Bay's security guy eyed us from the front passenger seat.

Out of the car came Holden, followed by Bay. She wore a shimmery skirt that looked part fish tail and fell to her ankles with a double-take inducing slit that disappeared under her coat. Her black pea coat hit her just below the hip, hiding the rest of the gap in her skirt.

Glitter sparkled around her eyes and the rest of her face. Starfish and coral-colored seahorse silhouettes were dotted all over her face.

She rushed forward, breathless and apologetic. "Sorry we're late. There wasn't much time to get ready after we left the tour fittings." An overwhelming, stunning kind of beauty people took for granted until they saw her up close.

Or maybe it was those old high school parking lot feelings that made me want to press her up against the car and kiss her like I had far too long ago.

Her eyes skimmed across the small group assembled near me and widened when they landed on Knox.

"Knox, good to see you." She teetered on the edge of a handshake hug before he opened his arms wide.

A moment of hesitation and she walked toward him, letting his arms envelop her.

I wished it could be that easy for us.

"Good to see you, Bay." He released her and her gaze locked onto me.

Beside me, the mouth-gaping and arm-punching told me no one else had expected Bay to show up here. Or know Knox. He'd been invited to a few of our events, vacations and hang outs, but this was showing a whole other side of my life I'd never spoken about.

I'd hidden it from them. The back of my neck burned from the stares I knew I was getting.

"You could've gone straight there if this was too out of your way." The suit had seemed like a good choice, but now the tie felt like it was choking me. I shoved a finger under the gap at the top of the knot resting against my Adam's apple. Old patterns had returned so quickly and easily with her, and so did the fear that bad came along with the good.

"Shit, sorry. Am I throwing off the schedule? I thought Gwen said we could meet here and follow you." She glanced over her shoulder at Holden.

A couple choked yelps squeaked behind me.

"No, it's okay. We were about to ride the last bus in. It's just us." I pointed to the other two couples. "These are some of the people I mentioned back during training camp. The guys I played with at Fulton U. LJ and Berk. And their wives, Marisa and Jules. We all went to college together. Everyone, this is Bay."

The four non-former Greenwood residents waved. I didn't miss the darting looks of shock bouncing between Bay and me. I might've forgotten to mention the whole knowing her thing. Inviting questions about what had happened between us had never been something I'd wanted, and I hadn't wanted it to come out like I was bragging about dating her in the past. What we'd had was more than that, and then it had been gone. I didn't need to invite anyone else into the maelstrom that had been raging in my head for years.

"You can ride with us, if you'd like. You can also take the SUV and follow, if you're busy or have things to do along the way." I wanted her to ride with us. Not in the SUV alone— well, not alone, but with her people. I'd never seen her with anyone else. Not that I'd seen her much outside of official events, but there was a lingering loneliness to her. She'd had to cultivate a separation over the past years, and it made me want to be closer to her.

Bay glanced over her shoulder again.

I hated how she looked to Holden for reassurance and direction. I hated that I wasn't the one she looked to. Hated that I wanted to be.

Holden nodded. "You should take the bus."

"Are you sure?"

"Yeah, when's the last time you had a chance to hang out? It's been a long day. Relax before you perform." Holden shooed her back toward the rest of us.

Her uncertain smile twitched. "Looks like I'm riding with you guys. Lead the way."

"We're headed to the last bus parked over there." It was less than fifty feet away.

Bay walked first with Knox, and Holden came out of nowhere to walk her to the bus.

My jaw clenched, but I relaxed it. I didn't want Holden to come along. I didn't want him hovering.

Walking to the bus, everyone else shot me a whispered 'holy shit' and wide-eyed looks of amazement that we'd all be riding together.

"Chill out." I gritted out. "She's going to turn back around, if you don't all stop acting like weirdos. You act like you've never met a famous person before."

"But not Bay. Even Berk sings some of her songs in the shower." Jules grabbed my arm.

"Fine, have your mini-freak out, and then promise me you'll treat her like a normal person." With all the ways her life had changed, that seemed to be the one piece missing. Normalcy. Not that my life was normal, but I could go about my day with only a few pictures and autographs. She didn't seem to have any interactions that anyone would consider normal.

We got onto the bus and the driver pulled the accordion door closed behind us.

Knox wandered around the bus like it was a relic in need of exploration. Bay took a two-seater three seats back from the first seat.

I sat in the three-seater across from her.

Berk and Jules took the three-seater behind me and LJ and Marisa rushed to the back of the bus, joining Knox in their middle school exploration.

Bay leaned forward, her eyes darting to the back of the bus. "Sorry if I made this awkward. I can go in the SUV. I don't want to ruin a fun night with you and your friends."

"You're not ruining anything. They'll calm down in a few minutes. I made them promise me they'd stop being so weird. I swear, they're not normally like this."

I sat on the edge of my seat, shoulders touching my seat back and the one in front of me. Shifting, I raised my arms and rested them on the cushioned vinyl tops. Had these seats always been so uncomfortable? Or was it being this close to her without the watchful eye of anyone else in a place that brought back all those old Greenwood memories?

Her legs were tucked into her row. If we'd both had out legs out in the aisle, they'd be brushing against one another. Or her knees would've been between mine.

She shrugged. "Occupational hazard. I'm used to it."

An ember burned in my chest.

Her acceptance of never being treated like a normal person, struck a match against my heart.

I grabbed for the normal.

"How was your day?"

She wedged her hands between her knees. "Work. Meetings. Phone calls. The same as always. How about you?"

"I worked out in the morning. We had a team meeting. I spent the rest of the day trying to stay out of the way of everyone planning tonight."

"The work your foundation does is truly exceptional. There are a lot of kids out there who could use the help."

"Unfortunately." I slumped against the padded bus seat. It shouldn't have to exist. My foundation should be unnecessary, but that wasn't the case. Part of me hated myself for wanting to take a salary cut to play in Wisconsin. My signing bonuses went to the foundation. Taking a step down for more time on the field was siphoning off money that could be put to good use.

My own selfishness won out there, but the conflict still raged inside my head. Maybe it was all still pretend. Maybe the guy I thought I was wasn't as good as I thought. Maybe I hadn't really made it past so many of the things I'd tried to put behind me.

Being here with Bay threw all the cracks and flaws into sharp focus, but I was drawn to her. She tugged at me like a gravitational pull I wasn't sure I wanted to escape. It would either be a safe landing or I'd burn up in her orbit.

It was getting harder to deny my past and deny the feelings she ignited.

14

BAY

Riding in the school bus brought back all kinds of high school feelings. I'd biked to school most days, but there had been the coveted field trip days when the entire class crammed into the elementary-school-sized seats. Voices had echoed off the metal walls and roof and excitement at missing a whole day of school had buzzed in the air.

The whole thing smelled like 8th grade algebra and lunch meat. As terrible as it was, the change of pace was refreshing. The nostalgia bombardment turned me into a seventeen-year-old version of myself with one whiff of school-lunch pizza.

Tonight, the bus was way less rowdy than any trip to a local farm or amusement park.

Knox had been an unexpected familiar face, but with his connection to Keyton, it made sense. He was here to support his friend.

Holden and Eric followed in the SUV. I'd felt a bit like a dork asking to ride in the bus with everyone else while my chaperones tailed us like overprotective parents.

The bus was a safe zone. Just Keyton and his pro football friends. No crazy fans or mob situations.

Our driver was a fan, though, and asked for an autograph. I did it quickly, glancing over my shoulder before everyone else made it to the bus doors. The last thing I needed was for them to all feel even weirder around me when we were just going for a low-key bus ride to a performance I was doing...okay, maybe not as low key as I'd have liked.

The rest of the gang loaded onto the bus. Holden tapping on my window to make sure I was okay was the only bump in the road to normalcy, apart from an actual bump where LJ and Marisa sat in the wheel well seat and tried to catch as much air as possible. They laughed and bickered more than any two people I'd ever seen, but the ring on her finger and the comfortable way they spoke to each other hit a chord of longing wrapped around my heart.

"He told us he knew you, but in a vague—we've-run-into-each-other kind of way." Berk, with the floppy hair and boyish demeanor shoved into a brick house of a man's body, rested his arm on the top of the padded seat in front of him. His Captain America costume seemed appropriate, if a little tight. Jules sat beside him in a killer forties Peggy Carter costume.

Knox took the three-seater behind Berk and Jules, propping his legs up on the seat.

"We did—do know each other. We went to high school together. Me, Keyton and Knox." I pointed to Knox, who touched his two fingers to his brow before flicking them toward everyone. "It's great you've all stayed friends even after college."

LJ came back up to the seats we had in the front with

Marisa. "We roomed together for senior year. The four of us." He pointed to Keyton, himself, Berk and Marisa.

I looked to her. "What was it like living with three guys?"

"It had its ups and downs for sure." She laughed. "Keyton probably had the worst time of the whole thing, right? LJ and I got pretty close that year."

Even in the dark interior of the bus, I could feel the beet red flush of his skin. "I have no idea what you're talking about."

"Come on. Not a single memory?" LJ leaned forward over the top of his seat, grinning and looming over Keyton.

He flung his arm across his face, covering his right ear, and slapped the other hand over the left. "Stop it. I hate you both."

I chuckled along, trying not to let the feeling of missing out sour the fun everyone was having. Other than Spencer and Felicia, I hadn't kept in touch with anyone from college. It was hard to be friends with people when every interaction started or ended with them asking for something. Felicia was doing her professor thing in New Orleans. She and Ethan had both scored positions. Spencer had cut a demo a year ago and touring seemed to be going well.

Keyton, on the other hand, had a whole team of peers, guys who'd gone through a lot of the same things he had and could be there to lean on.

It amplified how much I'd missed out on growing up with people like them around me. Peerless, they'd said in Rolling Stone when my last album released. But that wasn't always a great thing.

"Holy shit." Marisa jumped up, staring at me wide-eyed. "You're the girl."

Everyone's confusion meter spiked straight off the

charts, even mine. Normally, this kind of reaction happened when the pieces clicked into place and they realized it was me, not after we'd already been introduced and it had been established I was, in fact, *that* singer.

Jules bounced in her seat, clasping her hands over her mouth before dropping them and grinning wide. "You're the one Keyton drew all the time in college."

Berk and LJ turned to me, assessing me with new eyes. This wasn't the stranger fan gaze I was used to, but a you-mean-a-lot-to-someone-I-care-about gaze. It was one I hadn't encountered before.

He'd drawn me enough during college that the people around him recognized me. It rocked me to my core. Our time together in LA had been so quick. Only a blink of an eye when held up against the past six years and the four we were in college, but it had left an unreadable mark on me. It seemed it had on him too. Did he still think about me as much as he'd thought about me back then?

Did he still draw me?

So many of my songs were about him, and there wasn't a day I didn't think about him. But it felt like he'd moved on, determined to move past what we were. Now I was left wondering what we could be.

I focused on not squirming in my seat.

LJ spoke first, snapping. "It was your guitar he was always walking around with."

"You walked around with my guitar?" I turned to Keyton, who'd dropped back into the shadows of his seat across from mine.

Keyton's words were rushed. "Not all the time. Some-times I'd take it to a luthier to see if they could fix it. Or I practiced on other guitars to make sure I didn't fuck it up more than I already had."

"You fixed my guitar?" My heart squeezed even tighter. "I thought you'd paid someone else to do it."

He ducked his head. "Most people said it was a lost cause and there wasn't anything they could do, so I did it myself." A shadow shoulder shrugged.

"It had to have taken a long time." I wanted to reach out and take his hand. Run mine over his like the splinters and cuts would still be visible.

"It took far too long. It took a long time for me to gather up the nerve to even try." He stared at me, his gaze slicing through the darkness. This wasn't about how many hours he'd hunched over the broken pieces of wood to piece them back together.

Berk rested his elbow on his leg and propped his chin on his hand, looking straight at me. "I can't believe I never noticed you were the sketch girl."

Marisa leaned forward, resting her chin on the seat back behind me, less than a foot from my head. "He wasn't exactly waving that notepad around all the time."

"I didn't only sketch her." Keyton broke in, discomfort coating every syllable.

I tried to shift the focus. "Do you still draw?"

He broke off his tense glare at his friends, who were doing what friends did best, embarrassing the shit out of him. "I do. I paint sometimes, as well."

Marisa leaned forward this time with a menacing accusation. "You're painting and you didn't tell me."

Keyton laughed. "It's not exactly gallery quality. I keep telling you, no one will pay for these."

"They might for charity." She shot back.

"They're nothing special. Just something to do to relax." The shyness was back.

I dropped my head back against the seat. We'd spent so

many hours in his room or mine, him drawing and me scribbling in my notebook, both of us lost in what we created, but not needing to hide from each other. "You always had a way of capturing a moment with only a few pencil strokes."

LJ dropped his arm around Marisa's shoulder. "You've seen him draw other things? He'll barely show any of us."

Keyton's deadpan stare was directed at all his friends. "I can't imagine why I wouldn't want to."

But I wanted them to know he was talented. I wanted him to know too. "If he's kept it up since high school, then they've got to be gorgeous. He'd sketch everyday things and capture the thing that made them special."

"I just drew what I saw." A sidelong glance was all he chanced.

Berk inched forward, taking Jules with him like they were attached at the hip. "If I'd gone to high school with Bay, I'd start every conversation with that information."

"My first album didn't come out until after we'd graduated college. No one would've known who I was back then."

Keyton's gaze flicked to mine and I felt it skim across my skin. Now I was the one happy the dim interior of the bus provided enough shadows to hide every flush. And his gaze told me he'd known who I was. He'd always known.

"How are things going this season?"

Marisa and Jules groaned. "Don't get them started. From the second Keyton's trade announcement was made before last season, everyone's been hyped for every practice, every game. I swear some of the guys have already cleared space on their shelves for another championship ring."

"No pressure." Keyton mumbled under his breath.

"Everyone's really sure about you." I ducked my head trying to catch his eye. "That must be an awesome feeling."

"More like scary. I don't want to let my team down. I especially don't want to let these guys down, but there's nothing I can do when I'm not on the field."

"Just keep putting out those good vibes."

The conversation drifted from topic to topic as the ride progressed. Movies. The season. TV shows. Regular things I'd taken for granted once.

"We were watching House Hunters International and someone wanted to know if their 19th Century Paris walk-up—"

"Had a garbage disposal." I piped up.

Marisa smacked the back of the seat. "Yes! How insane are these people?"

"My budget is $3000 and I'd like an oceanfront beach house. I sure hope you like cardboard boxes."

The whole bus erupted into laughter. Uneasiness slid away with each mile until the bus slowed, gravel crunching under the wheels.

Trees had lined our path on the way to the farm, but the dark cocoon burst open with sky-high bright lights. Carnival rides, tents, and a stage transformed the flat land.

Instead of pulling up to the front of the building people were flowing in and out of, the driver took us around the back.

The bus crawled to a stop and the doors opened.

It was almost show time. For a few minutes I'd forgotten why I was here, why I'd been invited. I wasn't a friend along for the ride with everyone else. I was the main attraction in the three-ring circus, and it was Keyton's job to make sure I performed.

There was nothing more to it than that.

But the easy way we talked and laughed on the bus. The

way his gaze heated my skin. As much as I'd tried to deny it and pretend I was only doing this for altruistic reasons, I wanted him to still want me. Because I still wanted him.

15

BAY

Holden, Emily, Gwen, and Eric stood at the bottom of the steps. I cringed, hating how much this made me look and feel like a diva. I wanted to walk off the bus like everyone else and join in with the crowds of people laughing, singing and shouting on the other side of the farmhouse. The catering ramp and over-sized AC units in the back meant it also doubled as an event space.

"Bay, you've already met Gwen."

Another man rushed out of the back door. It was getting more crowded out here by the minute.

"And this is Everest and Hunter from the event planning company, SWANK."

"Hey, Everest. Long time, no see." My smile widened and I hugged Everest.

"Good to see you, Bay." He released me. "I'm surprised you were able to slip this event in. I know how busy Maddy and Holden keep you." Everest's green eyes lit up at the mention of Maddy. Someday soon, I'd have to sit her down and get all the details on the specifics of what brought them back into one another's lives.

"They definitely try."

Holden cleared his throat. Right, we were on a timetable.

I shook hands with everyone else.

Gwen and Holden ushered us all inside, and within minutes, my new riding buddies were gone. I'd hoped we could hang out, but the circus never stopped around me, and I couldn't blame them for wanting to enjoy their evening without all the extra hassles and commotion.

Through the heads of the people around me, I spotted Keyton, which made sense. It was his event. No need to get a big head over him playing a gracious host.

Inside the green room, I took off my coat. Sweat beaded on my skin, although the room had a chill. Sound guys came in to run me through the audio set up. It was a risk, performing without any time on the stage, but we hadn't had the time before the guests would arrive.

I'd have to wing it.

I was all wired up and ready to go, and Emily double-checked my makeup.

Someone placed a mic into my hand. I held onto the cool metal, which warmed in seconds from my clammy hands.

It might've been mid-September outside, but I was burning up. Nerves were running roughshod through my body. My stomach clenched and tightened.

Right about now, I wished Keyton wasn't here.

Holden's arm shot out with a trashcan in hand.

I bent forward. The little bit of food I'd had in the car came straight back up, burning my nose and mouth. Pulling my head back from the trashcan, I took the napkin Emily held out.

Before I could grab the water, a hand gently touched the back of my shoulder. "Are you okay?" Keyton stared at me, his face creased with worry.

"It'll be okay. I can still perform." I took a slug from the water and spat it back into the trashcan.

"I don't care about the show. Are you okay? Are you feeling alright?"

Emily handed me a breath freshener and helped me with my lipstick.

"Occupational hazard." I popped it into my mouth, happy the coral glitter and makeup could cover at least some of the embarrassed-as-hell flush currently overtaking my body.

"How often does this happen?" He looked from me to Holden and Emily.

They looked away, suddenly fascinated by finding a place for the trashcan.

"Most of the time before I perform." I chuckled, trying to play off the not-so-mild humiliation at puking in front of him.

"Most of the time?"

Ducking my head, I fidgeted with the scales on my dress. "Maybe every time..."

"You throw up before performing every single time."

"It's not a big deal, and it won't affect my performance." One quick check in the mirror. "See, good as new!" Clapping my hands to my sides, I slapped on a sunshine spotlight smile.

"We can wait a little longer, if you need it."

That would only lead to a second puke session. Better to rip the band-aid off. "No, let's go."

The stage staff and audio tech walked me through the

sound check through my earpiece, since I couldn't do it on stage with everyone already outside.

Keyton hovered nearby.

My reassuring smiles didn't seem to be convincing him at all.

I tried not to bask too hard in him caring, and chalked it up to him not wanting the performer for his big event and the meet-and-greet after to back out at the last second.

The chill increased the closer we got to the stage. Doors were propped open, and I bounced on the balls of my feet to warm up without the coat I'd worn on the way here. The sheen of sweat brought my temperature down even lower. I was simultaneously sweaty and freezing.

Keyton checked with me one more time.

I offered up a smile and nodded. A curtain was draped over the seven stairs leading to the newly erected stage. The backing band were guys I'd played with before.

Keyton stopped at the top of the stairs and looked back at me.

A thumbs-up was all I could muster. Gwen took off up the stairs behind him. The crowd cheered from the second the curtain was pulled back and he walked out on stage.

Even with the open space and non-packed event, their chants grew as Keyton read my introduction.

"Bay!" The stagehands pulled back the curtain and I jogged up on stage, swallowing the bile that always tickled the back of my throat during a solo performance.

There was nothing to be afraid of, but the panicking fear that was hard to shake until the second before the first song. Focus on the music. I rushed through my hellos and thank you's before launching into the first song.

The entire event was centered around the stage. Rides, games, food and pop-up bars surrounded the whole space.

The performance was seamless. Despite having no rehearsals with the local backing band, they didn't miss a beat.

Every person in the crowd was on their feet. People screamed and cheered from the Ferris wheel with their cameras out, filming the whole performance. This was my kind of party. Everyone was in makeup and masks, so it didn't feel like tons of people staring. This was just some friendly, ghoulish, and furry friends who'd come to have a great time. It didn't hurt that the booze was plentiful and the singing along got louder by the time I reached my final chorus.

I'd never been to an event like it before. In the distance, a helicopter took off and came back with partygoers. Carnival ride lights dotted the empty space. It was a summer carnival, rave, and Halloween all rolled into one.

We powered through five songs and I made the announcement written on the card Gwen had handed to me. The silent auction would be closing soon and I threw in a few extra prizes of my own, letting them know about the all-expenses trip to any of my upcoming concerts and front row seats that were up for grabs.

I glanced at the side of the stage. Holden rolled his eyes and laughed, leaning down to whisper to Emily, who launched into action to get whatever needed to be done to make it happen. That was why they were the best.

There may have been a small rush of people heading toward the silent auction area between the skee-ball and basketball shoot out with an adult-sized unicorn and taco hanging between them as the ultimate prizes.

The crowd cheered for another encore after I'd blown through two already. Checking in with the band, we came up with one other they all knew. Sweaty from my performance, rather than anxiety, I left the stage breathless and humming with excitement and relief. Another successful show with a satisfied crowd.

Emily shoved a bottle of water into my hand and Holden handed me a towel.

I dabbed so I wouldn't mess up my makeup and drained the plastic water bottle until it collapsed in my hand.

"You've got the meet-and-greet and then we're done." Holden flipped the cover closed on his tablet. "Great job out there. They had to add two extra sheets to your tour package auction item. People kept bidding."

"Awesome." I braced my hands on my hips and scanned the outdoor backstage area for Keyton, but the man who stood a head above everyone else wasn't here.

He had a lot going on tonight, and I didn't need my hand held.

With my energy setting cranked up, we walked into the meet-and-greet area for hundreds of pictures. Giving all the fans tons of shots to take with them, my cheeks ached by the end of the hour. It had been a long day and I couldn't ignore the throbbing in my feet any longer.

I collapsed into the chair in the now-deserted green room area. There had been no sign of Keyton since he'd introduced me on stage. I wanted to say goodbye. Maybe it was my way of being the one to leave first this time. We both had a way of making pretty dramatic exits.

I didn't want to disappear on him.

Holden and Emily kept pointing at each other's tablets. I sunk down in the chair enough to rest my head on the low back and closed my eyes. "The driver is on his way to the side entrance."

If I kicked my shoes off now, I'd have to walk out barefoot. My toes would mutiny if I tried to shove them back in. Decisions, decisions.

The door opened and the muted sounds of the party increased.

"Sorry." It was Keyton.

The melodic, rumbling timbre of his voice did crazy, dirty things to me. I shot up straight and opened my eyes. "Hey."

"Hey." He glanced over at Emily and Holden. "Were you leaving already or did you want to check out the party?"

An excited glow was quickly extinguished. As fun as it looked from the stage, I was a one-woman wrecking crew when it came to quiet enjoyment. "It's okay. I don't want to create a scene out there. I'm not exactly inconspicuous." Especially after standing on stage in this costume earlier tonight.

The door opened behind him and Gwen came in. She, Holden and Emily must have gone to a special celebrity handler school to pull off looking like they always knew what to do next.

"There won't be any issues." He glanced over his shoulder. "Gwen, do we have some extra costumes? Something Bay could use to go out incognito?"

She nodded. "I can make it happen."

"Really. You don't have to. I know you're so busy already." I called after her, but she was gone already. "I'd love to hang out longer, but I don't want to make extra work for everyone else. There are hundreds of people out there and lots of fires I'm sure she's putting out already. She doesn't have to. I'm sure she's got her hands full."

"I know. Gwen is more than capable and the event planning company is handling all the fires—big and small. You did us a massive favor, the least you can do is have some fun tonight, if that's okay..." His gaze drifted from me to Holden.

"I'd love to." I stood and winced. My toes angry at my premature celebration of near freedom. I wish I'd brought some more comfortable shoes.

Holden stepped forward and nodded toward Keyton now standing beside the couches on the far end of the room. "Are you sure about this?" He glanced over his shoulder. "The last time I left you two alone, you didn't look so happy when I came back." All the protective big brother instincts I loved about him were rearing their heads.

"I know. But Holden, if I don't go with him tonight, I'll look back and regret this moment. As scary at it might be. As hurt as I might end up. I can't not do this." My heart rate picked up, the anticipation of being on my own with Keyton making me a little dizzy.

"As long as you don't look back and regret not getting into the car with me and Emily."

I peered over at Keyton who did his best to pretend he wasn't watching us from ten feet away. "I won't." I sounded a lot surer than I felt. I might regret it, but there was no other choice. I'd have to take the leap and worry about the rest later.

"That's what I thought." He held out my phone. "You'll need this."

Gwen returned with a few different costume options. There were a couple half-face Venetian masquerade masks, a cat woman mask, and one plastic mask with a fluffy zippered onesie to match. It was soft and warm and comfortable—Wonder Woman in pajama form, complete with the costume and nude-colored fabric on the arms and legs. Maybe all my concert costumes should be in Snuggie form from now on. "This one."

Rushing into the bathroom, I stripped off my costume and hopped into the other. It was a warm hug. I slid my phone into the pocket—yes, there were pockets! —and zipped it up fully. Using a hair tie from Emily's bag of tricks, I put my hair up. My feet screamed at being shoved back into my heels, but maybe I'd slip them out later and let the cold ground numb them.

I peeled off the large glitter decorations around my face and scrubbed with soap and water to get the makeup off, but I'd learned a long time ago, glitter was forever. I did the best I could without the industrial makeup remover I had back in my hotel room.

Opening the door, I stopped short.

Keyton stood inside the alcove. His broad shoulders seeming to fill the whole space. His presence never failed to send my heart into overdrive. He dropped down in front of me, kneeling. "I thought you could use these." In his left hand, he had a pair of flats.

I could have cried.

He took my right foot in one hand and slid the heels off. The rush of relief was back.

His strong fingers kneaded the sole of my foot in a far-too-short massage. My toes got a little attention, too.

He slid the black, cushioned flat onto my right foot and repeated the pleasurable torture on my left. Picking up my heels, he stepped back with his arm out, letting me past.

I didn't want to walk past. I wanted to stay in this darkened cubby of a space with him.

But there was a room full of people on the other side of the wall and I didn't have much time before something came up and I couldn't stay.

Not wanting to lose a minute, I hurried back into the room.

Everyone stood, watching and waiting.

Keyton handed my heels to Emily.

Please don't tell me they're going to say I can't go out there.

I ran my hands along the fuzzy pajama Wonder Woman legs. "Are we good to go?"

"If you're sure about this." Holden set down his phone. "We can stay for a while if you'd like, in case you need some back-up."

Keyton stepped forward. "Once they see the SUV go, everyone will assume Bay's gone. I won't let anything happen to you." He held out his hand. "Trust me."

I stared into his eyes and slid my hand into his. "I'll be fine, Holden." I couldn't rip my eyes away from Keyton.

The pads of his fingers ran over the inside of my wrist. His eyes told me everything I needed to know. I could trust him. He wouldn't leave my side. And I'd regret leaving without spending this time with him.

We walked toward the door. I called out over my shoulder. "I've got my phone, Holden. It will be okay."

Without waiting for a response, we were out the door, Keyton leading the way.

Eric and Holden stayed behind. The doors to the green room closed behind us.

Excitement and nervousness were in an on-stage scuffle in my stomach.

Keyton walked through the event space with his head held high, no worries about what might be on the other side of the door.

It wasn't until that moment that it hit me how far I'd veered from the path of the life I'd had before. The anticipation of a shitshow on the other side of a door wasn't a given for most people, not even people who were famous like Keyton.

The sounds from outside got louder as we got closer. Shoving the doors open, he grinned and looked back at me.

I gripped his hand tighter, covering it with my other. It felt like I was sitting in the car pulling into an amusement park parking lot, gripping the seats and bouncing around, ready to have some fun—finally.

Outside on the lawn there were lights flashing and laughter and screams filling the air. The rest of the gang stood close by.

He whispered close to my ear. "I let them know you were staying. I hope that's okay."

The hair on my arms jumped to attention at his close talking and familiar scent. "It'll be fun. I'm sure you want to hang out with your friends too."

"And you." He still hadn't dropped my hand and I hadn't dropped his. His friends were right there though and it could invite questions, ones I wasn't prepared to answer.

Besides the rides, there was a full carnival set up, complete with rigged games and junk food galore. A fried food fantasy ran through my head.

Marisa showcased my outfit with her hand. "You're the coziest Wonder Woman I've ever seen."

"Warm too. And I've got pockets." I extracted my hand from his and stuck both mine in my pockets.

He stood beside me in a way that felt more like a declaration, one to rival me pulling my hand from his. My whole life was one big plan that I didn't feel clued into half the time. There were no plans for what any of this meant beyond tonight, but that didn't mean I couldn't enjoy it, that I couldn't savor every moment, no matter what the morning sun brought.

"What do you want to do first?"

Colorful lights, laughter and childhood flashbacks were in every corner of this place. "Anything. Everything."

With a whole group of friends, kind of like the ones I'd never had in high school, we ran through the carnival.

No money was needed for rides or the games, and the lime green lanyard was our VIP drinks package. We stood in line for the Gravatron, where our backs were stuck to the wall while *Welcome to the Jungle* blasted at top volume.

We raced from one attraction to another, everyone telling jokes and stories to keep us entertained while we waited for our turn on the next near-vomit-inducing ride. My cheeks hurt from laughing and smiling, although my disguise hid a lot of it. It also let me watch Keyton without feeling like everyone could see.

I didn't have to hide my smile when partygoers asked if I'd take a picture of them with him and the rest of the guys. It was nice being on the other side of the camera for once.

I could see his ease with who he was now, how easily he laughed, how much his friends cared about him, and he cared about them.

Tears welled in my eyes, but I blinked them back, willing myself not to get emotional. He'd finally found a family with a bond not even six years and cross-country moves could dampen. He'd finally found some peace.

We sat beside each other with our arms over our heads on the rollercoaster. Locked in a small car beside him, I rested my head on his shoulder, soaking up every moment.

He dropped his head down on top of mine. A gentle weight. Words said without opening our mouths.

I missed you so much.

A yearning I hadn't even let myself recognize slammed into me like two Mack trucks driving toward each other at sixty miles per hour. I missed him. I missed being with him, laughing with him, knowing him.

My feet were no longer in rebellion, but my legs were. Still, I didn't want to stop. It was one of the few times I'd been on my own, not tucked inside four walls, in so long I could barely remember the last time.

The food stand with beignets and crepes would be the death of me, and I shouldn't have ridden the Tilt-A-Whirl after ingesting what had to be a pound of powered sugar and Nutella.

All of us collapsed onto benches, Keyton beside me, a little sweaty and a lot happy.

It was the happiest I'd been in a long time.

I didn't want the night to end. I didn't want my time with him to end, but in the light of day would everything feel as magical as it did tonight?

16

KEYTON

Bay had to be tired. She'd been on the verge of passing out in the green room when I'd gone back to check on her, scared she'd left already. As tired as she'd looked, I hadn't wanted the night to end with a handshake and a 'thank you for coming'.

So I'd asked her to come out with me, expecting one of her handlers to jump in to say no, but she'd jumped in first.

Watching her enjoy herself without the weight of who she'd become tapped into a piece of me that longed to give her the world, longed to give her something no one else could. But tonight was one night.

A night for her to hang out with my friends and nearly deafen me with screams on the can drop ride. A night to be close to her.

Running around the transformed farm grounds with Bay, Knox, LJ and Marisa, and Berk and Jules felt like some alternate universe where we'd all grown up together. Here, we were eighteen again, hanging out at a fall fair, laughing and being goofy together without a care in the world.

It was a past I'd wished I'd had, but my true past had brought me to this moment.

The rotor of the helicopter across the farm sent shivers down my spine. My muscles tightened and I fought against the roiling acid in my stomach.

Bay jumped up and down and squeezed my arm. "A helicopter ride maze? Can someone explain what the hell that is?" Her eyes widened behind her mask.

Marisa tugged her forward. "Who knows? Let's find out."

"I thought it was just helicopter rides. That sounds awesome. Let's go." She tried to pull me toward the cordoned off landing pad area, but my knees locked.

Knox jumped in. "Bay, I've been trying to steal a couple minutes with you all night to catch up. I can take you up."

My vision narrowed onto the whirring blades of the helicopter. My stomach roiled, breath increasing into choppy pants and my muscles tensed. The helicopter rocked back and forth, hovering in the air before planting its landing skis down on the makeshift helipad.

Panic gripped my chest, wrapping its fingers of dread tight around my throat.

Marisa chimed in, her overly light voice sounded like it was at the end of a tunnel. "Let's do it as a girls' thing. The guys can get us more funnel cake."

Bay looked to me. "Are you okay with me going with them? Knox, are you okay with that? We can talk after."

He nodded. "Don't worry about it. Just wanted to catch up, we can do it some other time."

"Keyton?"

"We'll be fine. Hang out with them and we'll kick your butts in skee-ball for the giant dancing taco." My voice was strained.

A flicker of a question danced in her eyes.

My breath stalled in my chest and I worked to unwind the tight cording in my muscles. I offered her a smile that probably bordered on full-on serial killer to hide my panic. I licked my lips and cleared my throat.

"Seriously, we'll be here waiting with piping hot funnel cake once you guys land."

She smiled and let Marisa and Jules pull her away. Her fingers slid across my suit jacket.

I wished it was my bare skin.

They rushed forward under the whirring blades of the helicopter and the door was closed behind them.

I was seconds from bracing my hands on my knees so I didn't pass out.

Knox placed his hand on my shoulder. "She'll be fine. She'll be perfectly safe."

"Still not up for helicopter rides?" LJ stood shoulder to shoulder with me.

"One near-death experience was more than enough for a lifetime."

Berk stepped up to my other side like they thought my legs might give out from under me just from being in the vicinity of a helicopter. "Plummeting thousands of feet through the air in a helicopter with a stalled engine still got you scared of hopping into one of them again?" His attempt at a joke fell flat.

"I'll stick to commercial aircraft with multiple engines." My fingers had felt like they didn't unlock for at least a week after the sightseeing tour over the Grand Canyon three years ago had almost ended in a twisted, charred metal catastrophe. "Let's get the girls their funnel cake."

I kept my gaze on the sky. Fear gripped me by my throat so tightly I couldn't speak. All the scenarios of what could go wrong raced through my head, careening off the inside of my skull. If something happened to her...

Knox held onto my shoulder. "Breathe, man. She'll be okay."

I ripped my gaze away from the sky and stared back at him. "You can't know that."

"You're right. I can't, no more than any of us can know about anything, but she'll be alright. And you'll freak her out if you tackle her the second she gets off the helicopter. Calm down."

I closed my eyes and breathed through the irrational fear, taking each scenario of what could happen to her and putting it aside. Driving myself crazy in the few minutes she was gone wouldn't do any of us any good.

The sounds from the party slowly edged in over the tight, strained breaths that gave way to slower, steadier ones. Partygoers slipped further into drunken revelry around me, celebrating their charity. I couldn't blame them one bit, and the money we made here as their inhibitions over at the auction table loosened would do a lot of good over the next year and beyond.

For a while, I'd been worried about what would happen when I left the city mid-season. Leaving the guys in a lurch wasn't what I ever wanted to do, but I needed to take this step, and there was no guarantee we'd all be playing together after this season anyway.

It wasn't a situation I had to worry about anyway. Ernie's call that Wisconsin had reached their salary cap for the year and even my lowest trade salary couldn't be met had squashed my hopes of it happening. The money I got here would be well spent, and the foundation would start their planning as soon as all the numbers came in.

Being here with the guys and Marisa and Jules wasn't

the worst thing. It was the best. Maybe it was a sign I needed to finally stop looking for my chance on the field and focus on what was most important to me.

When the four-passenger helicopter landed, I was standing beside the roped-off area waiting.

She rushed toward me and flung her arms around my neck. "We solved it!" Her mask collapsed some against my shoulder. She pushed it up, lit up with excitement pouring off her. "We were guiding people on the ground through it. We got our whole team out without needing to double back." Pumping her hands overhead, she made mock crowd noises.

People walked behind us.

My back stiffened wanting to shield her.

"I'm glad you had fun." I slid the mask back into place.

Her fingers shot to the mask and her eyes darted around behind it.

"Don't worry, no one saw."

She nodded. "I forgot for a second."

My heart rate spiked in frustration that she had to remember that she needed to remember.

Knox left early, needing to get back for a mid-afternoon show tomorrow and he'd be nursing a chocolate chip cookie martini hangover.

I hugged him.

He thumped my back. "Good to see you, man. Let me know if you need anything and how you're doing." He released me and his gaze flicked to Bay. His wariness made sense after being the only one to keep the pieces of me in near human form after she left the last time. But this time I wasn't the complete and total bad news mess I'd been back then. Still nowhere near perfect, but not teetering on the edge anymore.

"I'll be good. Don't worry."

The noise he made didn't sound like he believed me, but he didn't push it.

The night wound down, going a little off the rails when Marisa finished her third bag of cotton candy and got on the Tilt-O-Whirl.

LJ wrapped his arm around her shoulder. "I'm going to take her back. Thanks for a great night. And it was nice to meet you, Wonder Woman."

Tucked under his arm, Marisa looked a whiff of funnel cake away from painting the ground with neon puke. She mumbled a goodbye.

"Nice to meet you too. Feel better, Marisa." Bay stood a little in front of me to the side. Close enough that the front of my chest touched the back of her arm with every breath.

"We'll head out too." Berk held Jules's hand. Their fingers intertwined. "See you at practice."

"Bye, Keyton and Wonder Woman. We had a lot of fun."

"I did too. And I'm happy I met you both. Maybe I'll see you again sometime." Her chin swung toward her shoulder like she was trying to check with me, but the mask kept her from catching my eye.

"That would be awesome." Jules beamed.

They disappeared into the after-midnight crowd, not one bit deterred by the dropping temperatures.

Sliding my hand into Bay's, an electric current shot up my arm, and the itch of anticipation crawled under my skin. I walked her back to the event center.

Her steps were as fast as mine. We were rushing toward something. What it was, I wasn't sure, and I didn't know if I wanted a heads-up.

One handed, I sent a message to Gwen to send a car to get us.

Her reply was immediate. We had five minutes before the car came to pick us up and the moment would be over. "The car will be here in a few."

Five minutes.

The green room was empty, darkened and left for the clean-up crews tomorrow.

Closing the door behind me, I spun her around and pressed her back against the wall. Running my fingers along her chin, I pushed the mask up over her face.

I stared into her hungry eyes with ones just as ravenous.

My arms braced on either side of her head.

Her soft, glistening lips called to me. Little flecks of cinnamon sugar stuck to the corner of her mouth to rival her already sweet lips, the ones I hadn't tasted in over six years. The ones I still dreamt about. "When was the last time you were kissed?"

"On or off camera?" Her gaze flicked from my lips back to my eyes.

"A real kiss." My voice dropped. I didn't care about pretenders in music videos or perfume ads. I wanted to know the last time a man had made her feel that deep down achey feeling which could only be quenched by more touches.

"The kind that lingers on your lips and etches into your memory."

Her breath hitched. "Six years, two months and twenty-eight days ago. The night—" She didn't get to finish the sentence.

My lips crashed down onto hers. The sear of our lips burned with a pent-up passion I'd tried to deny since the first moment I'd seen her. A hungry ache punched at my chest like my heart was staging a coup and ready to escape.

Her fingers yanked at the hair at the nape of my neck

and I crushed her against the wall, trying to meld us into one.

My hips pressed against hers.

She squirmed and shifted, wrapping her legs around my waist.

I ground against her, friction heating my body even more. My dick didn't appreciate the barriers between us.

"I should've kept the skirt on." She breathed against my mouth between blistering kisses.

My body was so hot it felt like liquid fire had been injected into my bloodstream.

Holding her against me with my hands on her ass, I ground against her.

The panting turned to moans and her grip around my neck tightened. "I've been wanting to do this all night."

"I've been wanting you to do this all night." She held onto me and stared into my eyes. "Will you take me home with you?" A question so naked we might as well have been standing in the fall air stripped down to nothing.

Had we ordered fireworks for tonight or were those going off in my chest? This was national-championship-style, with confetti cannons shooting in all directions. She was the most beautiful woman I had ever or would ever meet.

"You never have to ask." I attacked her lips with a ferocity only she brought out in me. Our bodies shook, vibrations traveled down my shaft, making it harder to remember we could be discovered at any minute.

"I think that's your phone, unless you're packing a vibrator in your pocket." She grinned and let her legs loose from my hips.

I'd been oblivious to the insistent buzzing in my pocket.

Rumbling with my phone, I pulled it out of my pocket. "The car's here."

"I figured." She smiled and picked up her mask, which had fallen to the floor.

We wedged against each other in the back of the car like it was a two-door 90s Honda. Our fingers brushed.

She peeked over at me. With one glance, she sent my heart rate skipping, my blood surging, and my hunger skyrocketing.

Keeping my eye on the driver, I bent and whispered, letting my lips caress her lobe and tickle the shell of her ear. "It's a good thing you're wearing footie pajamas."

She shivered even though the heat was cranked up. Her gaze darted to the driver as well, biting her lip.

"Are you saying you don't want a hand job right now?" The light innocent tone of her words sent whatever blood was left in my head straight to my cock.

The tease was there in her words, but I wouldn't expose her to any actions that might intensify the spotlight on her, like having a driver leak information about an illicit handy in the back of his car with the Philly good luck charm.

"What I want and what I'll do are two very different things. At least until we get to my place."

The rest of the drive was a torturous exercise in restraint. Every look and caress was an invitation to hold her in place while I kissed her breathless.

But I could wait until she was safely in my apartment.

She put her mask back on for the awkward walk across the lobby. I looked like a Secret Service agent protecting a furry version of Wonder Woman. We made it to the elevators on the residents' side of the building. Even after the doors closed behind us, I tamped down the urge to tear her mask off and press her up against the wall. There were still cameras there and someone would record that footage and sell it in a heartbeat.

I couldn't read her expression on the ride up, but her fingers were still threaded through mine, her thumb moving in maddening circles, tightening with each swipe until it moved across the side of my wrist like an ever-increasing countdown to an inevitable explosion.

The doors opened and we burst out of them, spilling into the hallway, both trying to pretend we were racing with me leading the way.

We fell into my apartment. I didn't even turn the lights on, barely got the door closed behind me.

Clothes hit the floor with reckless abandon and there was definitely a lamp or two as a casualty.

Backlit by the moon, she let the last article of clothing dangle from her finger before it dropped to the floor. My heart raced, my blood thundered in my veins, and my fingers itched to touch her again and never let go.

Scooping her up in a bear hug tackle, I headed straight for the couch.

I braced my arms to make it a soft landing for both of us —the couch for her and her for me.

My fingers skimmed from her collarbone down her chest, over the curve of her breast, and down past her waist to her hips. I lifted her leg, hooking it around the back of mine and palmed her ass. Squeezed it.

Under me, she writhed, groaned and had her hands all over me.

Above her once again, I couldn't help but feel how right this was. All I could think about was this moment never ending. Not just the sex and feeling her body against mine, the relentless pounding of my cock demanding release, but all of it. Every moment I was with her, I wanted to stretch it out into a sunrise that never ended.

Fumbling for the pants I'd thrown over the back of the couch, I grabbed for my wallet and pulled out a condom. Ripping into the wrapper like a man possessed, I took a steadying breath and rolled it on.

"Keyton, I need you." She reached between us and wrapped her fingers around my shaft, sliding me between her wet folds.

I shuddered, almost losing all strength in my arms. Dropping to my elbows on either side of her head, I kissed her and rocked my hips back, aiming and pressing forward, letting her slickness coat the head of my cock. Staring into her eyes, I dropped my weight and sunk into her.

The walls of her pussy clamped around me and I sucked in a breath through my clenched teeth.

Her back arched, pressing her breasts against my chest. Her pebbled nipples brushed against my skin, tickling and teasing.

Shifting my hips, I sank completely into her.

The fit was perfect. Tight, a teeth-gnashingly tight grip. I was being dragged under the waves of pleasure racing down my spine and shooting out from the soles of my feet.

A spasm of her pussy ripped a groan from my throat.

She clung to me, holding on through each rough thrust of my hips. So close to the edge, I wasn't gentle or slow, but feral and unhinged.

Her moans, yelps and gasps directed my movements and desire to make this a night she wouldn't forget.

It was one I wouldn't either. I wanted to stop the sunrise and keep her here with me forever.

Every gasp in my ear sent the tingling pleasure rocketing down my spine to the tips of my toes.

Her legs tightened around my waist, muscles seizing and her walls clamped around me with a rhythm too sweet to resist. Grinding, thrusting and colliding, our bodies created their own symphony.

I growled out her name and spots danced in front of my eyes before I lost the grip on my restraints and spilled into the latex between us. My heart thundered so loudly in my ears it blocked out all sound.

Dropping my head to her shoulder, I rocked against her gritting my teeth against the exquisite oversensitivity.

Sweaty and panting, I shifted to the side and held her against me.

Both of us slipped into recovery mode, silent and blissful.

She ran her fingers down my back. "When were you going to tell me you live in the same building I was staying in?"

17

BAY

"I wasn't sure if you noticed that." He shifted back, falling free from me and getting rid of the condom. The cold barely registered, my overheated bliss making my skin feel like it was a glowing beacon bright enough to light the night sky.

I propped my head up on my arm, watching him. "Hard to miss with the big Four Seasons logo everywhere. You weren't stuck in traffic when I invited you for coffee, were you?" I swung my legs onto the floor, not sure how to feel about that. He'd been so close for the past couple weeks. A short walk away.

He sat beside me, making the cushions dip under me. Bracing his forearms on his naked muscled thighs, he pressed his palms together and tilted his head, staring at me.

"I was scared to go."

His honesty now still caught me off guard. It sliced through all the thoughts racing through my head about what every move truly meant.

"I was worried that seeing you again would throw me

back into being the guy I was before. The one from Greenwood and LA."

Right now, I wished I had a blanket or my clothes back. The nakedness felt bone-deep now, the vulnerability so close to the surface. I was almost afraid to ask. Swallowing, I steeled myself.

"And now?"

He turned and ran his finger down the side of my neck. The sparks and flares were still there, burning hotter and deeper than before.

"And now I'm trying my best to not mess up tonight." He traced his thumb down over my lip.

"Me too." The sun would rise soon, and the fantasy dream world would fade. "But we still have a couple more hours until sunrise. Let's not waste them." I held onto his hand and sucked his thumb into my mouth.

His pupils dilated, swallowing the color surrounding them. Muscles tightened and his shaft stiffened against my leg. All that time on the practice field and in the gym paid off. Stamina for days—well, hopefully nights.

He shoved his hands under my legs and behind my back before I could catch my breath, and hauled me against his chest.

Moving through his darkened apartment like it was on fire, he shouldered open a door.

It smelled like him in here, more so than when we'd stripped each other down in the entryway of the apartment. Or maybe I'd been the slightest bit distracted.

My back hit the soft bed and his body covered mine, blanketing me in his warmth and strength.

The rough pads of his fingers ran over my body. They were callused and coarse, and sent shivers rocketing down my spine.

His hunger was unmatched, not even by my own. Our last session had done nothing to quell it, only sprayed a bit more lighter fluid on the raging fire. He fumbled in the bedside drawer and lifted my legs until my heels pressed against the back of his shoulders.

The cool air whispered across my clit and I squirmed, needing more contact.

My back pressed against the mattress. My legs locked over his shoulders. My body hummed in anticipation.

His cock brushed against my ass, weighty, thick, everything I remembered and dreamed about on the lonely nights I'd spent dreaming of him, dreaming of the raw, visceral pleasure coupled with the way only he could look at me. The kind of look that wrote songs without a single word. I couldn't look away and didn't want to.

He braced his hands on the bed beside me and stared into my eyes, catching the dim light filtering in from a cracked door.

"I missed you."

My breath caught and tears filled my eyes. I blinked them back and nodded, not trusting my voice.

Reaching between us, I wrapped my fingers around his shaft and ran my fingers across his thick mushroom tip.

His shudder sent a powerful feeling rushing through me.

I placed him at my entrance, hissing as his hips slowly pushed forward, stretching me like a slow invasion. "I missed you too."

I bit down on his shoulder as he rested his head in the crook of my neck with one hand on my ass. My fingers flexed and spread against his back, my body coming apart at the seams at the bliss radiating down my spine. I tightened my legs around him. I didn't want our time to end—not only the toe-curling pleasure, but the closeness to him.

Rocking my hips, I urged him to move, an insistent encouragement to recapture what we'd recreated out in the living room before. Had it been three minutes or three hours ago? I was lost in a sea of pleasure with emotions overwhelming me from every angle. Pleasure, excitement and deeper ones too scary to touch, but there nonetheless.

"Let me savor this," he mumbled against my neck, tickling my skin.

I didn't want him to savor it. I didn't want him committing this to memory. I didn't want him taking me like it was a one-time thing he'd look back on fondly. I wanted to get him addicted to every taste and touch like I'd been craving him.

Lifting me higher with both hands on my ass, he dropped his hips, spearing me with his solid length.

My back bowed and I moaned, gasping and holding on.

With me still impaled on his dick, he canted his hips and changed the angle of his thrusts. He came crashing down into me, thrusting and rocking his hips, sending pleasure racing down my body, centering on my clit. The grinding strokes when he bottomed out sent sparks so sharp they crested on the edge of pain ricocheting through me.

His fingers skimmed my waist and across my ribs before his palms scraped the underside of my breasts. His touch intensified, squeezing and tugging my nipples as his tongue plundered my mouth.

It was too much. It was not enough. I clung to him as he thrust into me with an unrestrained ferocity.

My orgasm exploded, coursing through me.

Spots winked in front of my eyes and my back bent, riding the tide of pleasure drowning out all my other senses.

My scream ended in a breathless pant riding out the rippling waves of pleasure as my walls clamped around him.

Inside me, he thickened and groaned, his thrusts sloppy and without the precision with which he'd brought me to climax.

He collapsed on top of me with both elbows still on the bed.

I wrapped myself around him, not wanting to let him go, not wanting this moment to end.

He stayed on top and inside of me, not fully losing his erection.

There were no complaints from me.

Our breathing evened out, sweat cooled, and with a curse under his breath, he slowly slid his hips back.

We both groaned as he fell free from me. He went into the bathroom.

I flopped onto the pillows, not hating the view of his ass, but hating to see him leave.

Since when had I become the clingy chick? I was Bay, the untouchable woman who'd actually been untouched for much of my professional career. Suddenly it all paled compared to one night with him.

Scooting up the bed, I sat against the headboard and waited for his return. The water turned off in the sink and he returned with a washcloth.

The damp cloth brushed against the insides of my thighs, and I did nothing to help him.

He watched me, parting my legs, teasing me. Every stroke added a little more lighter fluid to the blaze that had only been under control for a few minutes.

Just as quickly as he cleaned me up, we were sweaty all over again with my legs hitched around his waist and him sinking into me again.

Collapsed in a heap and cleaned up again, he held me close and brushed the hair from my face, tracing the waves running down my cheeks.

"Has anyone ever told you you're beautiful?"

There were social media posts and news articles saying something like that, but somehow this felt more real, just like everything did with him. The scary kind of real that, when let inside, could do real damage. A new reality was here. One where I was close enough to someone to bring up all these thoughts I'd felt so disconnected from for so long. And I felt like he was the only one who could reach me. The only one I'd ever truly wanted to let in.

"It's been a while."

For so long I'd believed he didn't want me anymore, that my place in his heart had closed up, but now with him staring down at me and his fingers brushing away the tears in my eyes, I knew there was a place for me in this world where someone loved me for me. Where he loved me as much as I loved him. The scary kind of love that was easier to run from than let it swallow you up whole and change you, but I didn't think I could stop it this time. I didn't think I wanted to.

"Then I'll have to do it more often."

It hit me with a jolt, sending my heart skipping so fast spots danced in front of my eyes.

I loved him. Like I had back in my bedroom in high school. Like I had when I'd kissed him one last time in California. I loved him, and it burned just as brightly in my chest as an end-of-summer sunset, bittersweet but filled with so many happy memories. I didn't want to look back on them with regret because they'd ended.

Snuggled up against him, this was all I ever needed in the world. How had I survived this long without it?

His fingers tightened on my shoulder. "What time does your chariot arrive?"

My throat tightened. For a moment, I'd forgotten there was a schedule to keep. Demands on my time outside of Keyton wringing another orgasm from me.

I looked up at him and traced my fingers across his muscular chest. The hair at the center between his pecs was new. He was older now and so was I. What was a few hours? A day?

"Hold that thought." Hopping off the bed, I rushed out into the living room, searching the floor for my red, blue, and flesh-toned onesie. I grabbed it and felt around for the phone tucked in the pocket. On my walk back to the bedroom, I sent a message to Holden.

A barrage of texts flew across my screen in response.

Me: I need this

Holden: If it's what you need, then let me handle everything. Do you want me to cancel Spencer too?

Keyton sat up against the headboard.

Me: No, keep Spencer. Cancel everything else.

Holden: Your wish is my command.

I waltzed into the room with my back pressed against the doorway. "Twenty-four hours. I have the next twenty-four hours off." Giddy laughter bubbled up and I hopped to the bed, jumping on my knees before sinking to my butt. "Is that okay?"

Here I'd run out and arranged to spend the whole day with him when he could've just been wondering how much longer until he'd have his bed back to himself.

Reaching up, his hand rested at the back of my neck. "What did that cost you?"

His caring and understanding almost brought tears to my eyes. There were always tradeoffs. When deals were struck months or years ahead of time, the dominos were set, and one change could throw it all into disarray, like it had with Piper's birthday, but how often did I do something for me? How often did I have a chance?

Other than my period reclusion, when I was usually hanging out in bed, chowing down on all the junk, my schedule didn't allow for much in the way of vacation. "I haven't had a day off in forever. It'll be worth it."

A beat of silence stretched out into an entire silence solo before he dragged me down beside him and wrapped his arms around me. They were locked tight. Not tight like he thought I would run away, but tight like he didn't want one inch of us apart.

The heady weight of him over me, warm and strong and here, was like a dream. It was a dream I didn't want to wake from, but the carriage was already turning back into the pumpkin, and my eyelids were droopy and heavy. I couldn't have moved a muscle even if I'd wanted to.

He dragged the blanket over us both and buried his face in my hair.

I rubbed against him like a cat after catnip.

"Then I guess when we wake up I'd better make it worth your while."

18

KEYTON

The morning sun filtered through the light curtains pulled across the windows in my bedroom. This would normally be when I'd roll out of bed and head to the gym. I'd go over my schedule, make a few phone calls, and figure out what I'd have for breakfast.

But this morning, the weight against my chest made me want to find the remote for the blackout curtains and pretend it hadn't risen. We had one day together.

One day to spend together pretending that tomorrow she wouldn't have to go back to her world and I to mine.

"Morning," I murmured, rubbing my cheek against the side of her face. She'd rolled over in her sleep, never getting more than an inch away from me, seeking out my warmth and my touch.

For so long, I'd sought out contentment, the quiet peace I'd never had growing up, but lying in bed with her, everything felt shiny-bright and made my heart race. It was unparalleled and unmatched, which made me hungry for more of these quiet moments. This contentment lit a fire in my soul, not like a quiet lake, but a mountain view after summiting and breathing in the new, fresh air.

"Morning," she grumbled against my chest. "How'd you know I was awake?"

I pulled back to brush the hair from her face and stare into her eyes. "You stopped snoring."

Her jaw dropped and she pushed at my chest. "I do not snore."

Laughing, I held her tight with her arms by her sides. "Who would tell you?"

She wriggled in my hold and worked her fingers against my sides, tickling me. "I've never snored in my life."

Still in the throes of laughter from her devious fingers, I wrestled with her until we were panting and more than wide awake.

She ended up on top of me, with only the thin white sheet between us. My morning wood was no longer based solely on the time of day. I wanted to yank the sheet from between us, wrap my fingers around her waist, and sink into her. I wanted to not spend a moment of today not touching her. I wanted to barricade the doors.

But I didn't want today to only be about sex. It would definitely be about sex, but not *only* sex.

Bending forward, her hair fell like a curtain being drawn around us. Her lips touched mine, so soft and sweet.

I slid my hand to the back of her neck, fingers rubbing against the smooth skin there. I rested my forehead against hers.

Her stomach rumbled.

"Let's get you fed." Lifting her, I rolled to the side of the bed and swung my feet over the edge while my body was screaming for her touch. Not letting temptation get the better of me, I put one foot in front of the other. I wanted her happy with a full stomach. I wanted to take care of her and make it a hooky day she wouldn't soon forget—then I could think about getting her back under me again.

"Fed?" She shoved her hair back with confusion scrawled across her face.

"We have plenty of time. Unless you'd like us to both be unable to walk at the end of our time together."

Her lips twitched and she shrugged with a glint of mischievous mock innocence in her eyes. "I mean, I wouldn't be opposed."

"Then it looks like I'll have to save you from yourself." I walked into my closet and grabbed a t-shirt and shorts for her and a pair of shorts for me.

She'd climbed off the bed and wandered around my bedroom. She was the ultimate temptation.

I wanted to kick my own ass for not suggesting we sequester ourselves in the bedroom, only leaving to answer the door for food delivery.

But today wasn't only about sex. It was about us and who we were now. I rubbed at the center of my chest, where the warmth threatened to turn into a lump. Whatever happened tomorrow would happen, but I had her for today.

With my t-shirt hanging down over her hips and shorts cinched at her waist, she followed me out of the bedroom.

"This is a beautiful place." She peered into the opened doors on the walk to the kitchen. No need to close them here. "How long have you lived here?"

"I bought it a little over a year ago. When I moved to Philly."

"Do you usually buy a place whenever you move teams?"

"No." I swallowed back the urge to shut down, to hide things about my past she might not like. A small step. "It was a sad attempt to make Alice happy. She wanted to settle down and feel a little less transient. But it wasn't what we needed."

She dropped back behind me. No longer at my side, but just behind my shoulder. The words were quiet, small. "What did you need?"

You. It was the real answer. The one I'd tried to hide from and work past, but there wasn't anything to work past when she was what I needed.

"To not be together."

"Were—were things bad?" Her steps slowed.

I turned to face her not sure how exactly to say I'd been with another woman, engaged to her and hadn't felt even a tenth of what I'd felt for Bay. "No, things were never bad. We didn't fight. We'd disagree or argue sometimes, but never fight. Things were never bad. They were good sometimes, generally fine. We were perfectly fine."

"What happened?" Her eyebrows were creased in thought and curiosity.

"I woke up one day and looked at her and couldn't bring myself to steal a lifetime of joy from her to prove to myself I could be in a stable relationship. She deserved someone who couldn't take their eyes off her. Who couldn't stop thinking about her. Who'd treasure her and felt the sun rose and fell with her every breath."

She tugged at the end of her hair falling over her shoulder. Her voice was barely above a whisper. "You didn't feel that way about her?"

"As much as I wanted to" —I looked away, shame burning the tips of my ears—"no, I didn't. I couldn't."

"Why not?"

Confessing how much she'd stayed in my mind, in my dreams, would be heaping my expectations on her. Trying to force things when she'd only come to terms with her guilt after we talked a few weeks ago. I wasn't going to manipulate her. I wasn't going to twist this into something ugly like me trying to cling to her again. "That's the kind of feeling that only comes around once in a lifetime."

We stood in the darkened hallway between the streaming sunlight of the two open doorways. The tingling energy radiated off her, so close to breaking through this barrier we'd erected between ourselves.

The barrier was there to protect us from expectations and reality, to preserve this bubble we were in. But I wanted this to be real outside of the walls of my apartment. I wanted her to feel like we weren't a fever dream of sex, and then to fall back into her old life without me. "Come on, let's get some food."

I took her hand, once again threading my fingers through hers, and we walked past the evidence of our late-night urgency on the way to the kitchen.

"Pancakes? French toast? Bacon? Sausage? What do you prefer?" I opened the fridge and pulled out a bottle of orange juice.

"Are you cooking or ordering room service?" She leaned against the counter beside me.

I smirked. "While it's a perk of living in the hotel," — stepping around her and crowding her against the granite counter, I rested my arm on the open fridge door—"I was thinking we could do it on our own."

Her hint of a smile spread to a full-on grin. "I'd like that."

Palming the loaf of bread, I set it down next to her. "Do you have a recipe or should I look one up?"

Her head swiveled toward me. "I thought you had a recipe."

"Looking it up, it is." We scrolled through the first few pages of recipes until we found one with good reviews, then went in search of all the ingredients I had on hand.

Grabbing everything we'd need out of the fridge, I set it down beside her.

She rummaged through the cabinets for bowls and pans.

I liked that she felt comfortable enough to go searching through my space, like it was a space she wanted to get to know and spend a little more time in.

Working as a team we got everything ready and started cooking.

I crouched in front of the oven using tongs to flip the bacon and sausages. The salty meat smell battled it out against the sweet, eggy fried bread aroma filling the apartment.

She flipped the French toast before relinquishing the spatula to me after a couple burned slices.

Soon, we had fresh strawberries, whipped cream, syrup, sausage, bacon and French toast, all piping hot and ready to devour. The freezer stockpile had come in handy. My cabinets were full and so was my freezer, although I stuck to protein and vegetable mainstays during the season. With everything laid out on the table, I couldn't help the pride brimming in my chest that I'd had all this here for us to make a meal together. I felt a bit more like I was further away from the kid she'd known in Greenwood whose fridge and cabinets had always been barren.

Bay poured us both a glass of juice and set it on the table. "Do you need some help?"

"No, I've got it." Setting out the spread on the table, I took the seat beside her, not across from her. The table always felt too small for this apartment, but right now it was the perfect size as her leg brushed against mine.

"I haven't had a home cooked meal since the last time I was at my mom's." She crossed her legs in the dining room chair and pulled the plate of breakfast meat toward her.

"You don't cook at home?" Maybe she had a chef back at her place. I imagined a chrome-and-glass beachfront property where she'd stand out on the balcony letting the wind whip at her hair, or a technology-filled house where Holden and Emily returned to their charging stations along with their tablets every night.

"Where's home?" she snort-chuckled, pouring a ridiculous amount of maple syrup over everything on her plate.

"You don't have a house? An apartment somewhere?"

"I haven't been in the same city for more than a few weeks at a time over the past six years." She tapped her fork against her lip.

"There hasn't been anywhere to call home?"

"Not a place I'd want to plunk down a boatload of cash for and shell out for security to babysit while I was gone. It's easier to live in hotels. Sometimes we'll rent out a house. You said to me back during training camp 'it's hard to know who actually gives a shit and who just wants your shit.' So the less stuff I have, the less there's to exploit. That's been my life."

The aching loneliness was palpable. The stinging sourness carried through the air.

"I barely have a phone anymore. The one I have, I rarely use. The wrong people always find it and make my life hell. It's easier this way. I have to send a new number to my mom every few months once the last one leaks."

Her shyness last night, like a kid running out to play with new kids, made more sense. Instead of having a great time riding bikes until sundown, she spent most interactions hoping none of them would record her every move and sell it to the highest bidder. She was alone.

"You're cut off from everyone."

She made a face, scrunching up her nose. "Poor little famous rich girl. Most people would punch me in the face for complaining about all I have. All I've done. I've gotten to travel the world, sing in front of stadiums of people, meet celebrities and royalty. It's been a life beyond what I could ever have imagined."

"Does it ever get to you? All the travel? All the pomp?" It wore on me sometimes, but mine was only for half the year, not every week and if I travelled outside of football cities or internationally, I was only the big guy taking up too much space on the sidewalk. Still, the travel, planes, and buses became monotonous after a while. One hotel room looked like the next, and room service food lost its luster within the first season. Lukewarm fries and soggy buns just didn't hold much appeal.

"It does sometimes. But I have a lot of people depending on me. Not just Holden and Emily, but Maddy who went to the mat for me on my first deal. So many artists get screwed when they start out, but she used the Without Grey leverage to get me a contract that's unheard of. Then there are all the backup dancers and singers. The road and audio crews. There are two hundred people involved in every show."

"That's a lot of pressure." Like my season. A whole stadium of people who worked if we made it to the playoffs, and bonuses that went around if we won again.

"It's what I always wanted." The words didn't spell dreamy excitement. They spelled resignation. She shoved a forkful of French toast into her mouth.

"Do you think you'll take a break sometime soon?"

"Will you?" Her words were pointed.

I shook my head. It was the truth. Football would leave me long before I left it. All it would take was one lost season with me on the bench and I'd probably be out. "No. Not showing up at the stadium during the season...I wouldn't know what to do with myself."

"I feel the same way about my music. When I'm scribbling down songs in my notebook or in the studio—when they finally come alive I feel this release, like the story's been told and that piece of me can rest for a little while until another song starts echoing in the back of my mind." She stared off, closing her eyes like just thinking about it transported her to somewhere else.

I was glad it meant so much to her, and that she had the chance to recapture that love of music and share it with the world. I hated the four years I'd stolen that from her.

"When you talk about your music that way, it sounds like it's haunting you."

She turned to me with a quirk of a smile. "Sometimes I feel like it is. The songs used to be easy to ignore. First, writing them down was enough, then getting the melody right and playing them was enough. Now, they want to be heard."

"They picked the right person to bring them to life."

"It's the only life I know now."

"Maybe I'll call in a favor to get front row tickets to watch one of your shows."

She licked her syrup covered lips. "You have a connection."

"I might be able to scrounge up an old phone number."

She laughed. "That phone was retired a long time ago. But I can give you the new one." Darting from the table, she came back with her phone and slid it across the table to me.

Her contacts only had six numbers: her mom, Holden, Emily, Piper, Felicia and Spencer. It was a handful of people for someone millions could identify on sight. And now me. I was one of so few she'd let into her life over the past six years. I held onto the reins of my emotions to keep from overwhelming myself and her.

I added myself and held it out to her.

"I'm on a short list."

She licked a bit of syrup off her thumb.

My gaze zeroed in on her lips wrapped around it. A jolt shot through my gut.

"Comes with the territory. Not many people make it into the inner circle."

"Then I'm glad to have made it into yours."

She tilted her head and ran her fingers over the back of my hand. She traced the lines of my veins from my wrist to my knuckles. "You never left."

I felt like we were both walking on the newly formed ice of whatever this was, slipping and sliding, unsure of what it was and how long it would last.

I tried to lighten the mood, relieved we were in the same boat rowing toward destinations unknown. "I'd say there was a solid four years you'd rather have lit me on fire than have breakfast with me."

Her fingers stilled and she laughed, nodding. "There's certainly been a rough patch or two in the story we've written together over the past decade."

So much lost time to make up for. I wanted to give her whatever she wanted for the day. Anything in my power was hers. I pulled her out of her chair and onto my lap. Wrapping my arms around her, she settled her knees on either side of my hips. "What do you want to do today?"

Her gaze darted to the hallway leading to my bedroom.

"What's something you haven't done in a long time? Something you've always wanted to do?"

"Honestly?"

"Always."

"I want to spend the day with you doing whatever it is you want. Show me your life."

I kissed her on the tip of her nose and held out my hand. "That I can do. Just remember, you asked for this."

Her eyebrows crinkled and she leaned back eyeing me before sliding her hand into mine. "I'm not sure what I just got myself into."

Sweat poured down my face. "This wasn't what I had in mind."

Keyton laughed, whirring away on the rowing machine beside me. "I know, but it helps me start my day off right. Although I normally do it before breakfast."

He'd shown me to his gym after we ate. My protests about not having shoes for exercising had been killed when a man in a hotel uniform showed up at his front door with a pair of sneakers and fluffy socks. A perfect fit. Dammit! My backpedal about doing everything he'd normally do in a day hadn't worked.

Stupid full service hotel, even to people on the residence side. The hotel was split in two, with the residences and the hotel rooms only linked through a doorway in the lobby.

"I thought it might be easier than you going back to your suite where Holden or Emily might find one of the thousand things on your schedule to sidetrack our day." There was a shyness to his words.

It was a sweet shyness that made me want to jump on him. He didn't want me to leave as much as I didn't want to leave. There was no doubt that if I showed up back in the suite, an emergency meeting, conference call, fitting, or something else equally not-as-important-as-this-day issue would arise. It was better to leave my phone off and not turn it on until the clock struck twelve—or six AM, in my case.

"Good idea, but the thirty-seven pieces of bacon may have been a mistake." The workout was on par with what my trainer usually put me through, but then I didn't have a hearty breakfast with syrup chugging through my veins. The salty deliciousness was kicking my ass right now.

His machine beeped in triumphant completion of his workout.

Mine slipped into the cool down. I had to admit, working out with him beat the sessions alone with my trainer or on the treadmill in the wings of the arenas before a show or a hotel gym.

My machine slowed to a crawl reminiscent of stepping off a moving sidewalk in an airport. Relief swept over me. I wanted to flop to the floor and kiss the non-moving ground.

He jumped up onto the treadmill and stepped up behind me, falling into perfect pace. His arms wrapped around me, resting on my hips and anchoring me to his chest. Lips tickled the shell of my ear, nearly knocking my legs out from under me when they turned to jelly. "Now..." The scruff from his morning stubble scraped against the side of my neck.

My breathing intensified like I was back at top speed.

He tapped the STOP button when I wanted to do anything but. "It's time to get cleaned up."

I whirled around and pushed his chest. "You tease."

With a wink, he hopped off the treadmill and held his hand out for me. "Don't pretend you don't like it."

That was beside the point, but I glared, mentally promising retribution later.

Our shower wasn't quick or efficient. It was more languid and thorough. So thorough, I was happy for the heated marble bench inside and even happier for Keyton's attention to detail when it came to soaping me up and down. Three times.

All thoughts of payback from earlier were gone with my fingers streaking across the shower tiles.

I repaid him, of course.

He groaned out my name with one hand braced on the glass and his fingers buried in my hair as he spilled into my mouth.

Toweling each other off was just as much fun as getting clean, but he put a moratorium on any more below-the-belt action until we'd successfully made it out of the apartment. My disappointment was edged out by curiosity at what we'd be doing today. My schedule normally involved being shuttled from place to place with a quick debrief before each call, interview, photoshoot. Today was a day of possibilities and excitement.

With even more deliveries from the hotel shop, I was outfitted for the day.

My disguise included a gray knitted hat, tortoise shell sunglasses big enough to cover half my face, a face-rubbingly smooth gray scarf, soft pink and gray sweater, jeans, and warm and comfy flats. "How do I look?"

He held onto me and stared at me with an emotion simmering beneath the surface.

All the electrifying feelings from the shower paled in comparison to the breath-stealing stare that traveled across time and space to solidify the rightness of this. Of today.

"You look perfect. We have six hours of sunlight and the

city is ours to explore at your leisure." He laced his fingers through mine and we walked out of his apartment.

The door slammed closed behind us and a needle of panic threatened to burst this happy little bubble we were in. It was the first time I'd been out without security or Holden in a long time. What if this all went south and someone recognized me? Drawing a crowd was once a worry I'd had. Would anyone show up to my shows? Now, drawing a crowd could mean danger, not just for me, but for others. Was this a stupid, irresponsible thing to do? Was I putting myself in harm's way? More importantly, was I putting Keyton in harm's way?

In the elevator, a man rushed for the slowly closing doors.

I shrank back against the wall willing myself to be invisible.

Keyton glanced back at me. The muscles in his neck flexed, not straining, but poised—ready.

Dual feelings of comfort and worry warred in my chest at the thought that he'd protect me and that he'd feel the need to.

The older gentleman glanced over with polite smiles for both of us and jabbed his finger into the button facing front with his newspaper in hand.

My heart skipped a few beats. Suddenly, I felt naked until Keyton edged in front of me, his arm brushing against my chest. The broadness of him shielded me.

The elevator stopped at the ground floor.

I held my breath, waiting for an onslaught. Instead, the doors opened to nothing out of the ordinary.

The older man tipped the paper toward us before stepping out. "Have a good day."

A couple people waited outside for their chance to get

in, but no one spared me a second glance. For so long I'd wanted to break out of the invisibility around me, but now the panic of being seen was a lot scarier.

Keyton took my hand and pulled me out of the elevator. "It'll be okay." He kissed me in a reassuring way that didn't sound patronizing or like I was a complete moron for being afraid to go outside. "What do you want to do first?"

"We're supposed to do what you do. If I'm with you, it'll be a good day."

On the other side of the lobby windows, people walked down the sidewalks in their light jackets and coats. Stores were open and people wandered in and out. Food trucks and carts dotted the street.

"And I wanted to do what you want to. Let me."

My gaze narrowed hating his argument. I already felt selfish enough, but I didn't want this to turn into a back and forth out in the open. My trainer would hate it and I'd pay for it with even more time on the treadmill, but why the hell not. "After working out, I feel we deserve a treat. Ice cream."

"At the end of September?"

"You said whatever I wanted."

We stepped out of the building to where the straight streets turned into wind tunnels. "I know a good place."

"It won't be busy, right?" Not wanting today to be ruined was on the top of my list. Needing to call Holden to be extricated from an overwhelming situation wasn't my idea of fun. Plus, the last time there had been an underestimation in a crowd situation outside of an appearance I'd been doing, two teens had ended up almost getting trampled. They'd been fine, but the fear of me or, even worse, someone else being hurt because of me weighed heavily on this day of reckless fun.

A muscle in his jaw twitched. "No, it won't be."

A trill of excitement rushed through me. We were doing this.

I covered our interlaced fingers with my other hand and kept my head down and burrowed into his side. My gaze darted around behind my sunglasses. Even with them on I felt exposed. I couldn't let the panic snatch away today.

He extracted his hand from mine and slid his arm around my shoulder, holding me close.

My nerves calmed, less frayed and more frazzled. The grip on his sweater under his jacket was less of a clutch and more of a hold by the time we got to the nearly deserted ice cream shop.

The ice cream shop was small, almost food-truck-sized with two ordering windows. The second was closed with an arrow pointing to the other with a metal screen over it that the ice cream store worker slid open. It was a quiet location near a park, probably a prime spot during the warmer months, but now there weren't many visitors.

There were three metal picnic tables off the sidewalk in front of the walk-up window. Two people sat at one, finishing up their treats.

Against my side, Keyton's chest rumbled.

Jerking back, I looked up at him.

He and the ice cream worker looked at me expectantly. "Sorry, what did you say?"

"What kind of ice cream are you getting?"

I licked my lips. "Coffee."

His hand settled against the small of my back. "That's it. Coffee ice cream in a cup. No cone?"

Stalling, I tried not to be mesmerized by how good he looked in his black wool coat. It wasn't the scratchy kind, but the smooth, buttery kind you wanted to rub against like a cat—or maybe that was just me. "What are you getting?"

"Today calls for a sundae." He leaned against the metal shelf in front of the window, bending to speak to the woman on the other side of the opening. He glanced back at me. "I'll take the Cookie Chaos with chocolate jimmies."

My face must've shown I had no idea what the hell he was talking about.

He laughed. "They get a little testy around here if you call them sprinkles."

"Right, jimmies." It felt surreal being here with him. Just going out to get ice cream like we did this every day.

He'd led the way with an easy air. I didn't know whether he always wore it, or he was putting it on for me. Either way, it helped a little.

"Are you sticking with a scoop of coffee ice cream in a cup or do you want to change your order?" He leaned in. His warm breath skated along my skin sending a shudder down my spine as I breathed him in. "Their hot fudge looks good."

Staring at him, it took a wide smile and gentle tap on my hand to remember why we were there in the first place.

"Coffee ice cream..." He started, his lips quirking.

"Right, sorry." I leaned back from the window, looking up at the menu above. "I'll take the two-scoop hot fudge sundae in a waffle bowl with coffee ice cream, peanuts, Reese's cups, and rainbow jimmies." Seeing his eyes filled with amusement and encouragement, some of my nervousness thawed. "And whipped cream and a cherry."

The woman in the pink Berries and Cream t-shirt over the long sleeved shirt nodded and closed the window before getting to work assembling our sugar bombs in a cup.

I couldn't have been more excited, my mouth already watering.

"Can I have a taste?" He took my hands in his.

Staring into his eyes full of playfulness and barely

contained desire, I wanted to start the day all over to redo the hours already gone. The afternoon had approached too fast and all I kept thinking about was how short it all felt.

"Only if I can have some of yours."

He brushed his thumb across my cheek. "Of course."

Stepping out of the way, we let another group of people in to place their orders.

There were no suspicious glances or extra attention focused on us. People shot a few quick looks at Keyton, but no one approached us.

It was the first time I'd felt normal in a long time, and it was refreshing and scary at the same time. A chance to be me with someone who had known me before my first name became internationally recognizable.

This was the kind of day we could have if I were an accountant by day and songwriter by night. Maybe I'd be playing in local coffee shops, or, better yet, hanging out in a studio way past a responsible adult's bedtime, tweaking a music track until it hummed with an artistic electricity.

"Do you think we can actually pull this off today?"

"Of course we can. If we can't, I'll handle it and get you back to my place. We can order in and watch TV." He said it as though he'd have no problems plowing through throngs of people like opposing players to get me to safety.

And I believed him.

More of my nervousness slid away with the certainty of his words. "That doesn't sound terrible."

"Only if our day out doesn't work. What else do you want to do?"

"It's probably not somewhere you want to go."

"I'll follow you anywhere." A ring of conviction radiated from his words, like a power chord on an amp cranked all the way up. It didn't feel like he only meant today.

Instead of latching onto his words and giving them more meaning than he'd intended, I opened my mouth.

The window slid open and two cups with a mountain of sugary sweet goodness slid toward us. "One Cookie Chaos and one coffee hot fudge sundae."

We walked over to the empty tables. The chilly metal seat numbed my butt in five seconds flat, but I dug into the ice cream, letting the hot fudge and peanut combo warm my insides while my outsides froze.

From across the table, his legs settled on the outside of mine, giving me extra heat.

"Do you know how long it's been since I've been anywhere on my own with someone who didn't work for me?"

"You don't have any friends to hang out with?"

"Not ones I don't pay." I laughed and jammed my plastic spoon into my hot fudge, gathering up even more peanuts. "Piper comes to my shows whenever I pass through Seattle. She, Felicia and I did a girls' trip to Fiji after I finished the tour with Without Grey a few years ago. Piper's married now."

Keyton let out a low whistle. "Wow, already?"

"Already. I was at the wedding. She wanted me to be in the bridal party, but I knew it would be a clusterfuck. No one wants paparazzi pictures of their big day showing up on gossip websites. But I gave her a kick-ass bachelorette party." A twinge nudged at my ribs that I'd be missing Piper's birthday. The scheduling gods had been against me there, but they took away and also gave back, making today possible. I pushed aside the thoughts of the spillover effect it would have on the rest of my schedule.

He scooped up a heap of his cookies and cream ice

cream with one of the Oreos and even more hot fudge, holding it out for me.

I hadn't even had to ask.

Why did this make him ten times sexier? Any sexier and he might spontaneously combust—or maybe that was me.

I took the bite he offered, wrapping my lips around the spoon.

His grip on the spoon tightened. Legs under the table squeezed mine tight together, sending a tingling pulse to my core.

Was it hotter out here all the sudden?

He dragged the spoon from between my lips in a way that sent the tingling into sizzling mode.

We were still in public.

I broke my gaze away from his and focused on my ice cream. Decadent. Divine. Delicious. A lot like him.

"She has two kids now. A four-year-old girl and a three-year-old little boy." I bit into a chunk of peanut butter cup. "They're adorable. Hilarious too. I'm her son's godmother."

"That's great you're still close."

If he meant not seeing her for over a year and missing out on her birthday party, then yes, we were close. I'd figure something out, lock down a date and ask her if we could have a day together and try not to feel I was barging into her life asking her to rearrange things for me. Maybe I could set some dates for after the tour. Another girls' trip. Yes! Proactive with lots of forewarning to make sure I wasn't pulling last-minute availability requests.

"How often do you get to see Felicia? I saw her name in your phone. She seemed nice."

My head shot up. "How'd you kno—"

He caught my eye with a knowing look.

A nip of guilt hit my heart.

"Oh. I forgot." Of course. She'd been the one to deliver the letter. And the one who had sent me the guitar after he'd given it to her.

"She finished her PhD. So did her husband. They're teaching in New Orleans. They came to one of my shows last year, but we didn't get to see each other for more than a few minutes after—I had to do a meet and greet and they had to get home to their kids."

"What about other friends?" He peered over at me.

I shrugged. What other response was there? "Spencer. You remember him. We'll see him later tonight. That's about it. After college, all the people I knew went in different directions, and I've been on the road nearly 1500 days out of the last 2000. Most people who did keep up with me only did it for things. Tickets to a show. A video message to impress their girlfriend. Stuff like that." It sucked that 99% of the messages Holden and Emily fielded for me were asking for things. It used to bother me more, but I'd adjusted to always waiting for the ask.

"Every day I'm writing songs. Tweaking them. Figuring out what makes them tick. When I'm not on tour, I'm in the studio recording a new album or doing the promo work to keep the machine going. There's not much time to make new friends when you barely know what city you're in. It's also hard to be real friends with someone when it feels like everyone has an angle." I swallowed the bitterness with a heaping spoonful of hot fudge and rainbow sprinkles.

"Do you love it?" He held the spoon in front of his lips like the question had just occurred to him.

No one had ever asked me that way before. Usually it was in a way that confirmed their ideas about how much I loved it, never a genuine question.

"The music?" I smiled, thinking of the first twenty

shows. "The first time I stood up on stage and held out my mic to have the crowd sing without me...I teared up. I remembered thinking of what it would be like for people to know my words. I've seen people with them tattooed on their body. That blows me away. It's still insane to me how a wave or a signed piece of paper can make someone's day. Lucky doesn't even begin to describe how all this has been for me." How would our life had been if I'd stayed? The question always rang in the back of my head and tugged at my heart.

"But there's no off-season for you, huh?" He ate another spoonful of ice cream and I offered him a perfectly proportioned one of mine. Dropping his hands, he let me feed it to him.

"Not at all. But you know about that." I nudged his arm. "I've seen you in a few cologne ad campaigns."

He groaned and slapped his hand over his face. "Those weren't in my head?"

"Whether they were or not, you looked damn good."

I offered him another spoonful of my ice cream. Somehow, him eating it backfired on me, and my body was no longer numb. We needed to go before I climbed over this picnic table and tackled him to the ground.

A few heads turned in our direction and I tugged my hat down lower, avoiding eye contact. Going out with a guy as tall as Keyton wasn't exactly the best way to blend in, but for some reason walking with him, I wasn't hit with the panic I was hit with even when venturing outside with security. Normally, there was always that first heart-stopping moment when the door to the car or building opened.

I felt safe with him, the kind of comfort bred over years of mundane moments strung together to create a mesh of protection that couldn't be faked or forged overnight.

"Where to next, milady?" He held out his arm.

"It's going to sound really stupid."

"Nothing could. Trust me. You tell me where and we're going."

I peered over at him wondering just how crazy he'd think I was. Taking a deep breath, I slipped my arm through his. "Just remember. You asked for this."

20

KEYTON

The football-field-sized giant box of blue and yellow wouldn't have been my first idea of where to take Bay for her day off.

But here we were at Ikea, wandering through the bedroom section, picking out furniture for an imaginary two-bedroom apartment, and she looked like I'd taken her on a shopping spree through Tiffany's. Her happiness spilled over, making it hard for me to stop grinning like a maniac.

"What do you think of the Bingsta chair?" She tapped the tiny pencil against her bottom lip. "Does it scream bedroom comfort?"

Her gaze swung to mine, looking for my actual opinion.

Stifling my grin, I nodded. "The perfect addition to any room."

"How about that one?" She pointed to the other set-up in the mini apartment, complete with a bathroom with large writing on the toilet stating this wasn't to be used as an actual bathroom. How many mishaps had it taken for them to put that sign up?

I sat in the chair with a higher back than most and kicked my feet up.

Bay sat on the edge of the Malm bed with a paper tape measure around her neck, tapping her golf pencil against the order card.

For a second, I could believe this was what we were really doing, finally moving in together after graduating college. Merging our lives and our things together and picking out some we'd both like.

She looked to me expectantly.

I came back to where we really were and what we were really doing. Playing pretend. A pretend I'd dreamed about on the nights Bay floated into my dreams even after I'd vowed I'd moved on.

"The chair feels great."

"Nice." Her eyes twinkled and her smile was megawatt-bright as she made a note on the card with the name and quantity.

"What about the bed?" She lay back on it. Her sunglasses rested on top of her head.

The first few steps inside the store, she'd been hesitant, holding onto me like she was afraid she'd be swept away at any second.

After we'd made it through the living room section, she'd popped her glasses on top of her head after I'd suggested she was drawing more attention to herself by keeping them on.

With them off, no one paid us any attention. They were all focusing on how the hell to pronounce the names of everything from the ottomans to the dishtowels.

I lay beside her, both of us with our feet still on the ground, a reminder of how inappropriate it would be to touch her the way I wanted to. "The bed feels fine, but I think we should do something about the ceiling. This will be a bitch to heat in winter."

She rolled her head to the side laughing. "That's what the cardboard from all these boxes is for."

"A woman with a plan. Where to next?" I'd buy the whole damn store for her, if that was what she wanted.

Sitting up, she rubbed her hands together. "Kitchens. Who doesn't love a good farmhouse sink?"

She took off in that direction, no longer keeping to my side. The change in her attitude between when we'd left my apartment to now was a complete one-eighty. At first she had been like a frightened puppy, and now she was bounding around like a poodle hopped up on Red Bull.

Walking backward, she beckoned me toward the grey-cabineted kitchen with glass doors with white dishes inside.

"This one looks like yours."

"No, it doesn't."

"The cabinets aren't the same color, but your kitchen is definitely this neat. Perfectly arranged."

"They're not perfectly arranged." *Were they?*

"I checked them for dust to make sure you'd actually used them before."

"I keep my kitchen neat. What's wrong with that?" Using one plate and one cup most days helped with the organization. Plus, I liked to keep the cabinets stocked, so I could see if I was running low on anything.

"It's just nothing like the messy dumps I remember from college. So many of the apartments were an absolute mess."

"That's the thing about getting older. Once it's your own stuff, you want to take care of it. I'm sure you're the same..."

And it hit me why we were here. Not only to run around and play for a bit, but she'd never done this before. No apartment. No house. No finding a place to live after college with a slapped-together mishmash of furniture, dishes and everything else from college and the first couple adult paychecks.

Even I'd had a taste of it. The first half of the season, I'd been on the practice team salary. It wasn't peanuts, but it wasn't pro football player money. Even rooming with Knox, I hadn't wanted to freeload, and he'd wanted to save up his money.

After my lucky charm status had been cemented and the bank account commas had multiplied, I'd saved every penny I didn't have to spend. Banking on money based on my touchdown mojo would've been stupid, so Knox and I had stayed roommates until I was traded the following year.

Anyone who'd visited our place was more likely to think we were two guys fresh out of college, not professional athletes. What would Bay have thought if I'd let her up the day she rang the intercom so long it had shorted out the circuits? I'd never know.

But she hadn't had any of those rites of passage. As proud of her as I was, I hated how her life had made it almost impossible to do the things most people did after college. Not that my journey had been normal, but I'd never been afraid to leave my apartment because of worries about what fans would do to me.

We wandered through the lit-arrow walkways, talking out where items would fit in our imaginary apartment, Bay jotting down even more notes.

She scooted ahead after grabbing a cart and adding more items.

I stopped to check out a shelf, checking the price and memorizing it for her. But it came in three different colors. I hated not knowing her tastes now, not knowing her well enough to pick it out without checking in.

Her hat-covered head was a few too many people away to call out her name. It would definitely be a day-ruiner to call out her name and watch the heads turn.

I wracked my brain before the answer smashed straight into me. "TNG!"

She stopped, jolting so hard her cart slammed into a metal crate filled with stuffed animals, sending a metal-on-metal crash through the space.

A couple people looked at me before moving along. Shit, not as inconspicuous as I'd hoped. I offered an apologetic smile and looked past them.

Bay's head lifted in slow motion with wide, disbelieving eyes.

Shit. That was probably not the best way to get her attention.

She rushed toward me with the cart and her head down.

"Sorry." I grimaced. "I was trying to get your attention. Short of calling your name it was all I had."

Her fingers tapped along the top of the plastic shopping cart handle, but she didn't look up. "Do you know how long it's been since someone called me that?"

Shit, definitely the wrong choice. Had I just ruined our day of fun? "I'm going to go with not long enough."

She peered up at me with an indiscernible look in her eyes. "Not since Greenwood."

"Sorry, I could've run ahead and caught you and brought you back. But there was a shelf here I thought you'd like." Which sounded completely stupid right now. Why did I *have* to know her thoughts on a particular piece of furniture for an imaginary apartment?

"I was thinking the navy." I tried to keep the cringe out of my voice.

She glanced from me to the shelf and her lips twitched

with a smile. "Turns out you already know my style." Her fingers brushed against mine. "And I don't mind the name when you say it. It's a nice reminder."

Who'd want a reminder of that? I'd given her the name in front of the entire school, and it stuck with her for three years. Hell, I didn't like my name from Greenwood. I still flinched if anyone called me Dare. "Of how much of an asshole I was back in high school."

She pulled on the front of my shirt, bringing me closer until our lips brushed. "No, of simpler times." Adding the shelf name and number to her list, we set off again.

Finally hitting the major prize of the whole trip, I took two trays and we lined up for our Swedish meatball jackpot.

"Can one person eat that many meatballs at one time?" She pointed her fork at my plate filled with mashed potatoes, gravy and an ungodly pile of meatballs.

"I'm not sure, but I sure as hell want to try."

"You're going to make yourself sick." She sliced a meatball in half, swirling it in gravy alongside some broccoli. Her small hum of satisfaction with her food tapped into a primal need I'd never felt before.

"Was it everything you hoped it would be and more?"

Her gaze scanned the cafeteria-style restaurant with folded plastic chairs for easy cleaning, tables all a little off balance, rocking whenever you rested your arm on them, and textured plastic cups filled with slightly flat soda. She stared into my eyes, reaching across the table to cover my hand and squeezing it. "It was even better, because I got to come with you."

The meatballs lodged in my throat and my heart soared like a ten-yard field goal punt flying through the sky.

With one look at her, I believed that coming to Ikea was a magical experience for her only made better because I'd been there. "If this is how you feel about Ikea, I can't wait to take you to a Target."

Soda spurted from her mouth and she covered it laughing. "If you take me to a Target, I might just have to marry you." She wiped up the mess on the table and shoved the dirty napkins under her plate on the tray.

I trapped the words I wanted to say: 'let's do it.' It had taken almost a year for Alice and me to agree to move in together, and another six months before I'd felt it was appropriate to start thinking about rings.

Knowing Bay wouldn't be in my bed tomorrow felt wrong, the kind of wrong I'd pretended hadn't been there and that I'd been able to cover since the last time I'd fallen asleep with her in my arms.

We had today. What happened tomorrow was still for us to figure out.

After sliding our trays into the food cemetery, a couple more heads turned in our direction. My hackles rose.

The place had gotten progressively more crowded. Her nervousness had faded, but the glances were getting closer together. With so many people around, autograph and selfie hunters could overwhelm us quickly. I'd told her I'd keep her safe and I intended to keep my promise. I'd sent a message to Gwen while Bay stopped off at the bathroom.

When she returned, I slipped her hat out of her pocket and tugged it down onto her head, over her eyes.

She grinned and shoved it up.

I slid her sunglasses on.

I didn't want her day spoiled by being recognized. I also didn't want to find out how the heart-racing, cornered feelings would rear their heads when Bay was involved.

We needed to leave now.

More people gathered closer to the doors. I'd told her I'd

keep her safe today. My muscles tightened as the cell phones were whipped out.

Taking her hand, I guided her out through the automatic doors. A car idled outside the entrance. "Where to next?"

21

KEYTON

After heading back to my apartment to recover from the Swedish meatball sedation, we'd stopped in the games room in the building. I beat her at pool and she kicked my ass at air hockey. Far too quickly, it was time to go to our only scheduled event for the day.

We sat in a studio wildly different than any I'd been in with her before. The room wasn't cramped. It wasn't dank. The equipment, furniture, even the walls didn't feel like they'd been in the same place for sixty years.

Everything was clean and sleek. Shiny and pristine. A curved desk was covered in electronics and computers.

Our ergonomic rolling chairs were soft. There wasn't a single crack in the plastic or leather.

Holden had dropped by before disappearing again. Bay fiddled with the electronics on the computer monitors. Huge speakers sat on top of the soundboard and I had no doubt they could blow out my ear drums if they were cranked all the way up.

None of it made sense to me, but she tested them out on

a short melody she'd sung when we first arrived. Her voice in a stadium filled with thousands or even on a stage in front of a crowd of hundreds didn't compare to her singing for me. Just the two of us, effortless notes with a sweet and smooth cadence. It brought me back to those days laying on her bed back in Greenwood or our time together in LA.

The desire to have more of this time hit me like a craving. I needed more hours in a day.

"And if I slide this up—" She touched the board, and her voice came out like Alvin and the Chipmunks on speed.

"Is this the sound you're going for on your new album?"

She laughed. "Fans would definitely be shocked."

The door to our left opened. In the doorway, a male silhouette froze, unsure.

"Spencer!" Bay threw her arms around the neck of the guy she'd run off with within seconds of seeing me back in California, and who had stolen my seat during my dinner with her before rushing away.

The bristling jealousy wanted to break free. It wanted to rage and roar at him to get his damn hands off her. But I pulled those feelings apart.

Bay and I had spent the whole day together. We'd talked, laughed, kissed, and had mind-blowing sex on multiple surfaces in my apartment. It had been a jam-packed day. Not once had she felt like she wanted to be anywhere else. He wasn't a threat.

I dismantled the warships cruising through my chest and took a deep breath.

"You remember Keyton from the summer after graduation." She walked him over to me. He had light brown hair, longish on top and short on the sides. He wasn't scrawny, but not bulky like most of the guys I hung out with. He fit the rocker musician profile, complete with a defined jaw and cheek bones flirting with the edge of feminine. He probably cleaned up with the ladies after his shows.

Sticking out my hand, I relaxed my muscles to make sure I didn't power-trip power-grip his hand. Slipping into destroy mode would put a damper on the great day we'd had. He was Bay's friend, and those were in short supply.

His eyes widened and he pumped my hand twice before letting go. "Yeah, I remember. The football player." He looked between us. "I didn't know you two still kept in touch."

Bay didn't clarify and neither did I. Part of me wanted to crow there was a lot he didn't know about her life, but for all I knew, he knew a hell of a lot more than me.

Stepping back and giving them their space, I sat on the couch along the back wall.

"How's it been on the road?" Bay sat on the couch right beside me, our legs pressed against one another.

Another win added to the keeping calm column.

Spencer flopped into one of the rolling chairs, digging his heels in to drag it closer. "Exhausting. Absolute chaos. A grind beyond all grinds." His face split into a huge grin. "It's been the best time of my life. A hell of a lot better than working at the twenty-four hour gym I was at during the two years I cut my demo."

"And now you're ready to do the whole album?" She glowed, pitched all the way forward with her hands trapped between her legs like she couldn't trust them if she didn't keep them contained. It was the excitement she'd talked about over ice cream. Not nervous or worried, but excited to talk shop with a friend.

"Trying to. I was shocked as hell when you offered to have me come down here." He stared at her like he still wasn't sure what he was doing here.

"After I watched the cover I mentioned to you, I watched a few more, and you sang one you want to put on your next album." She sounded impressed.

"Been checking up on me?" He teased.

I kept repeating in my head that their easy banter and joking wasn't a threat. Because it wasn't. Also, what was there to threaten? Bay and I had spent a total of twenty-four hours together in the past six years. I couldn't exactly grab a flag and plant it in her vagina, claiming it for me.

"It's what friends do, right?" She leaned against me and dropped her hand to my leg, reassuring without even realizing what she was doing. After the ease and happiness of our day, it didn't feel like we'd seen each other for less than forty-eight hours since our lives had collided once again. Being with her made it feel like the six years apart had only been a few hours, like I'd woken that morning in her apartment, kissed her, and gone off to meet my fate and held her tight after getting the news of my career derailment.

It was scary how real that version of my life felt in only a matter of hours with her.

Spencer's head dropped. "I'm glad you still think of me that way."

She scooted forward. "Of course, I do."

"Bay..." Spencer's mouth opened and closed. "I know I was shitty toward the end." He brushed his hands down over his jeans.

My protective instincts threatened to break through the calm I'd thought I'd created here. What the hell did he do that was so shitty?

"And asking you to give my demo to Walter was out of line, especially when you hadn't even signed the deal yet. I shouldn't have put you in that position."

Was that what they'd been talking about when I interrupted the conversation when we'd had dinner? His need to apologize felt laughable in light of me sitting beside Bay, of all we'd done to each other.

"How many times do I have to say it's okay? Look where you are now." Pride oozed from every word, like a sister watching her brother cross over into the end zone.

Would she watch me on the field? Scream in the stands and cheer me on, unable to look away? Would I ever get to play for her?

"Look where you are." He looked over his shoulder. "I can't believe they even let me in here. I'm expecting to be tackled by a security guard in the next thirty seconds."

"Ha ha. Very funny."

"So what exactly *am* I doing here? When I got the invite, I didn't think we'd be meeting at the studio. Are you recording? I'd love to sit in."

Bay hadn't explained it fully to me either, not that I'd needed much of an explanation for anything she wanted to do. Being together had been my top priority. I'd have been up for anything short of bungee jumping or a helicopter ride over the city.

Holden walked back into the studio.

Bay's head whipped around in his direction. "Great, you're here."

"Did you tell him already?" Holden waved his glowing tablet in Spencer's direction. "I needed to be here to block the door to get him to sign an NDA, if he's good with it."

My arm snaked around her back, fingers touching her hip. I hated how much Holden ran her life. At times it felt like she didn't have control over anything that happened to her. He was supposed to be looking out for her, but the irritation grated that she was always running ragged, never having time for herself, and could barely remember which city she was in. She should have a home, a place to escape the madness of the world she'd been plunged into.

Spencer's eyes bounced between the three of us. "Good with what?"

Bay leaned forward and plucked the notebook out of her bag. It wasn't the same one she'd written her songs about me in, but it was well worn. Broken in. "I have some songs I'd like to share with you. After watching your performances they came to me and I wanted to see if you liked them."

He fell straight out of the chair. It jammed into the wall-length mixing board behind him and his ass hit the floor. "Are you fucking kidding me?" Shooting up, his eyes looked a quarter of an inch from falling out. This was his shot, like a first-round draft pick after being a college walk-on.

A gift. She was giving him a gift, the kind a musician like her didn't need to give to anyone. Her words. Her songs. Her voice.

She and Spencer spent the next few hours working on music. I threw in my thoughts when asked, but for the most part I was happy to sit back and watch her work, see her immerse herself into the music, offering her tweaks through the mic to Spencer in the booth.

I hadn't seen her on this side of the glass directing someone else. A confidence stole over her unlike the kind she had up on stage. This wasn't for show.

Spencer found his groove after nerves seemed like they'd gotten the best of him. He shook it off and dug into the song Bay had written for him. It sounded good—better than good, perfectly matched to his voice even though they were her words.

She grabbed a guitar and they played the melody and rhythm of the song before she worked her magic to mix it all together with the vocals. They wrapped up the recording on one song and she told Spencer to come listen.

I was their sounding board. They both looked to me like I could provide more than a novice's thoughts.

Spencer crossed his arms over his chest, staring intently. "Would you crank this up in the car and sing along to it?"

I looked to Bay. "The chorus is an earworm I'll probably be singing for the rest of the week."

They exchanged looks and high fived with a "Yes!"

After they'd finished recording the three songs, Spencer was spirited away by Holden to rooms unknown, probably to sign away his first born for a chance to release these songs.

Bay sat on my lap while the replays spilled out of the speakers.

Being this close to her would never get old, but the night was stretching on, which meant our time would be coming to an end. I couldn't go another six years before holding her in my arms again.

"These songs are amazing."

Her arms looped around my shoulders. "Do you think so? I hope Spencer likes them."

"If he doesn't, he's an idiot." I nuzzled the side of her face.

She was comfortable on this side of the glass. The edge of anxiety that lurked under the surface whenever she went out, or even before a performance, evaporated. Instead, in the studio with Spencer, her excitement for making music was contagious.

I'd wondered if her love of music had died in her rise to stardom, but it hadn't. I could see it. I could feel it with every look and nod. The determined expression when she asked him to sing a line again or incorporated a tweak they'd come up with together.

She did love it. Which meant she'd never walk away from this life. And she shouldn't—it was where she came alive. But I had no idea what it meant for whatever came next for us.

Her fingers toyed with the buttons of my shirt. "Thanks for coming. I'm sure this wasn't what you had in mind when I said we could spend the day together."

I kissed her—not the way I wanted, but the only kind I could give her without dropping her onto the couch and giving her a tease of what would happen when we made it back to my place. "Today's about you having fun. I'm good with whatever that looks like."

"Should we go rescue Spencer?" She nibbled on her bottom lip. "I feel like Holden's holding him hostage at this point."

"Give them a few more minutes."

She rested her head against my shoulder and I trailed my hand down her back. If the world ended in this moment, I would be content.

But it didn't. Holden and Spencer returned before their minutes were up. Spencer looking like he'd seen a ghost waving winning lottery ticket numbers at him.

Bay got up and cued up the music before coming back to me, as happy to hear it as she'd been to play her own songs for me before Spencer arrived.

Spencer stood by the board with his eyes closed until the last note ended. When they opened, he stared at her like she was a miracle worker. "I'm still afraid I'm dreaming. These are next level. My voice doesn't do them justice."

"I wrote them for your voice." She tapped on my arms and I released them from around her waist. Shooting up, her hands shook Spencer's shoulders. "Are you not hearing what I'm hearing? Holden, back me up."

Holden looked up from his tablet, swinging around in the chair. "They're killer. Your singing and playing, Bay's production and lyrics. That's a top 100 hit right there."

Spencer turned to her, skepticism etched deep in his face. "And you want me to have this?"

"If you want it." She stepped back.

I brushed my fingers along the back of her leg like I had the first time she played in public back during training camp, lending her my strength and confidence that she'd kick ass in whatever she did.

"Are you fucking kidding me?" He shouted so loudly that someone outside must have heard, even with the soundproof walls. "Of course."

He flung himself at her, nearly knocking her over.

They both laughed, their bond solidified through the music.

I took in a deep breath and watched her with another guy squeezing her tight, poking around for the jealousy or insecurity to explain the way my heart raced.

But it wasn't there. It was happiness at how she'd been able to share her lyrics and create a song others would hear even if it wasn't her singing it. The feelings were unexpected. With Alice I'd thought I was over all those old, destructive behaviors. Now I knew it was because I hadn't felt for her like I did for Bay. There hadn't been an undeniable draw that made it hard to not think about her, not dream about her. This had been the true test. Maybe I could handle this. Maybe I could handle us.

We wrapped things up at the studio. Bay beamed while they went over the smaller details. Spencer could open for her in a few shows in the last leg of the tour in Europe. The contracts were crossed and dotted for Bay as the songwriter on the new lead track for his album. He'd finalize the songs when she was back in Philly next.

The trip to my apartment was uneventful. So much of today had been spent guarding against the other shoe dropping, against a worst case scenario where things all went wrong.

But now we were in my living room, sitting on a bunch of pillows on the floor with a bowl of Goobers and popcorn beside us. The TV was off, but we didn't need anything to keep us occupied other than each other.

She leaned against my chest. Her hair brushed against my cheek.

I stared into the fire crackling in the fireplace I hadn't ever used before. After a few failed attempts, I'd figured out how to turn it on.

After the few hours in the studio, the sun had long since set. Our day was winding down, almost over. The ticking closer to five AM, when she'd be leaving, was marked by each heartbeat.

The silence of my apartment felt like a comfort now, but it also meant there was nothing to drown out my thoughts. What had once been a jumble of so many emotions all wrapped up in Bay now had a singular focus.

The question had been replaying in my head all day. It had started as a whisper, but now it grew louder until it was a roar in my ears. "What happens now?"

My arms wrapped tighter around her waist.

She stared straight ahead into the fire. "I don't know." She nuzzled her head against the stubble on my chin.

Neither did I, but I knew this couldn't be the only night we spent wrapped up in each other.

A selfish sliver of my soul wanted her to lock the door

and tell me she wasn't leaving, that she'd made her decision and it was me, but that was a greedy dream that washed me with shame.

"The season ends in January. February, if my streak holds."

Shifting, she peered over her shoulder, sadness clouding her gaze. "I leave for London the first week of November. The tour goes until the end of July."

"Just in time for training camp."

She slumped back against my chest and wrapped her hands around mine with her head tucked against my shoulder like she was afraid at any moment someone would burst into the room and tear us apart. "And I'll be finishing up the next album."

"I can come hang out with you after the season's over. Join your roadie crew." I settled my legs over her outstretched ones, trying to envelop her. The season was 17 weeks, half a year including training camp and playoffs. I'd buy a jet if I needed it to see her whenever she had a break, however short it might be.

"The two of us bouncing around from hotel to tour bus to hotel for a few months before you leave for another season." She sounded far away, like we were already slipping away from each other.

A squeeze tightened around my heart like a fist constricting the blood flow.

"And you'd be happy with that? What kind of relationship would it be?"

I held on more fiercely. "Ours. Who says there are rules? It might not be perfect. But it would be ours."

"A few days ago, you were ready to say goodbye to me and never look back."

The mental ass-kicking for how I'd handled things

intensified. My fear over what being close to her again might drive me to might now stop anything new between us before it began. I wouldn't be satisfied with shared ice cream sundaes and a trip to IKEA. Desperation mounted to see her again.

"I was wrong. I should've handled it better."

"After how I left things, I don't blame you. How do you know I won't screw this up again? Do I even know how to be in a relationship? You were with Alice. You were engaged." She seemed to be talking more to herself than me, talking herself out of what we could have together.

"And I knew it wasn't right. For either of us."

She craned her neck and looked into my eyes. "And this feels right to you? My life isn't my own. Hundreds of people depend on me." Turning in my arms, she sat on my leg. "I've seen this play out with so many other people."

"We're not—

"Scheduling in a couple relationship days every month. Every dinner being interrupted. Every day another tabloid story or more paparazzi hunting you down. Schedules clash until seeing each other once a week turns to once a month, and then to once every few months." She traced her fingers over my knuckles. "Until things fall apart."

An urgency for her not to write us off gripped my heart. We wouldn't fall into their traps. After a decade of mistakes, we could finally get this right.

"We're not other people." I licked my dead-of-winter-dry lips. "I'm not saying we do anything crazy. We don't even have to put a name on this. But I want to see you." I lifted her chin with my finger. "I can't not see you."

A flicker of pain flashed behind her eyes. Pain and longing—the same two feelings clawing their way through my chest right now.

"When can we see each other next?" She wrapped her arms around my neck and inhaled deeply, like she was trying to imprint my scent. "I need to check my phone. Holden uploads my calendar there."

Hopping up, she went to retrieve her phone. The loss of her weight of her resting against me, the gentle curves of her body that fit to mine perfectly, her warmth overheating my body was sharp, and drove home how much I craved her near me.

I grabbed my phone out of my back pocket.

We reconvened. Bay sat on her knees between my legs.

She tapped away on her phone with her eyebrows furrowed. "I fly to LA tomorrow."

I ran my hands over her thigh. Looking down at my phone, my muscles stiffened. "When are you back?" Meetings, practices, travel for games and the games themselves had all been uploaded into my calendar by Gwen.

"In a week. Next Saturday." Her lips brushed against my skin. Soft and sweet.

I huffed. A half-hearted, humorless laugh.

She hadn't been wrong about the difficulty of seeing each other.

"What?" She tilted her head and stared at me.

"That's the day after I leave for LA."

Her fingers brushing against the base of my neck stilled. "When are you back?"

"Tuesday afternoon. What are you doing then?"

"I've got a recording session in the morning. Maybe we could have a late lunch? Or dinner?" The thought of spending two weeks without each other turned the needle of panic into a full cleaver to my heart. We'd just found our way back to each other. We'd both grown up so much, and now the things we'd always loved and dreamed about were keeping us apart.

"You'll probably be tired, but we can try." I brushed my lips against her forehead. "When do you leave for London?"

"November 3rd. It's a Tuesday. Are you here the weekend before?" Her hope lit eyes stared into mine.

"I have an away game in Georgia." I dropped my head back, cursing under my breath.

She perked up. "I could fly to Georgia."

I brushed my fingers down her arm. "No significant others are allowed in the game hotel before we play."

Her body sagged. "We're going to see each other for all of five days in the next six weeks, aren't we?"

"However long we get to see each other, I'll take it. You've got a life and a career. So do I. There's nothing we can do about it."

Isn't there? As quickly as the words shoved into my head, I pushed them away. I wasn't going to be the guy she'd left behind in LA who was willing to throw it all away to follow her around because I couldn't be without her. There was texting, phone calls, video chats, chartered flights if need be. We both had all of that at our disposal.

"We don't even know what this is."

"It's us getting to know each other again. Figuring out if we even like each other."

"At least part of you likes me a lot." She laughed, releasing some of the pressure tightening the valve on what would come after she left my apartment in the morning.

"We're both on the same page, but the jury might still be out on your end."

She turned in the circle of my arms and straddled my lap. "Oh trust me. Every part of me is in full agreement." Grinding against me, she smiled.

A hiss fell from my lips.

"Music to my ears."

I sat up and held the back of her neck. My erection, no longer accepting being ignored, pressed against the rough denim and zipper combo, which did nothing to stifle the blood rushing to my dick.

I kissed her, putting everything into it. I wanted her to remember it as a searing, crazy-about-you, can't-get-enough-of-you kind of kiss. The kind to spoil her for all other lips. All other men. All other love.

Our lives felt destined to intersect. Our timing had never been right. Our futures were speeding ahead in separate directions.

My heart was splintered when it came to her, but maybe a little heat and time could fill in those cracks, molding it into a new creation. Or the splinters would weaken and shatter, leaving me all alone once again.

22

BAY

We'd spent one full night together since SeptemberWeen. There had been a couple meet-ups in my hotel or his that made it feel like we were having an affair, rushing together, ripping off our clothes, and riding out a sweaty, can't-catch-my-breath orgasm before someone banged on the door and we had to part.

But on Tuesday I'd get to see him again when his flight touched down. Monday's schedule was light: only demo sessions, the fittings, test hair and makeup for the award shows in December, finishing the production on the songs I'd promised Spencer, and a photoshoot for my new album stood in the way to free up more hours to spend with him.

It turned out the timing for his trip had never been more perfect. Being in the same city and not seeing each other would've made it even harder to concentrate.

I'd watched his game over the weekend, which Philly had won, in between conference calls. If anyone had questions as to why all the TVs in the vicinity were tuned to the game, no one brought it up.

We'd had a few conference calls and interviews in the morning. Now, I was in the middle of my day of abdominal destruction, which meant I got a comfy robe, comfier socks, and all the candy I could stuff into my mouth to rest up for the brutal day Monday. That and a reenactment of The Shining in my super-sensible underwear.

Over the years, the week of my period had narrowed down to a few days, and then a couple of Armageddon-level ones, which sucked. Super sucked. But it gave me a consistent schedule of thirty-six hours of near-solitude and phone only activities and breathing room away from everyone when I didn't feel guilty for not being on.

Sure, I could've gotten on the pill or the patch or anything else to make it stop, but I'd also be giving up the vegging in bed time without the guilt.

Greasy food and sugar-packed sweets meant my ass would be kicked on Wednesday when I emerged from my cardiac arrest food cocoon in time for a commercial shoot for a product I couldn't even remember.

Didn't people get sick of looking at me? I sure as hell did. But every person on set made their money, including me. Complaints weren't what today was about. It was about solitude.

My phone buzzed in the blankets. Rummaging through the napkins and crinkly wrappers, I grabbed it.

D—Keyton.

"Hey, stranger."

He laughed. The warm baritone of it sent shivers down my spine. I missed him. "It's been less than twenty-four hours since we talked."

Gah! Was I already the clingy non-girlfriend? Part of me didn't care. I wasn't going to hide how I felt about him, and I needed him to know how much I missed him. The other part was scared he'd find it all too overwhelming or worse, suffocating.

"But I'm always glad to talk to you, especially on these long trips."

"Where are the guys?"

"They're in their rooms. There's nothing to do on game day except sitting and waiting. The bus will leave in a few minutes, and then we'll have more sitting and waiting at the stadium."

I rolled over on my bed, feeling like grounded high school me who hadn't gotten to see him outside of school for weeks.

"How do you occupy your time?" I hugged the pillow with a hot water bottle balanced on top of it against my stomach.

"The Foundation has a lot of plans for next year for me to sign off on. Ernie keeps me on my toes with pitches, deals, and trade talks."

"Trade talks?" My heart skipped a beat. We'd been looking at finishing the album here, so I could be closer to Keyton. Not that I wanted to go stage-five clinger on him after one night together, but him moving would make it even harder to see each other.

"Nothing for this season. Who knows from here on out?"

"Will you be in Philly next year? We've booked into the studio here to keep working on the album." Maybe we could make real plans. Ones where we saw each other for days and weeks at a time instead of hours. I hated adding any pressure to what we were doing, but Holden made plans one to two years out, and I wanted to make time not just for him, but for my mom and friends. It was time I made the people who were important to me more of a priority.

"I'd love to have you close by next season." He sighed,

his voice deflated. "There was some chatter, but it's died out now. Seems like our record this year has knocked the shine off my lucky charm status. Maybe I'll have a lot more time to spend with you after this season."

A clash of emotions hit me like a tide. The excitement of seeing him more was shattered by what it would mean for him. As much as I wanted him to be close, playing meant a lot to him. "On your terms."

He let out a long low breath. "We'll see. What are you up to tonight?" His voice bounced back.

"In my bed, watching TV and snacking. About to take a nap."

"It's about time Holden gave you a break. I swear, I don't know how you even have time to sleep sometimes."

I opened my mouth to correct him before snapping it shut. "I'll sleep soundly tonight after getting to talk to you."

"Would it freak you out if I told you I missed you?" There was a hint of tentative teasing to his words.

I wished I could be there with him now. He was an inescapable undercurrent rippling out through my life. No matter what was going on, who I was meeting, or where I was singing, I wanted to know I'd have the comfort of his arms to return to. It was too fast, insanely fast to have jumped straight back on the Keyton train.

"No, it wouldn't freak me out at all. Would it weird you out if I told you I'd stolen your scarf from the last time I saw you?" It had been a week ago in Memphis—or was it Houston? A precious four-hour window before our flights took off in opposite directions again.

Quirky would be a kind way to put it, but I loved to wrap his scarf around my neck when we left the hotel. It smelled like him, worked to hide my face if any photographers were out taking pictures, and helped calm me when everything felt overwhelming.

After only a matter of hours I'd become addicted to how he made me feel. But that wasn't true—he'd been sewn into the fabric of my being since I was eighteen years old. Falling back into love with him felt inevitable, like the sands of time had been waiting for their opening to shift and bring us back together. At least that's what I'd been telling myself. I could only hope the circus of my life didn't change how he felt about me.

He laughed, a full-on belly laugh that set the phone vibrating against my ear, sending flutters shooting through my stomach. "I wondered where the hell it went. And no, it wouldn't weird me out."

We talked late into the night and I woke up after midnight with the phone plastered to the side of my face and the gentle rhythm of his breathing comforting me. I loved him so much it hurt. Being away from him was like being dragged underwater and flailing for the surface. Seeing him again felt like I'd finally been able to surface and gulp down fresh, clean air. And now that I'd had my first lungful in forever, I couldn't go back.

The shoot stretched on. Extra lights were being set up because we'd lost the afternoon sun. Outside, it could be seven p.m. or midnight. I'd lost all sense of time. I kept nodding off and expecting someone to snap smelling salts under my nose to get me camera ready.

Spencer had loved the tracks I'd sent over, so the silver lining was a bit wider today. His freaking-out excitement was contagious and I couldn't wait to hear him perform the songs.

A team had transformed the industrial loft into a winter landscape. At least they hadn't tried to do it outside.

Keyton: Are you still doing your photoshoot?

Bay: Unfortunately

Keyton: No way out of it

Bay: Maybe if I gnawed my own leg off.

Keyton: Not happening. I love those legs. Especially when you wrap them around my waist trying to rush me to get inside of you

Bay: No fair! You're not allowed to get me hot and bothered when I'm in a room of twenty other people

Keyton: It'll keep your mind off things

Bay: More like it'll keep my mind on things...

I glanced around, holding my phone close to my chest, grinning like I had a secret. And I did. His name was Keyton and I missed him.

Keyton: And made you smile. That was my goal. I miss you

The wardrobe person came over with a new pair of heels.

For a total of five seconds, I had sweet relief. My toes rejoicing was cut off when the new pair were slipped on, pinching my already throbbing baby toe. At least I wouldn't have to stand for more than a couple minutes at a time.

I stared at the phone, longing squeezing my heart tight. We hadn't seen each other outside of video calls in two weeks.

Bay: I miss you too

Holden stomped across the studio space to shout at a couple label guys. They were wringing everything out of me they could for their last album before we renegotiated.

Going into a new round exhausted me and we hadn't even started. Holden and Maddy took the reins, but everyone looked to me for the final word. All eyes were on me with their futures on the line based on my thumbs up or down.

He marched back over to me with a bottle of water and a bowl of mixed nuts. "We were supposed to be finished three hours ago." He glared over his shoulder. "They're taking the piss at this point."

"You must be super angry to let your British-isms slip in." I pinched my lips together, failing miserably at keeping my smile under wraps.

"I can take these nuts back." He jerked the bowl back.

I scrambled forward and snatched the bowl. A few almonds spilled over the rim and fell into the mountain of fabric around me, lost in a sea of chiffon.

"Is this outfit thirty? I lost track when Emily and I had to call Berlin about the additional shows."

Drawing the horrified looks of the makeup artists and wardrobe assistants, I tossed the unsalted nut up into the air and caught it. "It's outfit number twenty-two, hairstyle number ten, and makeup look number twelve. The top five layers of my skin are gone." And it stung like I'd been out surfing and forgotten the sunscreen.

"I promise we'll have you out of here in the next half hour." His jaw was set and he meant business, but he was distracted. More distracted than I'd ever seen him. Every question was evaded, every prod shut down. every invitation to share turned around and refocused on me.

"Wasn't that what you said two hours ago? What the hell is going on?"

He ducked his head. "They're calling in some contract-level terms right now when it comes to this album. I know it sucks, I'm sorry. I'll do whatever I can to end this torture as soon as possible. We've been beyond accommodating and technically we've satisfied the terms—"

We were all working hard, and he was stressed as it was. I could sit around in pretty clothes and try to look interesting for a while longer. "It's fine. Everyone here is getting paid overtime at least."

A smile cracked the stony glare he cast over his shoulder. His phone buzzed. Glancing down, his frown deepened. "I'm taking this call then we're out of here." He hustled out of the room and the photographer turned back to me.

Holding a clear crystal tiger in my outstretched palm shouldn't be painful. It weighed maybe half a pound? A pound max. But my fingers were numb.

Holden hadn't returned, although it had to be way over the half hour mark.

My eyelids drooped. My feet ached. My body was rundown.

The photographer swapped out SD cards and conferred with the label suits. If there was ever a time to develop heat vision, now was the time.

Where the hell was Holden? How long could his call be taking?

The passenger elevator arrived on the floor. Heads turned at the rumbling from the wooden security gate raising.

Stepping out of the darkened area was the one man who never ceased to surprise me. He scanned the room and focused on me, sitting on the couch with a metric ton of fabric all around me.

Christmas morning excitement smashed into me, nearly toppling me over.

Keyton was here. How the hell was he here? How'd he

even know where to find me? I wanted to jump up, sweeping this dress along with me, and run to him. But I was pinned to the couch.

Working furiously, I unclipped, unpinned and unhooked the dress from the chaise lounge I'd been propped up on so long my right ass cheek was numb. A pin jabbed me. I kept going and sucked on the finger.

He crossed the space without a glance at anyone else. The corner of his mouth lifted and he crouched in front of me. "Looks like you could use a rescue, princess."

A thrill raced down my spine and I was ready to find a tower-long braid to throw out the nearest window.

I glanced down at my ridiculous dress and smiled, tramping down a giddy middle school laugh. "Come to get me from my tower?"

"That can be arranged."

"I thought you weren't coming back until Tuesday." Staring at him, I couldn't keep the starry-eyed look out of my eyes.

"Gwen worked her magic and here I am."

"Looks like someone's getting a whole case of wine for Christmas." To think at one point, I'd been melt-your-face-off jealous of her. She'd shot up to the top of my favorite people list.

"It'll be gone by New Year's." He laughed and looked at the warehouse of material around me like he was trying to figure out where the bottom half of me was.

"How did you know where I was?" I tried to stand, but caught on a few clips I missed.

He swooped in and freed me. "Holden. I messaged your phone and he gave me the location and said you could use a jailbreak."

"He's not here?" I whipped, shielding my eyes to look

beyond the lights on stands all around the set. The table he'd been set up at was empty. "He's not even in the building?"

"It didn't sound that way from his message. You didn't know he was gone?" A frown formed.

I shook my head.

"We can worry about that later." He held out his hand. "Come with me."

I glanced over my shoulder at the sea of people all here for me, but probably just as sick of being here as I was. And down at my dress—the twenty-third of the shoot. How many more pictures did they need to take? After eight hours they had to have found at least one that didn't make me look like an insecure high school kid. Had I ever even left that version of me behind, or was this all to try to cover up who I'd been back then?

It only seemed fitting that Keyton come to my rescue.

I slipped my hand into his.

The rough scrub of his callused fingers against my skin raised goosebumps all over my body.

His fingers squeezed mine like he hadn't thought I'd actually come with him.

"Where are we going?"

"Away." He glanced over his shoulder, his eyes shooting to the industrial elevator.

I nodded.

"Let's go." We both stood and leisurely strolled toward the elevator like no one would notice the football player and the woman in 157 yards of fabric making a break toward the exit.

I tried to keep my face neutral, but inside I felt lighter than ever, like we were busting out of detention.

"Bay?"

It was all it took from the unnamed person behind us for us to take off, dissolving into laughter and making our big break. Eat our dust!

23

KEYTON

I hadn't thought she'd say yes. I'd hoped—always—but never for a second did I think I'd be pulling down the wooden grate by the nylon strap and jamming my finger into the down button as a flood of people rushed toward us like I was a Viking who'd barged in and thrown her over my shoulder and stole her away to my village.

Holden had let me know where she'd be, almost like an invitation to get her out of there. Let's hope it didn't show up in the papers that I'd kidnapped Bay. It was by far the craziest thing I'd done in a few years. Exhilaration flooded my veins.

Bay held onto my shoulder, half tucked behind my body. Tonight she was as broad as I was. The poofiness of her dress—probably spanning at least six feet—wasn't exactly stealthy.

"Bay, where are you going?" A chorus of people called out from above.

Our heads disappeared below the floor and their calls were muffled.

Her fingers gripped tight to the sleeve of my jacket and she bent over at the waist. Her shoulders shook.

Was she having second thoughts?

I turned and put my hands on her shoulders. "Hey, we can—"

She peered up at me with tears of laughter in her eyes. Gasping, she clutched at the front of my shirt. "They're going to be so pissed." She brushed her tears away, smudging the makeup around her eyes.

The tension radiating through my body eased, replaced with a glowing ball of sunshine jammed straight into my chest.

The elevator hit the ground floor and I pulled up the grate, helping her step out.

She held onto me and bent, reaching under her dress and bracing one hand on my arm.

A pair of massive high heels emerged from under all the fabric, and she was no longer eye to eye with me, but half a foot shorter. She sighed and rolled her neck. From her sighs and groans, I could tell she was wiggling and flexing her toes.

Her gaze darted from me to the shoes. My disbelief at how she'd squeezed into those must've been written all over my face.

"I know, right? I keep asking why I need to wear them when no one will see them."

I took the heels from her.

She smiled at me, the kind of smile I'd won from her when we'd first become more than two reluctant planetary bodies circling each other. It was teasing. Shy. Perfect.

The vise tightened on my heart and I lead her toward the door, looping her arm through mine.

In front of the industrial steel door, weathered to give it a true industrial look, she froze. Her fingers tightened again. She glanced down at herself and back at the door. With a slight tug, she froze and leaned back away from her escape route. "I can't believe Holden left," she muttered, almost to herself.

It was a dick move on his part, but he'd tagged me in to get her out of there. At least he'd been trying to look after her despite whatever was going on with him. He didn't seem like someone who dropped the ball when it came to Bay.

Wasn't Holden supposed to be the one looking out for her? Who kept her from getting as exhausted as she was now? There were deep shadows under her eyes even the makeup couldn't erase.

"I have a car waiting outside." Part of me wanted to throw her over my shoulder now, whisk her away from her painful shoes, her non-stop schedule, her birdcage life. Which would probably earn me a well-deserved door slamming in my face.

Her gaze shot to mine with a quirk of her lips, but the worry still swam in her eyes. "I'm not exactly inconspicuous."

"You never were." I pushed open the door. An overcast evening greeted us. Humidity prickled my skin.

She never had been. From the first moment I'd heard her sing, she'd been the most conspicuous person in my life, always a part of me, like our souls had been stitched together one fiber at a time through each note from her guitar and her lips.

Gwen's go-to driver we had on retainer stood beside the black SUV with the back-passenger door already open.

Bay hurried across the sidewalk and climbed into the car. At least most of her body made it. It took a bit of shoving to the voluminous amount of fabric inside.

"How have you not gotten lost in this thing?"

"A flashlight and treasure map for any time I sit down." She beat down the gray material, spitting some out of her mouth.

I got in beside her with a department store's worth of cloth between us and slammed my door shut. "A compass too."

She nodded, wedged inside the car door.

The door we'd come through flew open and people poured out onto the sidewalk, heads whipping back in shock. I braced for the fallout, when Bay's sense of responsibility overcame the thrill of the escape and she trudged back inside.

Bay lunged forward. "Let's go."

I grabbed her around the waist to steady her from toppling into the space between the seats and being lost to the abyss of fabric.

The driver looked back at me and I nodded.

She rubbed her neck, squeezing her shoulders and rolling her head. "Is this what that couple felt like at the end of The Graduate?" She stared out her window with her back resting against the door.

The scene where Dustin Hoffman interrupts his ex's wedding after some behind-the-scenes machinations from her mother and she rushes off, catching a city bus still in the dress certainly came to mind with her outfit. "Not feeling like it was a successful escape?"

"For a few hours." She peered over at me, sagging against the seat. "I'm sure Holden will have a mountain of messages flooding his phone as we speak. Once he reappears..."

"I'm sure he can handle it."

"Too true. They'll probably reschedule what they didn't get for another minuscule gap in my schedule."

Why did she always seem like the last person on her list of people to do things for? "You can take time for yourself."

The fabric ruffled and shifted. Bracing her hands on the back of the driver's headrest and hers, she faced me. "Every job I turn down is money Holden or Emily or Maddy don't get to put into their pockets. Every show I turn down is money the road crew doesn't get to send home to their families."

"So you're only doing this out of the goodness of your heart?" Frustration mounted at how she couldn't separate herself from the work and weight and responsibility of everyone around her.

She shot me a glare. "Of course it also has to do with me, but there comes a point where the money is more than I could spend in a lifetime and it becomes about something else. You'd never walk away from your team in the middle of the season. Blowing off responsibilities for a few hours is fine, but they'll still be there in the morning." She slumped against me.

Her 'never walk away' comment was more of a direct hit than she knew. Leaving the team in a lurch was exactly what I'd been planning on doing, but it didn't feel the same. I literally had nothing to do with their wins.

But it wouldn't be the case. A hollowness formed in my chest. My issues with responsibility had to do with feeling like I had no control over any of the outcomes of the games my team played.

Bay had total responsibility. There was no show without her. There was no album. There was no tour employing hundreds of people and performing for more stadiums of people in a month than we did all season. Shouldering that kind of weight had to feel so stifling.

I could walk away from football right now. Pack my bags, find a nice place to live, and do whatever the hell I wanted with the rest of my life. But I still held onto the pipe dream of getting to play. Even after a handful of championship rings encrusted with diamonds, I kept going.

"But you don't sound happy about it." Searching for her legs under all the fluffy fabric, I grabbed her leg and spun her around. My fingers ran down the fine line of her leg to her ankle.

She rested her head against the window, a confused but curious dip to her eyebrows.

Taking one foot into my hand, I worked my thumbs into the soles of her feet.

She hissed and moaned.

My fingers stilled for a moment, unsure if I was hurting her.

Her eyes shot open, lips parting.

I'd seen that face before. My blood pounded harder, warming the veins headed straight for my groin. I pressed harder on her foot.

Another moan.

The driver's head jerked and the car swerved a little. Right about now, I wished I had ordered a car with a divider —for more reasons than one.

"Quiet or he's going to think I'm doing something inde-cent to you." I ran my fingers over her feet, massaging along the instep and pinches.

The tops of her toes were red. The sides, too.

Annoyance rippled through me. How long had she been wearing those shoes? Why had she been wearing them when no one could even see them?

Careful of the tender spots, I worked to release the tension in them.

Her hand shot out to her headrest, gripping it tight. "You are." She dropped her head back, pushing her breasts up in the dress. "One hundred percent indecent. How did you learn to do that?"

It shot out like an accusation.

My laughter couldn't be contained. "A long time playing ball will teach you a few tricks about human anatomy." Stretching to warm up for a game. Being ready for every block or pass in practice. Pushing myself harder than everyone else, hoping for my shot. I refocused on Bay, on giving her the relief she needed right now. What I needed was to be the one to give it to her.

Her squirms, moans, and sighs urged me to continue my ministrations on her feet even though my erection was about to take this from muscle relief to foreplay.

I rolled her toes between my fingers and she punched the roof of the SUV not even holding back her curse. It sounded a lot like other times I'd heard her scream, which brought with it a whole other slew of mental flashes, but the dress situation made any attempt at backseat sex—driver notwithstanding—impossible.

A rumbling, rolling laugh burst from my chest. I took my fingers off her feet before she smashed out a window.

"If you stop, I swear, I'll tweet out your home address to my fans and tell them there's a limited-edition Team Bay prize pack hidden in there."

"Pulling out the big guns, I see."

"This is the best foot massage I've ever had in my life." She groaned and collapsed into the seat.

"I've never seen you so relaxed."

Her eyes fluttered open and the corner of her mouth

lifted. She checked out the driver. "You and I both know that's not true."

Sliding her feet out of my lap, she swung around so we were sitting side by side. "You've used your skills in more ways than one to turn me into a boneless mess before."

The car jolted as we descended into the underground parking garage in our building. I whispered against the side of her neck. "Ready for me to do it again?"

She shivered and stared into my eyes with a blistering fire that promised we'd be lucky if we made it to the couch, let alone the bed.

Holding hands, we rushed into the elevator. The doors opened on a couple other floors, but the giant dress deterred anyone from getting on. There were a few double takes in the lobby, but no one said anything. No one screamed her name or chased after us.

Making it to my floor, I half-carried, half-hugged her to me.

She spoke against my lips. "We can't rip the dress. It's a Valentino. They'll be pissed enough I took it out of that room."

Careful of all the pins and clips, we frantically worked to get her out of the dress. I couldn't stop looking at her standing in nothing but boy shorts, smudged makeup, and a messy updo. I didn't want to stop touching her and hated to think about how little time we had together before we'd be separated again.

There was always a countdown timer on how long we had together, but instead of counting the months or weeks, our time was down to hours.

Hours I planned to make the most of. Cupping my hands around the sides of her neck, I stared into the eyes of the woman who owned me inside and out.

One look.

One touch.

One taste.

Bringing our lips together, the kiss started out as a graze, a gentle brush of her full and tender lips against mine. It was a soothing balm to all the aches created being apart from her.

Soon, it transformed back to the frenzied pitch that came from knowing our time together would be too short. Anything short of forever felt like it didn't last long enough.

Lifting her and cupping her ass with one hand, I carried her to the bedroom with her legs wrapped around my waist.

Each grind and moan sprayed lighter fluid on the flames of my desire, threatening to consume us both.

The head of my cock dipped inside her and my knees buckled. I braced our fall, covering her. My move to get up was stopped by Bay's kisses against my neck.

"Here's fine. I don't want to wait." Her breath whispered across my skin, spreading the heat and loss of control throughout my body.

Her hand reached down between us and she ran the head of my cock against her wet opening.

I sank into her hot velvety sweetness before coming back to myself. No protection. "Shit." Pulling out, I reached up and flailed for my bedside table, grabbing a condom and rolling it on like my hands were running a hundred-yard dash.

"I totally blanked." Her breathless words, glistening lips and roaming fingers beckoned me back.

"Sorry." The last thing I wanted to do was derail her life with my stupid mistake.

She urged me closer. "I'll forgive you, if you give me what I want." Her hips wriggled beneath mine.

Rocking my hips, I entered her again. My jaw clenched and I fought to keep my eyes from rolling back in my head. "What would that be?" My hunger and need for her grew. I clung to my slow, steady strokes, not wanting this to be over too quickly.

Her fingers gripped my shoulders tighter. "I think I'll let you figure it out."

24

BAY

The blunt thickness of his invasion sent raw, explosive bliss shooting through my body. The sparks threatened to fry every nerve ending swamped by the rush of sexual satisfaction.

His rough, rolling thrusts pushed the crescendo higher.

Words were lost to the power of his thrusts as he pinned my thighs down and bucked into me like these were our last hours on Earth.

My back arched, shooting off the floor, and I slammed my palms into the wood, so hard his downstairs neighbors would probably complain. My body hummed with unadulterated bliss.

Over me, his exacting thrusts became uncontrolled and sloppy, overflowing with the evidence of how good we were together.

Groaning, he collapsed on top of me, bracing his arms beside my head. The inescapable need and urgency faded into a blissed-out crash, sweaty, sated, and boneless.

I wrapped my legs around his waist, not wanting an inch between us just yet. "Did you miss me?"

He laughed, dropping his head against my shoulder, and rolled to his side. "Always."

My skin tingled. "Maybe next time we'll make it to the bed." I tilted my head back and took an upside down look at the neatly made gray-comforter-covered bed a few feet away.

"Baby steps, Bay." After taking care of the condom, we climbed into his bed. It was so much more comfortable than my top-of-the-line hotel mattress—maybe that was because I was here with him.

His fingers ran along the curve of my shoulder. "It's getting harder to be away from you."

My breath hitched. The fluttering in my stomach made me want to hammer the doors closed, so we could stay in this bed forever. "I know how you feel."

"You leave for London in three weeks."

A non-stop, grueling, rewarding, puke-inducing, euphoria-rushing tour. "And your season doesn't end for three more months." I brushed my fingers through the hair above his ear. "We should make the most of the time before I leave."

"Come to my next home game. It's a home game, so no travel needed."

"In two Sundays, right?" I might've memorized his schedule. *Might have.*

His lips twitched. "Right. If you're in town."

"Most likely. The studio has been taking up more of the schedule lately."

"Will you be back for Christmas?"

No point in making promises I couldn't keep. I shook my head. "I don't think so. My mom was asking the same thing. I was thinking of having her fly over to me instead."

His hum of understanding didn't hide his disappointment and drove home mine deeper in my chest.

"Could you come to me?"

"We'll be playing."

I propped my head up on my hand. "We could have our own Christmas before or after, complete with hot chocolate and Christmas movies. I might even pick up some stockings." Walking my fingers down his chest, I peeked over at him, hating that I couldn't say 'yes, of course I can see you and we can spend the whole day together'. Everything was compromises and making up for the things our schedules wouldn't allow for.

"You had me at hot chocolate." His deep, chocolate-sweet laugh made the fear of the distance a little less sharp.

We were making plans. Flexible plans, but plans for what happened when I left Philly and went out on the road. Some fears about how we'd navigate the next year were allayed—or did everyone else who dove head first into a relationship like this have the same level of hope that it would all work out?

His fingers brushed through. "You'll come to my game."

"I don't know if that would be a good idea..." A stadium full of people with me in the stands meant a logistical nightmare. Sadness rippled in my chest. I wanted to be there for him, cheering along with everyone else, but I couldn't pick up my ticket at Will Call and find my seat in the stands.

"How about a skybox? No one will bother you up there. You can relax, eat, drink and watch me not play." His smile and laugh didn't hide the glimmer of frustration that flickered in his gaze at his benched status.

"Maybe I'll be your good luck charm if I show up."

"How could you not be?" He brushed my hair behind my ear, tickling me with the strands.

We lay there in silence, not awkward or stifling, but content. I'd never felt that kind of silence, even sitting alone in my hotel room.

It wasn't until the tenth ring from Keyton's phone which rumbled against the living room floor that we knew our time was almost up.

He slipped out of bed.

I shifted and sat against the headboard with my legs crossed under the blankets when he came in. Even though I knew what was coming, I braced for the feeling of never having enough time.

"This isn't fair. You sitting like that in my bed makes me want to launch this out the window and become a hermit."

Same. "Is it Holden?"

"Of course it is. He's said we've had our fun, but it's time to return to the castle."

Crawling across the bed, I plucked the phone out of his hands. "He actually said that."

"I guess that makes you the princess for real now."

"Does that make him the dragon?"

"More like a very demanding fairy godmother."

"He did help make all my dreams come true." I sat staring at the glowing screen. It all felt so far away now with Keyton so close.

He slipped into the bed behind me and wrapped his arms around me. The heat of his bare chest against my back comforted me.

It's when I realized the promise I'd made to go to his game wasn't one I could even make off-handedly. Swiping my finger across the screen, I tapped out a message to Holden.

Me: This is Bay. I need to go to Keyton's game next Sunday. Can you make that happen?

Holden: Will you come back if I say no?

Me: No

Holden: Glad you're giving me multiple options.

Me: I need to go

Holden: That's all you had to say. We'll make it work with the pre-tour rest days built into the schedule.

Me: Thank you

Holden: Don't mention it. For real—like actually don't mention it. It'll ruin my reputation. We have some calls to make to Sydney and Japan tonight and at six in the morning. Do you plan on coming back or do you want us to come to you?

I leaned against Keyton, holding onto his strong, sinewy arm wrapped around my chest. Invading his home with my circus would buy me more time with him, but it would also subject him to more of my life's craziness.

Me: I'll be there in twenty minutes.

Dropping Keyton's phone onto the bed, I rested my head onto his shoulder.

His lips brushed against the side of my face. "You have to go."

I nodded.

"When will I see you next?"

"I'm not sure." I hated this feeling. Leaving him was bad, but knowing it would be so long until I saw him again, and the uncertainty of when that could even be, was even worse.

"But you can come to my game." He nuzzled my neck.

"Short of Holden locking me in my room, I'll be there." I looked up into his eyes and pulled his head down for a kiss, my fingers gently gripping the back of his neck.

"Let me get dressed, so we can walk over."

I pressed my palm against his chest. The beat under my palm increased the longer I held it there. With a bit a force, I straightened my arm.

He let me push him down to his elbows.

The walk wasn't far and he had to be tired after landing a few hours ago. He needed to rest. And I needed to think. "You stay. I can do it on my own. Plus, I like saving this view of you." I held up my fingers like I had an invisible camera. "Click. Just preserving this for later." I slid the imaginary polaroid into my nonexistent back pocket.

"At least let me walk you to the elevator."

"Front door." The fragile, scared bunny wasn't how I wanted him to see me. He shouldn't feel like he had to go into protective mode every time we were together. I could make it to the hotel side of the building by myself. It was a terrible idea. Anyone could recognize me, but I didn't want Keyton feeling like he had to go into protective mode the second we went out in public because I got so freaked out. Low stakes situations where I took precautions would relax me some. Baby steps.

Walking out into the living room, I stared at the mountain of fabric I'd showed up here in. "Shit." Not exactly a dress made to blend in.

Over my shoulder, Keyton held out a folded set of clothes. Sweaters, leggings, socks. "After I knew your sizes, I figured having some back-up clothes for when we could steal away together wouldn't be the worst idea."

"All this time you've been hiding your super genius powers from me." I wrapped my arms around his waist and squeezed my eyes shut, my heart leaping at his thoughtfulness and caring. Who knew sweaters, leggings and socks were the key to my heart?

He did.

"Purely selfish reasons. If you had clothes here, then you wouldn't have to go back as early."

I peered over my shoulder. "What do we do about the dress?"

He lifted his other hand. An oversized duffel bag swaying in his grasp.

"A Valentino in a duffel bag. I'm sure a designer somewhere is having an aneurysm without knowing why."

He rubbed his nose against mine and pecked me on the lips. "If you don't tell, neither will I."

With my new comfy clothes, wool-lined slip-on shoes, and duffel bag of couture, we kissed one more time at the elevator after more intensive negotiation, which may or may not have been waged with our lips and hands, nearly ending with me being late for my around-the-world phone call.

My hat pulled down over my hair and my head bent, I walked out of the elevator to the oversized mirror that acted as a door between the residences and the hotel, feeling like I was entering the movie Inception.

Panicked breaths tightened in my chest and my rigid muscles as the door glided closed behind me. I was on guard, but doing it, and people walked past me. Every set of approaching feet squeezed my lungs until they moved away. A simple walk through the lobby was terrifying and exhilarating all at once.

After taking the elevator up as far as I could, I switched to the stairs, rushing up them and sending Keyton even more mental appreciation, as my feet weren't screaming.

Eric stood, his eyes wide at my solo return, but he didn't say anything and opened the suite door.

Holden sat on the couches in the living room to the suite and closed a magazine, pretending to be nonchalant. I'd never seen him reading a magazine in his life. "How was your escape adventure?"

"You act like you didn't orchestrate it." I waved a totally

judgmental finger in his direction. "Where did you disappear to?"

"Nowhere."

"Oh sorry, were you there the whole time wearing your invisibility suit?" I teased.

His face fell, remorse written all over it. "Sorry I bailed. It won't happen again." He sounded miserable.

"I just wished you'd taken me with you." I rounded the couch and sat on the arm. "What's going on with you, Holden? Is everything okay?"

"Lovely." His smile couldn't hide the secretive tinge to the word.

"Holden, seriously, what's going on?" I leaned forward.

He leaned back. "Nothing that will affect you."

"If it affects you, it affects me. After six years of working together—six years of friendship—you don't know that?"

"I'm sorry about leaving during the photoshoot. It won't impact my work anymore."

"Holden...you can talk to me. You can tell me whatever is going on. Maybe I can help."

"I'm handling it. It's what I do." His easy smile was back. "Is the dress still at Keyton's?"

Way to roadblock me and change the subject, but I let it slide. He ran my life and I still knew so little about his. One more entry on the list of reasons I was a shitty friend, but I swore I'd do better.

"Emily can go get it. Em!" He called out over his shoulder.

"It's fine. I brought it with me."

The office door opened and Emily walked out, tablet in hand.

"With you..." The question trailed off and his gaze shot

to the bag in my hand, horror etching every perfectly chiseled line. "Is that the Valentino?"

Emily rushed forward like she'd seen blood seeping out of the bag. "What? No!"

～

Jet lag was more like jet drag, but Keyton was back tomorrow and I wanted to do something for him. It had been under a week since our great escape from my photoshoot from hell.

His trip to Miami overlapped with mine to New York in the imperfectly perfect way that meant we didn't even get to see each other at the airport.

But the idea hit me when I flipped through my old songwriting notebooks, which I always kept in one of my bags. The ones I'd written after the last show my senior year of high school. On the next page, I saw exactly what I needed. Without a second thought, I was up and out of the room, rushing into the office.

"I need a kitchen." The door to the suite office slammed behind me.

I jumped. We all jumped. Maybe that was a tad more dramatic than I'd intended.

Emily hopped up, stylus at the ready. "Chef's Table? For how many? Any particular cuisine you had in mind?"

"Not a restaurant. I just need a kitchen. And these ingredients." I held up the paper torn from my notebook.

"The chef in the kitchen downstairs is on call and can whip up whatever you want. Or we can have Emily pick something up from a restaurant."

"I don't want anyone to make anything for me. I just need a kitchen and the things on this list." Pointing to the list, I looked back at everyone, who exchanged looks of confusion. The frustration mounted.

"Why?" Holden asked like I'd asked him for a DeLorean and some plutonium.

My teeth clenched. "Because I want to make something."

"But—"

"*I* want to make something. Can you please help me do that, or do I need to figure it out myself? Going to the grocery store will be a shitshow, but I'll do it, if I need to." With my new disguise technique, I could pull it off. Slip in, rush through the aisles, and back out.

Holden spoke cautiously, enunciating every syllable more than usual like he was testing whether I actually wanted this. "I'll make it happen."

Relief that I wouldn't have to test out my disguise skills and excitement to get started made the next hour drag while Holden arranged everything.

An hour later, he stood beside me in a kitchen in a residence apartment just like Keyton's, eyeing my apron as I tied the fabric around my waist.

"Are you sure about this?" He tilted back the bag of sugar to examine it like I'd gone mad scientist.

I snatched it away from him and set it down on the counter. "I'm not cooking meth, Holden."

"Are you sure you wouldn't prefer I send the chef up here? He could help."

"You mean supervise. I should be offended, you jackass. I lived a life before I was Bay. I cooked and cleaned and even managed to dress myself. I know it's hard to believe."

"What's it been? Six years since you cooked anything for yourself?"

Being swept along in the wave of fame had happened so quickly, I'd forgotten what it was like to do things for myself.

I'd sometimes forgotten I was even allowed to do things for myself. When contract obligations were layered on top of exclusivity clauses piled onto travel coordination, me making a rash decision would add heaps of extra work and headaches for everyone, including me.

It was easier to give over the reins to everyone around me, easier to let me set the goal of being the biggest there was and let them lay out the plan to get there. Then I felt like I was just along for the ride, headed toward the destination I'd agreed to, but not thinking about everything it would take to make it happen. I wouldn't be where I was today if I hadn't let them handle it, and maybe that was part of the problem. I needed to relearn how to control my own destiny.

"I know my way around the kitchen." I ran down the list of ingredients I'd scribbled down after asking my mom for the recipe. "When's the last time you had something home cooked?"

"Home cooking doesn't always mean good." He shuddered.

"You haven't had my hot chocolate and cinnamon rolls." After Keyton had shown up the way he had, I wanted to do something for him. I needed to, to remind him that this wasn't always who I'd be.

"Okay. The trainer will be here in seven hours. Are you sure you want to start this so late?"

The dough could rise and proof in a couple hours. I wouldn't be getting much sleep tonight, but it would be worth it. "I've got it handled."

"Let us know if you need anything."

"I won't. I've made these tons of times. It's been a few years, but I can do things for myself." Making these for

Keyton was a small flex of the independence muscles I'd let atrophy.

All the kitchen tools were out and cleaned. Measuring all the ingredients, I got to work. My mom and dad had loved baking together. They'd both end up covered in flour or powdered sugar and I'd pretend not to notice the white hand prints on my mom's butt. Those quiet domestic moments were ones I'd taken for granted. Despite how much my dad loved music, we made him happiest.

How would he feel knowing I'd accomplished all he'd ever dreamed of in a music career, but had traded my love to get there?

During the first proofing of the dough, my eyelids drooped. The adrenaline rush of baking slowly faded. I set a timer on my phone, grabbed a few kitchen towels, and turned them into a makeshift pillow to crash for a little bit. The scratchy linen wasn't enough to stop my eyes from closing.

Keyton would love these. Watching him devour them in my kitchen back in Greenwood, I'd loved drizzling even more icing onto them for him. I remembered sending him home with a container full of them.

He could take them the next time he left town. Maybe I could make some for him to keep in the freezer.

I zonked out to dreams of him licking icing off my fingers while I fed him cinnamon rolls until my timer beeped. Bumping my head on the cabinets above me hadn't been in the plans, but I soldiered on with the top of my head throbbing.

When he got back into town tomorrow and came to visit me, we'd have morning cinnamon rolls and hot chocolate to celebrate making it through another week apart.

Once I left on tour it would be even worse. A pit knotted

in my stomach that had just been filled with excitement over seeing him again. Time would stretch into weeks, if not months apart, and thinking about getting up on stage was enough to bring on the watery-mouth feeling that proceeded every performance.

Sprinkling flour on the counter, I used a spatula to smooth out the generous heaps of cinnamon sugar filling. It brought back all those feelings from home, both Greenwood and Glendale, where we'd lived before. I remembered my dad trying to steal another finger scoop of icing before my mom smacked his hand away.

Those were the happy memories I poured into baking, memories of home and family. Rolling and slicing the dough, I set the cinnamon rolls in the pan and slid them into the oven.

Maybe I'd have Holden find me a kitchen more often, so I could bake for Keyton. Could I overnight deliver them to him while we were apart? The tabloids would smack me with the overly attached girlfriend moniker, if they ever found out. That sobered me up some. Once more people found out, the magnifying glass would swoop down over us, dissecting every bit of our lives. Every smile to a fan from both of us would be splashed up with giant headlines dripping with innuendo.

As much as I feared it, I didn't want to hide what he meant to me. I didn't want to pretend Keyton wasn't in my life. I wanted to announce it on mic or call a press conference to let everyone know, but it was a complication I'd be adding to his life, unfairly foisting it on him.

The next time we had a stretch of time together, I could make them in his apartment, leaving the lingering smell of them in his place, like I was trying to imprint myself on him even when I wasn't there. It could shrink that distance between us even when we were oceans apart.

Holden or Emily poked their heads in every so often, probably trying to make sure I hadn't set the place on fire.

The smells wafting from the oven intensified. I closed my eyes, envisioning my life as it had been. In my mind, Keyton and I were together, and I pulled these out of the oven after a day of song-writing and working in our home studio. He'd come back from practice all sweaty and tired, only to perk up and sneak into the kitchen to steal a cinnamon roll without me seeing.

It was crazy how dreams could change, and even crazier how they could feel so unattainable all the same.

25

KEYTON

I adjusted my travel game backpack, falling in line with the rest of the guys walking through the terminal. Seventy guys walking through the terminal to baggage claim weren't exactly inconspicuous, but the sparse early morning crowd kept stops for autographs and pictures to a minimum. All I wanted to do was get to Bay, to see her, hold her, kiss her. My steps quickened, and I was at the head of the pack on the way to baggage claim.

Berk and LJ were already on their phones to Jules and Marisa. Reece had taken off sprinting the second the doors opened. With Seph being pregnant, he'd gotten more anxious about being away.

As happy as I was for him, it freaked me out to know a baby would be around. A tiny little person, so small and vulnerable. Someone I knew I'd care about instantly because of who their parents were, and fear all the bad shit that could happen in their life.

It wasn't to say I ran screaming from the room any kid entered, but it was much easier to work with the foundation and handle the higher-level things, knowing it would help the kids, than to sit down one-on-one with them. I wasn't there yet. All I could think about when I looked at them was me growing up.

I remembered the chaotic, chilling uncertainty of never finding solid footing anywhere off the football field and always waiting for the next rollercoaster drop. My friends were breezing through life with each other, always looking ready to float away on a cloud. To me, having a child would feel like being dropped in the middle of the ocean during a hurricane without a life raft.

But the clock was ticking on the safe arrival of Reece's little guy or girl. I had a little over seven months to shake my fear of crushing a tiny baby I could fit in the palm of my hand.

The whole kid thing would be a long way off for me. Even if Bay and I made the big decision to give us a go, her schedule was so insane that kids wouldn't be in our future until years down the line. There was still time to work through my shit and get my head on straight. Maybe someday, I could be a good dad, but today wasn't that day.

My phone vibrated in my pocket. I fished it out.

Bay: Landed yet?

I cracked a smile, loving her checking in on me. Our text conversations stretched late into the night until one of us stopped responding only to wake up with the phone stuck to the side of our face.

Me: Walking toward baggage claim
Bay: Perfect. I have a surprise for you
Me: What's the surprise?

Maybe we'd have another full day together. Or she'd figured something out for Christmas. I loved making plans with her. Even as the gaps in our schedules narrowed, looking forward to the hours I could spend with her made it worth it.

No response to my text. Knowing her, she'd been pulled away by Holden. From time to time I wanted to lock him in a closet and snap his tablet in half, but he was only doing his job. The one Bay wanted him to do.

Our team duffel bags slid onto the baggage claim conveyor belt at a tired turtle pace. The name tags or colored tape on the handles were the only differences between all of them.

The chartered flight had been quiet, most of the guys still drained from the game and any celebrating they'd done after. I'd been tempted to call Gwen and pay my own way to come back to town early, but Bay had a full schedule and I didn't want to pressure her into ditching responsibilities or loading up her schedule for the next time I was away to steal time with me.

These road games felt longer than before. Every day away from the city, away from Bay, felt too long.

There was always a ticking clock over our time together. First, it had been to graduation back in Greenwood, then the end of training camp in LA. Now, the start of her tour in a few weeks hung over us. The urgency to cement what we had before she left was nearly insurmountable. I didn't want to leave a dangling thread between us so thin it could be severed again.

My bag with the DK on the tag rolled around. I grabbed it off the belt at the same time a hand wrapped around my elbow, squeezing. The initial snap of muscle tenseness took hold. Instead of following through, I took a beat and relaxed. Probably an eager fan.

Turning, I got one look at who I'd expected to be a fan and stumbled, falling backward onto the belt and staring at the surprise right in front of me—well, a little to the left of me—as I slid along with the rest of the team gear. The stunned silence was broken. This place was full of people. "TNG?"

In a hat, sunglasses and a sweatshirt like our first excursion out to IKEA, Bay was here, picking me up from the airport. She laughed and did a little jazz hands move. "Surprise."

Scrambling up, my heart kicked into overdrive. I wrapped her in my arms, hugging her tight.

"What the hell are you doing here?" My grin was cheek-spraining wide. Sheer joy ripped straight through me.

Her hat fell off her head, flopping to the floor behind her.

I buried my face in her hair, breathing her in.

"What? I can't pick my guy up from the airport?"

Her guy. Those words sent fireworks shooting off in my chest. Brushing her hair back from her face, I kissed her. "I like the sound of that." God, did I like the sound of it. I loved it. I grabbed the soft gray hat and stuck it back on her head, forcing her hair in front of her eyes like a curtain.

She swatted at my hands and yanked the hat off, shoving her hair out of her face. "Jerk." But her smile was as wide as mine.

Hovering over her shoulder a couple yards back, Eric and Holden stood sentry, conspicuously inconspicuous. For a split second, I forgot how careful she needed to be and was glad they were there keeping her safe on the way to me.

"Was that one yours?" She pointed to the belt jammed with bags.

"Yeah, let me..." I craned my neck looking for it. Sprinting down the line past my teammates, I spotted it.

With a clean yank, I got it free from the pile of bags and took off back to Bay. "Got it."

"Now are you ready for your surprise?"

"I thought you being here was my surprise." I couldn't stop looking at her, and slipped my arm around her waist, shifting to keep my bag on my shoulder. There was more? What more did I need when I had her here?

"No, it wasn't. This was." She bent, reaching for a bag I hadn't noticed at her feet. Out of it, she slipped a thermos and a small clear plastic container holding a cinnamon roll. "I wasn't sure if you needed to leave straight from here with the team or if you might be able to come with me, so I brought this inside."

"Did you pick this up for me?" Even with everything she had going on, she was thinking about me, maybe even half as much as I was thinking about her.

She held them out. "No, I made it."

Electric pulses rushed under my skin. She had made all this for me.

The woman who everyone wanted a piece of spent time making hot chocolate and cinnamon rolls for me. I took the thermos from her hand and opened the lid, sniffing the dark, rich scent. Memories of sitting in her kitchen, touching her under the table, and making sure her mom didn't see flooded my mind. The hearty, sweet liquid had coated the yawning pit of hunger in my stomach then. I'd made myself slow down and savor the tastes and smell instead of devouring them like I'd wanted to. "It's hot chocolate. Your hot chocolate."

She nodded.

"You made this too?"

The clear clamshell container sat in the palms of her hands. She nodded.

So many feelings rushed through me, burning deep in my chest. With everything going on in her life, she'd made this for me. Hell, I'd have been happy if she'd picked it up for me on the way here. But the time she took to make this…

"I can't wait to have it. I swear, nothing compares to your cinnamon rolls and hot chocolate." I wished I could see her eyes, hidden behind those sunglasses. And I wished she didn't have to hide herself away.

But the rest of her radiated happiness—happiness to see me. "Do you need to stay or tell someone you're going?" She tipped her head, looking down the line of football players and staff.

"We're good. This is the best surprise I've ever gotten." Normally, I hated them, but these were the kind I could happily experience every day. I wrapped my arm with the thermos around her shoulder. She held onto the cinnamon roll and my mouth watered—not only for the sweet treat in her hands.

"The car's out here." She pointed through the sliding set of doors where a black SUV idled with a driver standing on the curb. Even if it was only a ride back to the hotel, I'd take it. It was still time alone with her.

Holden walked in front of us and Eric behind.

Bay hugged me with one arm around my waist, under my coat, her giddy excitement was catching.

"Bay?" The question shot out like a scream when we were five feet from the door.

All four of us tensed. I could feel it in the air. This had gone from light and fun to potential disaster.

Her shining expression faltered. Worry seeped into her grip on me.

"Oh my god, it's Bay!" Another voice added to the

normal airport chatter and bustle. The hairs on the back of my neck stood on end and my muscles turned to granite.

A hand gripped both our shoulders. "Bay, let's move."

Bay looked over her shoulder and picked up the pace, I did too. The crush of panic swamped me. Voices rose, phones came out and people rushed toward us.

I dropped the thermos. It fell along Bay's side and bounced off the floor, spraying hot chocolate out the lid. I pulled Bay in tighter to me, shielding her and needing to get her out of here, fear rippling through me.

We made it through the doors. I checked over my shoulder to make sure we weren't about to get slammed. Eric stopped, spinning to hold back the crowd in the doorway, and Holden had the door open already and jerked my duffel from my grasp.

Bay jumped into the car and I followed behind her. Holden slammed the door before I could reach for the handle. His urgency ratcheted up my alarm. We needed to get her out of here.

Eric climbed into the front seat. The door slam rocked the car.

Emily let Holden in through the back door behind Bay. He shot into his seat and chucked my duffel over his shoulder into the back.

We peeled away from the curb. The driver had to veer around people who'd flooded into the road in front of us. That could've gone bad. Really fucking bad.

"Everyone good?" Eric looked back from the front.

"We're good. Just a little messy." Bay's brittle laugh sent all my protective instincts into red alert. She was putting on a brave face for me. Maybe even for herself. The handful of times she'd wanted to walk back to her room alone...I wasn't going to let her do it again. The spiral was starting. Catastrophizing and dread were working themselves into a needle-spiked ball rolling through my chest.

A hand extended from the back seat with a napkin. "Do we need to stop for a change?"

"No, it's all on my coat."

Bay popped open her buttons. A large white icing smudge smeared across the front of her black jacket. On one arm, hot chocolate dripped from shoulder to the end of the sleeve. From when I'd chucked it. The hot chocolate she'd spent her precious time on making. I went into freak out mode and tossed it aside like it was nothing to get her out of there.

"Shit, I'm sorry."

She shoved the coat off and folded it, keeping the stains from touching anything else. Her hand rubbed my leg. "It wasn't your fault. I could've stayed in the car and had Holden go get you."

I hated thinking about her sitting in the car, behind tinted windows, unable to step outside the bubble made to protect her. "You should be able to come and get me from the airport if you want."

She shrugged and smiled, her hand continuing the reassuring strokes up and down my leg. "I'm not sorry. We all make trades. And I wanted to see you."

Even if she hadn't been who she was, I couldn't keep her safe every minute of every day. How often did bad things happen to people going about mundane tasks in their lives? I took deep breaths. I couldn't control the situation. I couldn't control that crowd of people. All I could control was how I reacted to it, and I didn't want to spoil our time together by losing my cool. I'd talk to Holden and make sure she didn't take a risk like that again.

"I'm glad you did." I slipped my arm around her shoulder, holding her against me, while releasing the iron lock of my muscles and filling my lungs with her smell. "What's the rest of your day like?"

Her shoulders drooped. "It's packed. That's why I wanted to come this morning. There's no other time to see you today."

Her disappointment mirrored and amplified my own.

"Can I tag along?"

Her eyebrows shot up. "You'd want to? It's fittings, dress rehearsal for the tour, a few meet-and-greets. I won't have a lot of quiet moments."

My addiction to her meant any moments weren't ones I was willing to pass up. "I'd love to see what makes the Bay machine tick. Even a look across the room will be good enough for me. No babysitting required."

She peered over her shoulder. "Is that okay?"

Holden closed the cover on his tablet. "Of course. We'll get Keyton set up and comfortable. There's a chance we can do a solo lunch. We also need to go over the songs off the new album for the radio meet-and-greet tomorrow."

I ran my hand along her leg. "Don't worry about me. You don't need to entertain me."

We drove into the Wells Fargo Arena drop-off area. The SUV pulled up to a set of doors.

"The arena?"

"Where else to prepare for a stadium and arena tour?" Bay smiled.

All the doors in back and in front of us opened.

Holden opened Bay's door and she slid out. "It's going to be a long day. If you want to leave at any point, don't think I'll feel bad."

I followed behind her and took her hand. Not in a million years would I think of leaving, and I didn't want her thinking I would, adding me to the shit-Bay-has-to-worry-about-today list. "When I say I'm here, I'm here. Although I do wish I hadn't dropped my hot chocolate and crushed my cinnamon roll."

She smiled. "Don't worry. There's more."

That eased some of my anger at myself for ruining her surprises for me without even tasting them.

Emily handed her an identical bag to the one she'd had inside the baggage claim.

"I might have overestimated the hot chocolate and cinnamon roll recipes, so there's about three dozen rolls for your freezer and a whole winter's worth of hot chocolate mix." Her shoulder inched up in a slight cringe, like she was embarrassed to have spent so much time and effort on baking to make me happy.

Those feelings I tried to pretend we weren't ready for were pounding on the door to my heart, wanting to be let out. I wanted to bathe her in the flood of emotions barreling out of me, but I was afraid of overwhelming her. Instead, I settled for "I can't wait."

Inside, the hallways were a flurry of activity and people. It felt like game day all over again.

Every room down the hall was filled with people. Music echoed down the halls and rumbled the walls.

With my bag of treats, I followed Bay. Holden made announcements into the rooms we passed by, and the train of people grew. None of these were screaming Bay's name or grabbing for her. I wasn't on edge anymore. These were her people.

She hugged and smiled at everyone: dancers, wardrobe, sound technicians, and stage hands moving giant black-and-silver boxes.

Out on the arena floor, rows of tables were set up.

Bay stood at the front and the waves of people kept coming, filling in the space. At least two hundred people, maybe more. I stood off to the side, trying not to be in the way, but wanting to be close. The bag with her treats inside was still in my hand. It would be a breakfast of champions once things settled down and I found a spot to hang back and watch her work.

She grabbed a chair and stood on one of the tables so everyone in the back could see her. Holden stepped in behind her and I did the same, not waiting her to fall to the concrete floor.

"Hi everyone!" She waved and the crowd waved back. "I hope you all had a great break, but we're ready to do this one more time."

"Hopefully not just one!" A voice from the back shouted, and more people laughed and cheered.

"Let's make it through the next eight months in one piece. Then we'll talk. Everyone here is the best in the business, and I trust all of you to bring the songs in my head to life for an audience and give them one of the best experiences of their lives, and thank you for trusting me enough to come on this new journey and leg of the tour away from your friends and families. It means the world to me." Her eyes glistened.

The sea of expectant faces all stared at her. They were hopeful, excited and happy. So much hinged on her. Their livelihoods and their futures were in the hands of this one woman.

This wasn't a stadium like mine, where the games went on whether I was there or not.

"Now let's have an amazing rehearsal today and make this the best tour we've ever done."

Everyone cheered, clapping and chanting.

I held out my hand.

She smiled and took it, hopping down off the table, and joined in, jumping up and down in a chant that got louder and louder before breaking into screams and applause.

A game night ritual. I could feel it in my bones.

The people scattered back to whatever they'd been doing before Bay's pep talk.

After that, it was hard to keep up with where we were going.

Bay had wardrobe fittings in colorful, sequined, feathered, leather, sometimes lighted costumes. Alterations and changes were made on the fly.

Emily set me up in a spot in the wings of the stage. I finished my hot chocolate and cinnamon roll. Had Bay eaten before she picked me up? Other than a bite of my cinnamon roll after chugging half a bottle of water she hadn't eaten anything since I'd seen her.

Her face switched between smiles and laughter and intense focus whenever someone walked her through each facet of the stage. She practiced trips through the trap doors in the floor they'd be taking on tour and walked through choreography with the dancers. Lighting cues and sound cues were rehearsed until they were perfect.

And for one heart-squeezing moment, she took flight on a rig, flying out over the imaginary audience.

She kept her smile on, but by two her energy was flagging. She'd been at it for over six hours. We were in a smaller room, and Bay and twenty dancers were going over another dance routine.

Holden walked past me. I shot up from my folding chair and grabbed him. "Has she eaten?"

She hadn't been out of my sight for more than a few minutes, but I needed to make sure.

"Not yet." He dropped his tablet to his side with a tense look of annoyance, not at me, but for the same reason I'd asked him the question.

"Why not?"

"She wants to finish with the dancers, so they can go home instead of waiting for her to eat and finish things up. Trust me, I've tried to convince her three times already." From the way his nostrils flared with exasperation, I believed him. But she also signed his checks—how hard would he push against what she wanted, even if it was what she needed?

Her steps had been flagging, and breathers between running the routines stretched from a few seconds to almost a minute. Five minutes before I'd promised myself I'd step in, they finished. Everyone exchanged hugs and the dancers waved and rushed from the room.

Bay stopped for a second before she dramatically laid down on the floor with the back of her hand pressed against her forehead, chest rising and falling and her arms splayed out beside her.

She peeked with one eye open before closing it.

I got to her before Holden did, crouching beside her. "You need to eat."

Her eyes glittered with exhausted excitement and playfulness. "Only if you get a spatula to lift me up off the floor." Sweat glistened on her face and she stared deeper into my eyes. "You're not bored yet?"

I pushed a sweaty piece of hair from her forehead. "Not in the slightest."

The worried slant to her lips turned into a full-on smile.

I offered her my hands and she took them, letting me pull her all the way up.

"Hey, Holden. Can we get some food?" She braced her hands on her hips.

"Oh, you mean the food I've been trying to get you to eat for the past three hours? No, sorry, Emily ate it all." Their brother-sister vibe was in full force.

"Hey!" Emily called out from behind him.

He rolled his eyes. "Yeah, let's get you some food."

We grabbed food from the craft services set up, where there were trays of food as well as boxed meals, and found a room that felt more like a closet. It was quiet, though, and we were alone.

"You've been busy."

She nodded, unable to talk with her mouth full of turkey-and-cheese sandwich.

Finally, she was eating. I'd never been happier to see someone with mayo on the side of their mouth.

"Is it always like this?"

"Only leading up to and during a tour." She took two more bites, her cheeks filled up like a chipmunk. "There are a lot of moving parts and a lot of people to coordinate. I'm so freaking hungry. I should've grabbed another sandwich."

"I can get you one." I stood.

Her hand shot out and she grabbed me. "No, I'm good for now. I like being here with you."

The twin desires to stay with her and to get her more food warred inside me. The selfishness of wanting to stay won. "In case you didn't know, I like being here with you."

Outside the doors, the commotion was non-stop. "I had no idea all this went into a tour."

She laughed, covering her mouth with her hand. "Neither did I. The first tour, I think I slept for two days at my mom's house when I finished."

"Do you ever—"

A gentle knock broke into our quiet moment. Emily poked her head in.

"Bay, after you eat—Holden was very clear about this—after you eat, the little boy from the viral video is here. It'll be a quick meet-and-greet."

"I can go now."

Emily stared at the unfinished plate of food on her lap. "You haven't finished your food."

"I did." She handed the half-eaten sandwich to me. "I'm full. I don't want them to have to wait."

I grabbed her hand when she tried to pass me. "Bay, you haven't eaten."

She ducked down. "I know, but this kid is adorable and I want to make this special for him. He was bullied for singing my songs and I don't want to have to rush. And we only have the space for another two hours and they need to put me up into the aerial rig again."

"You're going to eat." I stood and held both our plates, following her and Emily.

The kid broke down into tears when he saw Bay. He was maybe a little over seven. The bruises on the side of his face from whoever had beaten him up had yellowed, but were still there.

A thud hit me in my chest, the kind I got right before I was dragged back to my childhood. I could feel how the stunned shock of a hit would bloom into a raging fire out from the spot where the fist had connected, spreading across skin and muscle, sometimes bone.

I gulped down air and flinched, trying not to envision the kind of hit it would take to leave a bruise that big. How his parents were standing, I'd never know. I was afraid of what I'd do if someone ever hurt my kid—I didn't know what I might be capable of. What darkness lurked in me that I'd never fully rid myself of, like a stain on my soul? Shaking it off, I focused on Bay.

She sat on the floor with the kid, showering him with so much attention and praise.

Now her determination made so much more sense.

Every few minutes, I'd sneak her another bite of something. She looked to me with thanks and spent her time singing along to her new best friend, signing every piece of tour swag they had on hand. He was ecstatic and so were his parents.

"He hadn't smiled since he was attacked, but I swear his lips were going to fall off from how happy he was from the moment the message arrived that he'd be meeting you." The little boy's mom held onto both Bay's hands with tears in her eyes.

My throat tightened. These were good parents, the kind who were torn up by someone hurting their kid. Their sadness was replaced by joy and gratitude at Bay spending a few minutes with them.

Both parents hugged her tight and posed for more pictures. Bay made the little kid promise to keep singing and told him she wouldn't be offended if they weren't her songs. They sang one together and she recorded a message to him, telling him to play it whenever he felt down.

She squeezed him tight in another hug before Holden showed up to whisk her away again back out onto the stage.

I followed and shoved a quarter of a sandwich into her hand.

"Thank you."

"You never have to ask."

She was rigged up again for another round of flying above the arena's concrete floor. The floor had no give, and Bay was currently dangling above it. I couldn't look.

Staring down at the floor, I tried not to freak the hell out.

"Not a fan of heights." Holden's shoes came into view.

"Not especially." I braced my hands on my thighs. "You're letting her push herself too hard."

"She does have a mind of her own."

Straightening, I kept my eyes focused on Holden. "And she's worried about letting the people around her down. Letting you down."

"It's a club big enough for all of us. She does what it takes to stay on top in this game."

"She's going to make herself sick."

"We've got an excellent team to make sure she doesn't this time."

"This time? Does that mean she's gotten sick before?"

Her boundary-setting needed work. People would continue to push her and take from her if she let them. And I was another person splitting her already precious time. Old hang-ups and mistakes were hard to shake, but I'd be good for her this time.

"Just learning her limits. We all need to." His gaze drifted above my head. "She'll be fine this time. You have my word."

I looked up at Holden, his gaze trained on Bay like a hawk. I believed him, but it didn't mean she'd know her limits and stick to them if there was one more thing she could do to make other people's lives easier or make them smile like that kid.

Two hours later, with the lights shutting off in the arena, we were back in the SUV and headed for our place. Not our place in the way I'd like, but as close as we could get right now.

"Your place or mine?"

She directed her gaze to the back seat. "Holden?"

The glow of the screen lit up his face. "You can sleep in longer if you stay in the suite tonight."

I made the decision before she could. "Suite it is."

"You don't have any clothes there."

"I'll figure it out. Don't worry."

She nodded sleepily, resting her head against my shoulder.

"What time does she have to be up tomorrow?"

Holden checked his tablet. "Five." He looked down again. "Six-thirty."

"Okay."

When we got to the hotel, a group of fans were camped out at the front. Eric directed the driver to the parking garage. This added more time on the trip up to the suite, but Bay sleepwalked the whole way. I didn't offer to carry her, but only because I knew she'd fight it.

Inside the suite, I led her to her bedroom, the one we'd spent a few hours in a couple weeks ago before she'd had to leave again. Undressing us both, I got her into the shower.

Her head rested against the tile, eyes barely opened, and she occasionally let out incoherent mumblings. If I hadn't been there, would she have passed out in there or lay down on the floor and gone to sleep?

More efficiently than the insistent erection between my legs would have liked, I ran the soapy loofah over her skin and down her curves.

"Thanks for spending the day with me," she mumbled.

Keeping one hand on her, I took a towel off the stack and dried her off, kissing the back of her neck and holding her against me. I wrapped the soft, fluffy fabric around her. She leaned back against the wall.

Not wanting to let her go, I wrapped my towel around my waist one-handed with the help of my teeth. By the time

I looked up, she was asleep in the corner, lips parted, legs barely holding her up.

Even after the games I did get to play in, I'd never been that tired.

Lifting her into my arms, I looked down at the woman who'd held my heart in the palm of her hand even when I didn't believe I had one. Maybe that was why—it had always been hers.

I set her down on the pillow-soft bed and grabbed a t-shirt from one of the drawers. Sliding it over her body, I climbed into bed beside her.

She sighed and curled into me.

Buried in blankets, I rested my head on hers, and the gentle wisps of her breath skirted across my neck. Leaving her would only get harder for me, and it would be so much worse when she left.

I sat on the edge of the bed, Bay wrapped around my pillow after reaching for me in her sleep. Apparently, my heated pillow was a suitable stop-gap substitute.

Being with her was like finding someone singing your name after a lifetime of silence. When I'd found her before it had been like clinging to a buoy in a hurricane. I'd been clinging onto her to keep my head above water, and it would've only been a matter of time before I'd dragged us both down.

Things were different now. We were different.

All those dreams we'd wished and hoped for had come true. So why was this the happiest I'd been in a long time? There had been moments of joy before, the kind that came from a big win or an impossible catch or checking my bank account and knowing I couldn't spend it all in a hundred lifetimes.

This contentment I felt around her was almost inde-scribable. It made me feel invincible. And it scared the shit out of me. Because living without this—having her ripped away again—after all the work I'd put in to be a man she could be proud of and the man she deserved, I wasn't sure what would happen if it all fell apart again.

Instead of focusing on those feelings, I recentered myself to right now, this moment with her. She was still here. I was still here.

I lay back down and brushed her hair off her shoulders.

She was the only woman I'd ever loved, the only woman who knew most of my story and secrets, and the only woman I'd risk everything I'd built for, not because I needed her to survive, but because that's all living would be without her—survival. Breaths taken, but not a life lived.

A gentle snore rattled in the back of her throat and she turned over.

Cracking a smile, I brushed her hair back from her face.

She rubbed her nose and snuggled in deeper to the pillow.

Sliding into the space behind her, I wrapped my arms around her and hugged her close.

Contentment settled over me like a blanket and I closed my eyes, breathing in her scent. Losing her wasn't an option this time, and I'd do whatever it took to make sure we didn't mess this up again.

~

"Are you sure we need to go?" I grabbed my cufflinks off her dresser.

Her laughter played on my heartstrings. "You don't have to come. It's a radio contest winner promo session. We'll be in and out in a couple hours. I'm sure you have better things to do." With her heels on, we were almost eye to eye. She draped her arms over my shoulders and ran her fingers through the hair at the back of my head. "Then I can come back to you."

"What could be better than spending time with you?" I kissed the tip of her nose and wrapped my arms around her. My hands brushed against her bare skin. "Is there something missing from your dress?"

The orange-and-navy dress was gathered in the high neckline, and hit just above her knee. With long sleeves, it wasn't exactly revealing, but I wasn't a fashion kind of guy.

"I need a little help." She turned, glancing over her shoulder, knowing exactly what seeing her unzipped would do to me. "Can you zip me up?"

Crouching, I decided to give as good as I got. If we were both waiting through the two hours until our night alone, I'd make sure she was just as antsy to get back to our room as I was.

I kissed her at the small of her back, holding onto her with my fingers spanning her waist.

She rocked forward, her breath hitching.

With one hand, I skimmed up her back, brushing away imaginary obstructions, only to plaster the area with whisper-soft, get-right-under–her-skin kisses.

She shivered and gasped.

I smiled against her skin and tugged on the zipper, slowly closing the metal teeth until I made it to the top. Once there, I wrapped one arm around her, pressing her tighter against me and kissed along the back of her neck before finishing the zip and closing the hook-and-eye closure.

My dick screamed at me for teasing all three of us.

Stepping in front of her, I met her glassy-eyed stare. Lips

parted, a little wobbly and flushed, she leaned into me and attacked my mouth.

I grabbed her ass, kneading and squeezing her tight.

A knock at the door was all that stopped us from ripping each other right out of our clothes.

"It's time to go." Holden's voice became my most hated sound in the world. "They just announced where we're meeting. The paparazzi are already on the move, which means fans will be next. We need to get there quickly before things become unmanageable. "

I brushed my thumb along her bottom lip. "You're going to need a touch up."

"You're going to be on Emily's shit list."

"It'll be worth it." Emily was a mini-Gwen in the making, but I'd bear her ire for a kiss from Bay any day. Taking her hand, we walked out of her bedroom. The whole team was there, coats already buttoned and ready to go.

Bay didn't have a coat. I wrapped mine around her shoulders, loving seeing her holding onto the edges of the lapels.

Inside the car, Eric sat up front. Emily and Holden were in the back row talking and texting. Bay and I sat in the middle, the seat she'd usually sit in on her own while the two in the back hammered out the details of her life and Eric took up sentry mode.

"Shit." Holden let out a long low breath.

Bay's laugh was cut short and she turned to him. "What's wrong?" Her fingers stopped kneading my thigh, meaning I could concentrate on more than her breast pressed against my chest. The tease was well worth it and kept me even closer to the edge of telling the driver to turn right around and get back to the hotel.

She followed his gaze out the tinted window to the car. "Shit."

Tension filled the car. What was supposed to be a one-hour meet-and-greet with contest winners and a first listen to a couple tracks off the album looked like a mob scene.

"I told them not to announce the location." Holden shoved his phone up to his ear, raising his voice at whoever was on the other end.

"What do we do?" My arm tightened around her waist.

Her hand, which had just been teasing me, stroked my leg to calm me.

I tried to calm myself, but it wasn't working. My pulse skyrocketed. My blood rushed in my veins with adrenaline spiking.

People were everywhere. They weren't screaming or shouting, but their anticipation was palpable from here. Photographers had also descended, large intrusive lenses primed and ready for the perfect shot.

"It'll be okay." She turned to me with a small smile and a flicker of fear. "This happens sometimes."

Eric leaned in between the front driver and passenger headrests. "We're going to circle the block. They're trying to get more security to the door. The parking garage is blocked off, so there's not another way in right now."

The building had restaurants along the bottom and offices up top. It was a standard twenty-story building of stone and glass except for the hundred people crammed in around the main entrance.

My jaw tensed.

Her hand smoothed down my shirt. "We'll be fine."

I wasn't sure if she was saying it to me or herself. My heart rammed into my ribs.

Worry thickened the air inside the car. The chatter and joking died during the four right-hand turns on the way back to the front of the building.

Every cell in my body screamed for us to turn the hell around and get her out of here.

The circle around the block didn't do much as far as security went. They were overwhelmed.

"We're going to go in through one of the restaurants instead." Eric called out from the front seat.

Our trip went straight past the main entrance, but by now people seemed to have noticed who the car belonged to, so the alternate entrance didn't stop the tide of people from swelling, only throttled it temporarily.

Bay took my coat off and handed it back to me, almost nibbling her lips before looking like she remembered her makeup and squeezing them together. "We promised the designer we'd get full shots of the dress."

She'd shivered when we got into the car, even under my jacket. My anger at the whole situation bubbled up. Why the hell would she agree to a deal where she'd freeze her ass off just for pictures?

"It's October."

"It has long sleeves. I'll be fine. We're just running straight inside." Her gaze darted out the tinted windows to the swell of people.

Bay squeezed my hand. Emily and Holden maneuvered to the door, and Eric jumped out.

The flashes went off, blindingly fast, before we even slid off our seats.

In seconds, the press was on. Whether it was strangers or Bay's team, bodies pressed against us, jostling and squeezing us on what felt like a charge up the field with a three-hundred-pound linebacker attached to each arm.

We were swept toward the entrance. The flood of people grew by the second.

Bay reached out as papers and markers were shoved into her face to try to sign memorabilia as we tried to shove toward the entrance. Her voice was strained. Her smile was stiff. Her gaze was filled with fear.

A spike of protectiveness slammed into me, shooting me straight to the edge.

More people rounded the corner. The thirty feet from the curb to the restaurant entrance felt like a fight against a riptide trying to drag us out to sea.

It happened in a blink, almost a flash. One second, she was smiling, signing autographs, struggling to move forward even with my arm around her. The next, my gaze snapped to a face. One that made the hairs on the back of my neck stand up.

It was beyond starry-eyed, bordering on unhinged.

A gap in the line of fans who clustered to squeeze in for another picture opened and the shot was taken.

The lunge was clean, snap-to-the-quarterback quick. His fingers wrapped around a shiny metal blade.

I jumped in front of her, sandwiching my body between her and the throngs of people pressing in so tightly I couldn't breathe. Or maybe I'd been holding my breath. Adrenaline screamed through my veins. White-hot rage burst free from my chest.

My fist slammed into his face. I hit him once. Twice.

The crowd parted. Screams ripped through the air.

I grabbed his hand, squeezing his wrist hard enough to crush bone until the knife clattered to the cement.

One more slam of my clenched fist into his face. Grabbing him by the shirt, I flipped him down onto the ground. He struggled to get up, face smeared with blood.

My hand shot to his throat, my fingers tightening. The cloud tinged with flecks of red and rage threatened the edges of my vision. I wanted to squeeze even tighter until his gasps and desperate clawing at my hand ended. I wanted to slam his head into the ground until he stopped moving. I wanted him to never be a threat to Bay again.

Bay. I needed to make sure she was okay.

Coming back to myself, I loosened my grip from crushing to restraining.

Eric crouched down beside him along with three other suited security guards with a set of zip ties and rolled the attacker over onto his stomach.

The adrenaline thundered through my veins, my heart sliding out of overdrive. I took a step back. Then another. A cavalcade of people flooded in, knocking into me.

A hand touched my arm. I flinched.

Bay stared at me. Not with fear, but concern. Her gaze searched my face.

I recoiled, not wanting her to look at me. Not wanting to have done this to her again. Bitter bile burned in my gut.

More security poured in around us. Holden and the rest of the team made room for the cops who'd just arrived. He caught up with us and hustled us both inside the restaurant.

No longer under the crush of people and danger, my hands shook. I clenched them and stared at the blood that covered my hands, dripping off my fingertips. The slow dotted pattern marking my path.

"Dare!"

I flinched.

"Keyton." Bay reached for me and I stepped back, banging into the table behind me. Silverware and glasses rattled.

"Bay!" Holden bellowed from the door, shoving through people. He was here. He'd take care of her.

I spun and took off. Past the tables of stunned diners through the double doors leading to the kitchen. The screams in my head quieted, leaving me only with what I'd just done.

I'd beaten a guy bloody, in front of onlookers and cameras, Bay. My hands shook, adrenaline still scorching its way through my veins. Escape. I needed to leave. To run.

Grabbing a towel from the stainless-steel rack, I wrapped it around my hands. I needed to get out of here. The glowing exit sign in the back corner called to me.

People jumped out of the way. There wasn't time to apologize for being the asshole with blood all over him in their kitchen. I wiped at my hands with the towel, staining it bright red, but the blood was still there.

I turned and rushed toward the sign. My heart raced even harder now. Bile rushed for my throat. And spots danced in front of my eyes.

In the alley, the wet grit crunched under my shoes. I checked down both ends of the alley.

The door slammed behind me, only to open a second later.

"Keyton!" Bay called after me.

My hand throbbed. I gripped the towel even tighter making my fist jump like it had a heart of its own.

"Go back inside." It was dangerous out here for her. Was she safe anywhere? "It's not safe."

Less than two steps later, she grabbed my arm, spinning me around. "Where are you going?" Her hair was mussed, the low, casual style ruined like I'd been running my fingers through it all afternoon.

Behind her, Holden and Eric hovered in the doorway. Why the hell couldn't we have come in this way?

"I need to get out of here."

She held onto my arm. "Okay, I don't think the car can fit down here, but we can meet the driver at the end of the alley." Her head whipped around.

Shaking her off, I stepped back. Wrestling with my demons wasn't over and I didn't want her near me.

"*I'm* going. You stay. Go back inside with Holden."

"You can't leave." She held onto me, her fingers gripped tight and panic in her voice.

Her worry softened me some, bringing me back to myself even more, but it still wasn't safe. She needed to go. "You'll be fine. They'll keep you safe. Just get back inside."

"I can't go back in there without you."

"You've done it for the past six years without me." I snapped, cursing myself for not being able to protect her.

She stared into my eyes and licked her lips. Her gaze dipped before shooting back up to mine. "I don't want to go back in there without you."

I ripped the towel from around my hand. "I've got another guy's blood all over me. I wanted to kill him, choke the life out of him for trying to hurt you."

"But you didn't. You stopped yourself." She pressed her hand against my chest. "No one blames you. I don't blame you. He could've hurt me. He could have hurt other people."

My heart pumped wildly against my ribcage. "I don't care about any of them. All I care about is you." I raised my hand and stilled before touching her face. Blood still covered my skin. It dripped down the side of my hand, dotting the crisp white cuff of my shirt.

Her gaze shot to my hand. "You're bleeding."

"It's not—" I stared at my hand. The bright red blood

continued to roll down my hand and off the tips of my fingers when I held it out in front of me.

Bay gripped my wrist, her fear palpable. "Holden! He's hurt." She jerked me forward, rushing toward the open door.

There was a flurry of activity, bodies and shouting, only this time, Bay held onto me. We were guided into a bathroom.

Holden cursed under his breath. "We'll have someone here in a couple seconds to get you checked out. There's someone at the door. No one who isn't supposed to come in here will get in." He gripped the edge of the window before disappearing.

Inside the bathroom, I shoved my hands under the faucet and pumped at the soap dispenser, rubbing my hand and hissing at the sharp burn. The water went from red to pink, but I kept my hands under the flowing water.

A slice down the side of my hand was where all the blood had spilled from. At least I didn't have to worry about this screwing up my non-existent playing time.

"Keyton." Bay's voice drew me from the furious scrubbing.

"I'm fine." I ran one hand over the other. The flow of blood wasn't as steady anymore.

In her hands, she clutched a handful of paper towels.

She reached for my hand.

I snatched it away, not wanting to get blood on her. "It's fine."

"Stop saying that. It's not fine. You were hurt." Her voice wobbled.

Jerking up straight, I reached for her with my uninjured hand. "It's nothing."

"It's not nothing." Her voice cracked and her eyes glistened, fingers tightening around the off-white paper towels. "You got cut protecting me."

Somehow her backing away with remorse and guilt filling her eyes like the tears she blinked back sliced even deeper than any wound.

"Hey." I lunged for her, keeping my hand away from her. Dragging her back to me, I pressed my hand against the small of her back and held her against me. "This isn't your fault."

The door burst open and the medic rushed in with a huge red bag.

After slapping on some gloves and sitting me in a chair someone brought in from the restaurant, he got to work.

The cut wouldn't even need stitches. A few butterfly bandages and some medical glue took care of it. He wrapped it in a bandage. The whole time, my gaze was locked onto Bay.

"Keep it dry. If it gets red and tender in the next week or so, you might need antibiotics. But you should go get it checked out by your doctor as well, since you work with your hands...and we need you this season." The medic offered a nervous smile and a fist bump before leaving. A gentle thud of the door signaling his departure.

Bay stood with her arms wrapped around herself. Holden had brought in another chair for her after she insisted on staying after letting us know the event had been cancelled and we'd be leaving as soon as I was checked out and we gave our reports to the police.

She slipped out of the bathroom and another officer came in to take my statement while Bay gave hers.

My gaze stayed trained on the door, waiting for her to come back and not wanting to look at my blood-stained sleeve.

Bay rushed back in and the officer asked her for her autograph. Her fucking autograph. She'd been attacked and people still wanted her. A dot of my blood stained the sleeve of her dress and here she was signing autographs for fans. I didn't want it to make me bitter, but a part of me wanted to lash out and lock her up in my apartment where she'd be safe.

The pit in my stomach widened into a cavern. "I'm sorry."

Her head shot up. The rest of her following along with it. "Stop saying that. You have nothing to be sorry about."

"I went after that guy."

"Are we doing this again? You mean you went after the attacker with the knife? The one who could've hurt me or anyone else out there?" Her cold hands cupped my cheeks as she crouched in front of me in her heels. "You took him out, restrained him and let the professionals take over. You have nothing to be sorry about.

"*I'm* sorry."

It was my turn to jerk my head back. "Mind filling me in on what *you* have to be sorry about?" I pulled her onto my lap, the throb and burn in my hand easily ignorable when I held her. Having her this close helped make everything feel less terrible. She hadn't backed away or looked at me like she was scared. She hadn't had to scream my name to get me off the guy.

There were no looks of recrimination from anyone.

A shudder shot through her. She stared at her shoes. A bit of bloody gauze rested beside her previously immaculate, but now scuffed and streaked yellow heels.

"He was coming after me. He could've hurt someone out there because of me." Anguish dripped from every syllable.

I ran my fingers under her chin and turned her toward me. "You don't get to blame yourself for that crazy guy."

She rubbed her nose against mine. "I'll make you a deal. You don't blame yourself and I'll try not to blame myself."

I didn't like that deal. I didn't like the way she said she'd try, when I knew it weighed heavily on her.

"Let's go ho—to my place."

27

BAY

"There's outdoor seating, if you wanted to watch from out there." The skybox attendant pointed toward the door leading out to the three rows of stadium-style seats on the mini balcony.

"Food is right over here." He pointed to the seven—seven!—chafing dishes. "If you'd like more, we can arrange for it to arrive right before kick-off. There's also a full-service bar and hot apple cider. The servers will be here in a few minutes."

Unless I'd been infected by a tapeworm, there was no way in hell I'd need more food. Did he think I was actually two pre-teens balanced on each other's shoulders looking for snacks?

"It's okay. I don't need anyone, I'm good to serve myself."

What would feel more awkward than being in this Presidential Club Suite on my own? Being here with a few servers and a bartender to watch me watch the game all by myself.

Those same people might surreptitiously take a picture or two of Bay Post Attack! While Holden and Emily usually handled my social media, I'd posted a note in the aftermath. The questions about Keyton being there with me and what happened given his past were mounting, and I wanted to set the record straight myself, to tell them exactly what happened, how he'd saved me and how the attacker was in custody.

Holden or Emily could've done it, but I felt the first post about me and Keyton should be from me. Everyone needed to know how much he meant to me and how grateful I was for what he had done. I didn't want anyone to think this was even the slightest bit of a return to the guy he'd once been. He'd truly changed, and I didn't want there to be a doubt in his mind that I believed that was true.

There was a deluge of support, millions of comments, likes, and shares. There were even more questions about me and Keyton. We were social media official now. The rest of the world had their window into us being together. I still wasn't sure how I felt about that, but I didn't want him to think there was a second thought in my mind about how much I needed him. How much I loved him.

My mom had been as shocked as anyone else to see him there. I'd never told her what happened between us back in Greenwood or LA, so she'd been happy we'd reconnected in time and he'd protected me. She even told me I should bring him to the house the next time I got there. She sounded happy I'd found someone, that someone was there for me. Someone not on payroll.

We'd also rescheduled the listen along event, inviting the radio winners to the hotel instead of going to them since we didn't want the location leaked again. It was a mess, but PR-wise, it had gone as well as it could. Mental health-wise, I could pretend with the best of them that I didn't feel like my heart might explode when more than a few people were around me or someone bumped into me.

"All our food and bar service is included with the suite." It was only then that I'd realized he'd been talking that whole time.

"And I appreciate it and I'm sure they'd do a wonderful job. There will be a hefty tip left behind for them, but I'd like to hang out on my own. No need to bring anyone else in.

"The food is already here, right?" I lifted the lid of the chafing dish. Buffalo chicken dip. I grabbed a plate and spooned some out, along with some celery. Taking a giant scoop, I shoved it into my mouth proving I could indeed serve and feed myself.

Covering my mouth with the back of my hand, I mumbled. "See. All good."

The man in the suit with a shiny silver name tag cycled through a few different reactions before settling on the best one. "If that's your preference. I'll let the team know."

"Thank you. And if there's anything anyone wanted signed, they can leave it outside with Eric. We'll also have some swag for the team as well." I extended my hand to shake his.

His whole demeanor shifted from defeated to delighted. He grabbed onto my hand with both of his and shook it like he was working an 1800s-water pump. "Thank you so much. And I wanted to say, I loved your last album. My *Remember Me* playlist has been on repeat for the past three months. It's helped me through some hard times." His eyes filled with barely contained tears.

These moments, when I saw how happy my songs made someone, were the best and hardest ones. My songs could be there while someone was facing down the rough patches in life. It made it all the more important to keep going. It made stepping back feel like an impossibility, if even one person could be touched by my music.

I squeezed his upper arm. "You're very welcome."

"Your lyrics—I love them so much. There's so much to them that everyone who covers you gives me goosebumps. I have a few of them mixed in there too. Have you heard any?"

"I've heard a few. Have you ever listened to Spencer Hayes?" He'd love the new songs—hopefully. Maybe I should talk to Holden about putting out more song-writing feelers.

"No, never, but I'll check him out on my next break." He backed out of the room, giddy and grinning.

Laughing, I went back to my plate of chicken dip, stealing another celery-loaded bite before dumping the plate. Maybe I could get them to give the staff all the leftover food too. There was no sense in it all going to waste.

I wandered around the big empty space all on my own. It was better than the alternative, but once again I was hit with the deserted loneliness of this moment. I wrapped my arms around myself and stared out at the stadium full of people in the stands sharing drinks, laughing, and cheering together.

I'd told Keyton, Holden and Emily over and over that I was fine after the attack, but being on my own had gotten harder, just like being around other people had.

Someone could've gotten hurt. Keyton could've gotten hurt beyond the small cut. Alone, I worried. I jumped at loud noises. Around too many people, I kept thinking of what would happen if someone else showed up wanting to hurt me.

Even now, outside the doors, Eric had brought on someone else for security. Holden had found a conference room to stake out. So much for being alone. Other than when I was with Keyton, this was as safe as I'd felt alone in the past week.

Behind me, the door to the suite opened. I jumped. Instead of the catering and bartending staff, it was two faces I hadn't expected.

"Bay!" Jules and Marisa walked into the skybox with giddy squeals. These weren't like the ones from fans, but like ones from friends—the same kind Felicia and Piper greeted me with in the far-too-infrequent visits we squeezed in. I was determined to make those more frequent after the tour, when I wouldn't be the shitty friend who always bailed or showed up an hour late.

They each hugged me and I hugged them back, happy I wasn't going to be the only one in this big box all by myself.

"What are you guys doing here?" I looked at them, trying to figure out if I'd missed a message about them coming.

"A last-minute thing. Keyton mentioned to LJ about you coming to the game, and of course, he told me. We didn't want you to have to sit through the game all by yourself, so here we are." Marisa did a showcase hand sweep. Her smile faltered a bit. "I hope that's okay." She glanced around the room like they might be intruding.

"It's perfect. I was wondering how I'd eat all this food myself. Keyton didn't have to spring for the twenty-person package."

"If we'd had more warning, we could've invited Elle and Seph, you didn't get to meet them yet, but they're awesome."

"He probably didn't want to spread the word around too much." I picked at the hem of my sweater until I realized how it might sound. Lurching forward, I waved my hands in front of me. "Not that he thought any of you would talk about it or anything. Just the more people who know...the more there's a chance..." I dropped my head. Frustration simmered in my chest that I couldn't be invited to a game like anyone else.

Jules rubbed my shoulder. "It's okay, Bay. We get it. Well, not 'get it' as in know what you're going through, but we understand. Especially after what happened earlier this week. Are you okay?" She offered a reassuring squeeze.

"I'm okay." My knee-jerk interview response.

"You're stronger than me." Marisa added. "A guy attacked me during senior year. Keyton came to my rescue there too. He knows how to handle himself."

"He does." I looked between the two of them. This was a conversation friends had, not someone looking for a juicy tweet or sound clip. They were concerned about me. Worried for Bay, their kind-of friend, not Bay, the singer.

"But he took the guy out and LJ got me home. I had to sleep in his bed that night, I was still so freaked out." She shuddered.

"When I'm with Keyton it helps with the nightmares. They're not so scary now. More like waking up from a dream where you feel like you're falling and less like a guy is coming after me with a knife. But I'll get there."

"If you ever need to talk, you have my number. Or you can get my number from Keyton." She laughed.

Jules hugged me again. "We're all just glad you're okay. I can't imagine. We thought Marisa's cooking was dangerous." Pulling back, her eyes were filled with glittery giggles.

"Hey!" Marisa piped up from behind me. "Under LJ's tutelage I've learned how to cook. I even made him dinner last night."

Jules leaned in. "Brave man."

Marisa glared. "I can hear you. We can't all be baking

virtuosos. If LJ and I ever get divorced, I'm marrying one of your chocolate chunk brownies."

"You bake?" I turned to Jules.

She ducked her head and tucked her hair behind her ear. "A little."

Marisa slung her arm around my shoulder. "She's being infuriatingly humble. Her cooking web series has racked up over fifty million views."

"Marisa..." Jules's warning chiding was smile-inducing. This was the kind of bragging only a person who loved someone else could do, the kind they'd never do for themselves.

"That's freaking amazing, Jules. Can I try some of your stuff?" I grabbed one of the buckets of popcorn. The salty-sweet caramel had been singing to me from across the room.

"You don't have to. It's not a big deal."

Marisa's arm blocked Jules's attempt at backing away. "It's a huge deal."

Jules's gaze shot to the ceiling. "Marisa. We're talking to Bay here. She's got fifty million views on one video. I've racked up fifty million over six years."

Here came the part I hated, the part where other people shied away from talking to me about their lives because they didn't live up to mine.

"Don't downplay what you've accomplished. People have a nose for talent. Do I get to try some of what you've made?"

"You don't have to. It's not a big deal."

"Her brown butter and toffee chocolate chip cookies are mind-blowing. Her salted caramel chocolate chunk cookies with the espresso chips are life-changing. Her caramel crunch cookies are soul-exploding."

"Please excuse her, the food poisoning over the years has poisoned her mind."

"You think I can't appreciate soul-exploding caramel crunch cookies?"

"No, but I'm sure people are always asking you for things or trying to get you to try them. I know you're busy."

"And you know who I love to do things for? People who never think to ask. Do you have a store?"

"No, I bake at home and donate it to local food banks. Once the online show took off, the volume of orders had me up almost 18 hours a day trying to fulfill them. Now I only bake for special events."

Marisa bit into a buffalo wing. "She charges through the nose for them too."

I laughed. "I'd gladly pay through the nose for some."

"You don't have to. Friends always eat free." Her last word was punctuated by a hip bump.

A heartwarming hip bump made me like the two of them even more.

Once Marisa discovered the full bar set up, she set our hot apple cider aside and moved straight to cranberry mimosas and snowflake martinis.

With our plates loaded up, we sat at the bar facing out over the stadium in the leather barstools.

"Do you two come to all the home games?" I inhaled a mini-cheeseburger slider.

"I try to." Jules pointed a mozzarella stick at herself. "Marisa likes to antagonize LJ and pretend she won't show, but she usually does."

Marisa crunched on some nachos. "I've got to keep him on his toes. Have you been to a game before?"

I shook my head. "Only the final one at training camp back when Keyton first started, but it wasn't a game like this." My hand swept out in front of me across the windows toward the stadium teeming with people.

Kick off began and the crowd was on their feet for most of the first quarter. It ended with a 16-14 score and no game play for Keyton.

"He's going to be upset he's not out there." I stress-munched the caramel corn.

"I know it upsets him, but man, what I wouldn't give for Berk to have a rest. I swear he spends more time in the ice bath than he does the actual bath."

"You should hear LJ walking down stairs. A skeleton on a xylophone would make less noise."

"How do you deal with all that?" I looked between them both. The slice on his hand had sent me into a panic, but watching him get hurt on a weekly basis would be so hard—even harder because I knew it was what he wanted. He'd dreamed of doing this his whole life. How could I keep myself sane and still watch him put his body on the line?

Marisa set down her drink with a wistful look out the massive window. "They love it. One-hundred-percent, no-regrets love it. Whatever happens after this season or the next, they only have a short window for their dream. I could never tell him not to wring every last ounce he can out of it."

Keyton got the superficial benefits but not the dirty, grimy, charging-down-the-field breathless kind of satisfaction. I could feel how much it hurt him not to live every bit of his dream. To feel he never got a shot.

It would be like asking me to get up on stage night after night and lip-sync someone else's words. Slowly, it would dismantle me brick by brick.

"Time to give you the full Philly football experience." Marisa slid off her stool.

"What does that mean?" I looked to Jules who laughed into her hand.

"It means gear up ladies, we're going outside." She

pointed toward the seats on the other side of the glass as if we'd be trekking up the Himalayas. "At least for a little bit, so I can tell LJ I haven't gotten too soft and stayed inside the whole time." A sheepish look crept onto her face.

Gathering provisions, we migrated outside, bundled up with parkas and blankets provided in the suite, our breath escaping in puffs in front of our faces. The seat warmers were handy, as were the gloves, hat and blankets over our laps, but my cheeks were icy. The three of us huddled together, laughing and sipping spiked apple cider.

"One of the downfalls of being up so high." Wind whipped at my cheeks.

"I love the man, but I'm lasting half a quarter out here, tops." Marisa bounced up and down in her seat.

Jules breathed into her hands. "None of us have to worry about freezing eggs. My ovaries have to be rock solid at this point."

"Have you looked into that?"

Both their heads swung in my direction. Totally not an awkward topic to bring up with two people I barely knew.

"Have you?"

My guard went up like it always did. I'd thought about it. I wasn't thirty yet, but I'd heard freezing them as young as possible increased the odds later on. Maybe my next album would flop and people would forget about me. Or maybe my life would get even more insane before I flung myself off the pop star train.

A part of me longed for a little girl with Keyton's eyes or a little boy with his devil-may-care smile.

"No, there was an article in Cosmo or another magazine. It was an interesting read. Are you guys planning on having kids soon?" My gulps were way too big for how hot the drink was. The apple cider burned on the way down.

Steam wafted up from Marisa's mug. "We're thinking about it, but LJ doesn't want to be traveling once they're here, so we're waiting to see how this season goes."

"Same. Berk is nervously excited about kids—even more now with Reece and Seph being pregnant."

Keyton had talked about them. "Those are the two who were supposed to come to SeptemberWeen. She's the one who put out the sex ad in college and he answered it?"

They laughed.

Marisa wrapped the blanket tighter around herself. "She's so lucky Reece showed up by mistake and not a total creeper."

Jules tucked hers up around her shoulders. "Do you think they'll tell that story to their kids?"

"Well, darling children, Mommy was looking to lose her vitginity, asked Daddy how big his dick was and that's when he fell in love."

The hot liquid burned on the way out my nose. I'd done more spit takes in the past month than I had in most of my life. Scrambling, I grabbed some napkins. Jules grabbed some and dabbed me down.

"She did not ask him that!"

Even more laughter. Jules wiped at the cider spot on my lap. "She did. It was question number one."

Marisa chimed in. "I think it was number three. The first was how long he could last. The girl knew what was important to her."

This time we all dissolved into laughter.

The quarter started with a teeth-rattling whistle blowing through the speakers—or maybe it was just the cold trying to rattle them out of my head.

The winter wind was way colder than I'd have expected for late October. It almost tasted like snow in the air.

Marisa waved. "We're on the big screen." She pointed at the massive screen opposite us in the stadium.

Jules waved too.

Their names popped up on the screen.

Marisa Saunders-Lewis. Wife - LJ Lewis.

Jules Vaughn. Wife - Berk Vaughn.

Bay.

No designation. Not that there should be. Keyton and I hadn't been hiding, but my post hadn't called him my boyfriend. I hadn't wanted to spring that on him. And our status had been semi-overshadowed by the man with the knife.

But seeing my name up there all alone didn't have the same appeal it once had.

For the first time, I wanted the notation, the modifier to my name showing I had some connection to the outside world, that I wasn't all on my own. That I was part of a couple. Part of one with Keyton.

28

KEYTON

The game had been close—so close I hadn't gotten my chance on the field. But the congratulations when the final play ended with a failed drive into the end zone by Atlanta had made it feel like I'd held back the whole opposing team on my own.

Anyone else would be jumping right along with the team, excited we were one game closer to the playoffs. But the gnawing in my chest grew with every second slipping off the game clock.

Leaving Berk and LJ behind, I left the locker room. There wasn't even a need to take a shower.

The post-game conference was a joke as always. A barrage of questions to me in my pristine jersey while the rest of the guys were grimy and still sweating from busting their asses out on the field.

Questions were lobbed my way like anything I'd done had an impact on the outcome. I always waited for the sneers or taunts from guys on the team about how useless I was, but they never came. They seemed as happy as anyone to bank on my good luck, either because they believed in it or because they loved using it to get inside the other team's head.

Knowing Wisconsin was out made the walls in the packed room of folding chairs feel like they were closing in on me, ready to twist and bend the metal. The trade deadline was in less than two weeks and there hadn't been a word from Ernie. And there wouldn't be.

I slung my duffel over my shoulder and left, even more eager to get to Bay, to make sure there hadn't been any issues, and to see what she'd thought of her first pro game.

Jules and Marisa waved from their spot beside the locker room door. Jules tugged the zipper up on her coat. "Thanks for letting us keep her company."

"Thanks for doing it."

Marisa rolled her eyes. "Like you'd have to ask twice. It's what we do when there's a new woman in a Fulton U guy's life. She's awesome by the way. But I'm sure you knew that already."

A feather-lightness filled my chest at how quickly they'd accepted her. They'd dropped everything after hearing she'd be watching the game all by herself. "I did."

Berk and LJ joined them a few seconds later and they all walked off toward the exits.

Instead of Bay waiting in the emptying hallway leading to the players' exit, Holden stood beside Eric with his hands shoved into his black pea coat. "Bay wanted to come down to congratulate you on the win."

Glancing up and down the hall, I saw that there were fewer people than during a game, but still a lot more than I'd like. After what had happened earlier in the week, her hesitancy about crowds made a lot more sense.

I strode over to him, unclenching my fists and battling against the anger burning in my chest. Had he forgotten what had happened less than a week ago? "Tell her no. It's not safe. I'll meet her." I searched the hall, hoping not to catch a glance of her.

His chin jutted out. "She wanted to greet you after your game."

"There are too many people."

"Obviously it was a risk she was willing to take."

"Isn't your job to make sure there aren't any risks?" I pointed to the two of them.

Holden's glower grew to a glare. "Removing risk is impossible. Mitigating risk is my job. She's not out here in a bikini singing into a microphone announcing she's here, is she?"

My jaw clenched.

"Do you want to see her or should we whisk her away and roll her in bubble wrap before coming back to carry you to her on a litter?" His caustic dryness grated my nerves.

I stepped back and loosened my grip on the shoulder strap of my duffel. My annoyance and anger at not playing was rearing its head at Holden being between me and Bay. I took a deep breath and another step back.

"Is she through there?"

Holden rocked back, caught off guard by my change in tactics. "Yeah. The car will be ready whenever you two are. She wanted to spend tonight with you."

I nodded, walking toward the door.

"It's costing her..." His lips tightened and his hand shot out, grabbing my arm. "All this time with you is costing her. I wanted you to know that. I wanted to make sure you weren't taking it for granted."

"I'm not." Our stare-off lasted for a few more seconds before his chin dipped and he let go.

The frosted window on the glass door was between me

and her. I shook off the tension from the game and my run-in with Holden, not wanting it to touch her.

She jumped when the door opened before smiling once I stepped inside out of the sharp light from the hallway.

"Great game." She glanced over my shoulder toward the closed door. Her shoulders were still tense.

I bit back the knee-jerk reaction to tell her all the reasons it hadn't been my game to win. "Thank you."

"Sorry for causing the sideshow out there with Holden and Eric, but I wanted to come down to see you like everyone else." Her steps toward me were slow and measured, unsure and timid.

A weight was hefted onto my shoulders at her uncertainty. "I'm always happy to see you. I'm glad you came down. How was it watching with Jules and Marisa?"

Some of the tension loosened. "They're hilarious. A lot of fun to hang out with. You're lucky you've got such a great group of friends around you." Noises picked up in the hallway.

"Everyone's finally showered up and changed, ready to celebrate their win."

Her half-hearted laugh didn't instill a lot of confidence in how well she'd handled the aftermath of the attack.

"Are you ready to get out of here?" I held out my hand.

Her gaze jumped from the door to my hand. Relief radiated off her and she took it, lacing her fingers through mine.

Pulling the hood on her sweater up over her head and pulling sun glasses out of her front pocket, she shoved them onto her nose. "Ready."

In the best disguise we had, we left the room. Eric took the front and Holden the back, both alert, same as me, but not conspicuous. Stadium security was also here, so my fear wasn't as heightened, but my concern for Bay was.

The trip to my apartment was fast, although I felt more like we were two kids being dropped off at the movies by our overprotective dads. In this case, though, every bit of help to keep Bay safe was okay in my book.

Inside, I flicked on the lights and scanned my apartment. Signs of Bay were here. A sweater she'd left. Comfy slippers she'd picked up a few weeks ago. A pair of throw pillows from Ikea on the gray couch. It felt like a home. Like our home.

I ordered pizza, poured us both a glass of wine, and sat on the couch beside her. She flicked through the movie selection.

"I might explode after all the food I had at the game." She cupped her hands in front of her stomach, puffing out her cheeks.

"No problem. You can watch me eat it, then."

"I've had more junk food today than I've had in a long time. It's been way too long."

"You have been living under unusual circumstances for a while."

"Totally missing out." She handed me the remote. "You choose."

Her fingers traced the rim of her wine glass. "November 3rd will be here soon." Her voice sounded faraway. Unfocused.

"It's when you fly out." The day I'd tried to prepare for, but I knew would hit me like a sledgehammer when it arrived.

"To London."

"How do you feel about it?" I knew how it made me feel —like I was preparing to lose the one person who I couldn't live without. The scary inevitability of our separation that could last weeks or months at a stretch loomed.

She hugged me tight, burying her face in my chest. Her heart pounded horror-movie quick. "I don't want to go without you, but you have a life and a career just like I do."

I brushed my hand over her head. "We've already made the plans for when we'll see each other next." After Christmas. After the end of my season, after playoffs, but before the National Championship. The only gap we could swing.

Her fingers tightened in my shirt. "I know."

I ran my hands across her back, wishing I could always protect her. "You're still freaked out about what happened."

She shook her head. "He didn't even get close to me. I know it's stupid." Her voice was riddled with embarrassment.

I tipped her chin up. "You have every right to feel the way you feel right now. It never should've happened. No one should have to live with the fear and situations you've been put in."

"Holden said the cops found out he'd been following me ever since I got to Philly. Not all the time, but enough that it's a little scary. He could've attacked at any time. He traveled up from Delaware."

Forcing my muscles not to clench, I held her close. "He's still in custody, right?" He'd been following her since she got here and I'd never seen him, never even thought an attack could happen. It showed how right she'd been to be wary of public situations, and here I was trying to get her out more. I was three seconds from wrapping her in bubble wrap and tucking her into my bed.

Rationality took over. I couldn't hide her away. She'd been living this life long before I reentered hers.

Brushing her hands against her red eyes, she sat up and nodded. "There were enough witnesses that they don't even need me there."

"Is Eric bringing on more security?"

"Yes, but on the tour it's different. I barely see the outside of the hotel, tour bus or stadium. It's a lot easier to contain."

A birdcage existence. I hated the necessity of it. I hated that it gave me the smallest bit of relief to know that without me around she'd probably go back to how she'd been living before, with fewer gaps for people getting close to her. And I hated how those connections were stolen from her to keep her safe.

"Can you do it?"

She laughed. "I don't exactly have a choice. Besides, that's what booze is for, right?"

"It'll burn like a motherfucker on the way back up if you're puking before every show." Was this how she normally coped on the road? Drinking to dull her nerves?

Her back stiffened and she shot up from the couch. "What's that supposed to mean?" With folded arms, she paced in front of me.

I scrubbed my hands down over my face. This wasn't about my question. It was about her fears and worries. I'd seen the difference between Performance Bay and Musician Bay. They didn't come close to each other in terms of how she lit up during each piece of her world. "Are you happy?"

"I'm living the life anyone would dream about. My face is on billboards. I get to see the world. I have people who'll do anything for me. Get anything for me."

"That wasn't the question I asked." I leaned forward, pressing my palms together and resting them against my lips.

Coming at her like this hadn't been the right way. I needed to back off, so she didn't feel like I was attacking her choices, but to show her I'd been there.

"My dad died four and a half years ago. Cirrhosis." I

tapped my pointer fingers against my lips. "He must've been on his last legs when he showed up in California."

She stopped pacing. My subject change catching her off guard. "I'm sorry. Had—had you spoken to him before then?"

"No. He tried to contact me a few times in LA, but I refused to let him cause more trouble for me. And I stopped letting me cause more trouble for me—at least I tried to." The sound escaping my lips teetered on the edge of laughter.

"That messed with my head for a while—him dying. The night I found out, I'd just finished my first season off the practice squad. I got a nice signing bonus. I'd been good with my money when I was on the practice squad, but felt like blowing it all." The edge of the cliff I'd been standing on had disintegrated out from under me in a snap.

"Knox and I had a wild night out in Vegas. Got blitzed beyond belief. Almost got into a few fights. I'd been coming to practice drunk too. What the hell did it matter if I wasn't playing? I made it on the team. Had the money. Had the championship ring. And I was trying my damnedest to flush it all away." The vise in my chest tightened telling her all this, opening myself up to let her know how fucked up I'd been.

"I thought it would be a great idea to take a helicopter ride over the Grand Canyon, show up somewhere and land like I was one of the guys out of Entourage. Knox had hit his limit and he was done for the night. We got into a fight. Something stupid." I squeezed my eyes shut. It had been him telling me it was time to go back to the hotel.

But my attitude had been 'fuck him'. My dad was dead, there was no one left on the planet who could tell me what to do.

"So I decided to go by myself. I didn't need anything or anyone."

I rubbed my hands together. "What I wanted was to be numb, and to test the depths of my numbness by doing something exhilarating. With a bottle of Jack Daniels and more money than a twenty-three-year-old should have, I went to look for my big adventure."

Her arm tightened around my shoulder. "What happened?"

"For the first twenty minutes, sweeping views, aerial tricks and a downturn in my alcohol tolerance. I sat with my head against the glass looking down at all the people living their lives. At the taillights moving through the streets. None of it felt real. I didn't feel real." Sweat beaded on my forehead. My pulse ratcheted up and my throat tightened.

"The life I was living was unrecognizable from what I'd had growing up in Greenwood. But there I was, alone with a bottle of booze, having fought with someone I loved like a brother."

She crouched in front of me, her hand reaching out. Fingers wrapped around my forearm. "And when you landed things were different."

"Not exactly." I closed my hand over hers, centering myself on this moment. I drew a shuddering breath to help me get through the rest. I was safe here with her.

She scooted around to sit back on the couch beside me.

"First, it took a little engine failure." I shuddered, sweat beading along my hairline thinking back to the stomach-plummeting feelings. My fingers gripped the edge of the couch, and it was hard to breathe.

I'd lived through a lot of shit, but I'd never doubted I'd make it to the other side. I might have been bruised, beaten, and battered, but I'd known I'd survive. Free-falling in the helicopter was the first time I'd felt the cold finger grip of death on the back of my neck.

"The pilot recovered, although he was probably just a few sheets in the wind behind me. But for the ten-second free fall—god, ten seconds feels like a long time when you think you're plummeting toward your death." There hadn't even been time to yell. No chance to scream or shout. All sound had been clogged in my throat by fear.

When we'd landed, I'd literally kissed the ground, sunk to my knees with my hands clenched on the back of my head and my nose touching solid ground. "I got a little clarity on what I was doing to myself. On who I was in danger of becoming.

"Drowning myself in alcohol, puking before practice from hangovers, I was trying to kill myself and ruin my life. I'd vowed to myself I'd never be like my father. I'd never do what he did." I'd started working with Monica a few days after that on a recommendation from some of the guys who'd had to see her for anger management sanctions.

"I worked my way through it. It sure as hell wasn't easy. It took a long time to figure out that he was never really my father. Not in the way I deserved, and not in a way that allowed him to teach me what it was to be a man. He had so much anger in him, and in a way, him dying freed me from so much of mine. If I hadn't changed, it would've eaten me up inside." There had been a lot of questioning of my humanity when I'd first realized how good his death had been for me.

"The helicopter gave me two gifts: a slap in the face to wake up and start seeing a therapist, and a crippling fear of helicopters."

Her head jolted a bit.

"Sometimes I'll wake up at night feeling like I'm free-falling, not only through the air, but also back toward my old path. Just hearing the rotor blades can send a cold panic running down my spine."

"At SeptemberWeen...that's why you didn't want to go up."

I nodded, feeling a bit like a coward. With my feet solidly on the floor I could be up high, like staring out my windows. But once my soles left the ground, all bets were off.

"But you let me go."

"My hang-ups aren't for me to force onto you. You were happy and excited to go."

"You were freaking out the whole time, weren't you?"

"Berk and LJ helped distract me, but yes. I was definitely losing my shit for a good portion of your ride. If you love what you're doing and can't imagine doing anything else, I'm behind you one hundred percent. But I know what it's like to have everything you've ever dreamed of and still feel like your life is spiraling out of control."

Her head dipped and her fingers brushed over the back of mine, sandwiching mine. She stared into my eyes and her mouth moved with soundless words, like they were being strangled from her throat. "I don't know what I want."

The silence became palpable, so thick I could taste it. It felt like a lance through my heart. I wanted her to choose me. Selfish as it was, I wanted her to say screw it, she wasn't going to London, and she'd call it all off to be with me.

"I came back." She clasped her hands together.

"To my apartment. You told me."

She looked back up at me with tears shimmering in her eyes. "No, before that." Her voice cracked.

I leaned forward, resting my forearms on my thighs. "What? When?"

A shuddering breath, whispered past her lips. "A month after I left."

"After you got the guitar."

Her nostrils flared and she looked down at her hands. "When I sent you the text. I was already back."

I sucked in a breath. "You were in town." She had come back, so much sooner than I'd thought—just as I'd begged her to in my mind.

"I was at the hotel. The one you stopped at with Knox's parents. The one by the beach. I saw you and I sent the messages to you."

My eyes slammed shut. The final 'please' of her message nearly toppled me.

But once Marcie and Dale arrived in town I had an easier time pretending. "It was a bad time for me."

"You looked so good. So happy. Lighter than I'd seen you the whole time we were together."

"Knox had spent two days sobering me up and forcing me to sleep. There had been a three-day break in practices, so I'd drowned myself in a bottle, more than a few. I'd felt like I was being fattened up like a Thanksgiving turkey."

"I-I didn't know."

"I know, that was the whole point. I'd already turned their son into my keeper, the least I could do was not add another person to the worry watch list." I had no illusions about what it was, but I couldn't slam on the brakes. If anything, I'd cut the lines and was looking for the steepest drop I could find.

"By the time I'd worked up the nerve to respond, I'd realized I had nothing to offer you. Then I finally changed my number to keep the temptation to call you back to me from the new life you'd started."

Tears glinted in her eyes. "I wanted to come back. I wanted to come back to you."

"I was a fucking mess, Bay." I cupped her cheek. "And know now how things worked out, I'd have snapped that phone in half, if it meant you didn't come back to play nurse maid to me."

Her eyes glistened. "Six years, Keyton. All I had was the music. It's what kept me going."

I brushed at the tears gathering at the corners of her eyes. "We're here now. We have the rest of our lives to make up for lost time."

But there was a part of me that wanted to keep her here and safe, keep everyone else away who might upset her or put the look of fear in her eyes. The music had been there for her when she'd thought she'd lost me, but my heart had always belonged to her.

She loved the music, but I didn't want her throwing up before performances or needing to be medicated to perform.

A knock sliced through the tension like a gasping breath freeing us from the crushing intensity of expectations and impending questions.

I grabbed the pizza and two plates for us.

She refilled our wine glasses and tucked her feet up under her legs on the couch.

"Your life is your life. Whatever you choose and however you want to live it, I want you to know I'm there for you. We'll make it work. We'll make us work." I squeezed her hand to reassure her I wouldn't be another person who wanted a piece of her without giving all of myself in return.

The conversation was slower. Gears turned in Bay's head. She was here with me, but also mulling over everything I'd said.

God, I hoped I hadn't fucked this up royally.

Going to my cabinets, I pulled out her favorite movie snack, Goobers and popcorn. I found the perfect movie. "I know it's a little early in the year for this, but I figured it's always time for the perfect Christmas movie."

She relaxed slowly, and by the time Nakatomi Plaza came into view on the screen, she'd shifted, resting her back against my chest. I wrapped my arms around her, but there was a hesitancy, almost like she was waiting for me to spring another bomb on her to rip us apart again.

I'd bide my time and do it the right way this time. I'd give her the time and space she needed, because I couldn't survive losing her again.

29

BAY

"I have a surprise for you." He turned off the engine and turned to me in the passenger seat.

The trip across the bridge to New Jersey had been unexpected, but never unwelcome. A short drive, sitting next to Keyton, listening to the radio and singing along to old favorites together was wonderful. Outside the city, where the houses became more spread out and people on the streets were fewer and farther between, it felt safer. Quieter. No overwhelming crowds were ready to emerge on a moment's notice.

It was almost a cruel joke that we'd found this window of time together right now and one couldn't be cleared in December to see Piper for her birthday. I'd sent her a message to check in on her, but hadn't heard back. Maybe Mark had told her I couldn't make it—again.

Peering out the front window, I looked up at the two-story red brick home nestled on a sprawling lot with trees and hedges around the perimeter of the property.

"Where are we?"

"Come on. You'll see." He popped his door open and jumped out.

It felt like everyone had jumped into distraction mode since the attack. They seized any chance to take my mind off it. The police reports had been filed. The social media response continued to be overwhelming. The emotional fallout was lessening, especially when I was near Keyton.

I opened my door. "What kind of surprise?" I asked over the hood of the car.

He rounded the front and brushed right past my question.

The house was a big question mark. Had he bought it? It allayed some of the fear I'd had about him possibly moving to another city. Philly being on the East Coast meant flight connections would be a lot easier.

"We have the whole day cleared."

"What exactly for?" My fingers walked up his arm to his shoulder, thoughts of why we had even left the bedroom simmering in my head, ready to crank the fire up a notch. However, he worked this out with Holden, and I was game, especially since we had less than a week left until London.

"So many questions. You're so impatient." His hiding-something smile sent my stomach into somersaults.

He led me up the stone-paved path lined with knee-high shrubs and fall flowers.

"Whose house is this?" I tugged on his arm.

"A rental for a special occasion." The smile wasn't any less mischievous.

A double knock and we waited. For what or who, I had no idea.

The door flew open. My gaze swung from Keyton to the doorway.

They could've probably heard the shrill scream from two states away.

Standing wedged in the doorway, Piper and Felicia stood beside each other with red-carpet-wide grins and the bouncy excitement that only came from seeing old friends.

We collapsed into a huddle of laughter and limbs, backstopped by Keyton keeping us from falling over onto the walkway bushes.

"What are you guys doing here?" I may have squealed. So sue me! This was Piper and Felicia.

"I flew in last night." Piper bounced and squeezed me harder.

Felicia squeezed my hands. "I got in this morning."

"But...what? How?"

They both looked past me to the man with his hand resting on the small of my back. "Keyton."

I turned and stared up at him. "You invited them to see me."

His gaze dipped, head tilted and caught my eye. "I thought you could use a ladies' day."

My eyes flooded with an emotional avalanche. Blinking and staring up at the sky in a technique I'd learned over the years to not ruin my makeup, I smiled and rested my hands against his chest. "You—" I cupped his cheek, trying to keep myself together. He was the reminder I needed. He was the past I'd lost. He was looking out for me in ways beyond what I could've imagined and in this moment, I knew I didn't deserve him. "Thank you. How long do I have?"

The countdown clock was always ticking. There were always demands on my time I couldn't get out of because missing one would cause a cascade.

"Like I said." He ran his fingers under my chin and kissed my lips, his firm-yet-soft ones drawing the flutters in my stomach out in full force. "You have the whole day. I'll come and get you tomorrow morning at 6 AM. There was an issue with some rigging for the stage, so you can't go to the arena today. Holden said you've got a rehearsal and prep for a New Year's pre-record tomorrow because the rental space was booked for today." His fingers laced with mine. "Have fun."

I nodded and looked over my shoulder at the two of them.

"You're good with that? A whole day with the worst friend in the world?"

They both rolled their eyes.

Piper grabbed my arm and dragged me toward the front door. "Don't worry, Dare."

He jolted.

"Sorry, Keyton. We've got her. We'll make sure she's good."

Our fingers left each other. Felicia pulled up the rear and closed the door.

"How'd he convince you guys to come?"

"Convince us?" Felicia frowned. "He didn't have to convince us. He asked and we said of course. It's been too long since we had a chance to hang out. I figured you were bored with hanging out with me since all I talk about is my kids and classes. It's nowhere near as exciting as your life."

Piper chimed in. "Yeah, potty training isn't the most spectacularly exciting topic."

"No, of course not. I love you both, and I've missed you so much. I thought me talking about traveling and what I had going on, plus never being around, meant you guys were most likely sick of me."

Our group hug continued. "Looks like we were all totally off the mark assholes!"

Felicia brushed a tear from her eye. "We were. This house is gorgeous."

"You both haven't had the tour yet." Piper couldn't contain her giddy excitement. "I swear, I've covered every square inch of this place and it's the gift that keeps on giving."

There was a heated pool, hot tub, full bar—complete with taps, bar stools, and a glowing neon light overhead—a rock climbing wall, skee-ball and mini basketball arcade games. Dance Dance Revolution had even been thrown in for good measure.

"Keyton said we have the full run of the place. He's also arranged for a chef to cook for us, a few masseuses to stop by, and a special surprise for later tonight." Piper glanced over her shoulder. "Do you think it's a stripper?"

Felicia shook her head. "You think Bay's boyfriend would hire a stripper for her?"

Piper shrugged and then her face lit up, eyes dinner plate wide. "Do you think he's the stripper?"

I burst into laughter and tackled her from behind once she reached the top of the basement game room stairs. "God, I've missed you."

She leaned back and held onto my arms. "Me too, Bay."

Damnit. Today wasn't going to be about tears. "What do you guys want to do first?"

The smell of breakfast meats and cheese flooded the room.

"Food!" We took off toward the kitchen with Piper leading the way.

Inside, a man in chef's whites with tattoos peeking out from under his collar and a whisk looked up as we walked into the kitchen. "Hello, ladies. I'm Wade."

"He's about to make me forget I'm happily married."

Felicia climbed onto her seat on the other side of the breakfast bar facing the stove. "Maybe Keyton *is* planning on sending a stripper."

The tattooed chef with light brown eyes was definitely easy on the eyes. He flung the kitchen towel over his shoulder and set a mimosa in front of each of us. "Today, I'm at your service."

Piper cleared her throat and dragged her drink closer.

"I can do plain, blueberry or chocolate chip pancakes. Coffee crunch brioche French toast is warming in the oven along with the sausages and bacon. Omelets can be made to order with whatever you'd like, or Eggs Benedict with thick honey-smoked bacon. There's also fresh fruit and for lunch—"

Felicia's hand shot up and she braced her other on the counter, shaking her head like she was about to pass out. "You're going to have to slow down, Wade. We"— she pointed between her and Piper—"are two working moms with kids. This level of pampering might kill us, so why don't we go slow? I'll have the French toast and sausages. Then the Eggs Benedict with more hollandaise sauce than you feel is appropriate. Then I'll need to jog around the backyard pool a few times before loading up on some more pancakes."

He grinned, showing off sparkling pearly whites. He certainly had his appeal. Who was I kidding? He was fucking hot. But knowing he was here for me because of Keyton added another tally mark to all the reasons this tour would be the hardest I'd ever been on.

"More." Piper waved her plate shaking the crispy bacon Wade had placed on it. "I see how much you've got over there. It's only the three of us here. Load me up, Wade."

Laughing, he added more strips to her plate.

She took her first bite and closed her eyes, lips still around the bacon. "Are these covered in maple?"

Wade nodded.

"Not just a pretty face." She looked after him wistfully as he worked on plating Felicia's French toast.

The morning ended with full stomachs and watching reality TV in the living room on oversized couches that threatened to swallow us whole.

Piper sipped her mimosa. "This is the first time I've been able to eat an entire meal uninterrupted in who knows how long."

Felicia laughed. "I went to the bathroom and almost left the door open out of habit. Anytime I close it there are suddenly fingers under the crack of the door screaming for me like I've been sucked into another dimension."

I rubbed my hands along the stem of my glass. "Glad to provide you with a little escape."

We went back to the kitchen for round two.

Wade came over and refilled Piper's glass and she clinked it to mine. "The security line at the airport was where my two days of freedom began. I love them more than anything in the world, but sometimes they're assholes."

"The kids?"

She relaxed back in her seat. "Hell, throw Mark in there too. I love him to death, but this couldn't have come at a better time. Right before all the holiday madness begins."

Felicia stood on the rungs of her chair and grabbed the bottle before Wade got to it, refilling her own glass with a wink. "Eve told me yesterday she wanted to change her Halloween costume. She doesn't want to be a Jack-in-the-box anymore, she wants to be an astronaut."

Piper nodded. "I swear—you know what? Nope! We're not doing this. Enough of us doing the mom complaining thing. How are you, Bay? Especially after what happened last week?"

"I want to hear, seriously. I love hearing about what's going on with you guys." And I did. I'd missed so much.

Piper folded one arm across her chest, holding out her glass like a prod. "You're not weaseling out. Spill."

I took a fortifying drink from my glass. "I'm good. Better. On my way to better. Keyton's helped a lot with that." I didn't want to pull the day down and make it all about me.

Piper shot up with a look of knowing. "I can't say I'm surprised. You two always had a connection."

"Yeah, sure. For the 2.75 years before he finally noticed me, we were definitely connected."

"You know what I mean. Once he saw you...he couldn't unsee you. The way he looked at you—part of the reason I fell for Mark was when I saw him look at me like Keyton looked at you."

"What?"

"All I'm saying is I'm glad you found your way back to each other."

Felicia set her glass on a coaster on the table-tennis-sized coffee table in front of us. "When he showed up with your guitar...I swear I've never almost burst into tears looking at someone before. It could've also been postpartum hormone craziness, but holy shit."

My stomach knotted with a yearning to reach out to him through time and tell him everything in person, not through a letter. I wished I could have figured out a way to have made it work without us both drowning.

Her hand covered mine. "I know you had your reasons for leaving. Given where you ended up, no one would begrudge you the hard choice you made. I'm happy he called me. I'm happy we get to be here with you."

Piper covered my other hand. "Me too. Mark told me about you not being able to come to my party."

I sucked in a sharp breath and stuttered trying to explain it all to her.

"I'm not upset. Of course I'm upset you won't be there. But I'm not mad at you, Bay. Just like our lives are hectic and feel out of control, I know yours is too, even more so."

Felicia poked me in the ribs like an older sister might. "It's different with family."

My chest tightened and tears burned in the backs of my eyes. I didn't deserve their understanding after all the times I'd let them down over the past few years.

Piper squeezed my shoulder. "Family's a lot more forgiving than hundreds of thousands, if not millions of fans demanding your attention."

I looked back and forth between them. "I don't want you two to ever think I've taken our friendships for granted or don't care about you."

Felicia patted my leg. "We know. And I think I speak for both of us here." She looked to Piper, who nodded. "Anytime you have a day or something, let us know. We might not be able to make it every time. If you're in Beijing or Melbourne, it's probably a no, but let us know and we'll come if we can. You're not being a diva by calling your friends and asking them if they want to hang out."

"Especially not if you've got top shelf booze." Piper drained the last of her glass and waved it around.

The pounding drum in my chest signaling all my failings over the years changed its tune to one of celebration. My friends were here with me. They loved me and cared about me. They didn't think I was the shittiest friend in existence and I hadn't damaged our bond. A new song played, one filled with joy and friendship and love for the people I'd never take for granted, and who made my life fuller.

We moved down to the game room before lunch. After a skee-ball face-off where Felicia won, I took the basketball shoot-out while Piper wiped the floor with us during the Dance Dance Revolution dance-off.

The copious drinks might have been part of the reason she won. Laughter bounced off the vaulted ceilings and we rushed through the house like it was the world's best amusement park.

After a lunch more delicious than it deserved to be and another food coma, we set off for the rock climbing wall treadmill (who knew that was a thing?), then a movie in the theater, complete with comfy theater seats, and we baked our own cookies before jumping into the hot tub before dinner.

Felicia topped up our glasses and leaned back. "Wade might kill me if dinner is as delicious as everything else we've had today."

Piper dragged imaginary glasses down her nose. "Staring at him, I'm wondering why I didn't decide to become a chef. Yum. Maybe he does virtual cooking lessons. If Mark learned to cook like that, I might never let him leave the bedroom, except to cook."

Felicia handed out the still warm cookies. "You two met in college, right?"

"Their freshman year. They lived across the hall from each other."

Felicia and I both *aww*ed.

Piper rolled her eyes. "He was so cluelessly cute with his newly pink shirts after he'd mixed white and colors in the wash. Adorable and the sweetest thing ever. We've been together ever since." She had a faraway, dreamy look on her face.

They'd been nearly inseparable since meeting. What would Keyton and I have been like if I hadn't left him in LA? Or if I hadn't left Greenwood right after graduation and we'd made up that summer? Would we have kids by now? A little girl and little boy who played with Violet and Parker?

A question rolled around my head. "If you hadn't gotten married to Mark, what do you think you'd be doing now?"

She peered over her shoulder through the windows framing the kitchen where Wade showed off his knife skills making our meal.

We burst into laughter. "*Other* than serving yourself up to Wade on a silver platter." I kicked her under the water.

"Ow!" She bent and rubbed her hand along her shin. "I don't know. Maybe I'd still be in Japan? Or Austria?"

"Felicia, what about you?"

"Probably elbow deep in research, trying to wrangle research assistants and chase grants. Oh, right, that's what I'm doing now, but with kids added to the mix. We met when we were both on this path, so things were already set. It's nice having someone there who gets it. We're tied to the same grant and funding deadlines. Parsing out similar cryptic comments on the papers we submit to journals."

"What about you, Bay?" Piper skimmed her hand across the water. "I'm thinking you don't have many regrets given where you are." She gestured to everything around me without any idea of how this question rolled through my head like a freight train.

"What would you be doing if you weren't 'Bay'?" She added extra sparkle to my name.

Wade saved me by announcing that dinner was served, but the question sat with me through the laughter-filled meal. Keyton's surprise turned out to be one of the newest blockbusters still in theaters. I don't know how he pulled it off, but a man showed up with a case under lock and key, worked his magic in the home theatre and before long the Dolby Surround Sound was rattling us all to our bones. It had been so long since I'd sat in a theater with my friends, eating boxes of theater candy, scarfing down popcorn and Cherry Coke. The movies was followed by collapsing out on the softest couch in the world in a junk food coma.

Piper and Felicia were asleep on the wrap-around couch wide enough to be a double bed.

I grabbed some blankets from the basket beside the TV and draped them over two of the best friends I had in the world.

My life was everything eighteen-year-old me could have dreamt of, but the things I loved—they'd changed right along with who I loved. The choices I had to make now would determine whether I looked back on moments like these as distant memories or just one of a long string stretching out over years until we were all gray and no longer able to comfortably pass out on the couch.

The question didn't leave me and demanded an answer. I just didn't know if I was strong enough to do it.

I walked into Maddy's office feeling like I'd been summoned to the principal. The room had a casual ambiance. Candles flickered, and low instrumental covers of artists she worked with were barely audible in the background. It felt more like a recording studio than a stuffy executive office.

But Maddy wasn't your typical power executive. She hugged me.

With her heels on, we were almost eye to eye. "How are you doing? I still can't believe what happened last week." She squeezed my arm and hugged me one more time. "Take a seat."

Walking to her bar set up, she poured me a glass of champagne and one for herself. I could swear she had it on tap.

Even though I had at least half a foot on her without the heels, Maddy always intimidated me with her drive and ability to walk out of any room with whatever she wanted.

The edges had been smoothed out over the years, but

she hadn't become the success she was now by letting things slide and not paying exacting attention to detail.

"What are we celebrating?"

"You didn't see the Grammy nominations?"

"Those were today?" Holden usually texted me with news like that. Where the hell was he? The disappearing acts he was pulling were getting more frequent. Anytime I tried to talk with him about it he ducked and dodged like a heavyweight boxing champion. "No, I hadn't seen." I set my glass on the table between the two comfortable black leather chairs and ran my clammy hands over my legs.

She took a sip of her glass and the twinkle in her eye dimmed. Her gaze leveled at me. "Three for you. Two for Without Grey. It's a great day!"

"Wow." I slumped back in the chair taking a sip from my glass. No matter how many albums I sold, I always felt like I was waiting for everyone to come to their senses and tell me it was all trash, to pick apart the lyrics and figure out I was a hack. I kept being proven wrong, and I still didn't know how I felt about it. Sometimes I thought I was just excellent at bullshitting my way through it all for a little while longer. The bubbles of the champagne tickled my nose.

"Try not to sound so happy about it." She sipped from her glass. "It's also perfect timing for the contract renegotiations. You're almost done with your third album. Nexus Records wants to talk about the next five!"

"Five?" It came out as a squeak.

"I told them not on my life was I wrapping you up in something more than three. But we also have Mixtape Records and Artistra interested, so I think we can get them off the five-album focus. We're also going to get an even better deal on streaming options, since I missed that last time around."

"My next three albums will take a lot longer to record. The first three—hell, even this one—were easier since I had so many older songs written." I'd fully plumbed the depths of heartbreak, betrayal, loss, hope, fear, and joy mined from my life before this life. Did I even have any real, true experiences left? A light shone through the worry. Keyton. He was real. But forcing myself to write about us felt wrong.

This wasn't why I wanted to be with him. Not for more material for my albums. Lying beside him with his arms wrapped around me, I didn't ever want to move. Even sitting with him in silence made my heart race. I knew what it felt like to be the center of his world, too—a world that would be ripped apart when I flew thousands of miles away.

"What about the song you did for..." She rummaged around on her desk finding a piece of paper. "Spencer? Holden sent it to me a couple weeks ago and it's Top-100-ready right now. Some of your best work. Are you sure you want to give it to him?" Her eyebrows dipped with skepticism.

The song for Spencer had been easier knowing I wouldn't be the one singing it. My well wasn't dry, but it was drying up for songs I want to perform.

"I can tell by how you're jumping for joy that you're ready to have me pull out all the numbers and talk negotiation strategy." Her glass scraped against the desk.

"It's not that. I'm...I don't know, Maddy." Even saying that felt scary. Monster-in-the-closet-when-you're-five scary. This was a looming unknown that could throw my entire life and the lives of all the people closest to me—who depended on me—into absolute chaos.

"You need a break." She sat back in her seat.

I froze and shot forward in my seat. "Do you have my rooms bugged or something?"

Standing, her smirk deepened. "That's a look I've seen before. The way you walked in here like your battery was inching closer to empty. After the attack, I can't blame you for wanting to take time off."

"What would it take to make that happen?" I couldn't decide now. The ground was shifting under my feet, so many changes happening all at once and not enough time to think it all through. Not enough time to be sure I was making the right choice. Maybe I should hold off until the tour finished and Keyton and I could see how we fared. My gut clenched at imagining a life where we were both always on the road, never truly able to find a place we could call home outside of each other's arms for another half decade or more.

She spun in her chair, facing her computer. "I can hold off on the negotiations for a few weeks. But once the numbers come in for this tour, whoever we sign with will want to make an announcement. After that, once things cool off it's harder to pick up the talks with the upper hand. Then there's determining touring schedules. We like to set up tours at least 18 months in advance. We need to book all the tech staff, roadies, back-up dancers, back-up singers. You know what goes into pulling it all off."

A few weeks wasn't enough. So many people. If I pulled the plug without warning, it would put people out of work. Piss people off. Disappoint them. Panicky dread tightened at the base of my neck. My ears heated. A few weeks to make decisions for my future. For the livelihoods of hundreds of people. And for my future with Keyton.

"A few weeks..."

"Maybe a couple months. You'll be busy with the tour. Holden will be in the loop too. Don't worry about that. But take the next few weeks and don't let him rush you. He'll get his percentage to feed his watch obsession in due time."

What would I do about Holden? If I just stopped, it would completely derail everything he'd built for me over the past six years.

My days had never been my own. Even my period rest days were bracketed by madness. I didn't know if I knew how to do nothing for more than a few days at a time. Maybe I could ease into things. "I'd like to maybe produce for other people. Like the work I did with Spencer." I braced myself for the scrutiny and confusion, maybe Maddy letting me down gently, but letting me know that no one would take me seriously.

Maddy's head tilted. "We can look into that. Are you sure you want to add another thing to your plate?"

"You know me. I can't stop working." The confession of wanting to pull the plug on everything else tickled the tip of my tongue, but not yet. I couldn't make a decision without talking to Keyton first and figuring out what he wanted his future to look like. I wouldn't just show up in his apartment saying 'hey, guess what? I quit being a pop star, let's be together for forever. No pressure'.

"Holden pitched Spencer as an opening act for the next tour. We could launch Spencer off your shows like we did for you. Imagine what it could do for him."

My stomach clenched. Would I be robbing Spencer of his big shot, if I stopped? This could be the opportunity of a lifetime for him.

I gripped the armrest of my seat. "What if we brought him on for this tour? For one of the last legs?" We could hang out. I could show him the ropes, bring him up on stage for duets and use my stage to help launch his career to the

new level now without hanging all that on the next tour—
the one that might never happen.

"We could make that work. We haven't finalized the
opening acts yet. You know how flighty acts can be."

"It would be perfect. His sound is distinctive and I think
my fans would love it too."

"Good, I'm glad. It'll also give you a buddy on tour. I
know it's rough doing this solo. At least Without Grey have
each other, no matter how much they've wanted to kill each
other over the years."

"Can you believe it's been a decade since I played on
their album?"

If I hadn't been working with Freddie, if I hadn't been
available that night, my life would be unrecognizable now. If
Keyton hadn't heard me singing on those back steps and
become the inspiration for a whole album's worth of songs.
If he hadn't shown up for training camp and pissed me off
so much I'd sung in front of everyone. So much of my life
was all wrapped up in him, and we had less than a week left.

A weight pressed down on my chest, an inescapable
pressure of crushing sadness closing in from all sides. I felt
the fear of what would happen when the schedules changed
and the cancellations racked up for us both, of what we'd
become when the reality for both of us came barging
back in.

"You're telling me." She sat in the seat beside me. "Mind
blowing. After bumming along with them on their first
summer tour, I definitely didn't think I'd end up here."
Gesturing with her glass, she checked out her office.

"The office is pretty swanky."

"You could certainly say I've got a bit of help with adding
some swank to this place."

"Are you hitting the road soon with the guys?"

"We'll see. We're all getting older."

Maddy was only four years older than me, but life changed quickly when priorities shifted. I knew that, and it became clearer with each passing day.

"After the madness of the last decade for me and the guys, they're finally maybe thinking about really settling down. What's the point of all the money and fame if you're sitting alone in a hotel room chugging from a bottle of Jack Daniels night after night?"

"Is this personal experience?" I finished my glass and sat it on the table between us.

She chuckled. "Personal experience of smacking bottles of Jack out of people's hands. If we can do a short tour and keep everyone from driving each other insane and losing their minds, we might try it in the spring. The album is coming together. Once it's closer to finished, we'll be able to figure out the rest of the logistics."

"We're all lucky we have you keeping us in line."

Her laugh was louder this time. "Only because I've never been great at keeping myself in line."

On occasion Manager Maddy slipped away and I got a glimpse of the messy 22-year-old who'd first introduced herself with the ratty backpack and the crinkled NDA. She'd gotten more relaxed over the years—mellowed after the Everest Era.

The phone on her desk beeped.

She leaned over it. "Shit. I've got to take this, Bay. You're welcome to hang out until I finish."

"It's okay. You've run out of booze."

"Never!" She gasped and glared. "How dare you insult me like that?"

I squeezed my lips together. "You're losing your touch, Maddy." With a quick hug, I left her to her call.

Eric waited in the reception area to usher me back to the car.

Taking my phone out, I laughed at the messages piled up in the group chat with Piper and Felicia. It was mainly gifs and random pictures from our day together, but it felt good knowing they were just a text away and they didn't feel they were bothering me by sending messages. I felt the same.

I sent a message to Emily to have someone go to the temperature-controlled storage truck that travelled with the tour. It was where all the things I hadn't wanted exposed to the ravages of day to day bumps and knocks were kept under lock and key. I'd said it was for when I got my own apartment, but that had been six years ago, and I needed it now.

Holden showed up five minutes before the conference call he'd set up with London, out of breath and flushed.

I slammed the folder closed. Was he literally running around putting out fires? Did he have a secret girlfriend? Was he on the run from a mob boss he'd pissed off? "Talk to me, Holden. What is going on with you?"

"Hmm, what? Nothing." He grabbed his tablet and set it on the conference room table.

"You keep disappearing."

He scoffed. "Busy, busy, keeping you busy."

The video chatting system chirped to alert us to an incoming call. My gaze narrowed at Holden who slipped right into the call with a smile full of charm and swagger like there wasn't anything the least bit weird with what he had going on.

After the call finished, Holden packed up and bolted out of the room.

Before I could rush after him and pin him to the floor to tell me what the hell was going on, Emily tapped my arm.

"I put what you asked for in your room."

My frustration was mounting with Holden, but I wouldn't take it out on Emily, and I was relieved it arrived so soon. "Thanks, Emily, you're a lifesaver."

Her cheeks went full pink ink blot, like I'd propositioned her, and her arms hugged her tablet to her chest. "Just doing my job."

"I couldn't do it without you. Really."

She peeked up. "I know you're not big into the fawning or gushing, but I wanted to tell you working for you has been the most exciting thing to happen to me in my entire life. Watching you perform never gets old."

"Even when you're holding my puke bucket?"

The tomato flush turned to fire engine scalding. "Everyone gets nervous. I could never do it. Once I tried to sing during a choir solo in high school and I puked so hard before, I burst a blood vessel in my eye and vowed to never sing again. At least you puke and keep going."

I jolted, rocked by her admission. Was everyone hiding things from me? "You sing?"

Her mouth opened and closed, and she shook her head like I'd asked if she'd murdered someone. "No, not at all. Never."

But I could see it. A flicker of want. She wanted to be able to do it without being clouded by the fear. I'd seen that same look when I'd stared at myself in the mirror, willing myself to sing, when nothing would come out.

She'd probably done the same thing herself. What kind of friend would I be if I didn't help her out?

"When are we in the studio next?"

Her throat tightened. She scrolled through the tablet, relieved to be back in her normal territory. "In two days."

"Perfect."

Maybe I could write a song for her. One that called to her in an irresistible way to get her over her fear. I'd been there. Helping her overcome the stranglehold on her voice was the least I could do.

31

KEYTON

I t was the picture-perfect scene.

Bay came over after two, using the key I'd given her. I wanted this to be a place she could escape to even if I wasn't here, even though she'd only be in town for a few more days. I'd needed to give it to her, needed to know this was a place she could always come back to.

"Hey, I thought you had a team meeting this afternoon. I was coming to get some quiet before you got back."

She hadn't come with her bag like she usually did. In her hand was the guitar case I'd had with me for four years, the one I'd spent hours with. I knew every nick and bump in the case. There was no mistaking it.

"We finished early. You brought your guitar."

My chest burned with the fires of regret and lost time. I'd pinned so many hopes and wishes on piecing it back together. For so long, I'd thought it wasn't possible, but here she was with me.

"Is that okay? I swear, I won't take long. I've had a few songs I need to get out, and sitting in the hotel room wasn't doing it." Beside the door, she kicked off her shoes and dumped them in a pile along with mine. Her coat came off and she opened the coat closet and hung it inside amongst my others.

Her arm wrapped around me. The case bumped against my hand.

I ran my fingers through her hair and kissed the top of her head. "Of course. I'll stay out of your way."

She grabbed my hand, searching my eyes with hers. "I didn't mean it that way."

I kissed her, teasing her lips with my tongue. "I know. Do your thing. Have you eaten?"

Her head ducked with a sheepish look. "Not yet."

"I'll make us some food."

Her smile was ice-cream-sundae-sweet. She rushed over to the living room, set down the guitar, and shifted the arm chair closer to the window. "I'll be quick."

After fishing her notebook out of her bag with a pencil clenched between her teeth, she fell into her music.

I'd never watched her create before. Not so nakedly. Back in high school, she'd been barely singing again, fumbling over the older songs, trying to find her voice. In LA, she'd been racked with worry and uncertainty.

This version of her wasn't nearly as worried about how she sounded—or maybe she was comfortable enough around me now to not hide any of the process.

All the missed notes, clashing chords, and groans of frustration were on display.

Lunch was ready and she ate one-handed, swearing she'd be finished in a few minutes. Watching her became my new favorite pastime.

I handed her a mug of the hot chocolate made with the mix she'd given me. I'd wanted to save it up to savor when she was gone, but her sniff of the cup and megawatt grin was a trade-off I could live with.

Her voice was no longer tentative tiptoeing from our first few nights in the studio together. There was no hint of hoping someone else didn't overhear, none of the nervousness that radiated off her before her performances.

Not wanting to feel like a full-fledged stalker watching her work, I grabbed my sketchpad and sat on the couch a few feet away from her.

Her focus was absolute, and I tried to capture it—not only the look on her face, but how our time together felt.

Once she'd left, I'd come home hoping to find her like this, absorbed in her music for so long she'd forgotten to eat, so I'd make her dinner and let her keep going until her muse was finally tired.

The sun had set and her phone chirped from her bag by the front door.

Her head popped up and she looked at me with wide eyes and whipped her head around staring outside. In the window, her reflection made double Bays. "Oh my god, it's so late."

She shot up, her notebook falling to the floor and pencil rolling onto the carpet. "I'm sorry. I didn't—I didn't even realize."

"Bay, it's fine. Answer your phone."

"Can you hold this?" She held out her guitar. The same one I'd broken. The same one I'd pieced together. And in that moment, I knew.

She'd forgiven me. Not only in her words or her thoughts. Not even consciously. But through and through to the depths of her soul.

I took the guitar, reverently trying to keep my emotions in check before letting them flow over me. Not shutting them away. But feeling all the ways this hit me. The joy. The pain. The fear. The love.

The love I felt for her now eclipsed every other love I'd had for her: my teen love born of my need to connect with someone, and my newly minted college graduate love heightened by the pedestal I'd put her on.

Now, I loved her from a place of wanting to spend the rest of my life with her, basking in her love for me, and being the best man possible for her.

She toyed with the ends of her hair after finishing her call. "I have to go now. But I can be back tonight, if that's okay with you. I know you have to leave early in the morning. And I'm sorry I took so long. I—this wasn't how I wanted to spend one of our last night's together."

"We'll have many more nights together." My throat tightened. Emotions raced through my body—regret for the time we'd lose when I left in the morning, happiness for how excited she was to come back to me. Love for her. "Of course. I'll wait up for you." I followed her to the front door.

"You don't have to." She grabbed her shoes and shoved her feet into them.

"I want to." Her grin spread and she draped her arms over my shoulders.

"Are you okay with me leaving my guitar here?"

I rubbed my nose against hers. "I'll look after it for you."

A quick peck on my lips. "I know."

She was gone too long, and the time I had with her was too short.

I spent my evening going over the hours we'd spent together. I wanted the years to stretch into eternity, to truly be with her. The only hitch in my head was the thought of a family. I wanted one with her and was terrified all at once.

A family. Not just Bay, but kids. I could tell she wanted them from how she talked about her future and how well she did with them. But we had time. She'd go off on her tour and I'd talk to Monica every damn day if that was what it took to get over the fears that woke me in the middle of the night.

The door swept open a little before one a.m.. I set down my sketch pad, my lone beer of the night long finished.

She rushed over to me. "I'm so sorry I'm late. It wasn't supposed to go that long." Her voice was frantic.

Standing, I set down the pad and folded her up in my arms. "You're busy. I get it. I'm up because I couldn't sleep. Trust me, I loved the idea of you sliding into bed beside me to wake me up."

Her body sagged with palpable relief. "What time do you leave in the morning?"

"Six."

"I leave in four days." Her eyes glistened with unchecked tears. "You're gone for the next two and a half." The waver in her voice clawed at my heart. There was never enough time.

"Then we need to make the most of this time. I'll give you something to remember me by."

Hand in hand, we walked to my bedroom. The one I wanted to be ours.

I peeled her clothes off, taking my time and savoring every inch of revealed skin.

Her hands were busy on my clothes.

There wasn't the urgency of our other times together, although the countdown clock loomed overhead.

This wouldn't be the end. This wasn't where we said goodbye, no matter how many miles there were between us.

In bed, we explored each other's bodies. My head buried between her thighs. Her mouth on my cock using her full sexual arsenal until I grabbed a condom and slid into her.

Rolling, grinding thrusts with our bodies so close together her breath fanned across my cheek.

Her climax was sharp, tightening around me so much stars danced in front of my eyes. We collapsed, sweaty and satiated.

Falling asleep beside her, the final piece of my peace in place, I knew what my life was like without her and with her. Without wasn't an option.

I woke when the sun was still a rumor to the horizon.

Sitting in my chair, I watched her sleep. The sketch pad sat balanced on my lap, not doing her the slightest bit of justice.

After slipping out of bed just before sunrise, I'd grabbed my pencil when the itch in my palms got to undeniable heights.

Her leg hung out from under the blankets, and she'd wrapped herself around the pillow I'd been using.

"Are you going to keep drawing me or are you going to get back in bed?" she mumbled against the gray pillow.

"How'd you know I was drawing you?"

One eye popped open, shining with amusement. "I've seen that look before. Back in Greenwood. You always have a look of intense concentration and contentment when you draw, like you're living in the moment, experiencing it and capturing it all at once."

This woman knew me unlike anyone else in the world. She owned every fiber of my being and lit every strand of my soul aflame. I set the notepad and pencil down on the floor and crawled into bed beside her. "There's something I need to tell you." Collapsing beside her, I cupped her cheek, skimming my fingers across her skin.

Her eyes widened, but she didn't say a word, waiting for me.

"I've known for a while how I feel, but I didn't want to rush things. I didn't want you to think I was forcing your hand or trying to pull something out of you."

"You wouldn't do that."

"I've had my moments." My thumb ran across her lip.

I stood on the edge of my cliff with the wind roaring in my ears. I wasn't afraid of the splinters or the shatter anymore. They couldn't hold me back from giving all of myself to her.

"Someone once said 'If I don't go for it, it'll be a question in my mind for the rest of my life.' You're my question, the one that's reverberated in my head since the first night I heard you sing. 'How can I be the kind of man she deserves?'"

She met my gaze, her eyes shining. "You already are. At this point, I don't feel I deserve you, but I don't ever want you to second guess how I feel for you. I hate the thought of leaving you."

I tucked her hair behind her ear. "But you have to."

Her throat tightened and she nodded.

"I love you, Bay."

A tear spilled over the edge of her eyelid.

I hated to see her cry, but her smile tempered the tightness in my chest.

She slipped her arms under mine and held me closer. "And I've loved you for as long as I can remember. Even when I fought it. Even when I tried to pretend I didn't. Even when I left. I've always loved you."

"I will always love you." I'd found my pre-dawn sunrise

in my own bed, draped in sheets and resting on my pillow. "There will never be someone as perfect for me as you."

"You might be overselling it. I'm sure there are plenty of women out there who could be perfect for you."

"Never. I could never regret a single minute of time I've had with you. From the first note you sang, you struck a chord in my chest that's reverberated over the past ten years. There couldn't be someone else out there because there is no other Bay out there."

"Maybe you should write a couple songs on my next album. They'd make killer lyrics."

I smiled, the mood lightening from soul-baring to serene satisfaction. "You can have them. Add them to your book, and when you're out on the road and you read them you can think of me."

"I don't need lyrics to do that." Her arms tightened. "How long until you need to leave?"

Lifting my head, I checked the clock. "Thirty-five more minutes." I brushed my hand over her hair and kissed her temple. The glow in my chest that made it feel like I was floating.

"Can I take your picture with me?"

"You want it?" My heartbeat skipped.

"I always love seeing how you see me. It'll make me feel like you're still here with me."

"Even when I'm not. I am."

We'd make this work.

32

BAY

I'd been tempted to fly to Wisconsin for his last game just to see him. Our time together was being gobbled up so quickly I'd wanted my never-ending days to actually never end, just to keep Tuesday from coming. But the weekend ended and he came back to me.

Getting on a plane had lost its thrill a while ago, but now dread curled deep in my belly.

While a quiet night at home at Keyton's place was what I wanted, there were obligations that came along with who I was, and they weren't all bad. Holden had disappeared again and Emily was recovering from a cold and had sequestered herself to make sure none of the rest of us got sick. She was power chugging orange juice and throat lozenges.

Keyton's trip felt like it had stretched on forever and happened too quickly all at the same time, signaling the countdown to my tour.

After a reunion in my suite, complete with a toe-curling orgasm, we'd put ourselves back together enough to be presentable. My phone dictated all nowadays, since Holden had taken his disappearing act to the next level.

I hoped he wasn't this distracted once the tour started. Stuck on a tour bus for hours on end, he wouldn't be able to evade my prodding questions for long. Maybe Emily and I could go on a recon mission when he snuck off with his London friends. I swore if there was a serious issue he was hiding from me, I'd kick his ass for not letting me know.

But tonight was about me and Keyton, not my pain-in-the-ass manager. Keyton and I wouldn't be cocooned up in my room or his apartment. We needed to come up for air, and I needed at least a full handful of hours to rest my vagina. She'd been put to work. There was never a shortage of things we could do outside our four walls, but now that people knew we were together, wherever he was spotted, they looked for me, which made incognito mode harder. So tonight we had dinner reservations. Who wouldn't want to show off this well-tailored piece of man candy?

As we walked through the kitchen, some of the sous chefs and other kitchen staff turned to track us past the flaming pans and stainless steel shelving units to the chef's table at the back of the kitchen.

"Holden asked for this as a favor. The restaurant wanted a big name drop before the Michelin star team came in to review. We don't have to stay the whole time."

"Let me enjoy a night out with my girlfriend." He whispered into my ear and slipped his hand around me, resting it at the small of my back.

The tingle from the touch traveled up my spine.

Hearing him saying that made me feel like I was back in high school, going out to dinner with the star football player. In a way, I was still that girl.

Other than my mom, Piper, Felicia and Spencer, he was

probably the only one who could see me that way—the real me without all the other larger-than-life things surrounding me, like Eric following behind us like I'd picked him up from the Secret Service surplus store.

The maître d' opened the door to the secluded room of half-windows overlooking the kitchen.

Eric procured a chair out of thin air like a street magician and plopped it outside the door.

I leaned out of the doorway. "You can come inside, you know."

"I'm good."

"Seriously, Eric. We can see you through the glass door."

His eyebrow quirked up. "Which means everyone can see you."

Touché. I'd gotten a lot less lax over the safety and security measures Eric and Holden insisted on since the attack. Walking to Keyton's was the length of my leash and even that was with my full winter disguise on.

I slipped the menu out of the maître d's hands and handed it over to him. "At least order dinner, so I don't feel like a complete asshole."

"I'm not eating on the job."

"We'll ask them to make it to-go."

He sat firm.

"Please."

He looked to me with a scowl and hesitated before taking it from my hands and taking his seat.

Keyton and I walked to the four-seater table with tea lights and a low fresh rose arrangement set in the center. He pulled out my chair for me and we glanced at the menu.

"Holy shit, there are twelve courses on this menu, all with wine pairings."

He laughed and dropped his hand onto my knee under the table.

"You'd be carrying me out of here over your shoulder if I drank this much."

His fingers brushed along my knee, sending rippling currents of desire flooding through my body. "It sounds like a perfect way to enjoy a nice dinner." His mouth said nice dinner, but his fingers said 'pin you against the wall in the bathroom'.

"Maybe we can ask for a to-go version of the meal like Eric's."

Before my escape plan could be hatched, the chef walked in and introduced himself.

Keyton and I took turns with the teasing through stolen brushes and caresses under the table. It was playful and fun in a way that felt like a new norm for us. I'd miss this closeness when I flew out on Tuesday, but it wouldn't be left behind.

We could do this. We could make this work. If we were still here together after a decade of the damage we'd done to each other, we could make it through a few months of separation due to work.

Once his season ended, I wouldn't mind sharing the tour bus bedroom with him, and he'd make every hotel room and every new city a new adventure. Maybe we could sneak out and explore a little. Disguises and Eric keeping his distance could let us wander the streets of Rome or the Winter Markets in Berlin. The thought of a rush of exhilaration at finding hidden treasures with Keyton helped temper some of the heartache trying to ruin the last couple days we had together.

Leaving the restaurant, he draped his arm over my shoulder and held me close. My puffs of breath hung in the air in front of my face, a perfect reason to snuggle deeper against him, holding onto the front of his coat to warm my fingers.

In the car, he traced my lips with his thumb. "You're beautiful."

From the way it made me feel to have him say that, you'd think no one had ever said the words to me before—that people hadn't screamed them at the top of their lungs in my face. But he said it and he saw me, every part of me.

"When I'm with you. I feel like me. I feel like the real me."

He brushed his finger down the side of my cheek. "I always want the real you. I want that with you for as long as you'll have me."

"And if that was forever?"

"Then your wish is my command." He captured my lips with his, pouring all of the love and passion into every caress of his tongue or nip of my lips.

"I want us to be real."

"Real and forever. Two promises that are easy to make."

I sunk into his hold with my head pressed against his shoulder. My future became clearer—one without the frantic, never stopping life and one with the man I'd given my heart to over a decade ago.

Fuller than I should be and a bit nauseous, I made it to the suite. With the early morning calls we had to make to London, it was easier to stay in my suite than Keyton's place tonight, although I'd much rather have been there. It felt more like a place people lived, not a place people passed through.

Even with my clothes in the drawers and closets in my bedroom I'd been in for nearly two months, this didn't feel like a place I'd ever call home.

Keyton's declaration yesterday had been the final push I'd needed to tell Maddy the truth and to finally decide what path I wanted to be on. Performing had once been all I could think about, but now it wasn't compatible with the life I wanted. The life I wanted was filled with friends and family, and wasn't dictated by a demanding schedule and a never-ending list of obligations only leading me further away from the people I loved.

It was a life with Keyton where I could have the best of the worlds I'd been shown. I could have my music and the man I loved, who loved me back just as fiercely and irrevocably as I loved him.

Inside the room, on the table was a basket. My basket of goodies for whenever I got my thirty-six-hour rest because of my period.

My phone pinged with a call from Holden.

"Hey, Bay, sorry the basket was late. I thought Emily was handling it, but with her sick, I had to scramble to get it to you. Is everything there that you need?"

Keyton stared down at the basket filled with tampons, pads, Goobers, soft baked peanut butter chocolate chip cookies and a note saying there were new seasons of House Hunters on the FireStick.

I stared at the basket as the ice-water realization spilled over me. "Yeah, I have everything I need. I'll talk to you later." My lips were numb.

"Do you need help with packing? We need to get on the plane at 6 tomorrow night."

"6 tomorrow night. Got it. I'll be ready." I ended the call and stared at the box that generally signaled my wanting to die for two days, but at least being able to do it in peace. My stomach knotted, not settling one bit, and not the kind of nausea I usually got when I had my period.

Keyton looked to me and back at the basket. "Are you on your period?"

I tilted my head. "You were literally inside me a couple hours ago."

His nostrils flared and the tampon box shook in his hand. "But you're supposed to be on your period."

"Yes." I took it out of his hand and shoved it back into the basket.

"And you're late."

I dragged my fingers through my hair and turned away, sitting on the couch. "Yes." Forty weeks from today would be August. The tour ended in July. What the hell was I thinking? I couldn't complete a full tour while pregnant. Delivering on stage in an arena filled with tens of thousands of people wasn't my idea of fun.

I shot up and paced, tugging on the ends of my hair.

"How late?" Keyton's voice broke through the avalanche of thoughts colliding in my head.

"A day. I'm a day late." The anticipation of Keyton getting back into town had wiped away all thoughts of my period, especially when the basket of goodies hadn't arrived. Distractions had been at an all-time high.

"How often are you a day late?"

I stopped pacing and stared down at the basket. "Never." Not through tours and time zones. I was regular enough to build a tour schedule around my break. I'd always looked forward to it to give me some time on my own, a chance to binge reality TV, eat crap, and be alone for a solid twelve waking hours.

"Oh." One word. Nothing else coming after it.

Unexpected. I waited for the panic about what to do next, but there wasn't any. There was a calm. This would be the perfect opportunity to take a step back, the chance I hadn't known I'd been looking for to jump off the hamster wheel and make something real for myself.

Then a pang of guilt shot through me that I wasn't thinking about this potential baby for them, but how it would allow me to weasel out of the life I'd built for myself and always dreamed of.

All the feelings I had were reexamined through a new lens. Were my nipples extra sensitive because Keyton's ministrations were even better or because I was pregnant? Was my stomach churning with way too much food or the morning sickness I'd heard never knew how to tell time? Was he looking at me in shock because this was shocking news, or had this changed everything about him wanting to be with me?

33

KEYTON

I sat up after Bay went to sleep. We'd both been slightly catatonic once the realization hit us. Neither of us seemed to have had the words. We'd taken separate showers, each lost in our own world of stunned silence and tumultuous thoughts.

We lay in bed, her head resting on my chest until she fell asleep. Her steady breaths whispered across my skin. I stared at the cream ceiling, trying to keep my grasp on the threads slowly unravelling, fraying, and snapping under the pressure.

I'd been careful for so long, not only because there were so many ways to get caught up in bad situations once a kid was involved, but also because I wasn't capable of being a good father. I was barely at the point of being a good human being.

The scars ran deep. I knew that now. I'd tried to pretend I was fine for so long. It had taken years to get me to this point, to be the man I thought I could be, the man she needed, even the husband I hoped to be.

I'd contacted a jeweler about a ring. Working in ideas

about her thoughts on rings over the next few months would have been tricky, but I'd wanted her to be blown away. I should've started ring shopping after our first night together, but we were supposed to have more time. I was supposed to have more time.

My chest got tight, breathing was a chore I hadn't felt since training camp. Panic swelled, overwhelming me. Sweat broke out on my forehead and my skin was clammy. Sliding out of the bed, I grabbed my phone.

Walking out of the bedroom, I braced my hand on the wall, shuffling the rest of the way. I closed the bathroom door without flicking on the light. The glow of my phone provided enough. The smooth case slid in my hand as I pulled up my contacts and pulled up the name.

Raking my fingers through my hair, I was wound tighter with each ring. I felt a sliver of relief as she answered on the eighth ring, groggy and grumpy.

"Monica? Hello, Monica? I need to see you."

"What the hell?" She yawned. "Do you know what time it is?"

"I need to see you."

"What happened? What's wrong?" Her voice was a bit more alert even though it was the middle of the night.

The throbbing in my head pounded even harder. "Can I come to you?"

"Of course. Keyton, what is wrong?"

"I'll be there in a few hours." I ended the call and opened the bathroom door.

I shouted, keeping myself from swinging on the figure. I clamped my hand to my chest. Just another reminder I was already in over my head. What if I'd hit her? What if I hit our kid? Being woken up in the middle of the night by a little kid and forgetting where I was wasn't out of the question. Bile rose in my throat, choking me.

Bay's shadowed form stood in the hallway, her hair bedhead-big and her arms wrapped around her waist.

"You're leaving." It wasn't a question.

I tried to slip past her, but she stood in front of me.

"There are some things I have to deal with."

She held her hand up toward my chest, but didn't touch me. "If I hadn't woken up, would you have told me you were leaving?"

My jaw clenched. "Maybe I wanted to be the one to walk away for once." Fuck. It was a low blow. But I needed to get out. The walls were closing in and I couldn't deal.

She gasped, her eyes wide even in the dim lighting from the seating area. "I might be pregnant and you're running for the door."

I scrubbed my hands down over my face. The tension was wound tight in me like a coil torqued past its factory recommended settings. "I need to handle some things first."

"Who were you talking to?"

My gaze snapped to hers.

She tilted her chin toward the phone clutched in my hand. "I came to see if you were okay. Things are going crazy inside my head too. And I heard you. That's not how you talk to any of your guy friends. Who are you going to see?"

There were so many things I wanted to say, so many things I wanted to do. I'd thought I had so much more time to work through it all, but I didn't. Feeling cornered with my mind on fire and thrown into chaos, I did the only thing I could.

With nothing more than my phone in my hand I turned and walked down the hallway to the door of the suite within a suite.

Holden and Emily were having their early morning meeting with schedules laid out on the table.

Their eyes widened. "Hey, Keyton. Did Bay need something? We can get it if you like."

I didn't stop. What excuses could I make? What explanations could I give?

And then I was out the suite door. It closed silently behind me with a soft hiss and click of the lock, and then I was off running.

The hallway was deserted and the plush carpet covered my thundering footsteps.

I ran straight for the stairs, my bare feet slamming into the concrete and metal steps, nearly jumping from landing to landing down twenty flights. I hit the bottom covered in a sheen of sweat.

I burst out the front of the hotel.

Paparazzi were stationed outside and caught off guard, giving me just enough time to dive for one of the hotel town cars.

"You okay?"

My heart jackhammered like it was seconds from splitting right through my sternum.

"Is something wrong?" The driver swung around with his arm behind the seat in front of me.

"Yeah, me." I stared at him dazed, numb, and in need of a brown paper bag. "I need to go to the airport. Now."

His eyes darted to the crowd gathering around the car with cameras flashing and back to me. With a grim look, he nodded.

I slammed the door and dropped my head between my knees.

"Do you want to talk about it?"

I shot up. "Does it look like I want to fucking talk about

it?" My glare just as blistering as my voice. And my face fell. I buried my head in my hands and yanked at my roots, trying to rip them out. The patch job I'd thought I'd done on myself was supposed to hold. I'd done everything I could to be the guy Bay deserved, and in a matter of hours I'd proven just how wrong I was.

"I'm sorry, man. I...I just need to get to Charlotte."

Gwen met me at the airport with clothes, shoes, my passport, a spare credit card and a profound look of concern. Not wanting to snap at her, I took the bundle and left without another word. The flight to Charlotte I felt like my brain was trying to lift out of my skull, like my skin was being peeled back from my flesh.

After the wheels touched down, I was in a cab and racing into the non-descript five story building I'd been into many times before. The shiny name plate beside her door matched all the others on this floor. When I pounded on the fifth-floor office door until Monica opened it, my shirt was soaked and it felt like I'd run all the way here from Philly.

"Now will you tell me what's going on?" She held open the door. The fifty-something woman with a no-nonsense bob and a nose for not wasting her time stared back at me with eyes filled with the concerned understanding she'd perfected.

Rushing inside, I glanced around the room wishing to god there was a bar. Those old habits were ready to rear their head. My stomach roiled and churned. But there was no bar. The office looked exactly as it had the last time I'd been there. The sameness had always helped center me, but nothing could do that right now.

Instead, I sank to the couch, rocking back and forth with my head in my hands. Panic smothered me and cold dread swamped my senses. My heart pounding in my ears threatened to drown everything else out.

She sat beside me and held onto my shoulder. "You're shaking, Keyton."

My head snapped up. "She's pregnant." Even without a test, I felt it was true. This was the one bit of kryptonite left in our relationship and it launched like a spear straight into my chest. A fear I'd thought I'd have more time to confront and deal with. Of course the universe would throw its head back and laugh, pushing straight into the giant open wound I hadn't yet gathered the strength to try and heal.

My eyelids felt like they were lined with glass. "And I don't know what to do."

"Bay is pregnant?" Monica's eyes widened behind her glasses and she dropped her hand from my shoulder.

I nodded, looking to her for that sage balm to fix this and help me off the ledge.

She shifted on the couch, turning to face me with one leg bent. "When did you find out?"

"A few hours before I called you." Standing in the middle of her hotel room feeling like my whole world had been shoved off its axis.

"Okay." Her head tilted. "Why did you call me?"

My head jerked back. "Why wouldn't I call you? A baby? I'm going to be a father. You don't see what the hell is wrong with that?"

"Let's take this step by step." Her lips tightened before smoothing back out. She got up and poured me a glass of water. Holding it out, she waited for me to take it.

My hand shook, but I grabbed it, downed it in three gulps and sat it on the table in front of me.

She sat in her chair. "Do you want to have a child with Bay?"

I shot up from my seat and stared out the floor-to-ceiling windows, scrubbing my hands down my face. "Of course I do. I want to have a family with her. I love her. I've always loved her." I turned and stared at Monica, hoping she'd have a book for me to read or a podcast suggestion. A magic spell. A potion. Anything.

I braced my hands on either side of my neck and squeezed my eyes shut.

"So what's the problem?"

"How can you ask me that?" My eyes snapped open. Breathing was a challenge. I was winded like I'd run halfway across the country in a sprint. "You know what the problem is."

She crossed her legs and folded her hands over her knees. Her degrees hung on her walls, and books she'd penned sat on the shelves. Those meant she should have better questions than 'what's the problem?'

"I won't know until you tell me."

"Isn't that your job?"

"How long have we been doing this?"

"Three years. Four? Since Vegas."

"Exactly."

I sat on the couch like I was teetering on the edge of a cliff. "I can't do what my dad did to me to a kid. A baby. Bay's baby. Our baby."

"And why do you think you would?"

"I feel out of control. When she told me, I got all panicky and hot. I was searching for the exits, not because I wanted to get away, but because I wanted to protect her from me."

"Why do you revert to those old feelings? Why do you think you'd be capable of hurting her now?"

"I've done it before. I've hurt her more than anyone, and I love her."

"And she's hurt you."

My gaze skipped to hers and I nodded.

"But you both still found your way back to one another."

"What if I love this baby and do the same things? I don't feel ready. I can't be ready."

Her face softened and she leaned forward and patted me on the back of my hand. "No one is ever ready to be a parent. Those panicky, scared shitless, out-of-your-mind feelings? Every parent has them. Feeling them doesn't make you a bad parent, and it doesn't mean you can't handle it."

"I don't want to mess this up."

"You know how you really mess this up?"

I squeezed my eyes shut feeling like my head was being held underwater and fought for breath, dropping my head. "Running away from the person I love instead of talking to them."

"Look at that. You don't even need me anymore." She patted my shoulder.

"What if I screw this up again?" I looked to her, trying to keep myself from falling apart.

"You think people who have their shit together don't ever worry about screwing their lives up? Do you think getting your anger issues under control means you'll never get angry again? Or you'll never make a mistake again? As a person, as a boyfriend or a husband, as a dad—let me put your mind at ease right now, you're going to fuck up. You'll probably fuck up big time, but a misstep when you're trying your best isn't a bad thing. No one has all the answers. I don't have all the answers."

I dropped my head.

"Keyton, look at me."

I dragged my eyes up to meet her gaze.

She stared back at me with a calm understanding. "You are not your father, Keyton. And how scared you are right now, how much you're worried about hurting the people you care about—that should tell you something."

Somewhere deep down I'd hoped my dad regretted what he'd done, that he was remorseful about it, but that dredged up the possibility that I could be that person, hurting the people around me and regretting it. But under it all, I knew he'd never cared. He wasn't the least bit repentant for what he'd done. He'd never cared about anyone other than himself. He'd never been capable of the type of fear I had about hurting the people I loved because he'd never loved anyone, least of all himself.

"You'll never be like him. If you love her, you need to tell her that and you need to be ready for the ups and downs. You can make it through them. You've done so much to heal yourself and work through everything you've been through. Don't deny yourself finding love with someone who loves you back just because you're scared."

"What if I fuck this up?" My fingers curled, fingertips digging into my palms.

She patted the back of my clenched fist and stared into my eyes. "The fact that you're here with me right now and not with her tells me you've already fucked up big time."

My stomach knotted, the pit deepening with every passing second.

The lines of censure eased and she patted me on the arm. "But it doesn't mean you can't come back from this. Think of it as your first trial run. Now get your ass back on another plane and stop being afraid of letting yourself be happy."

"What if she doesn't forgive me for this?" I stood and walked to her office door, opening it and turning back.

"Then you find a way to earn her forgiveness just like she earned yours and you earned hers before."

I left her office and bolted back downstairs for a taxi. Choking terror that I'd ruined everything Bay and I had built over the past couple months grabbed me, squeezing the breath from my lungs.

The moment I turned on my phone, a barrage of messages rolled in. Gwen. Ernie. Berk. Reece. LJ. Marisa. All bombarding me with question marks and all-caps messages referencing the same thing. *Wisconsin.*

I was plummeting off the edge of a cliff unable to catch my breath.

"No. No. No." I shook the phone and stared at it like I could somehow turn back the hands of time.

I needed to get back to Bay. I needed to explain. I needed her.

34

BAY

He left. The highs I'd been flying when he'd told me he loved me didn't compare to the tumble I'd taken, the plummet through the center of the earth. He left. I'd told him I was pregnant and he'd picked up the phone to call another woman and left.

I must have screamed. But I can't remember.

Holden and Emily burst into the room after he'd left. I don't know how long it was between when the door slammed shut behind him and when it sank in that he'd actually done it. Holden was in his button-down shirt with the sleeves rolled up and no tie. Emily's nose had a tinge of redness to it from blowing it so much.

They both stared at me with a mix of shock and worry.

Exchanging glances, they lifted me up off the floor, helping me onto the bed. Curled up, I buried my face in the pillow. Housekeeping had been in while we were out and changed all the bedding to fresh linens that smelled nothing like him. I cried even harder. So hard I felt like I was drowning.

It was like he'd shattered me all over again, only this

time there wasn't a guitar left to piece back together. "I'm late."

Silence consumed the room before I dissolved again.

A hand rubbed my back, and from the brush of the watch band at the end of each stroke, I knew it was Holden.

Finally, my hiccupping sobs slowed and my head pounded, anvils being dropped on my brain. I drifted off into a fitful, dreamless sleep, more like sliding into oblivion than a restful break from the world. My free-fall was plunging into darkness and loneliness.

I woke the next morning with my head throbbing like it had been shoved into a vise. Beside the bed there was a glass of water with condensation running down the sides and a couple ibuprofen.

The door to my room opened. Someone stopped in the bathroom and ran the water.

A flicker of hope pieced through the fog in my head. Had it all been a nightmare? Was that Keyton with breakfast?

But it wasn't him. Holden walked in.

I downed the pills.

He sat on the edge of the bed and held out a damp wash cloth.

It had all happened just the way I remembered it. This was my reality now.

"I look that bad, huh?" My voice sounded husky and scratchy like I hadn't used it in weeks, and I'd been crying so hard my stomach felt like I'd done a thousand crunches.

"Like absolute garbage." The corner of his mouth ticked in an attempt at a smile.

I laughed like gravel in a garbage disposal. After what had happened, I could still laugh. All wasn't lost, but the hollowness inside made me feel like I'd been scooped out, leaving me a shell. "What's on the itinerary for today?"

"Nothing, Bay. I...we don't have anything until the flight tonight."

"Right. I forgot." The pain in my stomach. The stabbing, angry feeling. "London. We're leaving tonight."

"Emily's also gone to get a pregnancy test." Holden lifted my hand and cupped his around it.

I flinched, curling in on myself. Was it too early? How long after a missed period would the results take?

"Whatever happens, we've got your back. Don't worry about anything. Just get some rest."

"I feel like I've been resting too long already. There's a lot to be packed, I'll do that."

He opened his mouth before slamming it shut and nodding. "Sounds like a good plan. I'll let you know when Emily's back."

I was alone again, with only my thoughts. All the ideas about how to make our relationship work were wiped away.

What did it matter? Keyton had already left.

After packing up my bags, I showered and tried to pull myself together. I turned on the TV to drown out the thoughts in my head. Better for things to be too noisy than to be alone with my own thoughts.

There would be people outside the hotel. There would be cameras and fans, autograph and selfie seekers. If I wasn't Bay than what the hell was I? Certainly not a girlfriend or a future wife. Maybe a future mother. I couldn't even think that far ahead yet.

He'd left at the slightest hint that I might be pregnant.

No, there was nothing else left but the music now.

I checked all the drawers under where the 65" TV sat.

"We have big news in the sports world. Renowned good

luck charm Darren Keyton has signed a three year deal with the Wisconsin Bison. This is shocking news only two days before the trade deadline. Most have already happened, but it looks like he'll need to invest in a winter gear wardrobe to make the leap from Philadelphia to Milwaukee. One thing we don't usually hear about with these trades is a payout. The tight end will be leaving a lot of money on the table with this move, but this is the first time he's signed a deal where he'll be joining the starting line-up."

I fell to the bed, staring at the TV as the newscasters bantered about what the move meant for him mid-season and how unusual it was.

Kind of like someone running away the first chance they got. Why was I surprised? Why hadn't I paid attention to the signs? When I'd seen him at the concert, he'd left. In my hotel suite after coffee, he'd left. After the guy attacked me, he'd rushed off. And I'd told him I might be pregnant and he was out the door.

If that wasn't a sign, I didn't know what was. I kept letting my past with him color how I saw him and how I saw our love. We were hurting one another. It was like a reflex. We couldn't help it.

He wasn't the Greenwood bad boy, who took interest in a stage crew geek. He was a guy who ran when he got scared. I was the girl who ran just as hard, but I thought together— this time we could conquer anything. That we were finally finished running from the big scary feelings that made us.

Only there wasn't an us. He'd seen to that when he'd left me to go to some other woman, sneaking out the first chance he got. I'd been ready to give it all up for him. Leave this life behind for him. A baby had been a perfect excuse to step back and take a breather.

The joke was on Keyton. He didn't have to flee the city to

get away from me. I was leaving tonight at 6 PM, ready to finish up the last leg of my tour and then figure out what was the next step for me.

The door to the suite banged open. Holden and Emily ran in like they expected me to be in a puddle again.

Wild glances shot to the TV and back to me.

"I saw it. I'm okay." That was the biggest lie I'd ever told, the kind I'd couldn't escape, but I'd keep saying it until I could believe the lie even for a few minutes. Falling apart wasn't an option, even though all I wanted to do was curl back up into my ball and forget everything existed. I wanted to forget I existed.

Like I had in LA after he refused to meet me, I'd fall back into the embrace of my music. The fans. The tour. The shows.

I'd do the same thing I'd done for the past six years. The show had to go on, even if all that remained of me was the shell of the person I'd once been, the vision I'd had of how things could go, of being a family with the one man who'd always seen me, destroyed. There was no one else who saw me like he had. Loved me like he had. Hurt me like he had.

35

KEYTON

The flight from Charlotte had taken forever. On the way to the airport, I'd picked up a last minute gift, a peace offering, a desperate bid to redeem myself in the slightest in her eyes and prove how wrong I'd been. I barged into the propped-open door of the suite and rushed into her bedroom.

Inside, a housekeeper shut off the vacuum and pulled off her headphones, staring at me with wide eyes. It was empty. Every sign of Bay and her team were gone.

"Sorry." I backed out of the suite.

She was gone.

I braced my hand on the wall to keep from dropping to my knees. Each breath burned my lungs. My head buzzed, woozy dizziness gripped me, and it felt like I was on the helicopter all over again, careening toward the ground.

Sucking down breaths that felt like shards of glass, I tried to focus. She hadn't disappeared into thin air.

Against every instinct and notion of decency, I plugged her name into a gossip site.

Bay headed out of the Four Seasons Philadelphia wearing an

Alexander McQueen asymmetrical long black coat, Valentino boots and Levi's jeans. She's so down to Earth! Add her outfit to your closet today!

She's making a big announcement in London before finishing up the last leg of her world tour! A second night was added to the Berlin show. Snap these tickets up before they're sold out!

I grabbed my phone and paced in the empty hallway.

"Gwen, I need you to find out what airport Bay's leaving from."

"When's she leaving and where's she going?"

"I don't know when she's leaving. I'm at the Four Seasons now. One of the paparazzi sites said she was headed to the airport thirty minutes ago. She's going to London."

"Okay, it might take some time."

"I don't have much. If she's leaving from Philly International she could be on a plane already. If she's going to Teterboro, if I break a few laws, I could beat them there or at least get there a few minutes after they do. Gwen, I need to see her before she gets on that plane."

"I'll see what I can find out."

The call ended and I raced down to the parking garage not wanting to lose a second as soon as Gwen called back. My heart thudded like it was trying to beat straight out of my throat. There had never been a slower eight minutes in my life.

Before the phone could ring, I answered. "Yes, did you find her?"

Panting, Gwen rushed out the words. "She's leaving from Teterboro at six."

I checked the time. Less than an hour to get there. There was no way I'd make it. Even breaking a land speed record with no traffic, I couldn't get there in time.

Deep breaths didn't stop the mind-numbing panic that overwhelmed me, and I braced my hands against the wall.

"A car's pulling into the garage now. It'll take you to the Philadelphia airport. There's a helicopter being fueled up right now. You can just make it."

I stood, unable to move, until the headlights of the SUV flashed over me and snapped me out of my freeze. "You're a miracle worker, Gwen."

"Remember, Christmas is just around the corner."

"I won't forget it." I jumped into the car before the driver could slide out of his side. "You know where we're going?"

"Yes, and I've been told a lead foot will be compensated."

"Doubled. Just get me to the airport."

Sailing through yellow lights, we made it just as the blades of the helicopter began spinning in the air.

Sprinting out of the car, I flew straight into the open door of the six-seater, pushing through the locked grip my muscles tried to enact. My stomach pitched, bile rushing for my throat. I locked my teeth. My hands were braced on the edge of the door. Prying them off, I flung myself onto the first seat. I scooted to the center of the three seats and buckled my belt. With a shuddering breath, I locked my fingers behind my neck and bent at the waist, not trusting my instincts wouldn't force me to jump out right back onto the helicopter landing pad to safety. I didn't have the time for a complete breakdown.

The helicopter lifted up off the ground and my stomach dropped like I was on a rollercoaster. Slamming my eyes shut and breathing deeply, I dug my fingers in deeper to the straining muscles of my neck. We were only a few feet off the ground.

I needed to get to Bay.

My stomach was knotted up and I dragged more air into my lungs.

The pilot's voice barged into my head and I jolted, forgetting I had the headset on. "We'll be there in fifty-seven minutes. We've already got the landing clearance for Teterboro."

I nodded, not trusting my open mouth with the pressure plugging my ears. We were high now. Much higher than a few feet. There was no jumping now.

My breath had frozen in my chest like I'd been shoved out into blizzard temperatures in nothing but a jock strap. Wheezing, sharp breaths made dots swim in front of my eyes. I stuck my hand into my pocket, centering my whole world on why I was doing this. Closing my eyes, I licked my dry lips and tried to buzz-saw through the clawing fear to the words I wanted to say to the woman I couldn't live without.

I recited what I wanted to say like a mantra, each time digging down deeper into the love I had for her. The need. Whether she believed me or not, whether she was willing to risk her heart again on me, the guy who'd broken it more times than should've been allowed, I wouldn't leave until I'd told her how much she meant to me. How much being a family with her meant to me. How much this baby meant to me.

And before long my torture had ended.

We landed and I almost got down on the tarmac and kissed the ground. Instead, I rushed across the tarmac, sprinting for the plane with the call number Gwen had texted to me. The winter air chafed my clammy, damp skin.

The Gulfstream 350 with the stairs down was lit up inside and a carpet was rolled out. A flight attendant stood at the top of the stairs.

A few people walked out of the airport hangar toward the stairs. Luggage was being loaded into the belly of the plane.

Holden walked out and stood at the bottom of the stairs, talking into his phone.

Then I saw her in the black coat, boots and jeans, with a hat tugged down over her ears.

My heart stuttered and I ran toward her.

She took a sip of a steaming drink in her hand and walked up the stairs to the plane.

"Bay!"

All heads swung in my direction, but my gaze was focused on her. Only her.

"Bay!" My breath collected in puffs in front of my face.

I stood at the base of the stairs beside Holden, who'd placed himself in the way. I could slam into him and he'd probably fly twenty feet. I could throw him across the tarmac for putting himself between us. I could destroy him to get to her.

And destroy whatever chance I had in the process.

She stood at the top of the stairs, her face neutral. I'd almost have preferred she fling her drink at me than stare at me with that impassive look.

"How did you know we'd be here?" Holden folded his arms across his chest. Although he was posh and the accent certainly threw me, from the fire in his eyes, I didn't doubt he'd try to take a swing at me if I tried to get to her through him.

"I need to talk to her." I looked at him.

After seeing how much he'd done for Bay and how he'd been someone she could lean on through all the madness that was her career, I didn't doubt he wanted me nowhere near her after what I'd done.

"I need to explain." Pleading with everything I had in me, I stared into his eyes. "Please."

Maybe he saw my pain, or the need to make things right. Or maybe he knew she'd never be able to move on without this conversation. Whatever the reason, he flicked his gaze over his shoulder.

The doorway to the plane was empty. Bay and the flight attendant were gone, probably not wanting to witness my abject humiliation on the airfield. Even the other people who'd been heading to the plane were nowhere to be seen now.

Holden's jaw clenched and he grimaced, deep and foreboding.

"You have ten minutes." He looked back up at the plane. "Do not make me regret this. I hope you brought the big guns, because you're going to need them." Shaking his head, he stepped out of the way.

Collecting myself for a handful of seconds, I took to the stairs, trying to remember all the things I'd planned to say as I climbed.

It never came out the way I wanted with Bay.

Inside the cabin, I scanned the interior for her. There were leather couches along one side of the plane, and two sets of four chairs with a table in the center of them.

Toward the back, there were two doorways. One most likely led to a bedroom and the other to a bathroom.

The bathroom door opened and Bay walked out in a sweatshirt and sweatpants, drying her hands on a towel with a pained expression on her face. "Is he gone yet?" She peered out the windows before standing up straight, staring right at me.

Her head jerked back and she dropped the towel. "What are you doing in here?"

"I needed to talk to you."

Her stunned expression faded back to the neutral blankness. "I don't have anything to say to you. Words never tell me half as much as your actions."

"I'm sorry." I walked down the aisle, needing to be close to her, needing her to know how badly I fucked up.

"You're sorry." Her face contorted into a mask of sadness and anger.

My chest ached, the pain spreading. "I know I screwed up."

"I told you I might be pregnant and you ran." Tears welled in her eyes and she brushed them aside. "You said being with me wasn't something you'd ever regret and you just left."

"It was wrong. I was wrong. And that's a regret I'll have for the rest of my life."

"I told you what I needed. I told you how much I wanted something real, and in an hour, you went from wanting to spend the rest of your life with me to walking out the door without a backward glance. How can I agree to spend the rest of my life with you if I don't even know if you'll be there in the morning? You'd have rolled out of bed and snuck out leaving me behind without even a note."

I dropped my head.

She was right. About everything. But we'd been doing this dance around each other for over a decade now.

"Do you think a note makes it easier?" I peered at her, my vision blurring with tears. "A note to parse every line of, looking for a secret code or message to tell you where things went wrong and how to fix them?"

"You left because you were scared. I did the exact same thing."

I stuck my hand into my pocket and wrapped my fingers

around the fabric. "I've never been more afraid of anything in my life."

Inside my pocket, I brushed my fingers over the letters printed on the front.

"Afraid of having kids. You talked about a family."

"*We* talked about it."

"Talks and reality are two very different things."

"Who's Monica?" Her voice stalled almost losing the end of Monica's name. She'd moved closer. Now she was standing at the end of the couch, no longer half a plane away from me.

"My therapist." I kicked myself thinking of how it all sounded to her. Not only did she think I'd run out on her while she was pregnant with my child, but that I'd run straight to another woman.

The despair at how incredibly screwed I was was only slightly edged out by the regret that I had come to her as a man who was still a work in progress, the kind who wasn't whole enough to be perfect for her. But I didn't look away, needing her to know it was true without a doubt or hesitation that there could never be another woman for me.

"You left to go see your therapist." Her head tilted and she dropped to the edge of the couch.

I nodded, shame burning in my chest that I'd walked out on the mother of my child the way I had because my head was still a fucking mess. All the work and self-talk and thinking I had it handled, and during a moment when most guys who loved the woman they were with and wanted to spend the rest of their lives with would've been jumping in the air pumping their fists. I'd left under the cover of darkness. "I was afraid of becoming him." A burning set in, deep in my nostrils.

"Your father? Keyton..." Her voice lost some of its razor's

sharp edge. The leather cushions shifted and she slid closer. "You could never, never be like him." Fierceness and vehemence ripped through her words. "The worries and fear I had about us, they were never that you'd turn into him."

"Whenever I see a little kid now, especially of someone I know or someone I'm close to—hell, even Felicia when she came to my door with her little baby strapped to her chest—all I can think of is that he looked at me when I was that small and vulnerable and he hurt me." I squeezed my eyes shut and clenched my fists, jamming them against my thighs before I took a shaky breath and released my grip.

"And it scares me to know anyone would be capable of that. It scares me to know I could be capable of that."

She shot forward and took my hands in hers. "You're not." Tugging me forward, she wouldn't let me evade her gaze. "You're not. I can't know what it was like to go through what you went through. I can't ever know that or truly understand what you've been through. No matter what happens here tonight, I need you to know I don't hate you. And I don't ever want you to think for a second that I believe you could hurt me like that or ever hurt your child." Her voice broke and she sniffled.

Setting my hands down, her lips pinched tight. "But what you did. How you just left the second you were freaked out...how can we have a relationship if you won't talk to me? If you run from me and don't even let me know what's happening? I thought we'd gotten past that and were finally able to trust one another. And then the news breaks that you're going to Wisconsin." Accusatory eyes sliced through me. "You didn't mention it once."

I hadn't. I'd shoved it to the recesses of my mind, not wanting to be disappointed again. My words to Ernie to go for it, no matter what, without checking with me, rang in my ears. I'd finally gotten the one thing I'd been striving for in my career, and it might cost me the one person who made my life worth living. "It was supposed to be a dead deal."

"Even if it was a deal to begin with, you should've told me. You should've been there for me. You should've let me be there for you."

36

BAY

The pounding in my head wouldn't go away. I wanted to throw my arms around him and him to hold me close. I wanted to kick him off the plane and tell him I couldn't do this anymore. Letting him in invited this soul-shredding pain I couldn't escape.

My heart ached for the boy who thought he could be capable of what he'd been subjected to, and I hated his father for ever pushing him to doubt himself, but there were no words from me to fix this. If he didn't believe it, he'd be scared of being that man forever; and I'd always have the fear in the back of my mind that one day it would all be too much for him and he'd leave to find an easier, less complicated life without the reminders of his past—without me.

"But you weren't there for me. You left me to deal with everything on my own. I get being afraid." Tears swam in my eyes again and I hated my treacherous tear ducts. My voice pitched higher, straining. "Hell, I'm scared shitless half the time of my life and who I'm leaving behind and what mistakes I've made, but I shared that with you."

My anger built again, making me fist my hands in my lap.

"All the talk about wanting our lives to be together and figure it out, but you were making plans before me and you didn't tell me what was happening. I started making plans for next year after the tour to be close to you, and you won't even be here. I talked to Maddy about stepping back from everything, winding things down over the next eighteen months, and you couldn't even tell me there was a chance, Dare." I gasped, my fingers flying to my lips.

He jerked.

Shit.

He dropped his head. "No, you're right. You're right about everything."

I looked up at him, seeing the anguish radiating from his gaze.

"And what kind of life would we have if you still have to be afraid of slipping up and calling me Dare? I never want you to be scared of me. In any way."

The tightness in my chest lessened. "Sometimes it's hard for me to remember."

"Sometimes it's hard for me to forget. Forgetting that part of my life, trying to leave Dare behind—I could never do it. I see that now and I accept it. It's part of who I am and I wouldn't have you without it."

He scrubbed his hands down over his face.

"I want to be there for you and the baby. My head is finally on straight and I'm okay." His lips tightened. "On my way to okay. I know what I did was screwed up. But I want to be here for you—you and the baby."

I scooted away. "If that's why you came back, then you're off the hook." I squeezed my hands between my thighs. The least funny laugh ever escaped my lips. "If you'd waited a few more hours, you'd have known you were in the clear. I took a pregnancy test and it came back negative and if that weren't enough confirmation, I got my period." I threw in a sweeping arm flourish that sent cramps punching at my stomach.

The hot water bottle sat on the couch beside me. I'd be sitting with it resting against me until I had to move again. It signaled that I wasn't going to become a mother. Keyton and I weren't bound together for the rest of our lives by a mini-version of him or me, or maybe the perfect combo of both.

He dropped to his knees in front of me, taking my hands in his. "I don't want to be off the hook. I never wanted to be off the hook. All I wanted was to never hurt you or our child like I'd been hurt." He squeezed his eyes shut and gripped my hands tighter. Looking up at me with tears in his eyes, he breathed deeply, like those old memories revisiting him had almost broken him all over again.

"Never doubt that I wanted to have a baby with you. I still want that in a desperate, almost scary way. I know we're not ready, but now I know we'll never truly be ready. You being pregnant wasn't the problem. My fear was the problem. Only now I see my real fear is living a life without you. I've done it. I've done it for too long and I don't want to anymore. I can't bear the thought of knowing you're not coming home to me."

"How do I know you won't do this again? I need people in my life I can count on."

"I know. There's nothing I can say to make you believe this. But I can prove it to you every day."

I shook his hands off mine. Running my hand over my forehead, I glanced out the window, half hoping Holden would come in insisting we needed to leave now.

Outside was a helicopter that hadn't been there before. The interior was still lit up, and the pilot sat in the cockpit.

I whipped back around to Keyton. "How did you get here?"

His Adam's apple bobbed. "The only way to make it from Philly to here in under two hours."

"You got in the helicopter?" He'd trembled telling me about the helicopter incident. He'd barely been able to look at it when I'd gone up during SeptemberWeen.

"I needed to tell you how I really felt before you left. It was the only way. And I needed to give you this." Out of his pocket, he pulled out a folded green bundle of fabric. It had a white ribbon around it.

I took it from him, my hands trembling.

Looking from him to the swatch of fabric, I tugged on the ribbon. It unraveled, falling over the sides of my hands.

Unfolding it, I cupped the soft green cotton in the palms of my hands and tried to read the words through my blinding tears. Screen printed on the front in white lettering was a little equation: "Mom + Dad = Me" with a little heart hanging off the "e".

"Whenever this happens, I want it with you." His fingers encircled my wrists. "There won't be a day I don't regret how I handled the news, even if it turned out to not be real. All I've been thinking about is how I could be the husband you deserve and could build a family with."

I couldn't rip my gaze away from the onesie. I'd dreamed about seeing a little, chubby, gurgling baby with his eyes.

But watching him leave—he'd run from that future, and who was to say he wouldn't do it again, even after I'd given everything up to live our life together? The music was all I had left. It filled me enough to keep going, but not the brimming overflowing feeling I had with him.

My chest ached, each pound of my heart making it harder to catch my breath. I slammed my eyes shut.

He'd laid it all out for me. All the fears and worries. So many of them I shared. The unknown of the future was scary when someone else wasn't running my life, when I let myself get close enough to him that he could hurt me in a way that rivaled the first time he'd rushed away from me in a hail of wooden splinters. Maybe the fears had always been there, like splinters, trying to work their way out of my heart to allow me to finally heal. To be the scared girl on the stage with the guitar, singing my heart out for the whole world, or for an audience of one.

Opening my eyes, I looked at the man who'd won my heart as a boy, had always been bound to my soul, and who was woven into the very fabric of my being.

The road we'd walked had been long and winding, traversing the spans of distance and time. Now that we were here together, this crossroads felt like one that would either split our story from here to eternity or forge it through the fire of past and present wounds.

But the question remained. *How did I want to live the rest of my life?*

Footsteps pounded on the stairs leading to the plane door.

Holden swung into the entrance of the plane. "Bay, sorry to interrupt, but we're about ten minutes from missing our take-off window until tomorrow."

I looked from Holden to Keyton, my pulse hammering in my veins. "I can't." My voice cracked. I scooted back, my nostrils burning with the building tears I couldn't let fall.

His head dropped and he sat back, resting his hands on the tops of his legs. He sat for long, excruciating moments where I couldn't be sure this was the right answer. I couldn't be sure I wasn't running by standing still.

"I understand." He got off the floor and took two steps, bending, he pressed his lips to the top of my head. "I hope you find happiness, even if it can't be with me. That's all I ever wanted for you, was for you to be happy, but no matter what, I want you to know I love you. I've always loved you and I'll always love you, TNG." His voice wavered and I slammed my eyes shut and clamped my lips together.

An ugly sob tried to break free of my throat.

And then the warmth of him was gone. He rushed past Holden and the plane rocked at his thudding footsteps down the stairs.

"Bay—"

"Don't." I held up a hand.

He took a step back and gripped both hands together. "We don't have to leave right now."

I brushed the tears from my cheeks. "We'll miss our window if we don't." It would delay everyone in London. Out of the corner of my eye, I caught the solitary figure walking away from the plane when everyone else was walking forward.

This life was safe. This life was chaotic and crazy. This life was free from ever letting anyone close enough to ever hurt me again.

Emily and Eric, along with a few other people, walked into the plane. The engines powered up, forcing more heated air through the vents. The muted voices of everyone around me sounded so far away. A flight attendant came out to gather everyone's coats and put them away. Eight hours over the ocean. In eight hours, we'd be a continent apart. In eight weeks, he'd shown me how different my life could be with someone I loved. In ten years, he'd proven there could never and would never be anyone I'd love as much as I had the broken boy watching me across our back yards.

The flight attendant walked down the aisle. "Could everyone please take their seats? We're ready to taxi."

37

KEYTON

For a time, plummeting to my death in a helicopter had felt like the most terrifying moment in my life. But after kissing the top of Bay's head, knowing that would be the last time I ever felt her again, I'd gladly have taken a fiery aircraft crash over the fire burning in my chest. It felt like the flesh was being ripped from my bones, and all I could dream of was the numbness to make this stop hurting so much. The pain almost brought me to my knees.

The sun set and the air went from cold to blistering on the wide-open tarmac with the jet turbines kicking up even more air.

I stared at the helicopter pilot across the tarmac and had no idea what to do next. How did I go on with my life without her? The engines to the jet powered up, and I locked my knees so I wouldn't turn and rush back to her.

She'd told me no. I wasn't forgiven. Wasn't that our MO by now? This felt like the dance we'd been sentenced to repeat every half decade.

Maybe she'd get a killer next album out of our couple months of paradise.

Her plane would taxi and take her back to her world of tour buses, adoring fans, and a non-stop schedule that would leave her no time to even think about me before she crashed into a sleep of blissful oblivion.

I'd—thinking of my life beyond this moment was too painful to bear. On wooden legs, I walked back toward the helicopter. The engine of the plane behind me got louder, and soon the wheels would leave the ground, and with them, my heart.

A voice nearly drowned out by the roar of the engine perked up my ears. "Wait!"

I whirled around.

At the top of the steps to the plane, Bay waved her arms. Leaping down the stairs in two jumps, she rushed toward me, running so fast, her feet barely touched the tarmac, puffs of breath escaping from between her lips. Her hair whipped behind her in the frigid air.

My heart stuttered, too afraid to dream. Too afraid to hope.

Her face was shiny and wet. "Wait." She rushed toward me, not stopping until she was a half step away from me. "I couldn't go, not without telling you," she shouted over the airport noise.

I clamped my hands to the sides of my legs to keep from touching her. "Telling me what?"

"That I could get on that plane and go to London and keep living the life I've been living for the past five years." She swallowed and her face fell, tears glistening in her eyes. "But I don't want to. I don't want to live another day without you knowing how much I love you and without feeling how much you love me. You scare me more than anything I've ever faced before because you're my one. I'm scared, Dare." She stared into my eyes, showing me exactly how I made her feel. The fear, the longing, the love. It burned so brightly it felt hot enough to singe the air.

I swept her up in my arms. "You scare me too, Bay. I've never loved anyone like I love you, and I never will, but I promise we'll get through this together and I'll never let my fear of how I feel about you force me to run again. The next time I run, I want you at my side running toward a future neither of us could imagine, a future that's beautiful and perfect and flawed and messy and ours."

I held her face between my hands.

She nodded with tears streaming down her face and gripped the front of my coat. "I want that with you. I need that with you. I love you, Keyton. I've always loved you and don't think I could stop if I wanted to, but I don't. And I never will."

"I love you too, Bay. Now and forever."

Holden hustled us both off the tarmac and back into the plane.

We made up in the bedroom in the back of the plane, holding each other on the double bed. There was more talking, laughter and tears. Finally, we were sharing all of ourselves without hesitation or reservation, the good, bad, and ugly. It was the only way we could tackle it all together, as a team.

And it was at the press conference to kick off Bay's tour that she announced it would be her farewell tour.

Shock rocked me to my core. In all our talking on the plane, she hadn't said anything about retiring.

The room had burst into a flurry of questions and raised

voices. Holden just grabbed his stylus and tablet, grumbling under his breath about being the last to know.

Someone in the room recognized me, maybe from one of the London games we'd played.

"Does this have anything to do with the American footballer in the room?"

Bay leaned in closer to the mic. "Absolutely."

The room erupted into even more madness, but with her gaze locked onto mine, it felt like we finally had our peace.

Holden stepped in when the questions continued like a firehose after she'd answered over twenty.

We sat in a car on the way back to the airport to catch my flight back. Flashes went off outside the tinted windows strobing the interior of the car in bright lights. People banged against the glass screaming her name.

"Are you sure about leaving all this behind?"

She stared into my eyes, unflinchingly and unguarded. "There's not a doubt in my mind."

"What comes next?" I stared down at our intertwined fingers resting on my leg.

"Whatever we want. Well, not whatever we want." She nibbled her bottom lip. "I'll have to finish the tour and wind down all the contractual obligations. My life won't be my own for at least a year, maybe more. I'm sure Holden's on the phone to Maddy right now, hashing it all out."

"I'll support you no matter what you decide."

She brought our joined hands up and kissed the back of my hand. "I know and that's most of the reason I'm brave enough to do this. I want to sit in the stands and cheer you on. I want to find a quiet studio and work on my music. I want to build a life with you."

"I've never wanted anything more in my life."

Our goodbye at the airport wasn't nearly as teary as it

was before our last take off. She clung to me with her legs wrapped around my waist and arms around my neck. The biting London freeze was no match for the heat of her body against mine.

"I love you, Bay." My fingers sunk into her hair and I held her to me.

"I love you too. Three weeks until I'll get to do this again." Loosening her hold, she slid down the front of my body.

"An eighteen-hour window, I can't wait for." Leaning against the railing to the stairs to the jet, I brushed her hair back and pulled her hat down lower over her ears.

She shook her head. "It won't be enough."

"No, but it'll be enough for now. We have the rest of our lives, Bay."

38

KEYTON

FIFTEEN MONTHS LATER

I spat out a piece of grass stuck in my mouth. My fingers ached, and the freezing cold seeped through my gloves. Down in a crouch, I stared back at the stacked row of defensive linemen.

The butterfly bandage above my right eyebrow was coming off from all the sweat pouring down my face, although it was so cold that it froze under the adhesive.

My body screamed for relief, screamed for rest, but the adrenaline surged to give me the motivation I needed. This was the season I'd wanted for so long.

Up in the skybox, Bay was watching me. Her forgiveness was a gift I'd never take for granted.

Someone slapped my helmet.

The play clock was running. We were down by one with twenty-two yards to go.

My blood screamed through my veins. I could feel my pulse in my eyelids. Two fingers were taped together after a near dislocation in the last play of the quarter.

Puffs of breath formed a cloud between the two lines of players.

The stadium came alive with fans, not worried about freezing their asses off.

I tested my cleats into the ground, waiting for the call.

The Wisconsin QB shouted it out and everything moved in slow motion. A pocket opened in our line and a linebacker headed straight for him. Digging deep for the last blast of adrenaline, I paced him and intercepted, ramming my shoulder into him and taking him down.

We hit the ground inches from the QB and the ball sailed overhead. I popped up, tracking the perfect spiraling arc streaking down the field.

My breath froze in my lungs, but it had nothing to do with the temperatures.

Everything stopped, and the whole stadium was on their feet in near silence.

A finger tip of the ball from one of our guys and he knocked it out of the air.

My hand slammed into my chest, gripping my jersey.

The QB grabbed onto the back of my shoulder pads.

And the recovery.

The running back palmed the ball in his gloved hands and slammed it against his chest before falling into the end zone.

Standing, dazed, I watched the stadium erupt, and my teammates rushed toward us.

Sideline benches cleared, and everyone poured out onto the field. The franchise that hadn't made it to the playoffs in over a decade had just clinched their second national championship—in a row.

Bodies piled on top of me. The team lifted me, hugging

me, screaming their excitement to the heavens right beside me.

Sweaty, tired and humming with the exhilaration of the win, I joined in with my team's celebration.

Hats were shoved onto our heads and cameras invaded the festivities. Interviewers shoved mics into our faces.

Through the madness, the trophy with a silver football perched on top was hefted overhead by our quarterback. He grabbed onto me and shoved it into my hands.

"I wouldn't have thought it would be so close with you with us for the whole season!" He grinned and shook me. "One more?"

I stared out over the sea of people, soaking in the energy, living in the moment of my second championship win after putting all my blood, sweat and tears into this team.

Through the fray of people and confetti raining down, the crowd parted.

Bay walked toward me, still in her halftime performance outfit complete with a jacket made from a Wisconsin jersey that was nowhere near warm enough. But she'd wanted to go out with a bang for her farewell performance.

"Enough." The word rang in my head. I handed the trophy back to the QB. "Next season you guys are on your own."

His face fell, but I didn't stay for the barrage of questions, instead I slipped my hands around the waist of my wife and spun her around, lifting her feet off the ground.

She laughed and hugged me back, even though I was sweaty and disgusting. "Congratulations, Mr. Keyton."

I wrapped my arms tighter around her and whispered into her ear. "Congratulations, Mrs. Keyton." A bombardment of bliss hit me on saying those words.

A hand landed on my shoulder and pulled me from Bay.

"We're here with Darren Keyton and his girlfriend and halftime performer, Bay. You two both had a stellar night."

I held Bay close to me, my heart pounding like I'd just finished the winning play. "We certainly did, and I couldn't have done it without her at my side."

"Any word yet on when you two will be tying the knot?"

Our rings sat on the dresser in our rented house not too far from the stadium. The private ceremony we'd held with fewer than twenty attendees on a private island away from prying eyes still wasn't public knowledge. Every night when we got home, I slipped the ring onto her finger and got to say 'I do' all over again.

I leaned into the mic. "We're still trying to decide on the perfect time."

The interviews were non-stop with microphones shoved in both our faces, but I couldn't hide my smile. I don't think I'd stopped smiling since she'd come running down the stairs of the private jet and into my arms.

The next few hours dissolved into a celebration procession. It was a blur of champagne showers, Gatorade baths, ten-second sound clip interviews, press conferences, and some time with the physio team getting patched up.

Bay fielded her own interviews throughout the night. Reporters grilled her on her next album, next tour, next product line. She kept the evasiveness up and directed them to two up-and-coming artists she was working with.

After the confetti cannons, we moved into the locker room. The floor was soggy with booze and sweat. I had stood in rooms like this for what felt like years of my life combined, and this might be one of the last times I was here.

Most of the players had cleared out, already celebrating the big win. I had enough rings to cover one and a half hands. The novelty of the party had long been eclipsed by my love of the game, but even that had waned.

Hands slipped around my waist.

Raising my arms, I turned in Bay's hold and dropped my arms around her. She was already in her coat.

Holden stood by the end of the lockers.

"Hey, you made it." I extended my hand.

He unfolded his arms. "Like I'd miss her possibly last performance."

We shook hands. "Thanks for coming back. She was a nervous wreck thinking about doing it without you."

"Like I'd let her."

Bay rolled her eyes. "Thanks for coming, Holden." She hugged him and kissed his cheek.

"Better watch out. That hubby of yours might get jealous," he whispered low enough for only us to hear.

She looked over her shoulder. "No, he knows he's got my heart."

"Alright, enough of the suffocating love exchange. I've got a plane to catch. I'll see you both after this next tour is done." And he was gone.

"Does it feel weird not seeing him every day?"

"I miss him. Thankfully, he's got that tablet surgically attached to his hand, so I know he's always there when I need him."

"He's a good friend."

"One of the best."

I buttoned the top two buttons of her coat and pulled her hat out of her pocket, pulling it on and down over her eyes.

Her lips pursed. She shoved it up and slipped her hands into my pockets, resting her chin against my chest.

"Great game."

"Great performance."

She scrunched up her nose. "It was all lights and fireworks. Smoke and mirrors."

"And you."

"Let's go home."

Home could've been in the back of a car. A studio apartment. An airport terminal. As long as I was with her, I was home. Snow began to fall on the drive. I could appreciate it even more since I wouldn't have to play in it ever again.

The early dawn sun was close to the horizon by the time we got to our rented house. We'd retrofitted it with a studio and anything else we'd need to make it through the blistering Wisconsin winter.

We kicked off our winter gear by the door still covered in Christmas decorations and went straight up to our bedroom in the three-bed cottage-style house.

Sitting beside the bed was a bottle of champagne in a bucket of ice. A tray sat on the dresser with food containers waiting for us.

I turned to Bay.

She tapped her fingers against her lips. "Okay, I might've called in a favor with Holden to make this happen."

"In that case, we can't spoil all his hard work." I grabbed the rings from the dresser and crawled into bed beside Bay.

She crossed her legs in the center of the bed with two glasses of sparkling wine ready on the tray.

"This never gets old." I held her hand in mine and stared into her eyes with the overlapping rings poised at the tip of her finger. We didn't do this every night, but only on those big nights, ones where we were reminded of how extraordinary our love was and how lucky we were to be together. "All my life, I've waited to find the one person who believed in everything I was enough that I could believe it, too. The day I found you was the day I finally stopping living and came alive." I slid the rings onto her fingers and turned her hand over, kissing her palm.

Her hand ran over the back of my head. Lips pressed against the top of my head.

She took my ring from my other hand and rested my palm against her chest. "You've made my dreams come true in more ways than one, and I would never have had the strength to do half the things in my life, if you hadn't believed in me first. I love you, Dare. I love you, Keyton. I love you, husband." She slid the ring onto my finger.

Tonight was a night for closeness. A quiet serenity fell over our little secret, in our home, which was with each other. We sipped our drinks and watched the snow fall outside the window.

"Every day, I thank the universe for putting me in my garage the night you first played. It scares me to think how things would've gone for me, if I'd never heard you sing." My life would be empty and I wouldn't even know it.

"And I might not have ever been brave enough to let anyone hear my voice, if you hadn't been the first to listen." She squeezed me tighter and sighed.

"Will you miss it? Performing?" I hated the idea of her giving up so much, of stepping away from a spotlight that pulled most people toward it like an inescapable tractor beam.

The light caressed her skin, outlining the curve of her nose and the slight parting of her lips. Her gaze stayed trained on the snow outside. "Maybe, someday? But right now, I'm happy to say it's the last performance of my career."

"Maybe next season, I'll be able to watch you from the freezing cold seats like everyone else."

I took her glass and set it down on the nightstand along with mine.

Shifting, I intertwined our fingers. "This was my last season."

She shot up, eyes wide and lips parted. Her head shook from side to side. "What? Why?"

"It's time." Being on the road away from her had been hard, especially when she'd given a life on the road up for me.

She tried to shake her hands free, but I held on tight. "But you've worked so hard."

"And proven to myself I could do it. There's nothing else left to do."

Her gaze intensified, almost outraged on my behalf. "Don't do this for me."

"I do everything for you." I kissed the back of her hand. "But this decision is all mine. It's time. Eight championship rings is enough. All I'm doing at this point is courting an injury that might take me away from you. As long as you're by my side, that's all I need."

"Dare..."

Now I loved it when she called me that. Another thing only for us. "There isn't a thing I regret about how I'd played. It's time to move on to the next part of my life. The best part."

She softened, holding our interlocked hands against her chest. "What part is that?"

"The part where I get to wake up next to you every morning, and go to sleep with you wrapped in my arms."

EPILOGUE

BAY

I turned up the music, making notes every few bars on the changes I needed to make.

The studio we'd had built had all the equipment and space that rivaled some of the best ones I'd ever worked in. But this one was mine. Waking up in the same place every morning and waking up beside Keyton was a winner over my touring life hands down.

The four-bedroom red-brick house with white shutters and details on an acre of land was close enough to a main street that we could walk to the grocery store. A small town, only a few minutes outside of the city, which was the perfect location to be in our little bubble. A lot of other athletes lived nearby, including the house Keyton had rented for my girls' night with Piper and Felicia only a few blocks away, so there hadn't been too many run-ins with fans since we moved into our house.

Our house. The words still felt strange, but so right. Being in Philly kept us close to Keyton's friends, who were now also my friends and kept him busy with the work at his foundation. It was a life full of simple pleasures, lots of quiet time and not so quiet time when we were both naked in a snap without the same demands that had run our lives for so many years.

The door burst open, thudding against the soundproof wall. Before I could spin my chair, I was whirled around so quickly I gripped the armrests so I didn't fly out. "Holy shit, Bay!"

"What happened?"

My heart shifted into overdrive.

"Holy shit." He wrapped his arms around me and pulled me out of my seat, holding me so tightly my arms were pinned at my sides. "You did it!" Jumping up and down, he shook me even more, still dizzy from the chair spin.

It wasn't urgency in his tone, but excitement. "I'm completely willing to take credit for whatever I did, but maybe you could tell me first." Laughing, I bent back to look at him.

He let me go, sitting me back in my seat, and shoved his phone in front of my face.

The glowing screen blinded me and my eyes, used to the dim light from the studio, I tried to focus on the words and images.

Seconds ticked by as I scrolled the screen looking for what might've lead to his wall-banging entrance.

My hand shot to my mouth. "Holy shit!"

He took the phone from my hand. "And the newcomer shocked the world with his debut LP, Fixtures, produced by none other than the hopefully-not-retired-for-much-longer pop powerhouse, Bay. Both will be up for a golden gramophone in February." His voice was full of awe.

His smile looked bigger than mine felt. "See, I told you."

He braced his hands on the armrest and sank to his knees in front of me.

I ran my hand along his cheek, looking at the man who'd never doubted me, even when I'd doubted myself. "You did."

My phone lit up on the console, a familiar name flashing on the screen. "Looks like Holden's losing his touch. You found out before he did."

"Are you going to answer it?" He nodded toward the phone.

I draped my arms over his shoulders. "No. I can call him back. First, I want to celebrate with my husband."

"You're still okay with keeping it quiet?" He stared intently at me.

He'd suggested we not broadcast the news. The media circus was finally dying down around us. News and social media cycles raced for fresh faces and juicy stories. We were becoming old news and the limelight was dimming. He was worried about how the news might thrust us back into the spotlight we were more than happy to step out of outside his foundation work.

At this point, I was amazed we'd managed it as long as we had.

"For as long as you want. I like having this secret with you. Something that's just ours."

He wheeled me closer. "I can't say I don't mind having TNG all to myself."

"Is that so, Dare?" I swept my hands over the thick column of his neck.

"That's so." His hands dropped from the arms of the chairs to my waist. "Have I ever told you you're breathtakingly talented?"

"Only once a week. I can't say I mind hearing it." As

confident as I'd pretended to be when I'd delivered the final tracks to Spencer and Holden, I'd been holding my breath to see how they'd be received. Four number one hits on a debut album wasn't too terrible.

Now there were managers and labels calling me from all over the country, but I was determined to take the time I needed to ease into this new life at a pace that worked for me. A pace that worked for us.

My phone pinged and vibrated with texts and incoming calls. I picked it up, holding down the button to power it off.

"You don't want to answer any of those?"

"No, I want to celebrate with you, here in our home."

He slipped his hands behind my knees and back and lifted me out of the chair, crossing the space to the not yet christened sofa. "And I didn't want to put a couch down here because I thought you'd never leave."

Holding onto his neck, I pressed my lips against his, smiling through my words. "Looks like you were wrong." The cool leather pressed against my back and a shiver traveled up my spine.

"But I was so right about you." He stared down at me with a loving adoration that brought tears to my eyes.

"Thank you for not giving up on us." My life without him had been a hollow shell of a life and now it felt like it was bursting at the seams with a happiness that had changed me in so many ways.

His weight settled on top of me. "Never."

I parted my legs and wrapped them around him. "I'm the luckiest woman who's ever lived to have you love me how you have."

"I'm just happy I'm the man who can give you the world. We were always meant to be, TNG."

AFTERWORD

Thank you for being a part of Keyton and Bay's journey back to one another. Their story was one I couldn't wait to tell and can't believe had finally made it into your hands. As I love to do for all my stories, I have a little extra scene of these two.

I hope you'll enjoy it and spending a little bit more time with them both.

～

Ready for some more college sports action?

Shameless King - Enemies to Lovers

Enemies to lovers has never felt so good!

Declan McAvoy. Voted Biggest Flirt. Highest goal scorer in Kings of Rittenhouse Prep history.

Everyone's impressed, well except one person...

I can't deny it. I want her. More than I ever thought I could want a woman. I've got one semester–only four months–to convince her everything she thought about me was wrong.

Will my queen let me prove to her I'm the King she can't live without?

Only one way to find out...

One-click SHAMELESS KING now!

❧

Want to start Fulton U where it all began?

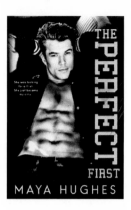

The Perfect First - Reece + Seph

"How long do you last in bed?" Those were her first words to me, swiftly followed up with, "And how big would you say you are?"

Cue the record scratching, what?!

Persephone Alexander. Math genius. Lover of blazers. The only girl I know who can make Heidi braids look sexy as hell. And she's on a mission. Lose her virginity by the end of the semester.

Grab The Perfect First today!

EXCERPT FROM THE PERFECT FIRST

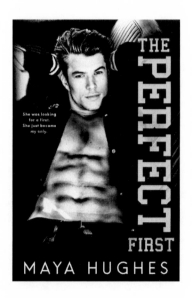

Seph - Project De-virginization

The jingle sounded again as the door to the coffee shop swung open. My head snapped up and my bouncing leg froze. The sun shone through the doorway and a figure stood there. He was tall, taller than anyone who'd come in before. His muscles were obvious even under his coat. He paused at the entrance, his head moving from side to side like he knew people would be looking back, like he was giving everyone a chance to soak in his presence. His jet black hair was tousled just right, like he'd been running his fingers through it on the walk over from wherever he'd come from. The jacket fit him perfectly, like it had been tailored just for his body.

I glanced around; I wasn't the only one who'd noticed him walk in. He seemed familiar, but I couldn't place him. He bent forward, and I thought he was going to tie his shoes, but instead he wiped a wet leaf off his pristine white sneaker. Heads turned as he crossed the floor toward me. Squeezing my fingers tighter around the notecards, I reminded myself to breathe.

He glanced around again and spotted me. The green in his eyes was clear even from across the coffee shop. Dark hair with eyes like that wasn't a usual combo. He froze and his lips squeezed together. With his hands shoved into his pockets, he stalked toward me with a *Let's get this over with* look. That didn't bode well. He stood beside the seat on the other side of the booth, staring at me expectantly.

My gaze ran over his face. Square jaw. Hint of stubble on his cheeks and chin. My skin flushed. He had beautiful lips. What would his feel like on my mouth? I ran my finger over my bottom lip. What would they feel like on other parts of me? My body responded and I thanked God I had on a bra, shirt, and blazer or I'd have been flashing him some serious high beams. This was a good sign.

He cleared his throat.

Jumping, I dropped my hand, and the heat in my cheeks turned into a flamethrower on my neck. "Sorry, have a seat." I half stood from my spot in the booth and extended my hand toward the other side across from me. The table dug into my thighs and I fell back into the soft seat.

Sliding in opposite me, he unzipped his coat and put his arm over the back of the shiny booth.

"Hi, very nice to meet you. I'm Seph." I shot my hand out across the table between us. The cuff of my blazer tightened as it rode up my arm.

His eyebrows scrunched together. "Seth?" He leaned in, his forearms resting on the edge of the table. He was nothing like the guys from the math department. They were quiet, sometimes obnoxious, and none of them made my stomach ricochet around inside me like it was trying to win a gold medal in gymnastics at the Olympics.

I tamped down a giggle. I did *not* giggle. The sound came out like a sharp snort, and I resisted the urge to slam my eyes shut and crawl under the table. *Be cool, Seph. Be cool.* "No—Seph. It's short for Persephone."

He lifted one eyebrow.

"Greek goddess of spring. Daughter of Demeter and Zeus. You know what, never mind. I'm glad you agreed to meet with me today."

"Not like I had much choice." He leaned back and ran his knuckles along the table top, rapping out a haphazard rhythm.

I licked my lips and parted them. Not like he had much choice? Had someone put him up to this? Had something in my post made him feel obligated to come? I hadn't been able to bring myself to go back and look at it after posting it.

Shaking my head, I stuck my hand out again. "Nice to meet you..."

He looked down at my hand and back up at me, letting out a bored breath. "Reece. Reece Michaels."

"Very nice to meet you, Reece. I'm Persephone Alexander. I have a few questions we can get started with, if you don't mind."

"The quicker we get started, the quicker we can finish." He looked around like he would have rather been anywhere but there.

Those giddy bubbles soured in my stomach. A server came by with the bottled waters I'd ordered. I arranged them in a neat pyramid at the end of the table.

"Would you like a water?" I held one out to him.

He eyed me like I was offering him an illicit substance, but then reached out. His fingers brushed against the backs of mine and shooting sparks of excitement rushed through me. Pulling the bottle out of my grasp, he cracked it open and took a gulp.

My cheeks heated and I glanced down at my cards, flipping the ones at the front to the back.

"I have a notecard with some information for you to fill out."

Sliding it across the table, I held out a pen for him. He took it from me, careful that our fingers didn't touch this time. I'd have been lying if I'd said I didn't want another touch, just to test whether or not that first one had been something more than static electricity. He filled out the biographical data on the card and handed it back to me.

I scanned it. He was twenty-one. Had a birthday coming up just after the New Year. Good height-to-weight ratio. Grabbing my pen, I scanned over the questions I'd prepared for my meetings.

"Let's get started." *Just rip the Band-Aid off.* Clearing my throat, I tapped the cards on the table. A few heads turned in our direction at the sharp, rapping sound. "When were you last tested for sexually transmitted diseases?"

Setting the bottle down on the table, he stared at me like I was an equation he was suddenly interested in figuring out. And then it was gone. "At the beginning of the season. Clean bill of health." He looked over his shoulder, the boredom back, leaking from every pore. *Wow.* I'd thought guys were all over this whole sex thing, but he looked like he was sitting in the waiting room of a dentist's office.

"When did you last have sexual intercourse?"

His head snapped back to me, eyes bugged out. "What?" I had his full attention now.

"Sex? When did you last have sex?" I tapped my pen against the notecard.

He sputtered and stared back at me. His eyes narrowed and he rested his elbows on the table.

I scooted my neatly lain out cards back toward me, away from him.

"No comment."

"Given the circumstances, it's an appropriate question."

The muscles in his neck tightened and his lips crumpled together. "Fine, at the beginning of the season."

"What season?" I looked up from my pen. That was an odd way to put it. "Like, the beginning of fall?"

"Like football season."

The pieces fit together—the body, the looks from other people around the coffee house. "You play football." That made sense, and he seemed like the perfect all-American person for the job.

"Yes, I play football."

"When did the season start?"

He shook his head like he was trying to clear away a fog and stared back at me like I'd started speaking a different language. "September."

"And..." I ran my hand along the back of my neck. "How long would you say it lasted?"

His eyebrows dipped. "It didn't last. It was a one-night thing. I don't do relationships."

Of course not. He was playing the field. Sowing his oats. Banging his way through as many co-eds as possible. Experienced. Excellent.

I cleared my throat. "No, I didn't mean how long did you date the woman. I meant, how long was the sex?"

The steady drumming on the table stopped. "Are you serious?"

I licked my Sahara-dry lips. "It's a reasonable question. How long did it last?"

"I didn't exactly set a timer, but let's just say we both got our reward."

"Interesting." I made another note on the card.

"These are the types of questions I'm going to be asked for the draft?" He took the lid off the bottled water.

The draft? Pushing ahead, I went to the next line one my card and cringed a bit. "Okay, this might seem a little invasive." I cleared my throat again. "But how big is your penis? Length is fine. I don't need to know the circumference, you know—the girth."

A fine spray of water from his mouth washed over me. "What the hell kind of question is that? I know you're trying to throw me off my game, but holy shit, lady."

～

Persephone Alexander. Math genius. Lover of blazers. The only girl I know who can make Heidi braids look sexy as hell. And she's on a mission. Lose her virginity by the end of the semester.

I walked in on her interview session for potential candidates (who even does that?) and saw straight through her brave front. She's got a list of Firsts to accomplish like she's only got months to live. I've decided to be her guide for all her firsts except one. Someone's got to keep her out of trouble. I have one rule, no sex. We even shook on it.

I'll help her find the right guy for the job. Someone like her doesn't need someone like me and my massive...baggage for her first time.

Drinking at a bar. Check.

Partying all night. Double check.

Skinny dipping. Triple check.

She's unlike anyone I've ever met. The walls I'd put up around my heart are slowly crumbling with each touch that sets fire to my soul.

I'm the first to bend the rules. One electrifying kiss changes everything and suddenly I don't want to be her first, I want to be her only. But her plan was written before I came onto the scene and now I'm determined to get her to rewrite her future with me.

Grab your copy of The Perfect First or read it for FREE in Kindle Unlimited at https://amzn.to/2ZqEMzl

ALSO BY MAYA HUGHES

Fulton U

The Perfect First - First Time/Friends to Lovers Romance

The Third Best Thing

The Fourth Time Charm

The Fulton U Trilogy

The Art of Falling for You

The Sin of Kissing You

The Hate of Loving You

Kings of Rittenhouse

Kings of Rittenhouse - FREE

Shameless King - Enemies to Lovers

Reckless King - Off Limits Lover

Ruthless King - Second Chance Romance

Fearless King - Brother's Best Friend Romance

Heartless King - Accidental Pregnancy

CONNECT WITH MAYA

Sign up for my newsletter to get exclusive bonus content, ARC opportunities, sneak peeks, new release alerts and to find out just what I'm books are coming up next.

Join my reader group for teasers, giveaways and more!

Follow my Amazon author page for new release alerts!

Follow me on Instagram, where I try and fail to take pretty pictures!

Follow me on Twitter, just because :)

I'd love to hear from you! Drop me a line anytime :)
https://www.mayahughes.com/
maya@mayahughes.com

Made in United States
North Haven, CT
22 December 2022

29926388R00262